# 大修館
# シェイクスピア双書
# 第2集

THE

TAISHUKAN

SHAKESPEARE

2nd Series

大修館書店

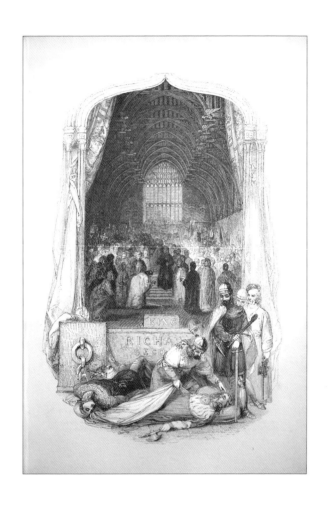

第 5 幕第 5 場リチャードの殺害
Charles Knight, ed., *The Pictorial Edition of the Works of Shakespeare* (1839)
の口絵より

ウィリアム・シェイクスピア

# リチャード二世

William Shakespeare

RICHARD II

篠崎　実
編注

## 大修館シェイクスピア双書 第2集（全8巻）について

　大修館シェイクスピア双書 第1集（全12巻）の刊行が始まったのは1987年4月。その頃はシェイクスピア講読の授業を行う大学もまだ多く、双書はその充実した解説と注釈において（手頃な値段という点においても）、原典に親しむ学生の心強い味方となり、教員の研究・教育に欠かせないツールとなった。

　そうした時代に比べれば、シェイクスピアよりも実用英語という経済性偏重の風潮もあって、シェイクスピア講読の科目を有する大学は数えるほどになったが、双書が役割を終えたわけでは全くなかった。そのことは発行部数からもよくわかる。2010年代になっても双書のほとんどは継続的に増刷を続けており、例えば『ロミオとジュリエット』の総発行部数は15,000に届く勢いだ。英文学古典の注釈書としてはかなりの部数と言える。

　これは大学の教員や学生のみならず、多くの一般読者にも双書が届いているからに他ならない。実際、周囲を見回せば、通信教育、生涯学習講座、地域のカルチャー・センター、読書会や勉強会でシェイクスピアの原典を繙く人は少なくない。そういう読者に双書が選ばれているのだとすれば、その主な理由は第1集編集委員会の目指した理念が好意的に受け取られているからだろう。

　原文のシェイクスピアをできるだけ多くの人に親しみやすいものにすること。とは言え、入門的に平易に書き直したりダイジェスト版にしたりするのではなく、最新の研究成果に基づいた解説や注釈により、原文を余すところなく読み解けるようにすること。そのために対注形式を取り、見開き2ページで原文と注釈を収めて読みやすさを重視すること。後注や参考文献により学問的な質を高く保ちつつ、シェイクスピアの台詞や研究の面白さを深く理

解できるようにすること。こうした第1集の構想が、第2集においてもしっかりと受け継がれていることは言うまでもない。また、表記の仕方などを除いて、厳密な統一事項や決まりなどは設けず、編集者の個性を十分に発揮していただく点も第1集と同様である。

　一方、重要な刷新もある。第1集では Alexander 版（1951）のテクストを基本的にそのまま用いたが、当時と比べれば近年の本文研究は大きな進展をみせ、現在 Alexander 版は必ずしも使いやすいテクストではない。むしろ編者が初期版本の性質を見極めた上で、そこからテクストを立ち上げ、様々な本文の読みを吟味しつつ編集作業を行う方が（負担は増すものの）、意義ある取り組みになるのではないか。そうした考え方に基づいて第2集では大きく舵を切り、各編者がテクストすべてを組み上げた。そのため作品によっては本文編集に関する注釈を煩雑に感じる読者もおられようが、注釈に目を通していただくと、問題になっている部分が実は作品の読みを左右する要なのだとご納得いただけると思う。

　第2集の企画を大修館編集部の北村和香子さんにご検討いただいたのは 2017 年秋。無謀とも思える提案に終始にこやかかつ冷静沈着に耳を傾け、企画全体を辛抱強く推し進めて下さった。第2集8巻の作品選定は大いに悩んだが、第1集『ハムレット』で編者を務めた河合祥一郎氏からのご提言もいただき、喜劇・悲劇・歴史劇・ローマ劇・ロマンス劇からバランスよく作品を選ぶことができた。ご両名にこの場を借りて心から御礼を申し上げる。「さらに第2期、第3期と刊行をつづけ、やがてはシェイクスピアの全作品を網羅できれば」という初代の思いが次に繋がることを願いつつ、あとは読者諸氏のご支援とご叱正を乞う次第である。


大修館シェイクスピア双書　第2集　編集者代表　　井出　新

# まえがき

『リチャード二世』は、編者がはじめて舞台で観たシェイクスピアの歴史劇だった。観たのは、1979年渋谷の小劇場ジャン・ジャンで上演された、出口典雄主宰のシェイクスピア・シアターによる舞台。出口によるシェイクスピア劇全作上演もゴールに近づいた頃のことだった。舞台下手に控えるロックバンドが演奏する、追放されたボリンブルックの心情を歌いあげる唄や、リチャード暗殺の場面のことを今も覚えている。ボリンブルックとリチャードという、劇のふたりの主要人物にまつわる場面が記憶に残っているのは、二重の焦点をもつこの劇の構造を考えると当然のことと思われる。

さて、本書はシェイクスピア作品を読みはじめて日の浅い初学者を主たる読者対象とし、『リチャード二世』本文のできるかぎり詳しく正確な注釈を提供することを目的としている。そのため、構文が複雑なところや現代英語と違う語法には文法的な解説をほどこし、語義が現代のものと違っている語には語注をつけるように心がけた。また、注釈では、語釈に当たって *OED* の語義を参照するなど、シェイクスピア研究において欠かせない基本的な参考文献に関する情報を意識的に多くおさめるようにした。こうしたツールを手にとってみて、有効に利用できるようになるきっかけとしたいからである。

『リチャード二世』という劇には、第4・四つ折本以降にしかおさめられていない部分があるという、書誌学上の問題がある。詳しくは解説の該当箇所を参照されたいが、そのため、テクストの異同に関して理解しやすいように、第1・四つ折本と第1・二

つ折版全集所収の本文に異同があるところには校注をほどこした。

シェイクスピアの歴史劇はホリンシェッドの『年代記』をはじめとする史書や先行作品を種本として書かれており、本作も例外でない。そのため、材源に関する注記を後注におさめた。頁数単位で関連箇所を示す一方、その本文を長々と引用することはしなかったが、それらを参照すれば、劇作家がどのように創作の腕を振るったのか、などといったことについて種々の発見があるだろう。余裕がある皆さんには是非材源の該当箇所やその前後を参照してほしいと願う次第である。

解説は紙数の制約上必要最小限のものとなったが、テクスト、創作年代、材源、作品の特徴や特記事項、上演史に関して必要不可欠な基本情報はおさめたつもりである。

シェイクスピア劇を読むことは、茫洋たる大海に乗りだす冒険のようなものである。行く手をはばむ困難もあるだろうが、それを乗りこえれば、さまざまな美しい光景に出会い、えがたい宝物を手に入れることができるだろう。そうした大海におもむく読者の皆さんにとって、本書が羅針盤のような役割を果たすことが、編者の希みである。

最後に、遅れがちな原稿の提出を辛抱強く待ってくださり、注の整理という面倒な編集作業を着実にこなしてくださった、大修館書店の北村和香子氏に心からのお礼を申しあげたい。

2022年秋

篠崎　実

# 目次

# 凡例・略語表

## 1. 凡例

### (1) 本文

　本書の本文は、Q1 に F1 の 4. 1. 154-317 相当部分を組みこむ形で、下記 Black、Gurr、Forker、Dawson & Yachnin を参照して、他の版本を確認のうえ作成した。ト書きは Q1 のト書きに F1 のものを補って作成し、必要に応じて書き足したものを [ ] に入れて示した。注の中で参照したシェイクスピアの他作品については、Oxford Shakespeare に基づいて引用および引用箇所の指示を行った。Q1 にない幕、場面割は F1 に依拠したが、F1 が新しい場面としていない第 5 幕第 4 場は Steevens に基づいて場面割りし、それ以降 F1 の場面番号よりひとつずつずれている。

### (2) 注釈

　注釈については、本文向かいの右ページには原則として語注など本文の意味解釈上の注および校注をおさめ、材源に関する注記は巻末に置き、右ページの注に「⇒後注参照」と指示した。

　本文中の箇所指定は幕、場面、行数をピリオドで区切って 4. 1. 154-317（第 4 幕第 1 場 154-317 行）などのような形で示し、同一場面のものについては 58 などのように行数のみを記す。

　ト書きの箇所指定は、そのト書きが出現する本文の行数のあとにピリオドとそのト書きのなかの行数を示す形で行う。たとえば第 1 幕第 1 場にほどこされた 15. 1 という箇所指定は本文 15 行目に加えられたト書きの 1 行目を意味する。そのため場面冒頭のト書きの 1 行目は 0. 1 という形で示す。

　頭書きの箇所指定は、その頭書きが出現する本文の行数のあとにピリオドと頭書きを意味する略語 SP（speech prefix）を書くことで行う。たとえば第 4 幕第 1 場にほどこされた 150. SP という箇所指定は 150 行目の頭書きであることを示す。

## 2. 略語表

### (i) シェイクスピアの作品

| | |
|---|---|
| *1H4* | *The First Part of King Henry the Fourth* |
| *2H4* | *The Second Part of King Henry the Fourth* |
| *3H6* | *The Third Part of King Henry the Sixth* |
| *LLL* | *Love's Labour's Lost* |
| *Mac.* | *Macbeth* |
| *R3* | *King Richard the Third* |
| *Rom.* | *Romeo and Juliet* |

(ii) 版本、校訂版

Black    Black, Matthew W., ed. *The Life and Death of King Richard the Second.* A New Variorum Edition of Shakespeare. Philadelphia and London: J. B. Lippincott, 1955.

Capell    Capell, Edward, ed. *Richard II.* In *Mr William Shakespeare: His Comedies, Histories, and Tragedies.* 10 vols. London, 1768. Vol. 5.

Chambers   Chambers, E. K., ed. *The Tragedy of King Richard the Second.* London and New York, 1891.

Clark & Wright Clark, William George, and William Aldis Wright, eds. *King Richard II.* Select Plays. Clarendon Press Series. Oxford, 1869.

Dawson & Yachnin Dawson, Anthony B. and Paul Yachnin, eds. *Richard II.* Oxford Shakespeare. Oxford: Oxford University Press, 2011.

Dyce    Dyce, Alexander, ed. *Richard II.* In *The Works of William Shakespeare: The Text Revised by Rev. Alexander Dyce.* London, 1864-67. Vol. 4.

Evans    Evans, Blackmore, et al. eds. *Richard II.* In *Riverside Shakespeare.* Boston: Houghton Mifflin, 1974.

F1     The First Folio, 1623.

Forker    Forker, Charles R., ed. *King Richard II.* Arden Shakespeare, Third Series. London: Thomson Learning, 2002.

Gurr    Gurr, Andrew, ed. *King Richard II.* New Cambridge Shakespeare. Cambridge: Cambridge University Press, 1984.

Halliwell   Halliwell, James O., ed. In *Works of William Shakespeare.* 16 vols. London, 1853-65. Vol. 9.

Hanmer   Hanmer, Sir Thomas, ed. *King Richard II.* In *The Works of Mr. William Shakespeare.* 6 vols. London, 1743-44. Vol. 3.

Irving    Irving, Henry, and Frank A. Marshall, eds. *King Richard II.* In *The Works of William Shakespeare.* 8 vols. New York, 1888-90. Vol. 2.

Johnson   Johnson, Samuel, ed. *The Life and Death of King Richard II.* In *The Plays of William Shakespeare.* 8 vols. London, 1765. Vol. 4.

Malone   Malone, Edmund, ed. *King Richard II.* In *The Plays and*

| | |
|---|---|
| | *Poems of William Shakespeare.* 10 vols. London, 1790. Vol. 4. |
| Newbolt | Newbolt, Henry, ed. *Shakespeare's Tragedy of King Richard II.* London and Edinburgh: Thomas Nelson & Sons, 1925. |
| Rowe | Rowe, Nicholas, ed. *King Richard II.* In *The Works of Mr. William Shakespeare.* 8 vols. London, 1714. Vol. 3. |
| Q1 | The First Quarto (1597) |
| Q2 | The Second Quarto (1598) |
| Q3 | The Third Quarto (1598) |
| Q4 | The Fourth Quarto |
| Q5 | The Fifth Quarto |
| Singer | Singer, Samuel Weller, ed. *Richard II.* In *The Dramatic Works of William Shakespeare.* 10 vols. London, 1855-56. Vol. 4. |
| Steevens | Johnson, Samuel, and George Steevens, eds. *The Tragedy of King Richard the Second.* In *The Plays of William Shakespeare.* 10 Vols. London, 1773. Vol. 5. |
| Theobald | Theobald, Lewis, ed. *The Life and Death of Richard the Second.* In *The Works of Shakespeare.* 8 vols. London, 1733. Vol. 4. |
| Ure | Ure, Peter, ed. *King Richard II.* Arden Shakespeare, Second Series. London: Methuen, 1965. |
| Verity | Verity, Arthur Wilson, ed. *King Richard II.* The Pitt Press Shakespeare for Schools. Cambridge, 1899. |
| Warburton | Warburton, William, ed. *The Life and Death of Richard the Second.* In *The Works of Shakespeare,* 8 vols. London, 1747. Vol. 4. |
| Wells | Wells, Stanley, ed. *Richard II.* Penguin Shakespeare. 1969; rpr. London: Penguin, 2008. |
| Wilson | Wilson, John Dover. *King Richard II.* 1939; rpr. Cambridge: Cambridge University Press, 2009. |
| Wright | Wright, Aldis Wright, ed. *King Richard II.* In *The Works of William Shakespeare.* 9 vols. London, 1891. Vol. 4. |

(iii) その他

| | |
|---|---|
| Abbott | Abbott, E. A. *A Shakespearian Grammar: An Attempt to Illustrate Some of the Differences between Elizabethan and Modern English.* London: Macmillan, 1929. |
| Arber | Arber, Edward, ed. *A Transcript of the Registers of the* |

|  | *Company of Stationers of London; 1554-1640 A.D.* 5 vols. 1875-94. rpr. New York: Peter Smith, 1950. |
| Crystal | Crystal, David. *The Oxford Dictionary of Original Shakespeare Pronunciation.* Oxford: Oxford University Press, 2016. |
| *CSPD Elizabeth,* Vol. 5. | Green, Mary Anne Everett, ed. *Calendar of State Papers, Domestic Series, of the reign of Elizabeth.* Vol. 5. London, 1869. |
| Davis | Davis, J. Madison, and A. Daniel Frankforter. *The Shakespeare Name Dictionary.* New York and London: Routledge, 2004. |
| Dent | Dent, R. W. *Shakespeare's Proverbial Language: An Index.* Berkeley: University of California Press, 1981. |
| Fryde | Fryde, E. B., et al. eds. *Handbook of British Chronology.* 3rd edn. Cambridge: Cambridge Universtiy Press, 1986. |
| Holinshed | Holinshed, Raphael. *The Chronicles of England, Scotaland, and Ireland.* 2nd. edn. 3 vols. in 2. London, 1587. |
| Jowett & Taylor | Jowett, John, and Taylor Gary. 'Sprinklings of Authority: The First Folio Text of *Richard II*'. *Studies in Bibliography* 38 (1985), 151-200. |
| Kökeritz | Kökeritz, Helge. *Shakespeare's Names: A Pronouncing Dictionary.* 1959; rpr. New Haven and London: Yale University Press, 1977. |
| Noble | Noble, Richmond. *Shakespeare's Biblical Knowledge and Use of the Book of Common Prayer, as Exemplified in the Plays of the First Folio.* London: Macmillan, 1935. |
| *OED* | *Oxford English Dictionary: Second Edition on CD-ROM* (v. 4.0). Oxford: Oxford University Press, 2009. |
| Onions | Onions, C. T. *A Shakespeare Glossary.* Enlarged and revised thoroughly by Robert D. Eagleson. Oxford: Clarendon Press, 1981. |
| Shaheen | Shaheen, Naseeb. *Biblical References in Shakespeare's Plays.* Newark: University of Delaware Press, 1999. |
| Sugden | Sugden, F. H. *A Topographical Dictionary to the Works of Shakespeare and His Fellow Dramatists.* 1925; rpr. Hildesheim, Georg Olms Verlag, 1969. |
| Tilley | Tilley, Morris Palmer. *A Dictionary of Proverbs in England in the Sixteenth and Seventeenth Centuries: A Collection of* |

*the Proverbs Found in English Literature and the Dictionaries of the Period.* 1950; rpr. Tokyo: Meicho-Fukyu-Kai, 1982.

*Traison*      *Chronicque de la Traison et Mort de Richart Deux, Roy Dengleterre.* Ed. Benjamin Williams. London, 1846.

大修館シェイクスピア双書　第2集

# リチャード二世

RICHARD II

# 解　説

## 1.　テクスト

　『リチャード二世』のテクストには、いわゆる「廃位の場面」
(deposition scene) または「退位のエピソード」(abdication
episode) (4. 1. 154-317) の出版検閲による削除の可能性という
大きな問題がある。本作は 1623 年出版の第 1・二つ折版全集 (F1)
におさめられる前に、1597 年出版の第 1・四つ折本を皮切りに 5
版の四つ折本 (Q1 〜 Q5) として出版されているが、問題のエ
ピソードが見られるのはジェイムズ朝時代に入って 1608 年に出
版された Q4 以降のテクストのみであるからだ。

　書籍商組合の出版登録は 1597 年 8 月 29 日にアンドリュー・ワ
イズ (Andrew Wise) の名のもとに行われ (Arber, III, 89)、同
年「宮内大臣閣下の僕<sup>しもべ</sup>たちによって上演されたとおりのもの」で
あることを謳う Q1 が出版されている。これはシェイクスピア劇
の単独出版としては 1594 年の『タイタス・アンドロニカス』、
1594-5 年出版の『ヘンリー六世・第 2 部』および『同・第 3 部』
に次ぐものであり、本作 Q1 出版と同年の 1597 年には『ロミオ
とジュリエット』が出版され、ワイズは同 10 月 20 日に『リチャ
ード三世』の出版登録をし (Arber, III, 93)、同年中に出版して
いる。

　ワイズは翌 1598 年にこの劇の 2 つの版を出版しており、シェ
イクスピア劇が同じ年のうちに 2 版を重ねたのはこの劇と『ペリ
クリーズ』の第 1 および第 2・四つ折本 (1609) の例しかなく、
この劇の人気の高さを物語っている。

　また、Q2 の標題頁には「ウィリアム・シェイクスピア作 (*By*

*William Shake-ſpeare.*）」との記載があり、同年同じワイズによって出版された『リチャード三世』の第2・四つ折本とともに標題頁に作者名としてシェイクスピアの名前を冠した最初の四つ折本となっており、前年3作のシェイクスピア劇が出版されたことと相俟って、この頃出版市場におけるシェイクスピアのネーム・ヴァリューがあがったことがうかがわれる。

　書籍商組合の出版登録簿には、1603年6月25日付けで『リチャード二世』、『リチャード三世』、『ヘンリー四世・第1部』ほか2点の劇の出版権がワイズからマシュー・ロー（Matthew Law）に移ったことが記録されており（Arber, III, 239）、ローは1608年に『リチャード二世』を出版している。このQ4には、これまでの四つ折本におさめられていない、問題の「退位のエピソード」がはじめて印刷されており、「議会の場面とリチャード王の廃位」という追加部分を収録していることを謳う標題頁がつけられている。1615年出版のQ5にもこの場面は収録されている。

　本作は、F1では『ジョン王』に次ぐ歴史劇2番目の作品として、23-45という歴史劇部分のページ番号を振られて sigs. b6-d5 におさめられている。

　Q1は、本文の正確さと、簡素だが演説的な台詞で密度があがる句読法上の特徴から、シェイクスピアの原稿（かその写し）から印刷されたものと考えられている。Q2以降は前の四つ折本をもとに印刷され、Q4は、行割りの不正確さや脱落、誤りの多さから、上演の再構成と思われる退位のエピソードを組みこんだものとされている。F1はいずれかの四つ折本（Jowett and Taylor によれば Q3）に劇団の後見用台本を参照して書きこみを加えたものから印刷されたと見られている。

　退位のエピソードがQ1になくて、Q4、Q5、F1におさめられるようになった経緯、ありていに言えば検閲による削除かあとか

らの附加かということが大きな問題であるが、そのことは他の問題とも関係するので、あとで論じる。

## 2. 創作年代

　本作は、『ヘンリー四世』二部作、『ヘンリー五世』へとつづく英国史劇第2・四部作の第一作である。シェイクスピアの初期キャリアーのなかで重要な位置を占める英国史劇のうち出版時期を明確に特定できるのは、エセックス伯のアイルランド遠征と帰国のあいだの時期に描かれたとされる『ヘンリー五世』のみである。本作に関しては1595年の執筆と推測されるが、完全に特定できる明確な証拠はない。以下に創作年代の上限、下限を決定する証拠を見ていくことにする。

　執筆時期の上限は、材源のうち最後のものが利用可能になった時期である。借用の証拠が認められるサミュエル・ダニエル（Samuel Daniel）の『ランカスター、ヨーク両家の内戦、最初の四巻』（*The First Fowre Bookes of the Ciuile Warres betweene the two houſes of Lancaster and Yorke*）の出版登録は1594年10月で、1595年11月3日付けのローランド・ホワイトのサー・ロバート・シドニー宛て書簡（*Letters and Memorials of State*, I, 357）にこの本を同送したとの追伸があり、ダニエルの著作が1595年11月には出版されていることが確かめられる。しかしながら、最近の研究では、戴冠式の際のリチャードのようすを語るヨークの「劇場で人気の役者が舞台からさがると、見物の目は次にあらわれる役者をぼんやりと見、その言葉を退屈なおしゃべりと思うように、いやそれ以上の侮蔑をこめて、人びとはリチャードにしかめ面を見せたのだ」（5. 2. 23-28）がダニエルの出版前の手稿に基づいている可能性が指摘され、シェイクスピアが少なくとも1594年頃から本作の執筆に取りかかっていたと推定されて

いる（Weiss）。

　E・K・チェンバース以来、私的な上演とはいえ、本作の上演に関するもっとも古い記録とみなされてきたのは、シェイクスピアのパトロンであるハンズドン卿ヘンリー・ケアリーの娘婿エドワード・ホービーが宰相サー・ロバート・セシルをキャノン・ロウの自宅での夕食に招待する際に書いた1595年12月7日付けの書簡にある、「火曜日〔12月9日〕にリチャード王があなたのもとにお目見えします（K. Richard present him selfe to your vewe)」（Chambers, II. 320-21）という言葉である。しかしながら、このリチャード王がどのリチャードを指すのか、また、これが劇への言及なのか、たとえば肖像画なのかもわからない。

　そのため確実に下限と言えるのは、1597年8月29日付けの出版登録とその年から翌年にかけて最初の3版の四つ折本が出版されていることである。また、フランシス・ミアズ（Francis Meres）は『知恵の宝庫』（*Palladis Tamia, or Wits Treasury*, 1598）のよく知られた一節で、シェイクスピアを当代のすぐれた劇作家とし、喜劇、悲劇に分けて12作の初期作品を挙げるなかで悲劇の最初のものとして本作をあげている。1600年には詞華集『イングランドのパルナッソス』（*Englands Parnassus*）にゴートのイングランド頌をはじめとする6箇所の引用がおさめられている。

　1594-5年はペストの猖獗（しょうけつ）を見た年で（1593年に1万人を超える死者が出ている）劇団の状況が不安定だったため、シェイクスピアは『ヴィーナスとアドニス』（*Venus and Adonis*, 1593)、『ルークリースの陵辱』（*The Rape of Lucrece*, 1594）の2作の詩を出版している。英国史劇の第1・四部作は1作ずつ異なる劇団によって上演されていたが、1594年に宮内大臣一座が結成されると、シェイクスピアはその団員となり、すべての劇をこの劇団に提供

するようになる。ケンブリッジ版の編者アンドリュー・ガーはこのような事情をあげて、シェイクスピアが第2・四部作を新しい劇団への加入の手立てとしたと考え、この四部作の制作はシェイクスピアの劇作家としての自身の芸術への自負とともに、自身の将来を切り拓くプロの劇作家としての腕前を示すものとみなしている（Gurr, 1-4）。

## 3. 材源

　シェイクスピアが本作を書くに当たってもっとも重要な材源としたのは、他の英国史劇創作の際にも参照しているラファエル・ホリンシェッド（Raphael Holinshed）の『イングランド、スコットランド、アイルランドの年代記』（*Chronicles of England, Scotland, and Ireland*）の第2版（1587）である。第3巻493ページに記された、1398年4月29日にウィンザーで開かれたボリンブルックによるモーブリー告発の聴聞会の記述から、515-17ページにおさめられた1400年におけるリチャードの暗殺とソールズベリー伯らの叛乱平定などの記述までを利用している。

　その利用の仕方は、ときには数ページ分の記述を凝縮して、ときには年代記にとどめられた王たちの言葉をそのまま利用し、ときには史実から離れるなど、融通無碍と言える。リチャード暗殺の際の「悪魔に取り憑かれろ、ランカスター家のヘンリーもお前も」（The devil take Henry of Lancaster and thee!　5. 5. 102）は、ホリンシェッドからそのままとられたものである。その一方、劇の大きな見せ場となっている、議会でリチャードがボリンブルックに王冠を渡し、王位を失ったみずからの境遇を嘆いて鏡を割るエピソードはまったくの創作である。第1・四部作は主材源をエドワード・ホールの『ランカスター、ヨーク両名家の和合』（*The Union of the Two Noble and Illustre Families of Lancaster and*

*York*, 1548）とする説もあるが、すでに第2・四部作の最初の劇で、シェイクスピアはホリンシェッドの年代記を自家薬籠中のものとしているように思われる。

　ホールの『和合』は、薔薇戦争の記述をボリンブルックとモーブリーのいさかいからはじめており、シェイクスピアがそれを参照している可能性はある。

　また、フランス人ジャン・フロワサール（Jean Froissart）による主として百年戦争期（1322-1400）の記録『年代記』（*Chroniques,* ?1495）のバーナーズ卿（John Bourchier, Lord Berners, c. 1467-1533）による英語訳（1523-25）も利用されている。第4幕1場でリチャードの王位委譲の意思を伝えるのをヨーク公としているのは、フロワサールなのである。

　シェイクスピアはまた、創作年代の項で触れたダニエルの『ランカスター、ヨーク両家の内戦、最初の四巻』を利用している。先にヨークの演劇の比喩がダニエルの手稿に依拠している可能性を指摘したが、フランスに帰る前のリチャードと妃を描いているのはダニエルだけで、第5幕第1場の別れの場面に影響をおよぼしていると考えられている。

　劇冒頭2幕の、ボリンブルックとモーブリーの決闘の原因となるグロスター公トマス・オヴ・ウッドストックの死、夫の死を悲しみゴーントに復讐をうながす未亡人、ゴーントの人格造形、王国領土の賃貸などのリチャードによる悪政は、作者不詳の先行劇作品『ウッドストック』（*Woodstock*）の影響を受けていると考えられている。

## 4. 作品
### (1) シェイクスピアの英国史劇における『リチャード二世』
　シェイクスピアは、リチャード二世の廃位（1399年）からヘ

ンリー七世の戴冠（1485年）までのイギリスの歴史を、8作の劇で描いている。描かれる時代順に並べると、本作『リチャード二世』（*Richard II*）と『ヘンリー四世』二部作（*Henry IV, Parts 1 & 2*）、『ヘンリー五世』（*Henry V*）、『ヘンリー六世』三部作（*Henry VI, Parts 1-3*）、『リチャード三世』（*Richard III*）の8作である。しかしながら執筆順では、『ヘンリー六世』（1589-92年頃）、『リチャード三世』（1592-3年頃）、『リチャード二世』（1595年頃）、『ヘンリー四世』二部作（1595-8年頃）、『ヘンリー五世』（1599年）となっており、この執筆順によって『ヘンリー六世』三部作と『リチャード三世』を第1・四部作、『リチャード二世』と残りの3作を第2・四部作と呼びならわしている。

　このふたつの四部作がカヴァーするのは、ボリンブルックによるリチャード二世の王位簒奪が、薔薇戦争（Wars of the Roses）と呼ばれるランカスター家とヨーク家の王位争いによる内乱の時代を招来し、リッチモンド伯ヘンリー・テューダーが内乱の時代の最悪の暴君リチャード三世をボズワースの戦いで破るまでの時代である。これを歴史記述のひとまとまりの単位とすることは、ポリドール・ヴァージルがヘンリー七世の求めに応じて執筆しヘンリー八世時代に完成した『イングランド史26巻』（*Anglicae Historiae Libri XXVI*, 1534）によってはじまり、ヘンリーの即位を神意に基づく平和の実現とみなす姿勢とあわせてテューダー朝神話と呼びならわされる。シェイクスピアの時代を統治したエリザベス一世へとつながる王家を称賛するこの歴史観は、シェイクスピアが材源として利用したホールやホリンシェッドなどの年代記作家に引き継がれている。

　シェイクスピアの歴史劇は同時代の問題をさりげなく劇世界に滑りこませるなどしており、個別に上演される劇作品が現王朝を礼讃する歴史観をひとえに体現していると言うことはできないに

せよ、この歴史理解の枠組みがシェイクスピアの歴史劇に創作の枠組みを提供していることは押さえておく必要がある。

## (2) エセックス伯の叛乱と『リチャード二世』検閲説

　『リチャード二世』という劇の性質を考える際に重要なことは、すでに指摘したように第4幕第1場のリチャードが議会でボリンブルックに渋りながらも王冠を引き渡すエピソードが最初の3つの四つ折本になく、出版検閲によって削除されたものと考えるのが、通説となっていることである。正統な王にたいする王位簒奪を描くこの劇は、世継ぎのいない老齢の女王が統治するイングランドにあって危険な劇だったと考えられているのである。

　この劇のそうした政治的紊乱（びんらん）性を示す証左として引きあいに出されるエピソードがある。エセックス伯の乱——アイルランドの叛乱平定の失敗などで女王の寵を失ったかつての寵臣エセックス伯ロバート・デヴルーが 1601 年に起こした、失敗に終わったクーデター計画——の前日にシェイクスピアの『リチャード二世』とおぼしい劇が叛徒たちの要望で上演されているのである。

　叛乱は 2 月 8 日日曜日に起こっている。劇団員オーガスティン・フィリップス（Augustine Phillips）の証言によれば、その前の金曜か木曜に、ノーサンバーランド伯ヘンリー・パーシーのふたりの息子チャールズとジョスリン（Charles and Josceline Percy）とモンティーグル男爵ウィリアム・パーカー（William Parker, Baron Monteagle）らが劇団員のもとを訪れ、「リチャード二世王の廃位と殺害」（the deposing and killing of King Richard II）の上演を依頼し、平常の額の倍ぐらいに当たる 40 シリングの支払いを申し出たという。劇団の面々は『リチャード二世』は古い劇で長いあいだ上演されていないので、客が集まらないと思い、ほかの劇の上演を決めていたが、この依頼を受けて

その劇を演じることにした、という（*CSPD Elizabeth*, Vol. 5, 578）。

　この記録が、シェイクスピアの『リチャード二世』を、エセックスの叛乱の際に叛徒側の要請で、クーデターへの支持を集めるための景気づけに上演された、政治的紊乱性をもつ劇とみなす根拠となっている。たとえばスティーヴン・グリーンブラットは、このときの『リチャード二世』の上演を例にとって、退位のエピソードが検閲によって初期のテクストから削除されたことを事実として引きあいに出し、劇作品がくり返し上演されることで、封じこめることができなくなり、政治的危険性をもつことを論じ、ジョナサン・ドリモアらとともに新歴史主義の鬨（とき）の声をあげている（Greenblatt, 3-4）。

　しかしながら、エセックス伯の周囲が『リチャード二世』の上演にどのようなことを期待したのかということには触れないとしても、これまで定説とされてきた、『リチャード二世』という劇の政治的紊乱性と不可分の関係にある退位のエピソードの検閲説は見直してもよさそうである。

　ひとつには、『リチャード二世』の政治的紊乱性を主張する際にかならず引きあいに出されてきた、エリザベス一世の「私はリチャード二世である」という発言の信憑性に関する疑義が呈されている。考古家のウィリアム・ランバード（William Lambarde）がエリザベスと会見して、ロンドン塔にある文書のリストを贈呈したとき、リチャード二世の項目に目をとめて「私はリチャード二世だ。あなたはそれを知らないのか」と言ったというエピソードである。この話の出所はランバード家の文書だが、その発言につづけてエリザベスは「この悲劇は往来や劇場で（in open street and houses）40回も上演された」と言ったことになっている（Chambers, II. 326-7）。ランバード自身がこの会見か

ら 15 日後の 8 月 19 日に他界しており、また、この劇が通りでの
上演も含めて 40 回も上演されているということなど信じがたく、
この記録の信憑性には疑義が呈されている。

　そうした周辺的なことはそろそろ終えて、検閲説の検討を行い
たい。検閲を見こしての自粛と考えるものも、出版のみの検閲と
考えるものも、上演上の削除も行われたと考えるものもいるが、
最初の 3 版の四つ折本に問題の退位の場面がないのは検閲による
削除であると考えるのがこの検閲説で、ケンブリッジ版、アーデ
ン版、オックスフォード版など現在使用される標準的な編集版は
すべてその説をとっている。

　早い時期の提唱者イーヴリン・メイ・オールブライト（Evelyn
May Albright）も、比較的近年のジョン・ジョウェットとゲイ
リー・テイラー（John Jowett and Gary Taylor）も、この部分
がないと場面に欠落が生じ、とりわけその出来事の直後にウェス
トミンスター大主教が発する「われわれは嘆かわしい一幕を見て
しまった」（A woeful pageant have we here beheld. 4. 1. 320）
の指すものがなくなると主張する。

　問題の退位のエピソードとは、リチャードの退位とボリンブル
ックの即位を決定する議会にリチャードが召喚され、渋りながら
も王冠や錫杖をボリンブルックに渡し、自身の罪状を読みあげる
ことを拒み、みずからの姿を映しだす鏡を割る、愁嘆場である。
とりわけ、鏡が映しだす自身の顔が王位にあったときと変わらな
いのを見て、王位を失った自身の境遇を悲嘆して鏡を割るリチャ
ードの姿は痛ましく、「嘆かわしい一幕」と呼ぶにふさわしい。

　だが、はたして Q1 は本当に欠落のあるテクストなのか。問題
の「退位のエピソード」の前後の部分を見てみよう。第 4 幕は議
会の場面で、貴族たちの決闘騒ぎのあと、リチャードのもとから
戻ったヨークが、王位委譲がリチャードの意思であることを告げ、

11

「ヘンリー四世万歳」と言ってボリンブルックに玉座に就くことを求め、ボリンブルックもそうしようとする。それにたいしてカーライルが正統な王位継承者でないボリンブルックが王位に就くと末代まで混乱と不幸の種になる、と反対演説を行う。Q3-F1ではそのあとに退位のエピソードがくるわけだが、Q1にはリチャードの召喚から愁嘆場までの約150行がなく、カーライルの反対演説を聞いたノーサンバーランドによるカーライルの逮捕命令に、ボリンブルックの「そうすることにしよう。いいか、次の水曜日に余は謹んで戴冠を宣言する。諸卿たちよ、準備をするのだ」(Let it be so, and loe on wednesday next, / We solemnly proclaime our Coronation, / Lords be ready all.) と F1 (4. 1. 318-9) とは違う返答がつづき、一同退場後舞台に残った修道院長の「嘆かわしい一幕を目にしてしまった」とカーライルの「悲惨なことがこれから起こる。まだ生まれておらぬ子たちが棘(とげ)のように痛みを与えるものと感じることになるだろう」という言葉がつづく。

　こうした出来事の流れを見れば、こちらのほうではリチャードの即位宣言とカーライルの逮捕命令が「嘆かわしい一幕」とされるのは自然な流れのように見える。また、カーライルは「〔ボリンブルックの即位を〕とめないと、子々孫々おおという嘆きの叫びをあげることになる」(Prevent it, resist it, let it not be so, / Lest child, child's children, cry against you <u>woe</u>. 148-49, underline added) という言葉で演説を終えており、ウェストミンスター自身の「嘆かわしい一幕」も、カーライル自身の「災いが訪れる。これから生まれる子供たちが今日という日を棘のように痛みをもたらすものと感じることになる」(The <u>woe's</u> to come. The children yet unborn / Shall feel this day as sharp to them as thorn. 321-22, underline added) も、演説の最後の語を受けての言葉となっている。

　材源となったホリンシェッドの『年代記』では、王は9月29日にロンドン塔で王位委譲の宣言を行い、立ちあったヨーク大主教が議会にその報告を行っており（Holinshed, 3: 504）、Q1のシェイクスピアはホリンシェッドの記述に従ってこのエピソードを書いたということができる。議会における国王退位のエピソードが「新しい附加部分」であるというQ4の標題ページの言葉を信じて、その後、劇作家はホリンシェッドの記述から離れる、国王が議会にあらわれ王冠を譲りわたす場面を加筆したと考えてもよいのではないだろうか。

　いまひとつ、検閲説を主張するものたちが説明していないのは、第3幕第3場でリチャードが退位の決心をするところでこの劇は廃位の劇となっており、王位をひき渡す彼の愁嘆場を削除することがなんの問題を回避することになるかということである。編者としてくり返し言うが、検閲説は定説である。ただ、疑ってもよい定説だと主張しておきたい。

## （3）韻文劇『リチャード二世』

　前節で触れたように政治的問題性がつねに最重要問題のように取り沙汰されてきたが、『リチャード二世』という劇はきわめて詩的な言葉で書かれた美しい劇である。本作は『ジョン王』、『ヘンリー六世・第1部』および『同・第3部』と並んで、シェイクスピア劇のなかで数少ないすべて韻文で書かれた劇である。用いられる韻律はシェイクスピア劇で通常用いられる弱強五歩格（iambic pentameter）だが、稀に六歩格（hexameter）のアレクサンダー格（Alexandrine）も見られる。さらに、シェイクスピアといえば無韻詩（blank verse）が連想されるが、押韻がこの劇の言語上の大きな特徴となっている。全19場面からなるこの劇で、第1幕第4場と第3幕第1場というふたつの短い場面（そ

れぞれ 65 行と 44 行）をのぞくすべての場面に押韻二行連句が見られ、4 つの押韻三行連句を含めて連続した行で押韻している部分の行数は総行数 2749 行にたいして 18％に当たる 502 行（二行連句と三行連句の数で言えば 249）、さらに交差韻が 18 行で見られるので、韻を踏んでいる行は全体の 19％に当たる 520 行（韻の数は 258）ということになる。シェイクスピア劇で押韻行の比率の高い劇としては、『夏の夜の夢』（*A Midsummer Night's Dream*）が 42％超、さらに『恋の骨折り損』（*Love's Labours Lost*）にいたっては 62％というから、それらには遠くおよばないが、台詞の最終 2 行だけで韻を踏む印象的なキャッピング・カプレットの使用がたびたび見られ、オーマールの叛逆をボリンブルックに報告する父親ヨーク公にたいして公爵夫人が息子を見逃してくれるよう新王に懇願する第 5 幕第 3 場 74-135 行のように、60 行を超えて押韻がつづく部分もある。とりわけ顕著なのはリチャードが韻となる語を 128 回、つまり劇全体の押韻行 520 行のうち 25％近くを発していることである。

　押韻が効果的に用いられているのは、第 3 幕第 3 場の、リチャードがノーサンバーランドの求めに応じて上舞台からおりていく件（178-83）である。この劇では、ボリンブルックとリチャードの運命の上昇と下降を、上下をあらわすさまざまな言葉の使用で主題化するが、この件ではそれが舞台演出上リチャードの動きによって可視化される。問題の台詞は、ノーサンバーランドの求めに応じてボリンブルックと相まみえるためにリチャードが（フリント城の胸壁に擬された）上舞台からおりるに当たって屈辱感をあらわにするものである。その言葉は base-grace、king-sing と押韻するふたつの二行連句で結ばれている。

**RICHARD** Down, down I come like glistering Phaëton,

Wanting the manage of unruly jades.

In the base court? Base court where kings grow base 180

To come at traitors' calls and do them grace.

In the base court? Come down? Down court, down king!

For night-owls shriek where mounting larks should sing.

　180行ではおりていく先の base court が二度くり返されたあと、「卑しめられる」という意味で base が押韻語となり、「頭を下げること」を意味する grace がそれを受ける。182-3行の king-sing の韻が用いられるのは劇中2度目で、前にこの韻が出てきたのは、ノーサンバーランドが、まさにこの場面でしているリチャードとの対峙を決心する台詞である。彼は、第2幕第1場262-64行でリチャードが死んだゴーントの財産を没収するのを目の当たりにして、アイルランド遠征の費用捻出のために酷税を導入する王との対決への決心をこう明らかにする。

**NORTHUMBERLAND** His noble kinsman, most degenerate King!

But lords, we hear this fearful tempest sing

Yet seek no shelter to avoid the storm.

「嵐の歌」にひるまず王との対決を決意するこの言葉が、王の没落を予兆する不吉な歌となってよみがえるのである。

　また、首句反復との組み合わせで、修辞的技巧が登場人物の苦悩を映しだすこの劇の特徴をよく表わしているのが、リチャードが鏡に映った自分の顔について語る第4幕第1場280-87行である。鏡が映しだす自分の顔が王であった頃のものと変わらないことで運命の残酷さに苛立ち、鏡を割るにいたる言葉が「これが…した

顔なのか」という文句を3度くり返し、この一節の最初の6行で6回出てくる face という音を用いたキャッピング・カプレットで締めくくられているのである（正確には台詞自体は、割れた鏡を見て我に返る3行がこのあとにつづいて終わる）。

Thou dost beguile me. Was this face the face            280
That every day under his household roof
Did keep ten thousand men? Was this the face
That like the sun did make beholders wink?
Is this the face that faced so many follies,
That was at last outfaced by Bolingbroke?            285
A brittle glory shineth in this face,
As brittle as the glory is the face . . ..

　そのほか、リチャードの台詞における押韻が印象的なのは、第5幕1場の王妃との別れ際のやりとり（79-102行）で、「別離」や「悲嘆」などに関わる語からなる part / heart（3回）、go / woe、groans / moans、brief / grief などの押韻から、ふたりの悲しみが惻々と胸に迫る。

　このように、要所要所で効果的な押韻を用い、リチャードの悲劇を整然とした韻文で伝えていることが『リチャード二世』の大きな特徴となっている。また、第2幕第1場における老齢のゴーントによる悲しい言葉遊びや、第5幕第5場における牢獄のリチャードの夢想など、詩人シェイクスピアの腕の見せ所が随所に見られる。

## 5.　上演史

　初演から清教徒革命による劇場閉鎖までの時期に、『リチャード二世』はさかんに上演されていた。第1・二つ折版全集が出版された 1623 年までに、標題頁の惹句で上演があったことを謳う四つ折本が 5 版を数えたことや、エセックス伯一味が叛乱の景気づけに上演を思いついたことなどがそのことを物語っている。また、創作年代の項で触れたホービーの 1595 年 12 月 9 日付書簡が私的上演の行われた可能性を示しており、1607 年には、アフリカ西岸シエラレオネに停泊中の、東インドに向かう船ドラゴン号で、船長ウィリアム・キーリングが訪問した僚艦の船長のために船員たちに『リチャード二世』（King Richard the Second）を上演させたとの記録（Chambers, I. 356, and II. 334-5）もある。また、1608 年出版の第 4・四つ折本の「最近国王一座によってグローブ座で上演されたように、議会の場面とリチャード王の廃位のあらたな附加部分を加えた」という惹句を信じるならば、その頃の上演もあったことになる。1631 年 6 月には祝典局長ヘンリー・ハーバートのために 2 度の寄附公演が行われている（Black, 568）が、このことは初演から 30 年以上すぎても本作が人気ある演目だったことを示している。

　その後約 1 世紀間、シェイクスピアの書いたとおりの『リチャード二世』は上演されなかった。記録に残るのは、シェイクスピア劇の改作者として知られるネイハム・テイト（Nahum Tate）と、のちにシェイクスピア全集の編纂者となるルイス・ティボールド（Lewis Theobald）による翻案劇のみである。テイトは 1680 年にこの劇の翻案を上演するが、王位を追われる王に同情的な劇であったにもかかわらず即座に上演禁止となり、直後に舞台をシチリアに移して上演した『シチリアの王位簒奪者』（The Sicilian Usurper）もすぐに同じ憂き目を見ている。ティボールドは 1719

年に、シェイクスピア劇の最初の2幕の内容がなく、徹底的に政治性を排除した翻案劇『リチャード二世の悲劇』（*The Tragedy of King Richard the II*）を執筆・上演して好評を博している。この劇はリチャードのアイルランドからの帰還にはじまり、舞台はリチャードとボリンブルックがはじめて会うロンドン塔に限定されている。ヨークはふたりのあいだで揺れることなく、最後までリチャードに忠誠を尽くし、リチャードの死後、傷心で命を落とす。こうした改作とその結果は、原作のもつ政治性に起因するものと言える。

　1世紀あまりの空白期間を経て『リチャード二世』が上演されたのは、1738年の、コヴェント・ガーデンの支配人ジョン・リッチ（John Rich）による舞台だった。1736年に設立されたシェイクスピア・レディーズ・クラブの要望を受けての上演で、第2・二つ折本所収のテクストに削除の印とアレグザンダー・ポープ編纂のテクストからの書きこみによって作られた台本で上演されており、カットされた部分は少なくシェイクスピアのテクストに忠実な上演だった。しかしその一方で、演劇統制を進める首相ロバート・ウォルポール（Robert Walpole）を国王を動かす佞臣たちになぞらえて揶揄するという政治的目的があった。

　ふたたび長い空白期間があり、次に記録が残っているのは19世紀の名優キーン親子による改作上演である。エドマンド・キーン（Edmund Kean）が出演したのは1814年のものである。この舞台はリチャード・ロートンによる改作で、大団円では、王妃の説得でボリンブルックがリチャードの復位を決意するが、リチャードはエクストンに殺されてしまい、王妃は夫の亡骸と対面し、リア王のコーディリアへの言葉を発して絶命し、あとに残されたボリンブルックが巡礼を誓う。しかし、19世紀の舞台の特徴をよくあらわしているのは、息子チャールズ・キーン（Charles

Kean）による『リチャード二世』（1857 年）である。この改作
劇は出来事の舞台となるイーリー・ハウスのゴーントの部屋やウ
ェストミンスター宮の枢密院議場、ウィンザー宮の聖ジョージ礼
拝堂などを歴史的正確性をもって再現した一大歴史スペクタクル
であった。その一方で、台本にはちぐはぐな部分があり、第 3 幕
第 4 場の庭師の場面より前にボリンブルックのロンドンへの凱旋
行進を第 5 幕第 2 場のヨークの台詞どおりに劇化し、第 5 幕第 2
場は大半をカットして舞台上でスペクタクル化された凱旋行進に
ついてヨークが語る台詞だけが残された。また、スペクタクル化
の裏では、第 5 幕第 5 場の幽閉されたリチャードの独白やゴーン
トのイングランド頌など重要な台詞の多くの部分をカットし、劇
の特徴である詩的興趣が失われている。1896 年からストラトフ
ォードでフランク・ベンソン（Frank Benson）が演出、主演し
た舞台も、大規模な舞台装置を用いスペクタクル性のある舞台だ
ったが、柔弱な臆病者と卓越した詩人というふたつの面を持ちあ
わせる、分裂的なリチャード像を造形し、リチャードの人格造形
に力点が置かれるようになる 20 世紀の傾向を先取りしていると
いう。

　20 世紀のシェイクスピア劇上演では、裸の舞台、速い台詞回し、
中断なしの上演というエリザベス朝の演技への回帰が大きな潮流
となるが、その中心的な担い手となるのがハーリー・グランヴィ
ル＝バーカー（Harley Granville-Barker）とジョン・ギールグ
ッド（John Gielgud）である。グランヴィル＝バーカーは、1899
年にエリザベス朝演劇協会の創設者ウィリアム・ポールによって、
ロンドン大学ユニヴァーシティ・コレッジにおける『リチャード
二世』公演に抜擢されている。彼は歯切れのよい台詞回しで俳優
として新しい演技スタイルを生みだしたが、のちに演出も手がけ
るようになり、素速い場面移行を可能にする、客席に突きだした

装置のない舞台の必要性を強調し、新しい演劇運動の担い手となる。1929年には若き日のギールグッドがオールド・ヴィック劇場の新しい演出家ウィリアム・ハーコートによってリチャード役に抜擢されている。この劇団も、グランヴィル＝バーカーが20年あまりにわたって進めていたこの運動の影響を受けていた。ギールグッドは1937年にウェスト・エンドで自身の演出した『リチャード二世』に出演し、1953年にはストラトフォードにおいてポール・スコッフィールド主演の舞台を演出し、グランヴィル＝バーカーが主張したように、台詞の細部に人格造形を見出そうとつとめた。

　主人公の人格造形を強調する舞台と対極にあるのが、四部作、あるいはふたつの四部作の一部として上演する方法である。はじめて第2・四部作全体を上演したのは、1951年のロイヤル・シェイクスピア・カンパニーだった。アントニー・クウェイル（Anthony Quayle）が演出を手がけたこの舞台は、イングランドを称える叙事詩的な舞台で、ボリンブルックを肯定的に描く一方、粗暴にして残酷な同性愛者というリチャード像を提示した。それと対照的なのは、ピーター・ホール（Peter Hall）演出のロイヤル・シェイクスピア・カンパニーによる1963-64年の『薔薇戦争』七部作（『ヘンリー6世』は2部にまとめられている）の、執筆順のため4作目として2年目に上演された舞台である。ボリンブルックが、とくにブシーとグリーンの処刑からリチャードの時代と変わらない性急な暴力性を発揮し、権力の行使による人間性の喪失という主題が、冷たく、耳障りな音をたてる金属を多用したセットによって強調される。リチャードをとおして現代社会を批判することによってリチャードに共感を集めるように演出されたのは、1986-89年のマイケル・ボグダノフ（Michael Bogdanov）演出、イングリッシュ・シェイクスピア・カンパニーによる七部作（こ

の七部作は 1988 年 4 月に東京グローブ座のオープニング・フェスティヴァルとして上演されている）の一部として上演された舞台。こちらも 7 作を、しかしホールの七部作とは違って描かれた時代の順に上演している。サッチャー政権下の同時代のイギリス社会と関連づける演出で、衣装は連作全体で 19 世紀風からはじまり最後が同時代のパンクファッションへと推移していくもので、『リチャード二世』はヴィクトリア朝の前の摂政政治時代に設定され、リチャード宮廷の面々にはきらびやかなシルクの服装、それにたいしてランカスター側には質素な軍服姿が用いられた。

　20 世紀後半の単独上演では、神のような王の地位から無名の人間への没落の悲劇とした、1968-69 年のプロスペクト・シアター・カンパニーによるリチャード・コットレル（Richard Cottrell）演出イアン・マッケレン（Ian McKellen）主演の舞台や、2000 年のジョナサン・ケント（Jonathan Kent）演出レイフ・ファインズ（Ralph Fiennes）主演のアルメイダ・シアターによる舞台（10 月に赤坂 ACT シアターで上演された）もあるが、個性の際立つ演出は、1973 年のストラトフォードにおけるジョン・ウォートン（John Warton）による舞台と、1995 年ナショナル・シアターにおけるデボラ・ウォーナー（Deborah Warner）演出フィオーナ・ショー（Fiona Shaw）主演の舞台である。ウォートンの舞台は、リチャードとボリンブルックの類似を強調した画期的な演出だった。この公演では、イアン・リチャードソン（Ian Richardson）とリチャード・パスコー（Richard Pasco）が交互にリチャード役とボリンブルック役を演じた。ふたりの対称性を強調するために、ウォートンは、シェイクスピアに扮した仮面をかぶった俳優が、舞台に向きあって立っているリチャードソンとパスコーのうち一方に鏡を渡し、このふたりが鏡をはさんで対峙する黙劇で劇をはじめ、台本を変えて暗殺者としたボリンブル

ックが退位のエピソードでリチャードが割った鏡の枠をリチャードに向ける大団円で同じ光景をくり返した。一方のウォーナーは、奇妙な演出で王権をめぐる物語を異化している。リチャード役に女優をキャストし、ちぐはぐにコーディネートされた衣装を着て、脈絡なく気分が変わる演技をさせている。リチャードとボリンブルックのあいだには過去に恋愛関係があるという設定で、退位のエピソードの、リチャードが王冠を渡す件は台詞回しは厳粛だが王冠をもたずに行われ、すべてが幻想のような『リチャード二世』となっている。

　今世紀のものには、2013 年のグレゴリー・ドーラン（Gregory Doran）が演出した、ロイヤル・シェイクスピア・カンパニーによる舞台がある。棺に取りすがって泣いているグロスター公夫人の姿から劇がはじまり、ボリンブルックの帰還から第 3 幕第 4 場の庭師の場面まで、劇中の雑草への系統的な言及にあわせて舞台背景が雑草の影となり、第 3 幕までのボリンブルックの行動を雑草駆除として肯定的に描くが、彼は退位のエピソードで高笑いによって野心を露呈する。一方リチャードは悲劇的な状況のなかで自己抑制を示すが、第 3 幕第 3 場におけるオーマールとのやりとりはどの舞台よりも感情的で、このリチャードの自己抑制と内面の混乱の対比は今世紀のテレビドラマでも顕著に見られる。また、リチャードがオーマールに殺されるという皮肉な結末となっている。

　テレビドラマ化に先鞭をつけたのは、1978 年から 85 年にかけてイギリスで放映された BBC テレビジョン・シェイクスピア第 2 弾の、デイヴィッド・ジャイルズ（David Giles）が演出し、リチャード役をデレク・ジャコビ（Derek Jacobi）が、ボリンブルックをジョン・フィンチ（John Finch）が演じたものである。すべて狭く暗いスタジオでの撮影であるが、俳優の顔のクローズ

アップが多いことも大きな特徴となっている。テレビの特性を活かした演出と言えるのは、ボリンブルックのノーサンバーランドへの堂々たる返事とオーマールへのとり乱した言葉が対比される第3幕第3場で、ボリンブルックと会見するために降りていくリチャードの「下へ、下へ、輝けるパエトーンよろしく」(3. 3. 178) が胸壁上で大声で、それにつづく部分が階段を降りていきながら泣き声で発せられることである。内面の苦悩と演技の対比や建物のなかにカメラが進んでいくことなどはテレビドラマ独特の表現と言える。

　2012 年に『ホロウ・クラウン／嘆きの王冠』(*Hollow Crown*) の第1作として放映されたルパート・グールド (Rupert Goold) 演出のテレビドラマ版では、ベン・ウィショウ (Ben Whishaw) がホモセクシュアルで神経質、エクセントリックなリチャードを演じた。とりわけ、第3幕第3場の胸壁上でノーサンバーランドに答える件は芝居の舞台装置のような金の天使の飾りの前でなされ、演技という側面が強調され、時折寄りすぎてピントがはずれる極端なクローズアップがリチャードの激しい発汗ぶりを映しだしている。聖セバスチャンに扮したモデルを描いているブシーにリチャードが親しげに腕に触る冒頭のタイトルバックの映像が、オーマールが弓で射殺するリチャード暗殺の場面で再現され、カメラはその後天上のキリスト磔刑像を映しだし、同性愛者の奇矯な王と救世主という二重の意味づけがなされている。

　イギリス以外で上演された初期の例は、1947 年フランス人演出家ジャン・ヴィラール (Jean Vilar) が自身の創始したアヴィニョン演劇祭で上演した舞台と、翌年のイタリア人演出家ジョルジオ・ストレーレル (Girgio Strehler) によるミラノのピッコロ劇場における舞台がある。1981 年の太陽劇団 (Théâtre du Soleil) のアリアンヌ・ムヌーシュキン (Ariane Mnouchkine) は、

バリ島のガムランや日本の文楽、歌舞伎などの影響を受け、俳優たちが台詞を観客に向かって朗唱する独特のスタイルで、個人性をもたない感情（states）をあらわすことを目指した舞台を演出している。2000年にブレヒトゆかりのベルリナー・アンサンブルが上演した『リチャード二世』は、テクストを大幅に刈りこんだ翻案で、リチャード暗殺をヨークにさせることや、廷臣たちを白塗りにすることで、政治の世界が人間性を喪失させるという主題を強調したもので、3面ベニヤで覆われた殺風景な舞台が、落書きをされ、仕舞いには泥が投げつけられてどろどろになってしまう。

　日本では1980年の出口典雄演出、シェイクスピア・シアターの舞台、1994年の村田元史演出、劇団昴による舞台、2002年の山崎清介演出、グローブ座シェイクスピア・カンパニーによる舞台、2020年鵜山仁演出、新国立劇場の舞台がある。

　こうして『リチャード二世』の上演史を概観すると、17世紀における人気と王政復古期以降の改作の横行、18世紀におけるシェイクスピア劇に忠実な上演のはじまり、19世紀のスペクタクル化、20世紀のエリザベス朝的上演への回帰、20世紀後半から今世紀にかけての演出の個性化と映像化などといった潮流を読みとることができる。

# 参考文献解題

## 1. 注釈付テクスト

近年の3冊の注釈付テクストは、それぞれの特徴があるが、どれも使いやすい。とりわけオックスフォード版が、注釈、解説ともすばらしい。

Dawson, Anthony B. and Paul Yachnin, eds. *Richard II*. Oxford Shakespeare. Oxford: Oxford University Press, 2011.

Forker, Charles R., ed. *King Richard II*. Arden Shakespeare, Third Series. London: Thomson Learning, 2002.

Gurr, Andrew, ed. *King Richard II*. New Cambridge Shakespeare. Cambridge: Cambridge University Press, 1984.

## 2. 材源

*Chronicque de la Traison et Mort de Richart Deux, Roy Dengleterre*. Ed. Benjamin Williams. London, 1846.

Daniel, Samuel. *The First Fowre Bookes of the Ciuile Warres Betweene the Two Houses of Lancaster and Yorke*. London, 1595.

Hall, Edward. *The Union of Two Noble and Illustrate Families of Lancaster & Yorke*. London, 1548.

Holinshed, Raphael. *The Chronicles of England, Scotland, and Ireland*. 2nd. edn. 3 vols. in 2. London, 1587.

## 3. 上演史

Shewring, Margaret. *King Richard II*. Shakespeare in Performance. Manchester: Manchester University Press, 1996.

1995年までの20を超える記録の残る舞台上演を簡潔に記述している。

Sprague Arthur Colby. *Shakespeare's Histories: Plays for the Stage*.

London: Society for Theatre Research, 1964.

　シェイクスピアの歴史劇全般についての上演史を概観している。上記 Dawson & Yachnin の解説にある上演史もすぐれている。


## 4. 批評史・批評集

Bloom, Harold, ed. *William Shakespeare's Richard II*. Modern Critical Interpretations. New York: Chelsea House, 1988.
　1972-86年までの7点の批評を集めたもの。

Forker, Cahrles R., ed. *King Ricahrd II*. Shakespeare: The Critical Tradition. Rev. edn. London: Arden Shakespeare, 2022.
　1780-1918年の82点を収録した評言集。

Lopez, Jeremy. *Richard II: New Critical Essays*. London: Routledge, 2012.
　18世紀以来の批評傾向をまとめた解説のあと、さまざまな視点からの最新の論文を集めた批評集。


## 5. 作品研究

Albright, Evelyn May. 'Shakespeare's *Richard II* and the Essex Conspiracy'. *PMLA* 42 (1927). 686-720.
　本作とエセックスの叛乱との関係をもとに検閲説を主張した基本的研究論文。

Barroll, Leeds. 'A New History for Shakespeare and his Time'. *Shakespeare Quarterly* 39 (1988). 441-64.
　本作の検閲説を否定し改訂説を主張する論攷。

Clegg, Cyndia Susan. '"By the Choice and Inuitation of al the Realme": *Richard II* and Elizabethan Press Censorship'. *Shakespeare Quarterly* 48 (1997). 432-48.
　本作の検閲説を、当時検閲を受けた、議会制定法が王位継承権を正当化するとする書物との関連で説明する試み。

Greenblatt, Stephen. Introduction. *The Power of Forms in the English Renaissance*. Ed. Stephen Greenblatt. Norman, Okla.: Pilgrim Books, 1982. 1-13.

　ルネサンス研究における新歴史主義抬頭の時期に編まれた論集の序文。ここでグリーンブラットは、エリザ女王をリチャードに擬し、エセックスの叛乱の際にこの劇の上演が大衆を扇動するために用いられたとして、演劇のもつ紊乱性について論じた。

Hawkes, Terence. *Shakespeare's Talking Animals: Language and Dram in Society.* London: Edward Arnold, 1973.

　言語のはたらきに注目してシェイクスピア劇を論じる本書で、本作については言葉に言葉を重ねるリチャードの言語のコミュニケーション能力喪失が分析される。

Holderness, Graham. *Shakespeare: The History Plays.* New York: St. Martin's Press, 2000.

　文化唯物論の立場から、シェイクスピアの歴史劇を、『リチャード三世』から『リチャード二世』という描かれた時代とは逆の順序で歴史を再話化し作りあげるものと論じる研究。

Jowett, John, and Taylor Gary. 'Sprinklings of Authority: The First Folio Text of *Richard II*'. *Studies in Bibliography* 38（1985）. 151-200.

　1986年のオックスフォード版シェイクスピア全集におさめられた本作のテクストに結実した、本作のもっとも行き届いた本文研究。

Tennenhouse, Leonard. *Power on Display: The Politics of Shakespeare's Genre.* New York and London: Methuen, 1986.

　シェイクスピア劇のジャンルを王権と反対勢力のイデオロギーとの関連から説明する試みで、歴史劇は体制転覆的なカーニヴァル的なものを肯定するものと考える。

Tillyard, E. M. W. *Shakespeare's History Plays.* 1944; rpr. London: Chatto and Windus, 1980.

　シェイクスピアの歴史劇を「存在の偉大なる連鎖」という世界観やテューダー朝神話という歴史観に基づくものとする20世紀中盤の代表的な歴史劇研究。

Weiss, David S. 'Did Shakespeare Use a Manuscript of Samuel Daniel's *Civil Wars* to Write *Richard II*?' *Huntington Library Quarterly* 83 (2020). 235-67

　シェイクスピアがダニエルの『内乱史』の手稿版を見て1594年頃には『リチャード二世』執筆をはじめていた可能性を指摘する論攷。

# 薔薇戦争系図

## エドワード3世の7人の息子たちと

⑦ プランタジネット王家
エドワード3世
(Edward III, 1327-77)

エドワード・黒太子
(Edward the Black Prince, 1330-76)

ウィリアム・オヴ・ハットフィールド
(William of Hatfield, 1336-37)

ライオネル・クラレンス公
(Lionel, Duke of Clarence, 1338-68)

ランカスター公ジョン・オヴ・ゴーント
(John of Gaunt, Duke of Lancaster, 1340-99)

ヨーク公エドマンド・オヴ・ラングリー
(Edmund of Langley, Duke of York, 1341-1402)

グロスター公トマス・オヴ・ウッドストック
(Thomas of Woodstock, Duke of Gloucester, 1355-97)

ウィリアム・オヴ・ウィンザー
(William of Windsor, 1348-48)

ランカスター王家

⑧ リチャード2世
(Richard II, 1377-99)

イザベル
(Isabel)

オーウェン・テューダー
(Owen Tudor)

キャサリン
(Katherine, daughter of Louis VI of France)

① ヘンリー4世
(Henry IV, 1399-1413)

サマセット伯ジョン
(John)

② ヘンリー5世
(Henry V, 1413-22)

③ ヘンリー6世
(Henry VI, 1422-61, 1470-71)

サマセット公ジョン
(John)

マーガレット
(Margaret)

エドマンド(伯)エドワード・テューダー
(Edmund Tudor, Earl of Richmond)

テューダー王家

① ヘンリー7世
(Henry VII, 1485-1509)

エリザベス
(Elizabeth of York)

オーマール公エドワード・オヴ・ヨーク
(Edward of York)

ケンブリッジ伯リチャード
(Richard, Earl of Cambridge)

ヨーク公リチャード
(Richard, Duke of York)

ヨーク王家

① エドワード4世
(Edward IV, 1461-70, 1471-83)

③ リチャード3世
(Richard III, 1483-85)

② エドワード5世
(Edward V, 1483)

エリザベス
(Elizabeth of York)

② エドワード5世
(Edward V, 1483)

―― 婚姻関係(線上の数字は結婚順)

王の名の上の丸数字は当該王家における即位順

王の名の下の( )内の数字は在位期間

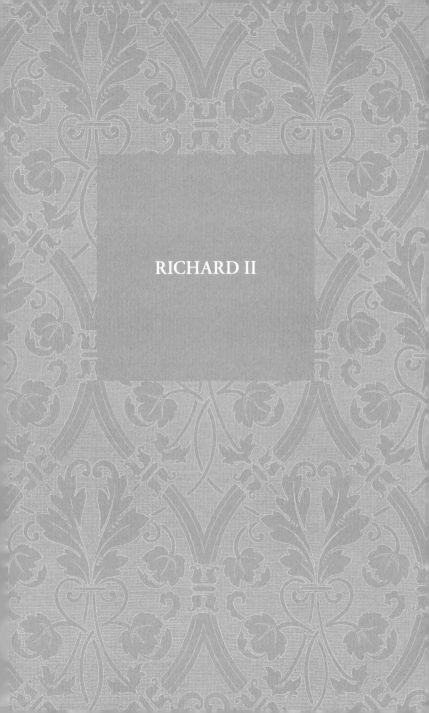

# RICHARD II

# DRAMATIS PERSONÆ

KING RICHARD II

QUEEN ISABEL, Richard's wife

JOHN OF GAUNT, Duke of Lancaster, Richard's uncle

EDMUND OF LANGLEY, Duke of YORK, Richard's uncle

DUCHESS OF YORK, his wife

DUCHESS OF GLOUCESTER, widow of Richard's uncle, Thomas of Woodstock

HENRY BOLINGBROKE, Duke of Hereford, Gaunt's son and Richard's cousin, later King HENRY IV

DUKE OF AUMERLE, York's son and Richard and Henry's cousin

THOMAS MOWBRAY, Duke of Norfolk

BUSHY
BAGOT } Richard's followers and counsellors
GREEN

HENRY PERCY, Earl of NORTHUMBERLAND
HARRY PERCY, his son

LORD ROSS

LORD WILLOUGHBY                                   } followers of Bolingbroke

LORD FITZWATER

ANOTHER LORD

LORD BERKELEY

EARL OF SALISBURY

BISHOP OF CARLISLE                 } allies of Richard
SIR STEPHEN SCROPE
DUKE OF SURREY
ABBOT OF WESTMINSTER

LORD MARSHAL

A Welsh CAPTAIN

# 登場人物

イングランド王リチャード二世　（1367-1400、在位 1377-99）

イングランド王妃イザベル　（1389-1409）

ランカスター公爵ジョン・オヴ・ゴーント　（1340-1399）リチャードの叔父

ヨーク公爵エドマンド・オヴ・ラングリー　（1341-1402）リチャードの叔父

ヨーク公爵夫人　〔ジョーン・ホランド Joan Holland（1366-1434）〕

グロスター公爵夫人　〔エリナー・ド・ブーン Eleanor de Bohun（c. 1365-99）〕

ヘリフォード公爵ヘンリー・ボリンブルック、のちのイングランド王ヘンリー四
　世　（1367-1413、在位 1399-1413）

オーマール公爵　〔エドワード・オヴ・ヨーク Edward of York（c. 1373-1415）〕
　ヨークの息子、リチャードとボリンブルックの従弟

ノーフォーク公爵トマス・モーブリー　（1366-1399）

ブシー　〔サー・ジョン・〜 Sir John（1399 歿）〕

バゴット　〔サー・ウィリアム・〜 Sir William（1407 歿）〕　　　リチャードの寵臣

グリーン　〔サー・ヘンリー・〜 Sir Henry（1399 歿）〕

ノーサンバーランド伯爵ヘンリー・パーシー　〔1341-1408〕

ハリー・パーシー　〔サー・ヘンリー・〜 Sir Henry（1364-1403）〕その息子〔*1H4*
　の Hotspur〕

ロス卿　〔第6代ヘルムズリーのド・ロス男爵サー・ウィリアム Sir William,
　sixth Baron de Ros of Helmsley（c. 1369-1414）〕

ウィロビー卿　〔第5代ウィロビー男爵サー・ウィリアム・オヴ・エルズビー Sir
　William of Eresby, fifth Baron of Willoughby（c. 1370-1409）〕

フィッツウォーター卿　〔第4代フィッツウォルター男爵ウォルター・フィッツ
　ウォルター Walter Fitzwalter, fourth Baron Fitzwalter（1368-1406）〕

もうひとりの貴族

バークリー卿　〔第5代バークリー男爵トマス・バークリー Thomas Berkeley,
　fifth Baron Berkeley（1353-1417）〕

ソールズベリー伯爵　〔ジョン・ド・モンタキュート John de Montacute（c.
　1350-1400）〕

カーライル主教　〔トマス・マーク（ス）Thomas Merke(s)（1409/10 歿）〕

サー・スティーヴン・スクループ　（1408 歿）

サリー公爵　〔トマス・ホランド Thomas Holland（c. 1374-1400）〕

ウェストミンスター修道院長　〔ウィリアム・オヴ・コルチェスター William of
　Colchester（1420 歿）〕

軍務伯

ウェールズ人隊長

Two HERALDS

GARDENER

Gardener's SERVANTS

LADIES attending on the Queen

KEEPER of the prison at Pomfret where Richard is incacerated

GROOM of Richard's stable

Sir Piers EXTON, Richard's murderer

Exton's SERVANTS and fellow murderers

Other noblemen, servants, attendans, soldiers

ふたりの式部官
庭師
庭師の徒弟たち
王妃の侍女たち
牢番
厩番
サー・ピアーズ・オヴ・エクストン
エクストンの従者たち
貴族たち、従者たち、お付きのものたち、兵士たち

[ACT I, SCENE I]

*Enter King Richard [and] John of Gaunt with other nobles and attendants*

**RICHARD**    Old John of Gaunt, time-honoured Lancaster,
    Hast thou according to thy oath and band
    Brought hither Henry Herford, thy bold son,
    Here to make good the boist'rous late appeal,
    Which then our leisure would not let us hear,       5
    Against the Duke of Norfolk, Thomas Mowbray?
**GAUNT**    I have, my liege.
**RICHARD**    Tell me moreover, hast thou sounded him
    If he appeal the Duke on ancient malice
    Or worthily as a good subject should       10
    On some known ground of treachery in him?
**GAUNT**    As near as I could sift him on that argument,
    On some apparent danger seen in him
    Aimed at your highness, no inveterate malice.
**RICHARD**    Then call them to our presence.    *[Exeunt attendants]*
                           Face to face    15
    And frowning brow to brow, ourselves will hear
    The accuser and the accusèd freely speak.
    High-stomached are they both and full of ire,
    In rage, deaf as the sea, hasty as fire.

*Enter Bolingbroke and Mowbray*

**BOLINGBROKE**    Many years of happy days befall    20
    My gracious sovereign, my most loving liege.
**MOWBRAY**    Each day still better other's happiness
    Until the heavens, envying earth's good hap,
    Add an immortal title to your crown.
**RICHARD**    We thank you both. Yet one but flatters us,    25
    As well appeareth by the cause you come,
    Namely to appeal each other of high treason.

〔**1. 1**〕**あらすじ**･････････････････････････････････････････････････････････

　リチャードの御前で、ボリンブルックが、すでに申し立てたとおり、モーブリーが兵士への前渡し金の横領、近年のあらゆる謀叛への関与、グロスターの殺害画策の 3 点で大逆罪を犯していると訴え、ふたりは激しい口論のすえ決闘を誓いあう。王は翻意を迫るが、双方決意が固いと知り、決闘の日取りを申し渡す。

**0. 1.** *Enter* 「〜を登場させること、〜が登場すること」シェイクスピア劇のト書きでは、登場、退場の指示に、動詞＋主語（直後の発話者である場合は省略される）の語順の、仮定法の命令的用法が用いられる。 ⇒15. 1 注参照。

**1. time-honoured** 「老齢ゆえに尊敬される」（*OED*, time-honoured, *a.* の初出例）。

**2. band** ＝ bond「約束」（*OED*, band, *n.*¹ 10）。

**3. Henry Herford** ⇒後注参照。

**5. our . . . us** 「余、朕」国王が自身をさして用いる royal 'we'.

　**leisure** 語そのものの意味は(廃)「（なにか特定のことをする）機会」（*OED*, leisure, *n.* †1）だが、文脈上「機会がなかったこと」の意。

**8. sounded** 「（人）をそれとなく探る」（*OED*, sound, *v.*² 6）。

**9. appeal** 「（人）を訴える」（*OED*, appeal, *v.* †1）。

**12. sift** 「（人）を問いつめる」（「篩(ふるい)にかける」の比喩的意味）。

**13. apparent danger** 「人に危害を与えそうな兆し」。

**14. your highness** 「陛下」現代語で国王に用いる尊称は Your Majesty のみだが、この時代には、現代語で王族、貴族に用いる highness、grace も使われた。

**15. 1.** *Exeunt* 「（〜を）退場させること」近代初期演劇の退場のト書きには、単数形 exit、複数形 exeunt が用いられる。exit は英語の動詞 exit の原形で仮定法の命令的用法。exeunt という、ラテン語動詞 exire の三人称複数・直説法現在形が用いられるのは、exit を同じラテン語動詞の三人称単数・直説法現在形と考え、その複数形をあてたためと思われる。16 世紀前半の劇では exat と exant という三人称単数、複数の仮定法現在が用いられていた。

**16. ourselves** royal 'we' の強調のための再帰代名詞形。ふつうは ourself（1. 4. 23 参照）。 　**18. High-stomached** 「意気軒昂たる」 　**ire** （古）「怒り」 　**22. still** 「つねに、変わることなく」（*OED*, still, *adv.* 3a）。

　**better** 「〜を上回る」（*OED*, better, *v.* 3）。

**23-24. Until . . . crown** 「天が、〔リチャードの居場所となっているという〕地上の好運をうらやんで〔彼を自分のものとするために〕その称号に『天界の王』を付けくわえるまで」。

　**immortal** 「天上の、神々の世界の」（*OED*, immortal, *a.* 1b）。

**25. but** ＝ only

Cousin of Herford, what dost thou object
Against the Duke of Norfolk, Thomas Mowbray?
**BOLINGBROKE**    First, heaven be the record to my speech.    30
   In the devotion of a subject's love,
   Tend'ring the precious safety of my Prince,
   And free from other misbegotten hate,
   Come I appellant to this princely presence.
   Now, Thomas Mowbray, do I turn to thee,    35
   And mark my greeting well, for what I speak
   My body shall make good upon this earth,
   Or my divine soul answer it in heaven.
   Thou art a traitor and a miscreant,
   Too good to be so, and too bad to live,    40
   Since the more fair and crystal is the sky,
   The uglier seem the clouds that in it fly.
   Once more, the more to aggravate the note,
   With a foul traitor's name stuff I thy throat,
   And wish, so please my sovereign, ere I move    45
   What my tongue speaks my right-drawn sword may prove.
**MOWBRAY**    Let not my cold words here accuse my zeal.
   'Tis not the trial of a woman's war,
   The bitter clamour of two eager tongues,
   Can arbitrate this cause betwixt us twain.    50
   The blood is hot that must be cooled for this.
   Yet can I not of such tame patience boast
   As to be hushed and naught at all to say.
   First, the fair reverence of your highness curbs me
   From giving reins and spurs to my free speech,    55
   Which else would post until it had returned
   These terms of treason doubled down his throat.
   Setting aside his high blood's royalty,
   And let him be no kinsman to my liege,
   I do defy him, and I spit at him,    60

**28. Cousin** リチャードとボリンブルックの関係は従兄弟同士であるが、この時代の英語では兄弟より遠い親戚一般に用いられた語（*OED*, cousin, *n.* 1）。

**30. record** 「証人」（*OED*, record, *n.* 3†d）。

**32. Prince** 「王、君主」（*OED*, prince, *n.* 1）。この時代の一般的語義。

**33. misbegotten** 「〔私怨などという〕誤った原因で生まれた」（「庶出の」の比喩的意味、*OED*, misbegotten, *ppl.a.* 1b の初出例）。

**34. appellent** 「上訴している、決闘の挑戦をしている（= accusing, challenging）」（*OED*, appellant, *a.* 1）。

　　**princely** 「国王の」。⇒ 32 注参照。

**36-37. what . . . good** 「〔決闘で勝って〕私の身体に私の言葉が真実であることを証明させるつもりだ」。

**37. shall** シェイクスピア劇では頻繁に見られる二人称、三人称の主語のときの話者の意思を表す用法（*OED*, shall, *v.* 6）。

**38. soul answer** あいだに shall が了解されている。

**40. good** 「高位の、身分が高い」（*OED*, good, *a.* 2a）。行全体の意味は「そう〔＝謀叛人に〕なるには高すぎる地位の持ち主であり、生きるに値しないほどひどい人間だ」。

**43. note** 「汚名、恥辱」（*OED*, note, *n.*² 8a）。この時代では一般的だった意味で、句全体は「〔お前の〕汚名をさらにひどいものにするために」の意。

**44. With . . . throat** 「お前の喉に謀叛人の名を詰めこんでやる」とは「反論できなくなるほど激しく謀反人と呼んでやる」の意。

**45. so please your sovereign** = if it please my sovereign「王様にお許しいただけるなら、王様がよろしければ」（*OED*, please, *v.* 3c）。

**50. Can** = that can　強調構文を構成する主格の関係代名詞の省略（Abbott, §244 参照）。

**51. cooled** 「決闘で死んで血が冷たくなる」ことが直接的な意味だが、当時の医学的知識では熱を下げると信じられていた瀉血（しゃけつ）のイメージを重ねあわせている。

**54-56. curbs . . . giving reins and spurs . . . post** ひとつの節のなかで、「轡（くつわ）をつけて（馬の）動きをおさえる」、「手綱をゆるめて拍車をかける」、「速駆けする」という馬の走りになぞらえる比喩が、「馬」によってたとえるものを「私」から「私の言葉」に、かつ「おさえる」から「思い通りに走らせる」という反対の意味に変えて用いられている。この比喩の乱れは、王が関与しているグロスター殺害が問題となっており、王の前で言葉を慎まなければならないが、その一方で自身の考えを主張したいというジレンマにさいなまれるモーブリーの心の乱れを表している。

**57. doubled**　Qq: doubled　F1: doubly

　　**down his throat**　44 のボリンブルックの言い回しをくり返している。

Call him a slanderous coward and a villain,
Which to maintain I would allow him odds
And meet him, were I tied to run afoot
Even to the frozen ridges of the Alps,
Or any other ground inhabitable                                    65
Where ever Englishman durst set his foot.
Meantime let this defend my loyalty:
By all my hopes most falsely doth he lie.
**BOLINGBROKE**    Pale trembling coward, there I throw my gage,

[*Throws down his gage*]

Disclaiming here the kindred of the King,                          70
And lay aside my high blood's royalty,
Which fear, not reverence, makes thee to except.
If guilty dread have left thee so much strength
As to take up mine honour's pawn, then stoop.
By that and all the rites of knighthood else                       75
Will I make good against thee, arm to arm,
What I have spoke or thou canst worse devise.
**MOWBRAY**    I take it up, [*Takes up gage*]
                  and by that sword I swear
Which gently laid my knighthood on my shoulder,
I'll answer thee in any fair degree                                80
Or chivalrous design of knightly trial.
And when I mount, alive may I not light
If I be traitor or unjustly fight.
**RICHARD**    [*to Bolingbroke*]
What doth our cousin lay to Mowbray's charge?
It must be great that can inherit us                               85
So much as of a thought of ill in him.
**BOLINGBROKE**    Look what I speak, my life shall prove it true:
That Mowbray hath received eight thousand nobles
In name of lendings for your highness' soldiers,

**63. tied** 「(人) に〜する（*to do*）義務を負わせる」（*OED*, tie, *v.* 5b）の過去分詞形。

**67. this** 指示対象は次行の内容。

**69. gage** 「決闘のしるし（通常は、相手への挑戦の意思を示すために地面に投げつける習慣があった手袋のこと）」（*OED*, gage, *n.*¹ 2）。

**70. kindred** 「血縁関係」（*OED*, kindred, *n.* 1）。

**72. except** 「〜を（考慮の対象から）除外する、ないことにする」（*OED*, except, *v.* 1）。*OED* はここを語義 †4「〜に抗議する」の初出例としているが、前行がモーブリーの 58 の言葉をくり返すものであるためにこの意味であることは明らか。

**73. have** Qq: haue F1: hath

**74. pawn** 「決闘のしるし」（*OED*, pawn, *n.*² 1†c）。⇒ 69 注参照。

**77. or thou canst worse devise** 解釈の分かれる難解部分。devise を「でっち上げる」ととれば、「お前が、おれのお前にたいする非難よりもひどくでっち上げていること（つまり私の罪状）」を決闘で負けることによって証明してしまう、という意味に。devise を「想像する」ととれば、「おれが実際に言った以上にひどく言っている、とお前が想像していること（つまりモーブリーの罪状）」を勝って証明する、という意味に。 **spoke . . . worse** Q1: spoke, or thou canst worse Q2: spoke, or thou canst Q3-Q5: spoke, or what thou canst F1: spoken, or thou canst Q1 が韻律どおり。

**78-79. that sword . . . my shoulder** 君主が剣で肩に触れて臣下を勲爵士に叙する習慣への言及。史実では、モーブリーは 1383 年にガーター勲爵士に叙せられている。

**79. laid** 「(人) を打つ、たたく」ただし文脈上「たたいて（勲爵士号）を授ける」の意（*OED*, lay, *v.*¹ †34）。

**80. degree** 「方法、仕方」（*OED*, degree, *n.* 5）。

**81. design** Onions は、語の本来的な意味は「計画（plan, scheme）」だが、その弱まった意味「意図（purpose）」から「企図、行い（enterprise）」という意味が派生する、と説明している。

**85. inherit** 「(人) に〜を（*of*）所有させる」（*OED*, inherit, *v.* †1）の比喩的用法。

**87-108. Look . . . spent** ⇒後注参照。

**87. Look what** = whatever（*OED*, look, *v.* 4†b）。

   **speak** Q1: speake Q2-F1: said

The which he hath detained for lewd employments 90
Like a false traitor and injurious villain.
Besides I say and will in battle prove
Or here or elsewhere to the furthest verge
That ever was surveyed by English eye,
That all the treasons for these eighteen years 95
Complotted and contrivèd in this land
Fetch from false Mowbray their first head and spring.
Further I say and further will maintain
Upon his bad life to make all this good,
That he did plot the Duke of Gloucester's death, 100
Suggest his soon-believing adversaries,
And consequently like a traitor coward
Sluiced out his innocent soul through streams of blood,
Which blood, like sacrificing Abel's, cries
Even from the tongueless caverns of the earth 105
To me for justice and rough chastisement.
And, by the glorious worth of my descent,
This arm shall do it or this life be spent.

**RICHARD** How high a pitch his resolution soars!
Thomas of Norfolk, what sayst thou to this? 110

**MOWBRAY** O, let my sovereign turn away his face
And bid his ears a little while be deaf
Till I have told this slander of his blood
How God and good men hate so foul a liar.

**RICHARD** Mowbray, impartial are our eyes and ears. 115
Were he my brother, nay, my kingdom's heir,
As he is but my father's brother's son,
Now by my sceptre's awe I make a vow
Such neighbour-nearness to our sacred blood
Should nothing privilege him nor partialize 120
The unstooping firmness of my upright soul.
He is our subject, Mowbray; so art thou.

**90. The which**　which が本来的には不定のものを表す関係形容詞であることから生じた用法とされる。すなわち、The better part of valour is discretion; in the which better part I have saved my life. *1H4.* 5. 4. 125 のように先行詞となる名詞を which のあとにくり返す関係形容詞的用法があり、そこから、前の部分に現れない名詞の前に用いる用法と、ここのように、複数の選択対象（nobles, lendings, soldiers）のなかからひとつの名詞（nobles）が先行詞として選べるような文脈で先行詞を which のあとにくり返さない、関係代名詞的用法が派生したと説明される（Abbott, §270）。

**lewd**　「邪悪な、無節操な（人または行い）」（*OED*, lewd, *adj.* †5）。

**92. battle**　「決闘」（*OED*, battle, *n.* 2a）。ここでボリンブルックが主張している、訴えの黒白を決闘でつけることを「決闘裁判（trial by battle）」と呼ぶ。

**95. for these eighteen years**　この数字は材源となっているホリンシェッドの年代記からとられたものだが、そこに具体的な説明はない。史実ではこの出来事は 1398 年であり、18 年間の最初の年は農民叛乱のあった 1381 年ということになる（Dawson & Yachnin）。

**96. Complotted**　「共謀した」（*OED*, complot, *v.* 2 の初出例）。

**97. Fetch**　Q1: Fetch　Q2-5: Fetcht　F1: Fetch'd

**head**　「源泉（＝ fountain-head）」の比喩的用法（*OED*, head, $n^1$. 16b）。

**100. Duke of Gloucester's death**　⇒後注参照。

**104-05. Which . . . earth**　ボリンブルックは、アベルが羊を生け贄として神に捧げ、神がそれを喜んで自分の捧げた穀物を顧みなかったことを怨みに思った兄カインに殺され、その血が土のなかから叫んだ、という Genesis 4: 1-10 の記述に基づいて、グロスターをアベルにたとえている。

**109. How high a pitch his resolution soars!**　「彼の決意はどれほど高く舞いあがることか！」王が、ボリンブルックの決意を、鷹狩りの鷹の飛翔になぞらえて、倨傲（きょうごう）と考えていることをほのめかす表現。ボリンブルックの台詞を締めくくる「下降」（文脈上の意味は「血筋」だが）を意味する descent（107）を含む韻の二行連句とリチャードの soars で終わる行の意味上の衝突が、リチャードのボリンブルックへの敵意を感じさせる。

**113. slander**　「面汚し（不名誉となる人物）」（*OED*, slander, *n.* 3†d）。

**116. my kingdom's**　Qq: my kingdomes　F: our kingdomes

**118. my sceptre's**　Qq: scepters　F1: my Sceptres　Qq が韻律どおり。

**119. neighbour-nearness**　neighbour の attributive の用法は通例人名、または人や場所を表す名詞を修飾するが、ここは抽象名詞を修飾する、現在では稀な用法（*OED*, neighbour, *n.* 4d）の初出例。実質上「近さ」を強調する言葉となっている。

Free speech and fearless I to thee allow.
**MOWBRAY**     Then, Bolingbroke, as low as to thy heart
   Through the false passage of thy throat thou liest.       125
   Three parts of that receipt I had for Calais
   Disbursed I duly to his highness' soldiers.
   The other part reserved I by consent,
   For that my sovereign liege was in my debt
   Upon remainder of a dear account       130
   Since last I went to France to fetch his queen.
   Now swallow down that lie. For Gloucester's death,
   I slew him not, but to my own disgrace
   Neglected my sworn duty in that case.
   For you, my noble lord of Lancaster,       135
   The honourable father to my foe,
   Once did I lay an ambush for your life,
   A trespass that doth vex my grievèd soul.
   But ere I last received the sacrament
   I did confess it and exactly begged       140
   Your grace's pardon, and I hope I had it.
   This is my fault. As for the rest appealed,
   It issues from the rancour of a villain,
   A recreant and most degenerate traitor,
   Which in myself I boldly will defend,       145
   And interchangeably hurl down my gage
   Upon this overweening traitor's foot,
   To prove myself a loyal gentleman
   Even in the best blood chambered in his bosom.

      [*Throws down his gage. Bolingbroke takes it up*]

   In haste whereof most heartily I pray       150
   Your highness to assign our trial day.
**RICHARD**     Wrath-kindled gentlemen, be ruled by me.
   Let's purge this choler without letting blood.

**124. as low as to thy heart**　44, 57 の表現を引き継ぐ「〔舌先だけでなく〕心か
ら」に「お前の心ほどの卑怯さで」(*OED*, low, *adv.* 1b) という意味が重ね
られている。107-09 に続いてふたたび高低に関わる表現が用いられている。

**126-41. Three . . . it**　⇒後注参照。

**126. Three parts**　「4分の3」(*OED*, part, *n.* 5a(a))。

**126. for Calais**　「カレーの守備のために」。

**127. I duly**　Q1: I duely　Q2-F1: I　Q1 が韻律どおり。

**128. by consent**　「国王の承諾のもと」。

**129-30. in my debt / Upon remainder of a dear account**　「私に多額の借金残
額があった」。

**132. swallow down**　44, 57, 124 を引き継ぐ表現。

**132-34. For Gloucester's death . . . that case**　⇒後注参照。

**133. my**　Q1: my　Q2-F1: mine

**137. did I**　Qq: did I　F1: I did

**150. In haste whereof**　whereof (= of which) の 先行詞は 148-49 の「ボリン
ブルックの胸に宿る最善の血までも流させて、自分が忠誠の士であることを証
明すること」。

**152. gentlemen**　Qq: gentleman　F1: Gentlemen　F1 による訂正。

**153. Let's purge this choler without letting blood**　51 に続き決闘による流血
と瀉血を重ねあわせた表現。choler = yellow bile(黄胆汁)は怒りの感情を
惹きおこすものとみなされていた。

This we prescribe though no physician:
Deep malice makes too deep incision;                                    155
Forget, forgive, conclude and be agreed.
Our doctors say this is no month to bleed.
[*to Gaunt*]
Good uncle, let this end where it begun.
We'll calm the Duke of Norfolk, you your son.
**GAUNT**    To be a make-peace shall become my age.          160
Throw down, my son, the Duke of Norfolk's gage.
**RICHARD**    And, Norfolk, throw down his.
**GAUNT**                                    When, Harry, when?
Obedience bids I should not bid again.
**RICHARD**    Norfolk, throw down, we bid; there is no boot.
**MOWBRAY**    Myself I throw, dread sovereign, at thy foot. [*Kneels*]    165
My life thou shalt command, but not my shame.
The one my duty owes, but my fair name,
Despite of death, that lives upon my grave,
To dark dishonour's use thou shalt not have.
I am disgraced, impeached and baffled here,          170
Pierced to the soul with Slander's venomed spear,
The which no balm can cure but his heart blood
Which breathed this poison.
**RICHARD**                                    Rage must be withstood.
Give me his gage. Lions make leopards tame.
**MOWBRAY**    Yea, but not change his spots. Take but my shame,    175
And I resign my gage. My dear, dear lord,
The purest treasure mortal times afford
Is spotless reputation; that away,
Men are but gilded loam, or painted clay.
A jewel in a ten-times-barred-up chest          180
Is a bold spirit in a loyal breast.
Mine honour is my life. Both grow in one.
Take honour from me, and my life is done.

**154. prescribe . . . physician**　治療の隠喩が前行に引きつづいて使用され、「（薬を）処方する、（治療法を）指示する」という意味が、文脈上の意味「命じる」に重ねあわされている。

**155. too deep incision**　瀉血の際につけられる浅い切り傷に比して、敵意によって流血沙汰となるときの傷の深さを限度の超えたものと表現している。

**156. conclude**　「（相手と）折り合いをつける」（*OED*, conclude, *v.* 13†b）。

**157. month**　中世においては特定の時期が瀉血に適しているとされ、暦に記載があり、それを口にする王の迷信深さを印象づける言葉となっている（Forker）。Qq: month　F1: time　どちらの読みにも優劣つけがたいという点で本文上問題のある一節。

**160. make-peace** ＝ peacemaker　（*OED*, make-peace, *n.*）

**162-63. When, Harry, when? / Obedience bids I should not bid again**　Popeによる校訂。Q1: Gaunt. When Harry? when obedience bids, / Obedience bids I should not bid againe　Q2-F1: Gaunt. When Harrie when? Obedience bids, / Obedience bids I should not bid agen　⇒後注参照。

**164. boot**「他の選択肢」（*OED*, boot, *n.*[1] †8）。

**167. The one**　前行の my life と my shame のうちの前者。

**170. baffled**「名誉を汚された」（*OED*, baffled, *ppl.a.* †1）。

**174. Lions make leopards tame**　王を獅子にたとえる伝統的な比喩を使って自然界の秩序を喚起する発言。

**175. but not change his spots**　「豹の斑点を変えることはできない」（A LEOPARD cannot change his spots）は諺的な表現（Tilley, L206）。spots には「汚名」の意味がかけあわされている。

**Take but my shame**　モーブリーは「ただ私の恥辱を身に引き受けてさえくだされば」という言葉で、暗にリチャードにグロスター殺しの罪を認めてほしいと思っていることをほのめかしている。

Then, dear my liege, mine honour let me try.
In that I live, and for that will I die.                                    185

**RICHARD**    [*to Bolingbroke*]
Cousin, throw up your gage. Do you begin.

**BOLINGBROKE**    O, God defend my soul from such deep sin!
Shall I seem crest-fallen in my father's sight,
Or with pale beggar-fear impeach my height
Before this outdared dastard? Ere my tongue                  190
Shall wound my honour with such feeble wrong,
Or sound so base a parle, my teeth shall tear
The slavish motive of recanting fear
And spit it bleeding in his high disgrace,
Where shame doth harbour, even in Mowbray's face.          195

*Exit Gaunt*

**RICHARD**    We were not born to sue, but to command,
Which, since we cannot do to make you friends,
Be ready, as your lives shall answer it,
At Coventry upon Saint Lambert's Day.
There shall your swords and lances arbitrate                     200
The swelling difference of your settled hate.
Since we cannot atone you, we shall see
Justice design the victor's chivalry.
Lord Marshal, command our officers at arms
Be ready to direct these home alarms.          *Exeunt*    205

[ACT I, SCENE II]

*Enter John of Gaunt with Duchess of Gloucester*

**GAUNT**    Alas, the part I had in Woodstock's blood
Doth more solicit me than your exclaims
To stir against the butchers of his life.
But since correction lieth in those hands
Which made the fault that we cannot correct,                     5

**186. Cousin** 劇中最初の呼びかけでボリンブルックを Cousin of Herford (28) と呼んだ王は、モーブリーの罪状を述べさせる際にも our cousin (84) と呼び、モーブリーに申し開きをうながす際には、公平さを強調するためにボリンブルックを our subject (122) と呼ぶが、ここでは、決闘を思いとどまらせるべく、ふたたびこの語を使って親しさをアピールする。

**up**　Qq: vp　F1: downe

**187. God**　Qq: God　F1: heauen　　　**deep**　Qq: deepe　F1: foule

**188. crest-fallen**　「恥辱をこうむった」、文字どおりの意味は「うなだれた」。

**189. pale . . . height**　「乞食同然にみじめな怖れによってわが気高い血筋を傷つける」。　**impeach**　「〜に危害を加える、〜を傷つける」（*OED*, impeach, *v.* †2）。

**190. outdared dastard**　「挑戦の言葉で言い負かされた臆病者」。
　　**Ere**　「〜するくらいなら（優先順位を表す）」（*OED*, ere, *conj.* 2）。

**191. my**　Qq: my　F1: mine

**192. sound . . . a parle**「講和交渉申し入れの合図として喇叭（らっぱ）を吹き鳴らす」。

**193. motive**「身体の動く部分」というシェイクスピア独自の意味（*OED*, motive, *n.* †6）。ここでは舌を指す。

**195. 1. *Exit Gaunt*** F のみにあるト書き。⇒後注参照。

**199. Saint Lambert's Day** 9 月 17 日。聖ランベルトゥス（Lambertus of Maastricht, c. 636-c. 705）はメロヴィング朝からカロヴィング朝への移行期の政争に巻きこまれ殺害された聖職者で、夫婦の絆の守護聖人。⇒ 1. 1 後注。

**202. shall** ⇒ 37 注参照。　　　**we shall** Q1: we shall　Q2-F1: you shall

**203. Justice . . . chivalry** 「正義が騎士道（＝決闘）の勝者を決めるようにしよう」。　　　**design**「〜を指名して選びだす」（*OED*, design, *v.* 2）。

**204. Lord Marshal**「軍務伯（＝ Earl Marshal）」（*OED*, marshal, *n.* 2a）。⇒後注参照。

**205. home alarms**「（海外の戦争でなく）国内の決闘での喇叭による戦いの合図」。


〔1. 2〕あらすじ……………………………………………………………………
　夫の殺害に悲憤慷慨（こうがい）し復讐を求めるグロスター未亡人にたいして、ゴーントは、殺害が王によるものであるため復讐は神にゆだねるしかない、と答え、息子たちの決闘が行われるコヴェントリーにおもむく。

………………………………………………………………………………………

**1. part** 「取り分、分与されたもの（＝ share）」（*OED*, part, *n.* 7）。
　**Woodstock's** Qq: Woodstocks　F1: Gloucesters　Qq で Woodstock という名が呼ばれるのはこれ 1 回のみで、F1 の読みは Gloucester という名に統一した結果とみなすことができる。

**4-5. correction . . . fault** 「処罰はその罪を犯した手にゆだねられている」との言葉が、はじめて観客にグロスター殺害がリチャードによることを告げる。

Put we our quarrel to the will of heaven,
Who when they see the hours ripe on earth
Will rain hot vengeance on offenders' heads.
**DUCHESS**   Finds brotherhood in thee no sharper spur?
Hath love in thy old blood no living fire?                          10
Edward's seven sons, whereof thyself art one,
Were as seven vials of his sacred blood,
Or seven fair branches springing from one root.
Some of those seven are dried by nature's course,
Some of those branches by the Destinies cut;                      15
But Thomas, my dear lord, my life, my Gloucester,
One vial full of Edward's sacred blood,
One flourishing branch of his most royal root,
Is cracked, and all the precious liquor spilt,
Is hacked down, and his summer leaves all faded                  20
By Envy's hand and Murder's bloody axe.
Ah, Gaunt, his blood was thine! That bed, that womb,
That mettle, that self mould that fashioned thee,
Made him a man; and though thou livest and breathest,
Yet art thou slain in him. Thou dost consent                     25
In some large measure to thy father's death
In that thou seest thy wretched brother die,
Who was the model of thy father's life.
Call it not patience, Gaunt. It is despair.
In suff'ring thus thy brother to be slaughtered                  30
Thou showest the naked pathway to thy life,
Teaching stern Murder how to butcher thee.
That which in mean men we entitle patience
Is pale cold cowardice in noble breasts.
What shall I say? To safeguard thine own life                    35
The best way is to venge my Gloucester's death.
**GAUNT**   God's is the quarrel, for God's substitute,
His deputy anointed in His sight,

**11. Edward's seven sons** エドワード三世（1312 年生、77 年殂<sup>ぼつ</sup>、27 年戴冠）
の 7 人の息子たちとは、エドワード黒太子（Edward the Black Prince、1376
年殂）、ウィリアム・オヴ・ハットフィールド（William of Hatfield、夭逝）、
クラレンス公ライオネル（Lionel, Duke of Clarence、1368 年殂）、ランカス
ター公ジョン・オヴ・ゴーント（John of Gaunt、1399 年殂）、ヨーク公エド
マンド・オヴ・ラングリー（Edmund of Langley, Duke of York、1402 年
殂）、トマス・オヴ・ウッドストック（Thomas of Woodstock, Duke of
Gloucester、1397 年殂）、ウィリアム・オヴ・ウィンザー（William of
Windsor、夭逝）のこと。この時点で生きているのはゴーントとヨーク公の
み。⇒ 29 ページ系図参照。

**12. sacred blood** 王権神授説に基づく表現。最初の言及は 1. 1. 119、この直後
（17）にも見られる。

**13. seven . . . root** 王家の血筋を木の枝にたとえるこの台詞のイメジャリーの
根底にあるのは、イザヤ書を淵源とするキリストの血筋を描いた「エッサイの
木（the Tree of Jesse）」の図像の伝統。イギリス王家の系図に当てはめたも
のとしてはジョン・ストウ（John Stow）『イングランド年代記』（*The
Annales of England*、1592 年）標題頁に描かれたものが知られている。

**20. leaves all faded** Qq: leaues all faded　F1: leafes all vaded

**23. mettle** 「材質」。metal の異綴りで、現代英語では、人の「性質」のような
比喩的な意味合いの場合にこの綴りが用いられるが、近代初期にあっては、こ
のふたつの語に区別はなかった（*OED*, mettle, *n.* 1; metal, *n.* 1f）。ここで
は、次に出てくる mould（「鋳型」）がゴーントやグロスターを産んだ母胎を
指し、こちらは子たちが引き継いだ形質、性質を指すことになる。ちなみに
Qq と F1 では異なる綴りとなっている。Qq: mettall　F1: mettle

**31. naked** 「無防備な」（*OED*, naked, *a.* 4b）。

**32. Murder** Qq: Murder　F1: murther

**33. mean** 「身分の低い」（*OED*, mean, *a.*<sup>1</sup> †2a.）。

　　**entitle** 「〜を〜と呼ぶ」（*OED*, entitle, *v.* 2）。

**36. venge** 「（犯された罪、不当な仕打ち）への復讐を行う」（*OED*, venge, *v.* 2）。

**37-41. God's is . . . minister** ゴーントは、グロスター殺害を犯したのが、神
の前で「聖油を塗られた」「神の代理人」たる王であるため、復讐は神の冒瀆
につながるとして、王権神授説を理由に復讐はできないと説明する。

　　**minister** 「代理人」（*OED*, minister, *n.* 2a）。

**37. God's . . . God's** Qq: Gods . . . Gods　F1: Heauens . . . heauens

**38. His deputy anointed in His sight** 「（戴冠の際に）王として聖油を塗る」
（*OED*, anoint, *v.* 2a）という動詞に、神の家たるウェストミンスター・アビー
で行われる戴冠式で新王の頭に聖油を注ぐ聖別の儀式が行われるため、「神の
見ているところで」という副詞句が添えられている。

Hath caused his death, the which if wrongfully
Let heaven revenge, for I may never lift                           40
An angry arm against His minister.
**DUCHESS**   Where then, alas, may I complain myself?
**GAUNT**   To God, the widow's champion and defence.
**DUCHESS**   Why then, I will. Farewell, old Gaunt.
Thou goest to Coventry, there to behold                            45
Our cousin Herford and fell Mowbray fight.
O, set my husband's wrongs on Herford's spear
That it may enter butcher Mowbray's breast!
Or if misfortune miss the first career,
Be Mowbray's sins so heavy in his bosom                           50
That they may break his foaming courser's back
And throw the rider headlong in the lists,
A caitiff, recreant to my cousin Hereford!
Farewell, old Gaunt. Thy sometimes brother's wife
With her companion, Grief, must end her life.                     55
**GAUNT**   Sister, farewell. I must to Coventry.
As much good stay with thee as go with me.
**DUCHESS**   Yet one word more. Grief boundeth where it falls,
Not with the empty hollowness but weight.
I take my leave before I have begun,                              60
For sorrow ends not when it seemeth done.
Commend me to thy brother, Edmund York.
Lo, this is all. Nay, yet depart not so.
Though this be all, do not so quickly go.
I shall remember more. Bid him, — ah, what? —                    65
With all good speed at Plashy visit me.
Alack, and what shall good old York there see
But empty lodgings and unfurnished walls,
Unpeopled offices, untrodden stones,
And what cheer there for welcome but my groans?                   70
Therefore commend me; let him not come there

**39. if wrongfully** 「もしそのことがなされたのが不当であるならば」。

**42. complain** Qq: complaine F1: complaint

**43. God, the widow's champion** Psalm 68:5 に基づく言い回し。

　**God . . . and** Qq: God . . . and F1: heauen, . . . to

**47. set** Qq: set F1: sit

**49. career** 「(馬上槍試合の) 1 回の勝負」(*OED*, careeer, *n.* †2a)。

**51. foaming courser** 「泡のような汗を流している (軍用または馬上槍試合用
の) 馬」(*OED*, foam, *v.* 1; courser², 1 )。

**52. lists** 「(馬上槍試合の競技場を観客席と仕切る) 柵」から転化して「馬上槍
試合の競技場」(*OED*, list, *n.*³ 9a)。

**53. caitiff,** Qq: caitiue F1: Caytiffe

**54. sometimes** (廃)「かつては 〜 であった (= sometime)」(*OED*, sometimes, *adv.* †2†b)。

**56. I must to Coventry** 方向を表す副詞(句)とともに用いられる運動の動詞
(go など) はしばしば省略される。Abbott, §405. 参照。

**58-59. Grief . . . weight** 「悲しみは、落ちたところで、空っぽで軽いせいでは
なく、重さゆえに弾む」公爵夫人は、悲しい心のうちを打ち明けたところ、心
は軽くならずに、なおさら悲しみがつのり、なおも言葉をつづけたくなる気持
ちをテニスボールのバウンドにたとえている。

**60-61. before . . . done** 「悲しみというものは終わったように見えても〔際限
なくなるから〕終わらないものなので、悲嘆しはじめる前に暇乞いをしなくて
はならない」。

**62. Commend me to thy brother** = remember me kindly to thy brother　こ
の時期の通常の表現 (*OED*, commend, *v.* 5)。

**65. ah,** Qq: ah F1: Oh,

**66. Plashy** 「プラッシー」エセックス州の村。州都チェルムズフォードの北東
7 マイルのところにあり、プラッシー城はグロスター公の居城 (Sugden)。
Q1-F1: Plashie　現代綴りは Pleshey だが Holinshed もこの綴りを用いてい
る。

**68. unfurnished walls** カントリーハウスを留守にするときのように、タペスト
リーや武具などの飾り物をはずした壁。

**69. offices** 食料貯蔵室や食器室、地下貯蔵庫、洗濯室など、邸の家事専用の部
屋 (*OED*, office, *n.* 9a)。

**70. cheer** Q1: cheere Q2-F1: heare

To seek out sorrow that dwells everywhere.

Desolate, desolate will I hence and die.

The last leave of thee takes my weeping eye. *Exeunt* [*severally*]

[ACT I, SCENE III]

*Enter Lord Marshal and Duke Aumerle*

**MARSHAL**   My lord Aumerle, is Harry Herford armed?

**AUMERLE**   Yea, at all points, and longs to enter in.

**MARSHAL**   The Duke of Norfolk, sprightfully and bold,

Stays but the summons of the appellant's trumpet.

**AUMERLE**   Why then, the champions are prepared and stay      5

For nothing but his majesty's approach.

*The trumpets sound and [Richard] enters with his nobles, Gaunt, Bushy,*
*Bagot, Green and others. When they are set, enter [Mowbray,] Duke*
*of Norfolk in arms defendant with [1] Herald. [Richard and nobels take*
*their seats]*

**RICHARD**   Marshal, demand of yonder champion

The cause of his arrival here in arms.

Ask him his name and orderly proceed

To swear him in the justice of his cause.      10

**MARSHAL**   [*to Mowbray*]

In God's name and the King's, say who thou art

And why thou com'st thus knightly clad in arms,

Against what man thou com'st, and what thy quarrel.

Speak truly on thy knighthood and thy oath,

As so defend thee heaven and thy valour.      15

**MOWBRAY**   My name is Thomas Mowbray, Duke of Norfolk,

Who hither come engagèd by my oath,

Which God defend a knight should violate,

Both to defend my loyalty and truth

To God, my King and my succeeding issue,      20

**74. The last leave of thee takes my weeping eye**　倒置構文でeyeが主語となっている。take (one's) leave of sb は「（人）に暇乞いをする」。of ＝ from（*OED*, leave, *n.*[1] 2a; of, *prep.* 10）。

〔1. 3〕あらすじ……………………………………………………………………………

コヴェントリーにおける決闘の場面。ボリンブルックとモーブリーはしきたりどおりに名乗りをあげ槍を受けとり、決闘を始めようとするが、開始の合図の喇叭が吹き鳴らされるとリチャードは決闘をやめさせ、ふたりにそれぞれ 10 年間と無期の追放を命じ、ゴーントの悲しみを見てボリンブルックの追放は 6 年に短縮する。

……………………………………………………………………………………………………

**4. Stays**　他動詞「〜を待つ」（*OED*, stay, *v.*[1] 19）。

**5. stay**　自動詞「待つ」（*OED*, stay, *v.*[1] 9）。

**10. swear him in the justice of**　「彼に〜が正しいことを誓わせる」（*OED*, swear, *v.* 10a.）。

**13. what**　Q1: what　Q2-F1: what's

**14. thy oath**　Qq: thy oth　F1: thine oath

**17. come**　Qq: come　F1: comes

**18. defend**　「（目的語節をとり）を禁じる」（*OED*, defend, *v.* †3†c）。

**20. my**　Qq: my　F1: his

Against the Duke of Hereford that appeals me,
And by the grace of God and this mine arm
To prove him, in defending of myself,
A traitor to my God, my King and me.
And as I truly fight, defend me heaven.                           25

*The trumpets sound. Enter [Bolingbroke,] Duke of Hereford appellant*
*in armour with [2] Herald*

RICHARD   Marshal, ask yonder knight in arms
  Both who he is and why he cometh hither
  Thus plated in habiliments of war,
  And formally according to our law
  Depose him in the justice of his cause.                         30
MARSHAL   [*to Bolingbroke*]
  What is thy name? And wherefore com'st thou hither
  Before King Richard in his royal lists?
  Against whom com'st thou? And what's thy quarrel?
  Speak like a true knight, so defend thee heaven.
BOLINGBROKE   Harry of Hereford, Lancaster and Derby          35
  Am I, who ready here do stand in arms
  To prove by God's grace and my body's valour
  In lists on Thomas Mowbray, Duke of Norfolk,
  That he's a traitor foul and dangerous
  To God of heaven, King Richard and to me.                       40
  And as I truly fight, defend me heaven.
MARSHAL   On pain of death, no person be so bold
  Or daring-hardy as to touch the lists
  Except the Marshal and such officers
  Appointed to direct these fair designs.                         45
BOLINGBROKE   Lord Marshal, let me kiss my sovereign's hand
  And bow my knee before his majesty,
  For Mowbray and myself are like two men
  That vow a long and weary pilgrimage.

**26. ask**　Qq: aske　F1: Aske　Irving: demand of　Qq、F1 の読みでは音節数の足りない行となるために Irving によってほどこされた校訂を Gurr、Dawson & Yachnin、Forker らは受け容れている。

**28. plated**　「鎧に身を固めた」（*OED*, plated, *a*. 1）。Qq: plated　F1: placed

　**habiliments of war**　「軍装」（*OED*, habiliment, *n*. †3†b）。

**29. formally**　Q1-4: formally　Q5, F1: formerly

**30. Depose**　「（人）に宣誓させる」（*OED*, depose, *v*. †6）。

**32. lists**　1. 2. 52 注参照。

**33. quarrel**　「訴えの原因」（*OED*, quarrel, *n*.³ 2）。

**34. so** = in order that　so という語だけで so that と同様にこの意味になる（*OED*, so, *adv*. 23）。

**37. God's**　Qq: Gods　F1: heauens

**39. he's**　Qq: he is　F1: he's　F1 が韻律どおり。

**43. daring-hardy**「大胆不敵な」*OED*, daring, *ppl*. *a*.¹ †3 は、この daring をほぼ同じ意味の形容詞 hardy にかかる副詞的用法ととり、その用法の唯一の用例としている。

Then let us take a ceremonious leave                               50
    And loving farewell of our several friends.
MARSHAL    The appellant in all duty greets your highness
    And craves to kiss your hand and take his leave.
RICHARD    We will descend and fold him in our arms.

*[Descends and embraces Bolingbroke]*

Cousin of Herford, as thy cause is right,                          55
    So be thy fortune in this royal fight.
    Farewell, my blood, which if today thou shed,
    Lament we may, but not revenge thee dead.
BOLINGBROKE    O, let no noble eye profane a tear
    For me if I be gored with Mowbray's spear.                     60
    As confident as is the falcon's flight
    Against a bird do I with Mowbray fight.
    *[to Lord Marshal]*   My loving lord, I take my leave of you,
    *[to Aumerle]*   Of you, my noble cousin, Lord Aumerle,
    Not sick although I have to do with death,                     65
    But lusty, young and cheerly drawing breath.
    Lo, as at English feasts, so I regreet
    The daintiest last, to make the end most sweet.
    *[to Gaunt]*   O thou, the earthly author of my blood,
    Whose youthful spirit in me regenerate                         70
    Doth with a two-fold vigour lift me up
    To reach at victory above my head,
    Add proof unto mine armour with thy prayers
    And with thy blessings steel my lance's point
    That it may enter Mowbray's waxen coat                         75
    And furbish new the name of John a Gaunt
    Even in the lusty haviour of his son.
GAUNT    God in thy good cause make thee prosperous.
    Be swift like lightning in the execution
    And let thy blows, doubly redoubled,                           80

**50-51. take a ceremonious leave / And loving farewell of**  ⇒ 1. 2. 74 注参照。

**57. my blood**  「わが身内」（*OED*, blood, *n.* 11a）。直後の which の先行詞は my blood だが、そちらは文字どおりの「血」を意味するものとしてこの表現を受けている。

**59. profane a tear**  「誤った理由で涙を流す」（決闘での敗北は偽証を意味するため）。profane の意味は「〜を濫用する」（*OED*, profane, *v.* 1b）。

**60. gored**  「（槍などの武器で人）を突き刺す」（*OED*, gore, *v.*¹ †1）。

**65-6. Not . . . breath**  直接的にはオーマールへの言葉だが、まわりにいるものたち全員に向けられている。

**67. regreet**  「〜に挨拶を返す」という意味ではなく「〜に挨拶をする」（*OED*, regreet, *v.* 2 の初出例）。文脈上、「配膳されたデザートを受けとる」ということ。食後にデザートを食べるのはイギリス独自の習慣だった。一番大切な父親への挨拶を最後にとっておいた、の意。

**69. the earthly author**  「（創造主である神にたいして）地上において私を生みだした人」（*OED*, author, *n.* 2†a）。　　**earthly**  Qq: earthly  F1: earthy

**70. regenerate**  （廃）「再生された、生まれ変わった」（*OED*, regenerate, *ppl. a.* 1）。

**71. with a two-fold vigour**  自分のなかに再生されている父の力と自分自身の力をあわせて「二重の力」となる。　　**vigour**  Qq: vigour  F1: rigor

**73. proof**  「槍を通さない鎧の強さ」（*OED*, proof, *n.* 10a）。

**74. steel**  「〜の穂先を鋼で硬くする」（*OED*, steel, *v.* 1a）。

**75. waxen coat**  「蠟（ろう）のように柔らかい鎖帷子（かたびら）」（*OED*, waxen, *a.* 2a; coat, *n.* 1a, 5）。

**76. furbish**  Qq: furbish  F1: furnish

**78. God**  Qq: God  F1: Heauen

**80. And let thy blows, doubly redoubled**  Q1-F1: And let thy blows, doubly redoubled  Qq、F1 ともに、redoublèd であったとしても音節数が足りない。

Fall like amazing thunder on the casque
Of thy adverse pernicious enemy.
Rouse up thy youthful blood, be valiant and live.
**BOLINGBROKE**    Mine innocence and Saint George to thrive.
**MOWBRAY**    However God or Fortune cast my lot,                    85
There lives or dies, true to King Richard's throne,
A loyal, just and upright gentleman.
Never did captive with a freer heart
Cast off his chains of bondage and embrace
His golden uncontrolled enfranchisement                    90
More than my dancing soul doth celebrate
This feast of battle with mine adversary.
Most mighty liege and my companion peers,
Take from my mouth the wish of happy years.
As gentle and as jocund as to jest                    95
Go I to fight. Truth hath a quiet breast.
**RICHARD**    Farewell, my lord. Securely I espy
Virtue with valour couchèd in thine eye.
Order the trial, Marshal, and begin.
**MARSHAL**    Harry of Hereford, Lancaster and Derby,                    100
Receive thy lance, and God defend the right.

[*An officer bears a lance to Bolingbroke*]

**BOLINGBROKE**    Strong as a tower in hope, I cry amen.
**MARSHAL**    [*to an officer*]
Go bear this lance to Thomas, Duke of Norfolk.

[*An officer bears a lance to Mowbray*]

**1 HERALD**    Harry of Hereford, Lancaster and Derby
Stands here for God, his sovereign and himself,                    105
On pain to be found false and recreant,
To prove the Duke of Norfolk, Thomas Mowbray,
A traitor to his God, his king and him,

**81. amazing**　「恐ろしい」（*OED*, amazing, *ppl. a.* †1)。

**82. adverse**　Qq: aduerse　F1: amaz'd　F1 の読みは前行 amazing に影響を受けた誤植の可能性がある。

**84. Mine innocence and Saint George to thrive**　「わが潔白と聖ジョージ（イングランドの守護聖人）の力で好運をえられますように」（*OED*, thrive, *v.* 2a)。聖ジョージは 3 世紀後半パレスチナのリュッダ（Lydda）でギリシャ系キリスト教徒の家庭に生まれ、ディオクレティアヌス帝の命じる棄教を拒んだため殉教したとされる聖人。記念日は 4 月 23 日。

**innocence**　Q1-F1: innocence　Capell: innocency　QF の読みでは音節数の足りない行となるために Capell によってほどこされた校訂を Gurr は受け容れている。

**85. God**　Qq: God　F1: heauen

**86. King**　Qq: King　F1: Kings

**90. enfranchisement**　「（拘禁、隷属などからの）解放」（*OED*, enfranchisement, *n.* 1)。

**95. As gentle and as jocund as to jest**　「楽しみに興じに行くときのように穏やかで陽気に」（*OED*, jest, *v.* 4†b)。

**97. Securely**　espy と couchèd のいずれにかかるか曖昧な「やぶにらみ的副詞（squinting adverb）」（Dawson & Yachnin)。

**99. Marshal**　Qq: Martiall　F1: Marshall

**101. God defend the**　Qq: God defend the　F1: heauen defend thy

**102. Strong as a tower**　For thou hast been my hope and a strong tower against the enemy. (Psalm, 61: 3) を踏まえた文句。

And dares him to set forward to the fight.

**2 HERALD**   Here standeth Thomas Mowbray, Duke of Norfolk,   110
On pain to be found false and recreant,
Both to defend himself and to approve
Henry of Hereford, Lancaster and Derby
To God, his sovereign and to him disloyal,
Courageously and with a free desire,   115
Attending but the signal to begin.

**MARSHAL**   Sound trumpets, and set forward combatants.

*A charge [is] sounded. [Richard throws down his warder]*

Stay. The King hath thrown his warder down.

**RICHARD**   Let them lay by their helmets and their spears
And both return back to their chairs again.   120

*[The combatants disarm and sit down in their chairs]*

*[to the Nobles]*
Withdraw with us and let the trumpets sound
While we return these dukes what we decree.

*A long Flourish. [Richard confers apart with Gaunt and other nobles,
then addresses combatants]*

Draw near,
And list what with our council we have done.
For that our kingdom's earth should not be soiled   125
With that dear blood which it hath fosterèd,
And for our eyes do hate the dire aspect
Of civil wounds ploughed up with neighbours' sword,
And for we think the eagle-wingèd pride
Of sky-aspiring and ambitious thoughts   130
With rival-hating envy set on you
To wake our peace, which in our country's cradle
Draw the sweet infant breath of gentle sleep

**109. forward**　Q1: forward　Q2-F1: forwards

**117. 1** *warder*　「職杖」は王や指揮官の地位を表す象徴物であるが、このように戦闘や武術試合などで戦いの始まりや終わりを命じるために用いるのが本来の使用法だった。

**122. return**　「(評決など) を伝える」(*OED*, return, *v.*¹ 16a)。

　**decree**　「(判決) を下す」(*OED*, decree, *v.* 3)。

**122. 1-2.** *Richard . . . combatants*　⇒後注参照。

**124. list**　「(人の言葉) に耳を傾ける」(*OED*, list, *v.*² 2)。

**128. sword**　Qq: sword　F1: swords

**129-33. And . . . sleep**　Qq のみに見られる行。上演台本に照合された可能性が指摘される F1 にこれらの行がないのは、関係代名詞がくり返される台詞全体のわかりにくさのため、上演に当たって削除されたためと想像できる。これらの行を含む王の台詞のわかりにくさの中心にあるのは、our peace (132) が、削除されたとおぼしい部分の次行にある Which (134) の先行詞と見え、そうであれば、眠っていた「平和」が軍鼓や喇叭、剣のたてる斬撃音によって起こされ、「平和をわが平穏なる領地からたたき出す」となることである。しかしながら、先行詞が rival-hating envy (131) であれば、それが戦いの音に目覚めさせられ、「平和をたたき出し」、われわれに身内の血を流させる、ということになる。とはいえ、この Which の先行詞のわかりにくさは、たてつづけに for をくり返して 3 つの理由を重ね、さらに関係詞節も重ねる、この台詞が混乱した印象を与える大きな要因となっている。そのことは、自身の決定によって行われることになり、しきたりどおりの手順を踏んではじめられようとしている決闘を、内戦の引き金となるという理由でやめさせるリチャードの牽強附会さを示している。

**131. set on you**:「お前たちふたりに襲いかかるようけしかけられている」とくに猟犬に用いられる表現、set は過去分詞形 (*OED*, set, *v.*¹ 148c)。

Which so roused up with boist'rous untuned drums,
With harsh-resounding trumpets' dreadful bray                    135
And grating shock of wrathful iron arms,
Might from our quiet confines fright fair peace
And make us wade even in our kindred's blood,
Therefore we banish you our territories.
You, cousin Herford, upon pain of life,                          140
Till twice five summers have enriched our fields
Shall not regreet our fair dominions,
But tread the stranger paths of banishment.
BOLINGBROKE    Your will be done. This must my comfort be:
That sun that warms you here shall shine on me,                  145
And those his golden beams to you here lent
Shall point on me and gild my banishment.
RICHARD    Norfolk, for thee remains a heavier doom,
Which I with some unwillingness pronounce.
The sly slow hours shall not determinate                         150
The dateless limit of thy dear exile.
The hopeless word of 'never to return'
Breathe I against thee, upon pain of life.
MOWBRAY    A heavy sentence, my most sovereign liege,
And all unlooked-for from your highness' mouth.                  155
A dearer merit, not so deep a maim
As to be cast forth in the common air,
Have I deservèd at your highness' hands.
The language I have learnt these forty years,
My native English, now I must forgo,                            160
And now my tongue's use is to me no more
Than an unstringèd viol or a harp,
Or like a cunning instrument cased up,
Or, being open, put into his hands
That knows no touch to tune the harmony.                         165
Within my mouth you have engaoled my tongue,

**136. wrathful** Q1: harsh resounding　Q2-F1: wrathfull yron　Q1 の読みは明らかに前行の harsh-resounding trumpets による汚染。

**140. upon pain of life** 「～してはならない」という趣旨の文に添えられる「さもなくば死刑に処す」という意味の副詞句。on pain of . . . は 42 のようにあとに処罰を書くのが普通だが、ここのようにあとに失うものを書く場合もある（*OED*, pain, *n*.<sup>1</sup> 1b）。

**life**　Qq: life　F1: death

**142. regreet** 「～に再会の挨拶をする」（*OED*, regreet, *v*. 1）。文脈上「～に帰国する」の意。

**148. doom**　Qq: doome　F1: dombe

**150. determinate** 「～を終わらせる」（*OED*, † determinate, *v*.<sup>1</sup> 1）。

**156. dearer merit** 「もっとよい褒美」。dear は「高価な、貴重な」（*OED*, dear, *a*.<sup>1</sup> †4）。merit は「相当の賞罰」（*OED*, merit, *n*. †1）。

**156. maim** この語はもともとは、かならずしも手足の（機能の）消失をともなわない重度の負傷を指して使われた（*OED*, maim, *n*.）。

**158. deservèd** 「（賞罰）を与えられるにふさわしい行動をする」（*OED*, deserve, *v*. †1）。 merit (156) が目的語。

**159. learnt**　Q1, 2: learnt　Q3-F1: learnd

**these forty years**　歴史上のモーブリーは追放を言いわたされた時点で 30 代前半だった。

**162. viol** 「ヴィオル」この劇の描く時代には存在しなかった、弓で弾く 4 ～ 7 弦の擦弦楽器でヴァイオリンの前身。Qq: violl　F1: Vyall

**163. cunning** 「たくみに細工された」、しかし同時に「（演奏に）技術を要する」の意も（*OED*, cunning, *a*. 2b, 5b）。

Doubly portcullised with my teeth and lips,
And dull unfeeling barren ignorance
Is made my gaoler to attend on me.
I am too old to fawn upon a nurse,                              170
Too far in years to be a pupil now.
What is thy sentence then but speechless death,
Which robs my tongue from breathing native breath?

**RICHARD**   It boots thee not to be compassionate.
After our sentence plaining comes too late.                     175

**MOWBRAY**   Then thus I turn me from my country's light
To dwell in solemn shades of endless night.

[*Starts to leave*]

**RICHARD**   [*to Mowbray*]
Return again and take an oath with thee.
    [*to Bolingbroke and Mowbray*]
Lay on our royal sword your banished hands.

[*They place their hands on Richard's sword*]

Swear by the duty that you owe to God —                         180
Our part therein we banish with yourselves —
To keep the oath that we administer.
You never shall, so help you truth and God,
Embrace each other's love in banishment,
Nor never look upon each other's face,                          185
Nor never write, regreet nor reconcile
This louring tempest of your home-bred hate,
Nor never by advisèd purpose meet
To plot, contrive or complot any ill
'Gainst us, our state, our subjects or our land.               190

**BOLINGBROKE**   I swear.

**MOWBRAY**                   And I, to keep all this.

**BOLINGBROKE**   Norfolk, so far as to mine enemy:

**167. portcullised** 「落とし格子によってさえぎられた」(*OED*, portcullised, *ppl. a.* 1)。Q1-3: portculist Q4-F1: percullist percullis は portcullis の 異綴り。

**172. sentence then** Qq: sentence F1: sentence then

**173. Which . . . breath** 「私の舌に母国語を話せないようにする」from = of、 breathing は動名詞形、Which の先行詞は前行の thy sentence。

**174. compassionate** 「嘆き悲しんでいる」(*OED*, compassionate, *a.* 1†c)。

**175. plaining** 「悲嘆」(*OED*, plaining, *vbl. n.*)。

**178. Return again** 「こちらに向きなおれ」again は、「もとのところへ」とい う動作、行為の方向を表す副詞で、しばしば return、answer など反対方向 の動作、行為を表す動詞とともに用いられる(*OED*, again, *adv.* 2)。

**180. you owe to God** Qq: y'owe to God F1: you owe to heauen F1 の読み が韻律どおり。

**181. Our part therein** 「私にたいする忠誠心」part = share、therein は前行 の the duty you owe to God を受け「神に示すべき忠誠のうちの」というこ とを指す。

**182. administer** 「(誓い)をするように勧める」(*OED*, administer, *v.* 5 の初 出例)。

**183. so help you truth and God** 「信心(または忠誠心)と神がそうなるよう 手助けしてくださりますように」。

**God** Qq: God F1: heauen

**185. never** Qq: neuer F1: euer

**186. never . . . nor** Qq: neuer . . . nor F1: euer . . . or

**188. never** Qq: neuer F1: euer

**advisèd** 「意図的な、熟慮のうえの」(*OED*, advised, *ppl. a.* 4)。

**192. so far as to mine enemy** 「敵にたいして言えるかぎりのこと〔を言おう〕」。

By this time, had the King permitted us,
One of our souls had wandered in the air,
Banished this frail sepulchre of our flesh,                    195
As now our flesh is banished from this land.
Confess thy treasons ere thou fly the realm.
Since thou hast far to go, bear not along
The clogging burden of a guilty soul.

MOWBRAY    No, Bolingbroke. If ever I were traitor,            200
My name be blotted from the book of life
And I from heaven banished as from hence.
But what thou art, God, thou and I do know,
And all too soon, I fear, the King shall rue.
Farewell, my liege. Now no way can I stray.                   205
Save back to England, all the world's my way.        *Exit*

RICHARD    [*to Gaunt*]    Uncle, even in the glasses of thine eyes
I see thy grievèd heart. Thy sad aspect
Hath from the number of his banished years
Plucked four away. [*to Bolingbroke*] Six frozen winters spent,    210
Return with welcome home from banishment.

BOLINGBROKE    How long a time lies in one little word!
Four lagging winters and four wanton springs
End in a word; such is the breath of kings.

GAUNT    I thank my liege that in regard of me                 215
He shortens four years of my son's exile.
But little vantage shall I reap thereby,
For ere the six years that he hath to spend
Can change their moons and bring their times about,
My oil-dried lamp and time-bewasted light                     220
Shall be extinct with age and endless night.
My inch of taper will be burnt and done,
And blindfold Death not let me see my son.

RICHARD    Why, uncle, thou hast many years to live.

GAUNT    But not a minute, King, that thou canst give.         225

**194. had wandered** ＝ would have wandered 帰結節に would などの助動詞を使わない単純形（simple form）の仮定法。Abbott, §361 参照。

**195. Banished this frail sepulchre of our flesh** 「肉体というもろき墓から追放されて」banished は、二重目的語〔人を場所から〕をとる他動詞の過去分詞形。

**197. the** Qq: the　F1: this

**199. clogging** 「動きを妨げる」文字どおりの意味は「足におもり木をつける」（*OED*, clog, *v.* 1, 2）。

**201. book of life** 「命の書」'He that overcometh, the same shall be clothed in white raiment; and I will not blot out his name out of the book of life, but I will confess his name before my Father, and before his angels.' (Revelation, 3: 5) に基づく。「命の書」から名を消されると永劫の罰を受けるとされ、罪をあがなわれたものはそこから名が消されないことが約束される。

**203. God** Qq: God　F1: heauen

**207-08. even in the glasses of thine eyes / I see thy grievèd heart** 「目は心の窓」（The EYE is the window of the heart）という諺的表現がある（Tilley, E231）。

　**glasses** 「窓ガラス」（*OED*, glass, *n.*¹ 3a）。

**208-10. Thy sad aspect . . . Plucked four away** ⇒後注参照。

**215. in regard of me** 「私を思いやって」（*OED*, regard, *n.* †14b の初出例）。

**221. extinct** ＝ extinguished 動詞 extinct の過去分詞形（*OED*, †extinct, *v.*; extinct, *pa.pple.*）。Q1: extint　Q2-F1: extinct

　**night** Q1-3: nightes　Q4-F1: night

Shorten my days thou canst with sullen sorrow
And pluck nights from me, but not lend a morrow.
Thou canst help Time to furrow me with age
But stop no wrinkle in his pilgrimage.
Thy word is current with him for my death,                    230
But dead thy kingdom cannot buy my breath.

RICHARD    Thy son is banished upon good advice,
Whereto thy tongue a party-verdict gave.
Why at our justice seem'st thou then to lour?

GAUNT    Things sweet to taste prove in digestion sour.       235
You urged me as a judge, but I had rather
You would have bid me argue like a father.
O, had it been a stranger, not my child,
To smooth his fault I should have been more mild.
A partial slander sought I to avoid,                          240
And in the sentence my own life destroyed.
Alas, I looked when some of you should say
I was too strict to make mine own away,
But you gave leave to my unwilling tongue
Against my will to do myself this wrong.                      245

RICHARD    Cousin, farewell, and uncle, bid him so.
Six years we banish him, and he shall go.

                    *Flourish. Exit [Richard with his train]*

AUMERLE    [*to Bolingbroke*]
Cousin, farewell. What presence must not know,
From where you do remain let paper show.        [*Exit*]

MARSHAL    [*to Bolingbroke*]
My lord, no leave take I, for I will ride                     250
As far as land will let me by your side.

        [*Bolingbroke fails to respond. Lord Marshall stands apart*]

GAUNT    O, to what purpose dost thou hoard thy words
That thou return'st no greeting to thy friends?

**226. sullen**　Qq: sullen　F1: sudden

**229. his** ＝ Time's

**230-31. Thy word is current with him for my death, / But dead thy kingdom cannot buy my breath**　「お前の言葉は『時』から死を買うのに通用するが、私が死んでしまえば、お前の王国をもってしても私の命を買いもどすことはできない」228-29 とほぼ同一内容。

**232-33. Thy son is . . . a party-verdict gave**　⇒後注参照。

**233. party-verdict**　「陪審のひとりとしての評決への関与」（*OED*, party, *n.* 18a）。

**235. Things . . . sour**　Tilley は What is sweet in the MOUTH is oft sour (bitter) in the maw (stomach)（M1265）というかたちで収録している。

**238-41. O . . . destroyed**　Qq にはあるが F1 にない、削除されたとおぼしい部分。

**239. smooth**　「言いつくろう（＝ gloss over）」（Onions）。

**240. partial slander**　「身内贔屓との非難」（Wilson）。

**242. looked when**　「～するのを心待ちにする」（*OED*, look, *v.* 3c）。

**248-49. What presence must not know, / From where you do remain let paper show**　「あなたと一緒にいてあなたから聞いて知ることができないことを、あなたのとどまっているところから、手紙で知らせてください」。

**253. return'st**　Qq: returnest　F1: return'st　F1 の読みが韻律どおり。

**BOLINGBROKE**  I have too few to take my leave of you,
When the tongue's office should be prodigal                    255
To breathe the abundant dolour of the heart.
**GAUNT**  Thy grief is but thy absence for a time.
**BOLINGBROKE**  Joy absent, grief is present for that time.
**GAUNT**  What is six winters? They are quickly gone.
**BOLINGBROKE**  To men in joy, but grief makes one hour ten.    260
**GAUNT**  Call it a travel that thou tak'st for pleasure.
**BOLINGBROKE**  My heart will sigh when I miscall it so,
Which finds it an enforcèd pilgrimage.
**GAUNT**  The sullen passage of thy weary steps
Esteem as foil wherein thou art to set                        265
The precious jewel of thy home return.
**BOLINGBROKE**  Nay, rather every tedious stride I make
Will but remember me what a deal of world
I wander from the jewels that I love.
Must I not serve a long apprenticehood                        270
To foreign passages, and in the end,
Having my freedom, boast of nothing else
But that I was a journeyman to Grief?
**GAUNT**  All places that the eye of heaven visits
Are to a wise man ports and happy havens.                     275
Teach thy necessity to reason thus:
There is no virtue like necessity.
Think not the King did banish thee
But thou the King. Woe doth the heavier sit
Where it perceives it is but faintly borne.                   280
Go, say I sent thee forth to purchase honour,
And not the King exiled thee; or suppose
Devouring pestilence hangs in our air
And thou art flying to a fresher clime.
Look what thy soul holds dear, imagine it                     285
To lie that way thou goest, not whence thou com'st.

**255. prodigal** 「ふんだんにある」(*OED*, prodigal, *a.* 2)。

**261. travel** この語にはもともと同一語の異綴りだった travail の「労苦、骨折り」という意味ももち、ゴーントが「旅」という意味で言ったものをボリンブルックは「労苦」という意味で受けとめる (*OED*, travel, *n.* †1, 2a)。

    **travel**　Qq: trauaile　F1: trauell

**265. as foil**　Q1: as foyle　Q2: a foyle　Q3-F1: a soyle　　**foil** ゴーントは「下敷き箔（宝石の輝きを増すためにその下に敷く金属片）」の意味で言うが、ボリンブルックは「挫折、妨げ」という意味で受けとめる (*OED*, foil, *n.*[1] 5a; foil, *n.*[2] 2)。

**267-92. Nay, . . . sets it light**　Qg にはあるが F1 にはない、削除されたとおぼしい部分。Wilson は、この部分の削除によって、つらい旅路を宝石の輝きを増してみせる下敷き箔にたとえるゴーントの言葉（264-66）にたいして、ボリンブルックが答えた部分（267-69）が削除され、極寒のコーカサスのことを思えば火を手で持つことができるのか、という問いかけ（293-94）がつづくことの唐突さを指摘している。また、301-02 も、削除されたゴーントの291-92 に答えて言った言葉である。

**268. remember** 「（人）に～を思いおこさせる」(*OED*, remember, *v.*[1] †8a)。

**270. apprenticehood** 「徒弟奉公（= apprenticeship)」(*OED*, †apprenticehood, *n.*)。

**272. freedom** 「一人前の職人としての権利」(*OED*, freedom, *n.* 13a)。

**273. journeyman** 文字どおりの意味は「徒弟奉公を終え、親方（master）に雇われる職人」で、比喩的には「～の支配を受けるもの」。この語の journey は職人の労働にたいする対価が発生する「一日」という意味だが、追放によって「旅」に出るという意味もかけあわされている (*OED*, journeyman, *n.* 1, 2b; journey, *n.* †1, 3a)。

**274. the eye of heaven** = the sun (*OED*, eye, *n.*[1] 1b)。

**276-77. necessity . . . necessity** 「困窮…必然性」(*OED*, necessity, *n.* 10a, 2a)。

**277. There is no virtue like necessity** 「必然にまさる美徳なし」(Make a VIRTUE of Necessity) という諺的な表現がある (Tilley, V73)。

**284. clime** = climate 「国、地方」(*OED*, clime, *n.* 2)。

Suppose the singing birds musicians,
The grass whereon thou treadst the presence strewed,
The flowers fair ladies and thy steps no more
Than a delightful measure or a dance,                          290
For gnarling Sorrow hath less power to bite
The man that mocks at it and sets it light.
BOLINGBROKE   O, who can hold a fire in his hand
By thinking on the frosty Caucasus,
Or cloy the hungry edge of appetite                            295
By bare imagination of a feast,
Or wallow naked in December snow
By thinking on fantastic summer's heat?
O no, the apprehension of the good
Gives but the greater feeling to the worse.                    300
Fell Sorrow's tooth doth never rankle more
Than when he bites but lanceth not the sore.
GAUNT   Come, come, my son, I'll bring thee on thy way.
Had I thy youth and cause, I would not stay.
BOLINGBROKE   Then England's ground, farewell. Sweet soil, adieu,   305
My mother and my nurse that bears me yet.
Where'er I wander, boast of this I can:
Though banished, yet a true born Englishman.
            *Exeunt [Gaunt and Bolingbroke, followed by Lord Marshal]*

[ACT I, SCENE IV]

*Enter [Richard] with [Green and Bagot] at one door, and Aumerle at
another*

RICHARD   We did observe. Cousin Aumerle,
How far brought you high Herford on his way?
AUMERLE   I brought high Herford, if you call him so,
But to the next highway, and there I left him.
RICHARD   And say what store of parting tears were shed?       5

**288. presence** 「謁見の間」(*OED*, presence, *n.* 2†c)。

**292. sets it light** 「それを軽いものとみなす」(*OED*, set, *v.*¹ 88a)。

**294. Caucasus** 「コーカサス山脈」黒海からカスピ海にいたる、ヨーロッパとアジアの境界となる山脈。エリザベス朝時代には極寒の地と考えられた。

**298. fantastic** 「空想上の」(*OED*, fantastic, *a.* 1†a)。

**299. apprehension** 「認識」(*OED*, apprehension, *n.* 5)。

**301. never** Qq: neuer F1: euer

　**rankle** 「化膿させる」(*OED*, rankle, *v.* †2)。

**302. he** Q1: he Q2-F1: it

　**lanceth** 「ランセットで切開する」(*OED*, lance, *v.* 6)の直説法三人称単数現在形。

**306. that** Qq: that F1: which

〔1. 4〕あらすじ………………………………………………………………………

　リチャードとその側近たちのあいだの宮廷におけるやりとり。リチャードは、追放されたボリンブルックを見送ったオーマールから別れのようすを聞いて、民衆にたいして腰の低いボリンブルックの人気を懸念する。王は顧問官のひとりグリーンにアイルランドの叛乱への対応を迫られると、徴税権と引き換えの国土の賃貸と、金額を白紙とした徴税勅許状の発行によって資金を調達し、自身で外征する意志を表明する。イーリー・ハウスでゴーントが危篤との報をブッシーがもたらすと、リチャードは戦費捻出のためにゴーントの財産の横取りを指示する。

…………………………………………………………………………………………

**0. 1 *Enter . . . another*** Qq: *Enter the King with Bushie, &c at one dore, and the Lord Aumarle at another.* F1: *Enter King, Aumerle, Greene, and Bagot.* ⇒ 1. 4. 23. 後注参照。

**1. We did observe. Cousin Aumerle** 音節数の足りない行(8音節)。最初の文は observe の目的語がない断片となっているが、その前に話されていた、リチャードたちが気づいていたこととは、ボリンブルックの大衆への取り入りぶりであることが 23 以降からわかる。

**2. high** 「驕り高ぶった」(*OED*, high, *a.* 14a)。

**4. next** = nearest(「近い」を意味する形容詞 nigh の最上級、*OED*, next, *a.* †1)。

**5. store** 「(*of . . .*)多量の〜」(*OED*, store, *n.* 4a)。

**AUMERLE**    Faith, none for me, except the north-east wind,
   Which then blew bitterly against our faces,
   Awaked the sleeping rheum and so by chance
   Did grace our hollow parting with a tear.
**RICHARD**    What said our cousin when you parted with him?    10
**AUMERLE**    'Farewell.'
   And for my heart disdainèd that my tongue
   Should so profane the word, that taught me craft
   To counterfeit oppression of such grief
   That words seemed buried in my sorrow's grave.    15
   Marry, would the word 'farewell' have lengthened hours
   And added years to his short banishment,
   He should have had a volume of farewells.
   But since it would not, he had none of me.
**RICHARD**    He is our cousin, cousin, but 'tis doubt,    20
   When time shall call him home from banishment,
   Whether our kinsman come to see his friends.
   Ourself and Bushy, Bagot here and Green
   Observed his courtship to the common people,
   How he did seem to dive into their hearts    25
   With humble and familiar courtesy,
   What reverence he did throw away on slaves,
   Wooing poor craftsmen with the craft of smiles
   And patient underbearing of his fortune,
   As 'twere to banish their affects with him.    30
   Off goes his bonnet to an oyster-wench.
   A brace of draymen bid God speed him well
   And had the tribute of his supple knee
   With 'Thanks, my countrymen, my loving friends',
   As were our England in reversion his,    35
   And he our subjects' next degree in hope.
**GREEN**    Well, he is gone, and with him go these thoughts.
   Now for the rebels which stand out in Ireland,

**7. blew**　Qq: blew　F1: grew

　**faces**　Q1, 2: faces　Q3-F1: face

**8. sleeping**　Q1, 2: sleeping　Q3-F1: sleepie　Q3 以降の四つ折本の読みと一致する F1 の読みは、プロンプトブックに由来すると目される F1 独自の読みでないため、信頼性は低い。

**12. for**　この時代には従属接続詞であった for は、主節の前に理由を表す節を導くことができる（*OED*, for, *conj.* †1）。

**13. profane**　「～を濫用する」（*OED*, profane, *v.* 1b）。⇒ 1. 3. 59 注参照。

**15. words**　Qq: words　F1: word

**18. a volume**　「一冊の本となるほどのもの」（*OED*, volume, *n.* 3）。

**19. of** = from（*OED*, of, *prep.* †3）

**20. cousin, cousin**　Qq: Coosens Coosin　F1: Cosin (Cosin)

　**doubt** = doubted　-t、-d で終わる動詞の過去分詞形の屈折語尾 -ed は省略されることがある（Abbott, §342）。

**23. Bushy, Bagot here and Green**　Q1-5: Bushie　Q6: Bushy, Bagot here and Greene　F1: *Bushy*: heere *Bagot* and *Greene*　⇒後注参照。

**24. courtship**　「おもねり」（*OED*, courtship, *n.* †5 の初出例）。

**25. dive**　「深く入りこむ」（*OED*, dive, *v.* 4）。

**27. What**　Qq: With　F1: What

**28. craft**　「巧妙な術策」（*OED*, craft, *n.* 4a）。

　**smiles**　Qq: smiles　F1: soules

**29. underbearing**　「耐えること」（*OED*, underbear, *v.* 1）。

**30. As 'twere to banish their affects with him**　「人びとの好意も追放されるわが身とともにたずさえていくかのように」。

　**As** = As if（*OED*, as, *adv.* 9a）

　**affects**　「好意」（*OED*, affect, *n.* 3）。

**32. A brace of draymen**　「ふたりの荷馬車夫」（*OED*, brace, *n.*² 15d; drayman, *n.* 1）。

**35. As** = As if　⇒ 30 注参照。

**35. in reversion**　「現在の所有者の死を前提として」（*OED*, reversion, *n.* 1c）。ボリンブルックをイングランドの継承者になぞらえることになるこのリチャードの言葉は、劇的皮肉となっている。

**36. our subjects' next degree in hope**　「わが臣民の望む次の王位継承者」degree は「梯子の一段」（*OED*, degree, *n.* 1）の比喩的用法。

Expedient manage must be made, my liege,
Ere further leisure yield them further means                    40
For their advantage and your highness' loss.

RICHARD   We will ourself in person to this war,
And for our coffers with too great a court
And liberal largess are grown somewhat light,
We are enforced to farm our royal realm,                       45
The revenue whereof shall furnish us
For our affairs in hand. If that come short,
Our substitutes at home shall have blank charters
Whereto when they shall know what men are rich
They shall subscribe them for large sums of gold               50
And send them after to supply our wants,
For we will make for Ireland presently.

*Enter Bushy*

Bushy, what news?

BUSHY   Old John of Gaunt is grievous sick, my lord,
Suddenly taken, and hath sent post haste                       55
To entreat your majesty to visit him.

RICHARD   Where lies he?

BUSHY   At Ely House.

RICHARD   Now put it, God, in the physician's mind
To help him to his grave immediately.                          60
The lining of his coffers shall make coats
To deck our soldiers for these Irish wars.
Come, gentlemen, let's all go visit him.
Pray God we may make haste and come too late.

[ALL]   Amen.                                        *Exeunt*   65

**39. Expedient manage** 「早急な対策」manage = management (*OED*, man-age, *n.* †5)。

**42. ourself** ⇒ 1. 1. 16 注参照。

**43. coffers** 「財源」(*OED*, coffer, *n.* 1b)。

**45-52. We are . . . make for Ireland presently** ⇒後注参照。

**45. farm** 「(土地)を賃貸する」(*OED*, farm, $v.^2$ 2 の初出例)。借用者は借地料を払い、土地の租税収入をえる。

**48. blank charters** 金額を特定しない徴税権の勅許状 (*OED*, blank, *a.* 10)。

**50. They . . . gold** 「代理人たちに、多額の金を要求するために〔裕福とわかったものたち〕の名を書き入れさせるのだ」shall については 1. 1. 37 注を参照せよ。

**52. make for** 「〜に向かう」(*OED*, make, $v.^1$ 78b)。

**presently** 「ただちに」(*OED*, presently, *adv.* 3)。

**52. 1. *Enter Bushy*** Qq: *Enter Bushie with newes.* F1: *Enter Bushy*

**53. Bushy, what news?** F1 のみの行。

**54. grievous** Qq: grieuous F1: verie

**58. Ely House** ロンドン北部の現在のイーリー・プレイスにあった歴代のイーリー主教の邸。1388 年に建造された門がホールボーン側にあり、イーリー主教たちはしばしば貴族に貸借しており、ゴーントはそこに滞在中他界した (Sugden)。

**59. God** Qq: God F1: heauen

**in the** Q1: in the Q2-5: into the F1: in his

**61. lining** 「内張り」だが比喩的には「中身」を意味する (*OED*, lining, *vbl n.*$^1$ 3)。

**65. Amen** Qq のみの行。

[ACT II, SCENE I]

*Enter John of Gaunt sick, [carried in a chair,] with Duke of York [and attendants]*

GAUNT    Will the King come that I may breathe my last
In wholesome counsel to his unstaid youth?
YORK    Vex not yourself nor strive not with your breath,
For all in vain comes counsel to his ear.
GAUNT    O, but they say the tongues of dying men                    5
Enforce attention like deep harmony.
Where words are scarce, they are seldom spent in vain,
For they breathe truth that breathe their words in pain.
He that no more must say is listened more
Than they whom youth and ease have taught to glose.            10
More are men's ends marked than their lives before.
The setting sun and music at the close,
As the last taste of sweets, is sweetest last,
Writ in remembrance more than things long past.
Though Richard my life's counsel would not hear,             15
My death's sad tale may yet undeaf his ear.
YORK    No, it is stopped with other flattering sounds,
As praises, of whose taste the wise are fond,
Lascivious metres, to whose venom sound
The open ear of youth doth always listen,                    20
Report of fashions in proud Italy,
Whose manners still our tardy-apish nation
Limps after in base imitation.
Where doth the world thrust forth a vanity —
So it be new, there's no respect how vile —                  25
That is not quickly buzzed into his ears?
Then all too late comes counsel to be heard
Where Will doth mutiny with Wit's regard.
Direct not him whose way himself will choose.

〔2. 1〕あらすじ‥‥‥‥‥‥‥‥‥‥‥‥‥‥‥‥‥‥‥‥‥‥‥‥‥‥‥‥‥‥‥‥‥‥‥‥‥‥‥‥‥

リチャードが王妃らを引き連れて見舞いにやってくると、死に瀕したゴーント
は息子の追放が原因でやつれてしまったと抗議し、王による国土の賃貸とグロス
ター暗殺について批判してさがる。ゴーントの訃報が伝えられると、王はアイル
ランド遠征の費用をまかなうためにその財産の没収を決定する。これを聞いて堪
忍袋の緒が切れたヨークは、世襲財産の剥奪は王位継承制度の根幹を揺るがすと
抗議するも聞き入れられず、王の前を辞す。王は、ヨークに留守を任せてアイル
ランドにおもむくことにする。ボリンブルックに同情を寄せるウィロビー、ロス
らが国情を憂えるが、ノーサンバーランドはボリンブルックらが艦隊を組んで北
方から上陸する計画が進んでいることを告げ、一同ラヴェンスパーに向かう。

‥‥‥‥‥‥‥‥‥‥‥‥‥‥‥‥‥‥‥‥‥‥‥‥‥‥‥‥‥‥‥‥‥‥‥‥‥‥‥‥‥‥‥‥‥‥

**1-2. I . . . youth**　ゴーントの健康状態と、彼のアドヴァイスの道徳的な健全性
を対比する、この場面の状況を集約的に示す表現。
　　**breathe my last**　「事切れる」と「最後の言葉を伝える」(*OED*, breathe, *v.*
10c, 12a)。　　**unstaid**　「言うことをきかない」(*OED*, unstaid, *a.* 2)。

**5-6. the tongues . . . deep harmony**　Dying MEN speak true (prophesy)
(Tilley, M514) のヴァリエーション (Dawson & Yachnin)。

**9. listened**　「～の言葉に耳を傾ける」(*OED*, listen, *v.* 1a) の過去分詞形。

**10. glose**　「巧言を弄する」(*OED*, gloze, *v.*¹ 3)。glose は 15-17 世紀の綴り。

**12. at the close**　Q1: at the close　Q2-5: at the glose　F1: is the close

**15. life's**　Qq, F1: liues　liues (lives) は 13-18 世紀の life 単数所有格の異綴
り。

**16. sad**　「厳粛な、真摯な」(*OED*, sad, *a.* 4†a)。
　　**undeaf**　「(人) の耳が聞こえるようにする」(*OED*, undeaf, *v.*)。用例はここ
と 19 世紀のもののみで、この語はシェイクスピアの造語とされる。

**17. flattering**　Qq: flattering　F1: flatt'ring　Q が韻律どおり。

**18. of . . . fond**　「賢明なものでさえもその味わいに心を奪われてしまう (称賛)」。
　　**fond**　Collier による校訂。以下のような本文の変遷は汚染の進行とされる
(Gurr)。Q1: of whose taste the wise are found　Q2: of whose state the
wise are found　Q3: of his state: then there are found　F1: of his state:
then there are sound.　　**19. venom**＝venomous (*OED*, venom, *a.* 1)。

**22. tardy-apish**　「時代遅れになってから流行を猿まねする」。

**24-26. Where . . . ears**　「世の中が人に押しつけたつまらないことは、かならず
すぐに彼の耳にささやかれる」修辞疑問文、冒頭の Where は人を表す。

**24. vanity**　「つまらないこと」(*OED*, vanity, *n.* 1a)。

**26. buzzed**　「しきりにささやく」(*OED*, buzz, *v.*¹ 4)。

**27. Then**　Qq: Then　F1: That　　**28. mutiny with**　「～と争う」(*OED*, mutiny, *v.* 1†d の初出例)。　　**regard**　「熟考」(*OED*, regard, *n.* 6a)。

'Tis breath thou lackst and that breath wilt thou lose.   30
**GAUNT**   Methinks I am a prophet new inspired
  And thus expiring do foretell of him.
  His rash fierce blaze of riot cannot last,
  For violent fires soon burn out themselves.
  Small showers last long but sudden storms are short.   35
  He tires betimes that spurs too fast betimes.
  With eager feeding food doth choke the feeder.
  Light vanity, insatiate cormorant,
  Consuming means, soon preys upon itself.
  This royal throne of kings, this sceptred isle,   40
  This earth of majesty, this seat of Mars,
  This other Eden, demi-paradise,
  This fortress built by Nature for herself
  Against infection and the hand of war,
  This happy breed of men, this little world,   45
  This precious stone set in the silver sea,
  Which serves it in the office of a wall
  Or as a moat defensive to a house
  Against the envy of less happier lands,
  This blessèd plot, this earth, this realm, this England,   50
  This nurse, this teeming womb of royal kings
  Feared by their breed and famous by their birth,
  Renownèd for their deeds as far from home
  For Christian service and true chivalry,
  As is the sepulchre in stubborn Jewry   55
  Of the world's ransom, blessèd Mary's son,
  This land of such dear souls, this dear, dear land,
  Dear for her reputation through the world,
  Is now leased out, I die pronouncing it,
  Like to a tenement or pelting farm.   60
  England, bound in with the triumphant sea
  Whose rocky shore beats back the envious siege

**30. 'Tis . . . lose** 「お前は（病人で）息切れしているのに、その息（で話す言葉）を聞きいれられず無駄にする」breath に「生命」を維持する「呼吸」と「話す言葉」の意味をかけた「笑えない言葉遊び（uncomic quibble）」（Ure）。
**lose** 「〜を無駄にする」（*OED*, lose, *v.*[1] 6a）。

**32. expiring** = dying（*OED*, expire, *v.* †4）文字どおりの意味は「息を吐きだす」ことで、前行の文字どおりには「息を吹きこむ」ことを意味する inspiring（「霊感を与える」）とのあいだに言葉遊びが見られ、ヨークの直前の言葉遊び（前項参照）を受けて発されたもの。

**33. riot** 「放縦」（*OED*, riot, *n.* 1）。

**34-39. For . . . itself.** 激しく抵抗してもすぐに自分の言うことを聞くと考える根拠として、5つの警句的な表現が、度合いがエスカレートするように並べられていることについて、Ure は増幅、増加によって論点を強調する auxesis という修辞技法がこの台詞では以後もつづくことを指摘している。

**36. betimes . . . betimes** = soon . . . early in the day（Kittledge）
**tires**（自）「疲れる」（*OED*, tire, *v.*[1] 2）。

**40-66. This . . . itself** リチャードが強大で名高い王国イングランドの領地を賃貸に出していることを嘆くゴーントの長台詞はイングランド頌としてよく知られる名句であり、40-55 は詞華集 *Englands Parnassus*（1600）に 'Of Albion' の見出しで収録されている。王が治める、神の恩寵を受け、武力にすぐれ、ヨーロッパ中に名高い、と言葉を重ねてイングランドをたたえる主部が 64 行目前半までつづき、それが今やリチャードによって地代をえるために賃貸に出されているとする述部がわずか1行半となっている構文のアンバランスさが、母国がその素晴らしさに似つかわしくない扱いを受けていることにたいするゴーントの嘆きの大きさを伝える文となっている。

**40. sceptred** 「王によって治められている」（*OED*, sceptred, *ppl. a.*）。

**48. as a moat** Q1-3: as Q4-F1: as a Q4-F1 が韻律どおり。

**51. teeming** 「豊穣な」（*OED*, teeming, *ppl.a.*[1] 2）の初出例。

**52. by . . . by** = on account of
**by their birth** Qq: by theyr byrth F1: for their birth

**55. stubborn Jewry** Jewry はユダヤ人の国ユデア（Judea）、「頑迷」という形容詞が冠されるのはキリスト教信仰を受け容れなかったため。

**56. the world's ransom** Mary's son から明らかなように人類の罪を贖（あがな）ったキリストを指す。

**60. tenement** 「借地」（*OED*, tenement, *n.* 2）。
**pelting** 「とるに足らぬ」（*OED*, pelting, *a.*）。

**62. envious** 「悪意ある」（*OED*, envious, *a.* †2）。

Of watery Neptune, is now bound in with shame,
With inky blots and rotten parchment bonds.
That England that was wont to conquer others                     65
Hath made a shameful conquest of itself.
Ah, would the scandal vanish with my life,
How happy then were my ensuing death!

*[Flourish.] Enter [Richard], Queen, Aumerle, Bushy, Green, Bagot,*
*Ross and Willoughby, [with attendants]*

**YORK**   The King is come. Deal mildly with his youth,
For young hot colts being reined do rage the more.               70
**QUEEN**   How fares our noble uncle Lancaster?
**RICHARD**   What comfort, man? How is't with agèd Gaunt?
**GAUNT**   O, how that name befits my composition!
Old Gaunt indeed and gaunt in being old.
Within me grief hath kept a tedious fast,                        75
And who abstains from meat that is not gaunt?
For sleeping England long time have I watched;
Watching breeds leanness, leanness is all gaunt.
The pleasure that some fathers feed upon
Is my strict fast — I mean my children's looks,                  80
And therein fasting hast thou made me gaunt.
Gaunt am I for the grave, gaunt as a grave
Whose hollow womb inherits naught but bones.
**RICHARD**   Can sick men play so nicely with their names?
**GAUNT**   No, misery makes sport to mock itself.                85
Since thou dost seek to kill my name in me,
I mock my name, great King, to flatter thee.
**RICHARD**   Should dying men flatter with those that live?
**GAUNT**   No, no, men living flatter those that die.
**RICHARD**   Thou now a-dying sayst thou flatterest me.         90
**GAUNT**   O no, thou diest though I the sicker be.
**RICHARD**   I am in health, I breathe and see thee ill.

**63. watery** Q1, 2, 4, 5: watry Q3: waterie F1: watery Q1 が 11 音節、F1 が 12 音節。

**bound** 「抵当に入れられた」「証文（bonds）によって」（64）という副詞句を添えて、敵の侵攻をはばむ海に「囲まれた」という意味の bound（61）と対比的に用いられている。

**68. were** = would be ⇒ 1. 3. 194 注参照。

**70. reined** Qq: ragde F1: rag'd Singer（1856）: rein'd

**72. What comfort . . .?** 「ご機嫌いかがですか」（*OED*, comfort, *n*. †1 の初出例）。

**73. composition** 「心身の状態」（*OED*, composition, *n*. 16b の初出例）。

**74. Old Gaunt indeed and gaunt in being old** 「痩せ衰えた」（*OED*, gaunt, *a*. 2）という語をゴーントの名にかけた言葉遊び。

**76. meat** 「食糧、糧」（*OED*, meat, *n*. 1）。

**77. watched** 「寝ずにいる」という意味の自動詞（*OED*, watch, *v*. †1）の過去分詞形。

**83. Whose hollow womb inherits naught but bones** 屍体が墓に葬られることを、墓を主語として、生きている子が亡くなった親にたいして行う「相続する（inherit）」という動詞を使っている点と、「子宮（womb）」という言葉によって妊娠のイメージを喚起している点で、二重に倒錯的な綺想。このような「相続」、「子宮」の比喩の使用は、息子ボリンブルックを追放に処され、後継者を失ったゴーントの心情を示すものとなっていることが 85 以降から明らかになる。

**84. nicely** 「微妙に、精妙に」の裏に「おろかに、ばかばかしく」の意も（*OED*, nicely, *adv*. †3, †1）。

**85. No, misery makes sport to mock itself** 「いいえ、（病ではなく）自分のみじめさが、みずからを茶化して気晴らしのたわむれをしているのだ」しばしば悲惨な状況が登場人物に言葉遊びをさせる、この劇の特徴を端的に示す言葉となっている。

**86-87. Since . . . thee** ゴーントは、さらにつづけて自分の惨めな状況とはリチャードに息子を追放されて自身の後継者がいなくなったことであることを明かし、自身の名をおとしめるような自身の冗談は王への追従だと告げている。

**88. with** Q1: with Q2-F1 なし

**92. and** Q1: and Q2-F1: I

GAUNT Now He that made me knows I see thee ill:
 Ill in myself to see, and in thee seeing ill.
 Thy death-bed is no lesser than thy land,  95
 Wherein thou liest in reputation sick,
 And thou, too careless patient as thou art,
 Commit'st thy anointed body to the cure
 Of those physicians that first wounded thee.
 A thousand flatterers sit within thy crown,  100
 Whose compass is no bigger than thy head,
 And yet encagèd in so small a verge
 The waste is no whit lesser than thy land.
 O, had thy grandsire with a prophet's eye
 Seen how his son's son should destroy his sons,  105
 From forth thy reach he would have laid thy shame,
 Deposing thee before thou wert possessed,
 Which art possessed now to depose thyself.
 Why, cousin, wert thou regent of the world,
 It were a shame to let this land by lease.  110
 But, for thy world, enjoying but this land,
 Is it not more than shame to shame it so?
 Landlord of England art thou now, not king.
 Thy state of law is bondslave to the law,
 And thou —
RICHARD  A lunatic, lean-witted fool,  115
 Presuming on an ague's privilege,
 Darest with thy frozen admonition
 Make pale our cheek, chasing the royal blood
 With fury from his native residence.
 Now by my seat's right royal majesty,  120
 Wert thou not brother to great Edward's son,
 This tongue that runs so roundly in thy head
 Should run thy head from thy unreverent shoulders.
GAUNT O, spare me not, my brother Edward's son,

**94. Ill . . . ill** 「見ている私が病んでおり、お前が病におかされているのがわかる」前行 I see thee ill の 2 つの意味についての説明、行末の ill は名詞。

**95. Thy death-bed . . . thy land** 「王国全体がお前の死の床となっている」。

**lesser** = less（*OED*, lesser, *a.* 1a）

**thy land** Q1: thy land Q2-F1: the Land

**98. anointed** ⇒ 1. 2. 38 注参照。

**99. those physicians** 次行の flatterers のことを指す。

**102. encagèd** Qq: inraged F1: incaged

**verge** 「（金属などの）環」（*OED*, verge, *n.*[1] 13 †b）。'The inclusive verge / Of golden metal that must round my brow.'（*R3*, 4. 1. 54-55）参照。 さらに、王室執事長（Lord High Steward）が管轄する宮廷の周辺地域（*OED*, verge, *n.*[1] 10）を意味する verge は、王冠と宮廷と英国全土という 3 つの領域を重ねあわせ、「王冠を頂く王が、宮廷で佞臣（ねいしん）たちに取りまかれて、賃貸に出すことによって国土を失うも同然」という趣旨のこの文の鍵語となっている。

**104-05. thy grandsire . . . his son's son** 祖父とはエドワード三世のこと、その息子たちについては 1. 2. 11 注を参照せよ。

**106. From forth** 「〜のそとへ」（*OED*, forth, *prep.* 2b）。

**107-08. Deposing thee . . . to depose thyself** 「〔王位継承者の地位を〕お前から奪う … お前みずからが〔王位を〕失う」（*OED*, depose, *v.* 3b, 3）。 劇作家は、この劇でリチャードがおかす最大の失態「廃位（deposition）」を観客に予期させるように、ゴーントがその原因となるリチャードの行動を非難するに際して鍵語となる depose という動詞を早々と使わせている。

**wert possessed . . . art possessed** 「（王位継承により国の）所有を許された … 悪魔に取り憑かれている」（*OED*, possess, *v.* 5b, 8c）。

**109. wert** Qq: wert F1: were **regent** 「支配者」（*OED*, regent, *n.* 1b）。

**110. It were** ⇒ 1. 3. 194 注参照。 **this** Qq: this F1: his

**111. for thy world, enjoying but this land** 「〔お前は〕自分の世界としてこの国しかもっていないのだから」。

**113. now, not** Q1-4: now not, not Q5: now not, nor F1: and not Thoebald: now, not

**115. And thou —** Q1: And thou Q2-5: And thou. F1: And ——— Capell: And thou—

**A lunatic** Q1: A lunatike A2: A lunatick Q3, 5: Ah lunatick Q4: Ah lunaticke F1: And thou, a lunaticke

**118. chasing** Qq: chasing F1: chafing

**119. native residence** 頬のこと。

**121. great Edward's** リチャードの父エドワード黒太子のこと。

**124. brother** Q1, F: brothers Q2-5: brother

For that I was his father Edward's son.                                      125
That blood already, like the pelican,
Hast thou tapped out and drunkenly caroused.
My brother Gloucester, plain well-meaning soul,
Whom fair befall in heaven 'mongst happy souls,
May be a precedent and witness good                                          130
That thou respect'st not spilling Edward's blood.
Join with the present sickness that I have
And thy unkindness be like crookèd Age
To crop at once a too-long-withered flower.
Live in thy shame, but die not shame with thee.                              135
These words hereafter thy tormentors be.
[*to attendants*]    Convey me to my bed, then to my grave.
Love they to live that love and honour have.

Exit [carried in the chair]

RICHARD    And let them die that age and sullens have,
For both hast thou and both become the grave.                                140
YORK    I do beseech your majesty, impute his words
To wayward sickliness and age in him.
He loves you, on my life, and holds you dear
As Harry Duke of Herford, were he here.
RICHARD    Right, you say true. As Herford's love, so his.                   145
As theirs, so mine, and all be as it is.

Enter Northumberland

NORTHUMBERLAND    My liege, old Gaunt commends him to
    your majesty.
RICHARD            What says he?
NORTHUMBERLAND                    Nay, nothing. All is said.
His tongue is now a stringless instrument.
Words, life and all, old Lancaster hath spent.                               150
YORK    Be York the next that must be bankrupt so.
Though death be poor, it ends a mortal woe.

**125. For that**　接続詞 that には、現代英語で従属接続詞として用いられる語（because, if, etc.）のあとに節を導く語として添えられる用法があった（*OED*, that, *conj.* 7）。⇒1. 4. 12 注参照。

**126. like the pelican**　ペリカンの母鳥は自分の胸を嘴^(くちばし)でつついて流した血を雛に与えるとされ、自身の血で死者を再生させたキリストを象徴するが、ここでは叔父の血を流したリチャードの忘恩を親鳥の血を吸う雛鳥にたとえている。

**127. Hast thou**　Q1-5: Hast thou　F1: Thou hast

　**out**　Qq: out　F1: なし

**129. Whom fair befall in heaven**　「その冥福を祈る」befall は「（出来事が人の身）に起こる」という意味の動詞（*OED*, befall, *v.* 4e）の無人称構文、仮定法現在、Whom は与格でその間接目的語。

**133. unkindness**　「人情にもとる振る舞い」（*OED*, unkindness, *n.* †1）。

**133. crookèd**　老齢による「腰の曲がった」姿勢と擬人化された「時」がもつ、刃の「湾曲した」大鎌をかけあわせた形容。

**137-40. Convey . . . grave**　137-38 の grave / have と 139-40 の have / grave の連続する押韻二行連句で韻を踏む語が逆転した形となっており、ゴーントの「愛も名誉も失った自分は死にたい」という絶望的な言葉にたいして、リチャードが「老齢で不機嫌なゴーントは死んでしまえばよい」という冷酷な言葉を追いかぶせるように言うリズム感を強調している。

**138. Love . . . have**　「王の愛と敬意をえているものはよろこんで生きればよい」。

**139. sullens**　「不機嫌」（*OED*, sullen, *n.* a）。

**143-44. He loves you . . . were he here**　「命にかけて、彼（ゴーント）は、（息子である）ハーフォード公ハリーがここにいたら愛し大事に思うのと同じように、あなた（リチャード）のことを愛し大事に思っています」。

**145. As Herford's love, so his**　「ゴーントの私への愛は、ハーフォードの私への愛と同じだ」リチャードは、直前のヨークの、ゴーントの愛の対象として息子ボリンブルックと王を比較する言葉（「彼は息子同様にあなたを愛している」）を、意図的に歪曲して、自身に追放されたボリンブルックとその父ゴーントそれぞれの自分にたいする愛を比較する言葉に変え、親子ともども自分を憎んでいる、と言っている。

**149. a stringless instrument**　⇒1. 3. 162 参照。

**150. Words . . . spent**　この場面序盤での、死に際の言葉で王を諌めると主張するゴーントにたいするヨークの「言葉も息も無駄にすることになる」という警告（30）が、ふたりのやりとりを経てゴーントの死という形で実現する約 100 行の劇行為の意味を端的に要約するかのような言葉（⇒30 注参照）。

**151. brankrupt**　前行の spent を受けて「破産」を「死」になぞらえているが、ゴーントの財産を没収するという王の心づもりを知らないノーサンバーランドとヨークのやりとりは劇的皮肉となっている。

RICHARD    The ripest fruit first falls and so doth he.
His time is spent; our pilgrimage must be.
So much for that. Now for our Irish wars.                         155
We must supplant those rough rug-headed kerns,
Which live like venom where no venom else
But only they have privilege to live.
And for these great affairs do ask some charge,
Towards our assistance we do seize to us                          160
The plate, coin, revenues and moveables
Whereof our uncle Gaunt did stand possessed.
YORK    How long shall I be patient? Ah, how long
Shall tender duty make me suffer wrong?
Not Gloucester's death, nor Herford's banishment,               165
Not Gaunt's rebukes, nor England's private wrongs,
Nor the prevention of poor Bolingbroke
About his marriage, nor my own disgrace
Have ever made me sour my patient cheek
Or bend one wrinkle on my sovereign's face.                      170
I am the last of noble Edward's sons,
Of whom thy father, Prince of Wales, was first.
In war was never lion raged more fierce,
In peace was never gentle lamb more mild
Than was that young and princely gentleman.                      175
His face thou hast, for even so looked he,
Accomplished with the number of thy hours.
But when he frowned, it was against the French
And not against his friends. His noble hand
Did win what he did spend and spent not that                     180
Which his triumphant father's hand had won.
His hands were guilty of no kindred blood
But bloody with the enemies of his kin.
O, Richard, York is too far gone with grief,
Or else he never would compare between.                          185

**154. pilgrimage** 「人生行路」(*OED*, pilgrimage, *n.* 1c)。

**156. supplant** 「～を根絶する」(*OED*, supplant, *v.* †4)。

**156. rug-headed kerns** 「蓬髪のアイルランド人軽歩兵たち」。

　**kerns** Q1, 2: kerne　Q3-F1: Kernes

**157-58. where no venom else / But only they have privilege to live**　聖パトリックがアイルランドから毒をもつ蛇や爬虫類を根絶したという言い伝えがある。venom は「毒蛇」を表す提喩（synecdoche）。

**160. seize** 「（封建領主や王が臣下の財産）を没収する」(*OED*, seize, *v.* 5a)。

**166. England's private wrongs** 「イングランド王の人びとへの不当な仕打ち」。

**167-68. prevention of poor Bolingbroke / About his marriage**　⇒後注参照。

**168. my own disgrace**　詳細不明。

**169. sour** 「（顔）を不機嫌な表情にする」(*OED*, sour, *v.* 4†c)。

**171-72. I am the last . . . was first**　⇒ 1. 2. 11 注参照。

**177. the**　Qq: a　F1: the

**182. kindred**　Q1-4: kinred　Q5: kindred　F1: kindreds

**185. compare** 「比較を行う」(*OED*, compare, *v.* 1c の唯一の用例）。

**RICHARD**   Why, uncle, what's the matter?

**YORK**                                 O my liege,
  Pardon me if you please; if not, I, pleased
  Not to be pardoned, am content withal.
  Seek you to seize and gripe into your hands
  The royalties and rights of banished Hereford?                    190
  Is not Gaunt dead, and doth not Herford live?
  Was not Gaunt just, and is not Harry true?
  Did not the one deserve to have an heir?
  Is not his heir a well-deserving son?
  Take Herford's rights away, and take from Time              195
  His charters and his customary rights;
  Let not tomorrow then ensue today;
  Be not thyself, for how art thou a king
  But by fair sequence and succession?
  Now, afore God — God forbid I say true —                    200
  If you do wrongfully seize Herford's rights,
  Call in the letters patents that he hath
  By his attorneys-general to sue
  His livery and deny his offered homage,
  You pluck a thousand dangers on your head,                  205
  You lose a thousand well-disposèd hearts
  And prick my tender patience to those thoughts
  Which honour and allegiance cannot think.

**RICHARD**   Think what you will, we seize into our hands
  His plate, his goods, his money and his lands.              210

**YORK**   I'll not be by the while. My liege, farewell.
  What will ensue hereof there's none can tell,
  But by bad courses may be understood
  That their events can never fall out good.            *Exit*

**RICHARD**   Go, Bushy, to the Earl of Wiltshire straight.      215
  Bid him repair to us to Ely House
  To see this business. Tomorrow next

**186-88. Why . . . withal.** Theobald による行割り。Qq は . . . matter? / . . . please / with all で終わる 3 行、F1 は . . . Vnckle / . . . matter? / . . . if not / . . . with all で終わる 4 行。

**189. gripe** 「〜をつかむ」(*OED*, gripe, *v.*[1] 2.)。

**190. royalties** 「国王から委譲された管轄権」(*OED*, royalty, *n.* 6a)。

**192. just** 「〔臣下として〕信義に篤い」(*OED*, just, *a.* 2†b)。

**true** Forker は「(嫡子として) 正統である」と「(息子として) 忠実である」(*OED*, true, *a.* 4c, 1a) の意味がかけられている可能性を指摘している。

**199. sequence** 「連続」(*OED*, sequence, *n.* 1a) の初出例。

**201. rights** Q1: rightes Q2-F1: right

**202-04. Call . . . livery** 「彼〔ボリンブルック〕がえている、相続する土地の譲与を代理人によって要求する訴えを起こすことを許可する開封勅許状を無効にする」。

**Call in** 「〜を撤回する、失効させる」(*OED*, call, *v.* 29a)。

**the** Qq: the F1: his

**letters patents** 「開封勅許状」(*OED*, patent, *a.* 1)。

**to sue / His livery** 「(相続人が土地の) 譲与を要求する訴訟を起こす」(*OED*, livery, *n.* 5a)。

**204. deny his offered homage** 「捧げた臣下の誓いを却下する」王にたいして臣下の誓いを行うことが、相続人が土地の譲与を認められる際に必要なプロセスだった (Forker)。

**213. by** = concerning, with respect to (*OED*, by, *prep.* 26)

**courses** 「振る舞いぶり」(*OED*, course, *n.* 23b)。

**214. events** 「結果」(*OED*, event, *n.* 3a)。

**215. Earl of Wiltshire** ウィリアム・ル・スクループ (William le Scrope 1351?-1399)。この劇には登場しないが、大蔵卿を務めており、ブシー、バゴット、グリーンと並ぶリチャードの 4 人の腹心のひとり。

**straight** 「すぐに、ただちに」(*OED*, straight, *adv.* 2a)。

**216. Ely House** ⇒ 1. 4. 58 注参照。

**217. Tomorrow next** 重複的な表現と見えるが、morrow は本来「朝」を意味し、この句全体で「翌朝」を意味する (Black)。

We will for Ireland, and 'tis time, I trow.
And we create in absence of ourself
Our uncle York Lord Governor of England,                    220
For he is just and always loved us well.
Come on, our Queen. Tomorrow must we part.
Be merry, for our time of stay is short.
    *Flourish. Exeunt [Richard], Queen, [Aumerle, Green and Bagot]*
**NORTHUMBERLAND**    Well, lords, the Duke of Lancaster is
    dead.
**ROSS**    And living too, for now his son is Duke.          225
**WILLOUGHBY**    Barely in title, not in revenues.
**NORTHUMBERLAND**    Richly in both if Justice had her right.
**ROSS**    My heart is great, but it must break with silence
    Ere't be disburdened with a liberal tongue.
**NORTHUMBERLAND**    Nay, speak thy mind, and let him ne'er
    speak more                                                       230
    That speaks thy words again to do thee harm.
**WILLOUGHBY**    Tends that thou wouldst speak to the Duke of
    Hereford?
    If it be so, out with it boldly, man.
    Quick is mine ear to hear of good towards him.
**ROSS**    No good at all that I can do for him,               235
    Unless you call it good to pity him,
    Bereft and gelded of his patrimony.
**NORTHUMBERLAND**    Now, afore God, 'tis shame such wrongs
    are borne
    In him, a royal prince, and many mo
    Of noble blood in this declining land.                    240
    The King is not himself, but basely led
    By flatterers, and what they will inform
    Merely in hate 'gainst any of us all
    That will the King severely prosecute
    'Gainst us, our lives, our children and our heirs.        245

**218. We will for Ireland** ⇒1. 2. 56 注参照。

   **trow** 「(〜と)思う、確信している」(*OED*, trow, *v.* 4b)。

**219-20. we create . . . England** 「不在中にわが叔父ヨークをイングランド摂政に任じる」⇒後注参照。

   **create** 「(人)に(位階、官位)を授ける」(*OED*, create, *v.* 3)。

   **Governor of England** 「摂政」を意味すると思われるが、*OED* はその語義をたてていない。2. 3. 77 では regent という語が用いられている。ホリンシェッド『年代記』では lieutenant generall と lord gouernor という語が使われている(3: 497)。

**226. revenues** Qq: reuenewes F1: reuennew

**228. great** 「(心が思い、感情で)満ちあふれている」(*OED*, great, *a.* †4)。

**229. liberal** 「喋々しい、口の軽い」(*OED*, liberal, *a.* 3†a)。

**230. ne'er speak more** = die (Forker)

**232. Tends . . . Hereford?** 「お前の話したいことはヘレフォード公に関係することか」。

   **Tends . . . to** = relate to (*OED*, tend, *v.*² †9)

**233. out with it** 「かまわず話せ」動詞を省略した命令的な用法(*OED*, out, *adv.* 13b)。

**237. gelded** 「(重要なもの)を奪う」の過去分詞形(*OED*, geld, *v.*¹ †2)。

**238. God** Qq: God F1: heauen

**ROSS**    The commons hath he pilled with grievous taxes
    And quite lost their hearts. The nobles hath he fined
    For ancient quarrels and quite lost their hearts.
**WILLOUGHBY**    And daily new exactions are devised,
    As blanks, benevolences, and I wot not what.       250
    But what a God's name doth become of this?
**NORTHUMBERLAND**    Wars hath not wasted it, for warred he hath not,
    But basely yielded upon compromise
    That which his ancestors achieved with blows.
    More hath he spent in peace than they in wars.     255
**ROSS**    The Earl of Wiltshire hath the realm in farm.
**WILLOUGHBY**    The King's grown bankrupt like a broken man.
**NORTHUMBERLAND**    Reproach and dissolution hangeth over him.
**ROSS**    He hath not money for these Irish wars,
    His burthenous taxations notwithstanding,     260
    But by the robbing of the banished Duke.
**NORTHUMBERLAND**    His noble kinsman, most degenerate King!
    But lords, we hear this fearful tempest sing
    Yet seek no shelter to avoid the storm.
    We see the wind sit sore upon our sails     265
    And yet we strike not but securely perish.
**ROSS**    We see the very wrack that we must suffer,
    And unavoided is the danger now
    For suffering so the causes of our wrack.
**NORTHUMBERLAND**    Not so. Even through the hollow eyes of Death    270
    I spy life peering, but I dare not say
    How near the tidings of our comfort is.
**WILLOUGHBY**    Nay, let us share thy thoughts as thou dost ours.
**ROSS**    Be confident to speak, Northumberland.
    We three are but thy self, and speaking so     275
    Thy words are but as thoughts. Therefore, be bold.
**NORTHUMBERLAND**    Then thus: I have from le Port Blanc,
    A bay in Brittany, received intelligence

**246. pilled** 「～から略奪する、強奪する」(*OED*, pill, *v.*¹ 1a)。

**248. quarrels** 「訴訟」(*OED*, quarrel, *n.*³ †1)。

**250. blanks** = blank charters (*OED*, blank, *n.* 6a) ⇒ 1. 4. 48 注参照。

**benevolences** 「善意献金」1473 年にエドワード四世王が法的根拠なく強制した拠出金の呼び名で、14 世紀末の出来事を描くこの劇に出てくることは時代錯誤となっている。エセックス伯の叛乱の際、同じ時期の出来事を扱い、この劇との関連も取り沙汰された歴史書 Sir John Hayward, *The First Part of the Life and Raigne of King Henrie IIII* (1599) にもこの表現が出てくる。

**250. I wot not what** 「私にはなんのことかよくわからないもの」(*OED*, what, *pron.* 8b)。

**251. a God's name** 「神の名にかけて」(*OED*, a, *prep.*¹ †10; god, *n.* 11)。Qq: a Gods name　F1: o'Gods name

**252-54. Wars ... blows** リチャードは 1397 年にブルターニュ半島の海港都市ブレスト (Brest) をブルターニュ公に戦わずして明け渡している。

**254. his ancesters** Qq: his noble auncestors　F1: his Ancestors　F1 が韻律どおり。

**256. hath the realm in farm** 「国土を〔地代目当てで〕賃借している」(*OED*, farm, *n.*² 3)　⇒ 1. 4. 45 注参照。

**257. King's** Q1, 2: King　Q3-F1: Kings

**258. dissolution** 「破滅」(*OED*, dissolution, *n.* 9)。

**260. burthenous** 「重い (= burdensome)」(*OED*, † burdenous, burthenous, *a.* 1a)。

**265. sit** 「(風が) 吹く」(*OED*, sit, *v.* 13d)。

**266. strike** 「帆を下ろす」と「たたく」の二重の意 (*OED*, strike, *v.* 17c, 25)。

**securely** 「油断して」(*OED*, securely, *adv.* †1)。

**268. unavoided** 「避けられない」(*OED*, unavoided, *ppl. a.* †2)。過去分詞には -able という意味になる使い方がある (Abbott, §375 参照)。

**277. le Port Blanc** 「ポール・ブラン」 ブルターニュ半島北岸の海港都市。Qq: le Port Blan　F1: Port *le Blan*

**278. Brittany** Q1: Brittaine　Q2-4: Brittanie　F1: *Britaine*

That Harry Duke of Herford, Rainold Lord Cobham,
Thomas, son and heir to the Earl of Arundel,                          280
That late broke from the Duke of Exeter,
His brother, Archbishop late of Canterbury,
Sir Thomas Erpingham, Sir John Ramston,
Sir John Norbery, Sir Robert Waterton and Francis Coint,
All these well furnished by the Duke of Brittany                      285
With eight tall ships, three thousand men of war,
Are making hither with all due expedience
And shortly mean to touch our northern shore.
Perhaps they had ere this, but that they stay
The first departing of the King for Ireland.                         290
If then we shall shake off our slavish yoke,
Imp out our drooping country's broken wing,
Redeem from broking pawn the blemished crown,
Wipe off the dust that hides our sceptre's gilt
And make high majesty look like itself,                              295
Away with me in post to Ravenspurgh.
But if you faint, as fearing to do so,
Stay and be secret, and myself will go.
**Ross**   To horse, to horse! Urge doubts to them that fear.
**Willoughby**   Hold out my horse, and I will first be there.        300

*Exeunt*

[ACT II, SCENE II]

*Enter Queen, Bushy and Bagot*

**Bushy**   Madam, your majesty is too much sad.
You promised, when you parted with the King,
To lay aside life-harming heaviness
And entertain a cheerful disposition.
**Queen**   To please the King I did; to please myself            5
I cannot do it. Yet I know no cause

**280. Thomas . . . Arundel**　Qq、F1 どちらにもない行で、Evans が植字工に
よる見落としと考えてホリンシェッドの記述をもとに再構成したもの。

**281. Duke of Exeter**　ジョン・ホランド（John Holland, c. 1352-1400）。ハン
ティンドン伯でもあった。1386 年にボリンブルックの姉エリザベスと結婚し
ている。　⇒5. 3. 136 注参照。

**284. Coint**　Qq: Coines　F1: *Quoint*　Coint はホリンシェッドの綴り。

**287. making**　「向かう」（*OED*, make, *v.* 35b）。

**289. stay**　「〜を待つ」⇒1. 3. 4 注参照。

**291-96. If . . . Ravenspurgh**　リチャード廃位、ボリンブルック擁立の意図を示
す劇中最初の言葉。

**292. Imp**　「（鷹の翼）に羽毛をつけ足して繕う」（*OED*, imp. *v.*[1] 4）の比喩的用
法。

**293. broking pawn**　「高利貸しにとられた借金の形」。
　**broking**　「高利貸しの、ぺてんの」（*OED*, broking, *vbl. n.* 3）。ちなみに
*OED* はこの一節を限定的用法の用例として引用しているが、出典源を **1594**
SHAKES. *Rich. III* と誤記している（Black）。

**296. Ravenspurgh**　「ラヴェンスパー」イングランド北東部ヨークシア州イース
ト・ライディング地区（East Riding）の海岸線にある低湿地ホールダーネス
（Holderness）の、ハンバー川（the Humber）河口近くにあった町。海水に
よる浸食によって 16 世紀には消失した。追放中のボリンブルックがここから
上陸することになる（Sugden）。⇒2. 2. 49-51 後注参照。

**299. Urge . . . fear**「恐れるものにたいしてお前たちなど信じないと言い立てる
のだ」（*OED*, urge, *v.* 1b の初出例）。

〔2. 2〕あらすじ‥‥‥‥‥‥‥‥‥‥‥‥‥‥‥‥‥‥‥‥‥‥‥‥‥‥‥‥‥‥‥‥‥‥‥‥‥‥
　遠征に出た夫の身を案じ嘆き悲しむ王妃のもとに、ボリンブルック侵攻とノー
サンバーランド伯、ウスター伯ら離反の報がもたらされる。次いで武装したヨー
クが現れ、リチャードのもとで国を守らねばならないが、状況は厳しいことを告
げ、息子オーマール離反の報、次いで軍資金の出所と当てにしていたグロスター
未亡人の訃報を従者から受ける。リチャードとボリンブルックのはざまで思い悩
むヨークは、徴兵を命じて、王妃とともにバークリー城に向かう。あとに残り民
心の変化を嘆いていたリチャードの 3 人の側近のうち、ブシーとグリーンはブリ
ストルへ、バゴットはアイルランドへ向かう。

■■■■■■■■■■■■■■■■■■■■■■■■■■■■■■■■■■■■■■■■■■■■■■■■■■■■■

**3. heaviness**　（廃）「悲しみ、憂鬱」（*OED*, heaviness, *n.* e）。

Why I should welcome such a guest as Grief,
Save bidding farewell to so sweet a guest
As my sweet Richard. Yet again, methinks
Some unborn Sorrow ripe in Fortune's womb                    10
Is coming towards me, and my inward soul
With nothing trembles. At something it grieves
More than with parting from my lord the King.

BUSHY    Each substance of a grief hath twenty shadows
Which shows like grief itself but is not so.                 15
For Sorrow's eyes, glazèd with blinding tears,
Divides one thing entire to many objects,
Like perspectives, which rightly gazed upon
Show nothing but confusion; eyed awry
Distinguish form. So your sweet majesty,                     20
Looking awry upon your lord's departure,
Find shapes of grief more than himself to wail,
Which, looked on as it is, is naught but shadows
Of what it is not. Then, thrice-gracious Queen,
More than your lord's departure weep not. More's not seen,   25
Or if it be, 'tis with false Sorrow's eye,
Which for things true weeps things imaginary.

QUEEN    It may be so, but yet my inward soul
Persuades me it is otherwise. Howe'er it be,
I cannot but be sad, so heavy sad                            30
As, though on thinking on no thought I think,
Makes me with heavy nothing faint and shrink.

BUSHY    'Tis nothing but conceit, my gracious lady.

QUEEN    'Tis nothing less. Conceit is still derived
From some forefather grief. Mine is not so,                  35
For nothing had begot my something grief,
Or something hath the nothing that I grieve.
'Tis in reversion that I do possess,
But what it is that is not yet known; what

**9. methinks** ＝ it seems to me　人称代名詞・一人称単数与格の me と主語を書かずに使用する無人称構文の動詞 think からなる複合語。過去形は methought（*OED*, methinks, *impers. v.*; † think, *v.*[1] 2）。

**10. ripe**　「(胎児について) まもなく生まれる」（*OED*, ripe *adj.* 2c）。

**12. nothing . . . something**　予期される不幸な事態を、まだ起こっていない「実体のないもの」という意味で nothing と、それが現実に起きていることを大きく上回る「重要な意味をもつもの」という意味で something で表している。Forker は、劇中 25 回使われる nothing が劇の大きなモチーフとなっていることを指摘している。　　**16. eyes**　Qq: eyes　F1: eye　　**glazèd**　「窓ガラスをはめられた」（*OED*, glazed, *ppl. a.* 1）。

**17. entire**　「まるのままの」（*OED*, entire, *a.* 2a）。

**18. perspectives**　①レンズと鏡の組み合わせで複数の像を見せるのぞきからくり（16-17）と②ハンス・ホルバイン（Hans Holbein the younger）『大使たち（*The Ambassadors*）』（1533 年）のように、特定の角度から眺めるともの姿が認められるように描かれただまし絵（18-20）の、ふたつの perspective が混同されている（*OED*, perspective, *n.* †2, 4†b）。

**25. More's**　Qq: more is　F1: more's　F1 の読みで 1 行 12 音節。

**27. for**　＝ instead of　　**weeps**　Qq: weepes　F1: weepe

**30-32. so heavy sad . . . shrink**　「浮かんでくる想像のことを考えないようにしても、実体のない悲しみによって、私に気を失い、やつれはてさせるほど、ひどく悲しい」で、直前の sad（30）を言い直した形容詞句となっている。文の構造が、thinking . . . thought . . . think（31）のくり返しによってみずから意図して意味のあることを考えるということを強く否定し、Makes（32）ではじまる使役の構文を使用することによって、不幸な事態の予感という実体のないものによって否応なく悲しみに暮れることを余儀なくされている王妃の心情をよく表している。　　**31. though**　Q1: thought　Q2-F1: though

**33. conceit**　「あだな想像」（*OED*, conceit, *n.* 7）。

**34. still**　＝ always　⇒ 1. 1. 22 注参照。

**36. something**　「実体をもつ」代名詞 something の形容詞的用法。

**37. hath**　＝ hath begot（前行を受けて）　　**38. in reversion**　⇒ 1. 4. 35 注参照。

**39-40. But what it is . . . nameless woe I wot**　「それがなにであるかはまだわかっていない。私に名づけることができないものは、名前のない悲しみであると私にはわかっている」Q1: But what it is that is not yet knowen what, / I cannot name, tis namelesse woe I wot.;　Q2-F1: But what it is, that is not yet knowne, what / I cannot name, 'tis namelesse woe I wot.

34-38 の、まだ生じていない、現実の出来事を超える大きな不幸の予感が悲しみの原因となっている、という王妃の綺想につづく部分で、Q1 では難解な王妃の考えがパンクチュエイションに混乱をもたらしている。

I cannot name 'tis nameless woe I wot.                                    40

*Enter Green*

**GREEN**   God save your majesty, and well met, gentlemen.
I hope the King is not yet shipped for Ireland.
**QUEEN**   Why hopest thou so? 'Tis better hope he is,
For his designs crave haste, his haste good hope.
Then wherefore dost thou hope he is not shipped?          45
**GREEN**   That he, our hope, might have retired his power
And driven into despair an enemy's hope,
Who strongly hath set footing in this land.
The banished Bolingbroke repeals himself
And with uplifted arms is safe arrived                         50
At Ravenspurgh.
**QUEEN**                    Now God in heaven forbid!
**GREEN**   Ah madam, 'tis too true and, that is worse,
The Lord Northumberland, his son, young Harry Percy,
The Lords of Ross, Beaumont and Willoughby
With all their powerful friends are fled to him.              55
**BUSHY**   Why have you not proclaimed Northumberland
And all the rest revolted faction traitors?
**GREEN**   We have, whereupon the Earl of Worcester
Hath broken his staff, resigned his stewardship,
And all the household servants fled with him                 60
To Bolingbroke.
**QUEEN**   So, Green, thou art the midwife to my woe,
And Bolingbroke my sorrow's dismal heir.
Now hath my soul brought forth her prodigy,
And I, a gasping new-delivered mother,                        65
Have woe to woe, sorrow to sorrow joined.
**BUSHY**   Despair not, madam.
**QUEEN**                              Who shall hinder me?
I will despair and be at enmity

**41. God**　Qq: God　F1: heauen

**44. crave**　「(事物、事態が)～を要求する」(*OED*, crave, *v.* 6))。

**46. retired**　「(軍隊)を撤退させる」(*OED*, retire, *v.* 7a)。

**49-51. The banished Bolingbroke . . . is safe arrived / At Ravenspurgh**　⇒後注参照。

**49. repeals himself**　「追放先からもどる」「～を追放先から呼びもどす」を意味する他動詞の再帰用法(*OED*, repeal, *v.*¹ †3†b)。

**52. Ah**　Qq: Ah　F1: O

**53. son, young**　Q1: son yong　Q2-F1: yong sonne

**54. Beaumont**　Q1-F1: Beaumond　Halliwell: Beaumont

**57. all the rest**　Q1: al the rest　Q2-F1: the rest of the

**58-59. the Earl of Worcester . . . stewardship**　the Earl of Worcester は初代ウスター伯トマス・パーシー (Percy, Thomas, Earl of Worcester d. 1403, second son of Henry, third baron Percy of Alnwick, 1322-1368) のことだが、この劇には登場しない。his stewardship は王室家政長官 (Lord Steward of the [King's] Household) 職のこと。　⇒後注参照。

**59. broken**　Q1: broken　Q2-F1: broke

**62-66. midwife . . . heir . . . prodigy . . . new-delivered mother / Have woe to woe . . . joined**　王妃は 10-11 (Some unborn Sorrow ripe in Fortune's womb / Is coming towards me)、36-37 (For nothing had begot my something grief, / Or someting hath the nothing that I grieve) で用いた、自身がいだいている予見的な悲しみを出産にたとえる比喩をつづけ、予感の実現について、不幸の予感で悲しみにくれていた自身を子を身ごもった母親に、その実現を告げる報せをもたらしたグリーンを助産婦に、侵攻という恐ろしい結果をもたらし彼女の予感を実現させたボリンブルックを怪物のような子になぞらえている。Forker は、66 について、怪物を産んだため、出産後も産みの苦しみにつづいて悲しみと苦しみを味わっていることと解している。この意味の sorrow については、Genesis 3:16 (Geneve Bible) の 'Unto the woman he said, I will greatly increase thy sorrows, and thy conceptions. In sorrow shalt thou bring forth children . . .' を参照 (*OED*, woe, *n.* †2a, sorrow, *n.* †5a)。

**62. to**　Q1: to　Q2-F1: of

**64. prodigy**　= monstrous creature (*OED*, prodigy, *n.* 2†b)

With cozening Hope. He is a flatterer,
A parasite, a keeper-back of Death,     70
Who gently would dissolve the bands of life,
Which false Hope lingers in extremity.

*Enter York*

**GREEN**    Here comes the Duke of York.
**QUEEN**    With signs of war about his agèd neck.
  O, full of careful business are his looks!     75
  Uncle, for God's sake, speak comfortable words.
**YORK**    Should I do so, I should belie my thoughts.
  Comfort's in heaven, and we are on the earth,
  Where nothing lives but crosses, cares and grief.
  Your husband, he is gone to save far off     80
  Whilst others come to make him lose at home.
  Here am I left to underprop his land,
  Who, weak with age, cannot support myself.
  Now comes the sick hour that his surfeit made,
  Now shall he try his friends that flattered him.     85

*Enter [Servingman]*

**SERVINGMAN**    My lord, your son was gone before I came.
**YORK**    He was? Why so, go all which way it will!
  The nobles they are fled, the commons they are cold,
  And will, I fear, revolt on Herford's side.
  Sirrah, get thee to Plashy, to my sister Gloucester.     90
  Bid her send me presently a thousand pound.
  Hold, take my ring.
**SERVINGMAN**    My lord, I had forgot to tell your lordship
  Today, as I came by, I callèd there —
  But I shall grieve you to report the rest.     95
**YORK**    What is't, knave?
**SERVINGMAN**    An hour before I came the Duchess died.

**71. bands**　「複数要素からなるものの全体をつなぎ止める<ruby>紐帯<rt>ちゅうたい</rt></ruby>」（*OED*, band, *n.*[1] 4）。

**72. Which**　先行詞は life（71）。

**Hope lingers**　Qq: Hope lingers　F1: hopes linger

**lingers**　「〜を長引かせる」（*OED*, linger, *v.* 7†a）。

**in extremity**　「いまわのきわに」（*OED*, extremity, *n.* 8）。

**74. signs of war about his agèd neck**　鎧の喉あて（gorget）のこと。平服に着用されることもあった。

**76. speak comfortable words**　Shaheen は、comfortable words を一般的な表現としながらも、国教会聖餐式の式文 'Heare what comfortable wordes our Sauior Christ saith vnto all that truely turne to him' およびサミュエル記の一節 'The word of my lorde the King shall nowe bee comfortable'（2 Sam. 14: 17）を引用し、シェイクスピアが聖餐式で頻繁に聞かれる日常的表現を使用していると指摘している（371）。

**God's**　Qq: Gods　F1: heauens

**77. Should I do so, I should belie my thoughts.**　Qq: Should I do so I should bely my thoughts　F1 なし　Qq のみの行。

**belie**　「〜のことをいつわって伝える」（*OED*, belie, *v.*[2] 4）。

**79. crosses**　「厄介ごと」（*OED*, cross, *n.* 10b）。

**cares**　「悲しみ」（*OED*, care. *n.*[1] †1a）。　　Qq: cares　F1: care

**85. shall**　⇒ l. 1. 37 注参照。

**86. your son was gone before I came**　⇒後注参照。

**90. Plashy**　⇒ 1. 2. 66 注参照。

**94. as I came by**　Q1: as I came by　Q2-F1: I came by and

**97. An hour before I came the Duchess died**　⇒後注参照。

**YORK**     God for His mercy, what a tide of woes
Comes rushing on this woeful land at once!
I know not what to do. I would to God,                                    100
So my untruth had not provoked him to it,
The King had cut off my head with my brother's.
What, are there no posts dispatched for Ireland?
How shall we do for money for these wars?
[*to Queen*]     Come, sister, — cousin, I would say — pray
pardon me.                                                                           105
[*to Servingman*]     Go, fellow, get thee home, provide some carts
And bring away the armour that is there.

                                                    [*Exit Servingman*]

[*to Bushy, Bagot and Green*]     Gentlemen, will you go muster
men?
If I know how or which way to order these affairs
Thus disorderly thrust into my hands,                               110
Never believe me. Both are my kinsmen.
Th'one is my sovereign, whom both my oath
And duty bids defend; tother again
Is my kinsman, whom the King hath wronged,
Whom conscience and my kindred bids to right.          115
Well, somewhat we must do. [*to Queen*] Come, cousin, I'll
Dispose of you.
Gentlemen, go muster up your men
And meet me presently at Berkeley Castle.
I should to Plashy too,                                                       120
But time will not permit. All is uneven,
And everything is left at six and seven.

                                           *Exeunt* [*York*] *and Queen*

**BUSHY**     The wind sits fair for news to go for Ireland,
But none returns. For us to levy power
Proportionable to the enemy is all unpossible.             125
**GREEN**     Besides, our nearness to the King in love

**98. God**　Qq: God　F1: Heau'n

**99. Comes**　Qq: Comes　F1: Come

**100. I would to God**　would は一般動詞 will の仮定法の形（＝ wish）である
が、I would to God . . . という言い方は、あとに that 節の目的語をとって
「神の思し召しで～あればよいのに」という意味となる。Would God . . .（＝
O that God would . . .）との混同から生じた語法とされる（*OED*, will, *v.*[1]
36, 37）。

　**God**　Qq: God　F1: heauen

**101. So** ＝ so long as　so that の that が省略された形（*OED*, so, *adv.*, 26）。

　**untruth**　（稀）「（王にたいする）不忠」（*OED*, untruth, *n.* 1）。

**102. my brother's** ＝ Gloucester's

**103. no**　Q1: no　Q2-5: two　F1 なし

**105. sister, — cousin, I would say —**　ヨークは義妹グロスター未亡人の訃報
に心を奪われ、目の前にいる王妃に「妹よ」と呼びかけてしまい、誤りに気づ
き言い直している。

**108. go**　Qq: go　F1 なし

**113. tother** ＝ the other　現在は方言に残る語（*OED*, tother, *pron.* 1）。Q1-2:
tother　Q3-5: t'other　F1: th'other

**115. kindred**　⇒ 1. 1. 70 注参照。

**116-19. I'll / . . . Castle.**　Wilson による行割り。Qq は . . . men, / . . . Barkly:
で終わる 2 行、F1 は . . . men / . . . Castle: で終わる 2 行。

**119. Berkeley Castle**　グロスターシアの市場町バークリーに現在も残る城
（Sugden）。Qq: Barkly　F: Barkley Castle

**120. I should to Plashy too**　⇒ 1. 2. 56 注参照。

**122. everything is left at six and seven**　「すべてが混乱状態にある」骰子（さいころ）のふ
たつの最大の目である 5 と 6 に由来する「運を賽（さい）の目にまかせる、一か八か
の勝負に出る（to set on cinque and sice）」から派生した表現。もともと
「運命を賭する」という意味だったが、数詞を最大の目を超える 7 に変えるこ
とによって「混乱におとしいれる」という意味に転化した（*OED*, six, *n.* 5;
Forker, LN）。Tilley は To set ALL at six and seven という形で収録してい
る（A208）。

**123. sits**　「（風が～の方角から）吹く」。　⇒ 2. 1. 265 参照

　**for**　Qq: for　F1: to

**125. Proportionable**　「釣りあった」（*OED*, proportionable, *a.* 1）。

　**unpossible**　Qq: vnpossible　F1: impossible

Is near the hate of those love not the King.

**BAGOT**   And that's the wavering commons, for their love

Lies in their purses, and whoso empties them

By so much fills their hearts with deadly hate.                    130

**BUSHY**   Wherein the King stands generally condemned.

**BAGOT**   If judgement lie in them, then so do we,

Because we ever have been near the King.

**GREEN**   Well, I will for refuge straight to Bristow Castle.

The Earl of Wiltshire is already there.                             135

**BUSHY**   Thither will I with you, for little office

Will the hateful commons perform for us,

Except like curs to tear us all to pieces.

[*to Bagot*]   Will you go along with us?

**BAGOT**   No, I will to Ireland to his majesty.                   140

Farewell. If heart's presages be not vain,

We three here art that ne'er shall meet again.

**BUSHY**   That's as York thrives to beat back Bolingbroke.

**GREEN**   Alas, poor Duke! The task he undertakes

Is numbering sands and drinking oceans dry.                        145

Where one on his side fights, thousands will fly.

Farewell at once, for once, for all and ever.

**BUSHY**   Well, we may meet again.

**BAGOT**                                    I fear me never.

*Exeunt* [*Bagot at one door, Bushy and Green at the other*]

[ACT II, SCENE III]

*Enter Bolingbroke and Northumberland*

**BOLINGBROKE**   How far is it, my lord, to Berkeley now?

**NORTHUMBERLAND**   Believe me, noble lord,

I am a stranger here in Gloucestershire.

These high wild hills and rough uneven ways

Draws out our miles and makes them wearisome.                      5

**128. that's** Qq: that is F1: that's

**131. Wherein** = in which「そのことで」理由を表わす。

**132. so do** = stand condemned

**133. ever have been** Qq: euer haue beene F1: haue beene euer

**134. I will . . . to Bristow Castle** ⇒ 1. 2. 56 注参照。

**Bristow Castle** 「ブリストル城」Bristow は、Bristol の近代初期に一般的だった異形。Bristol, Bristow の当時の発音は［'brɪstoː］(Crystal)。初代グロスター伯ロバート (Robert, 1st Earl of Gloucester, b. before 1100, d. 1147) が再建し、イングランドでもっとも強固な砦のひとつであったが、1656 年に革命政府によってとり壊された (Sugden)。Qq: Brist. F1: Bristoll 2. 3. 162 では Q1, F1 とも Bristow Castle となっており、Qq の Brist. を Bristow の略と考え、こちらの読みをとった。

**134-42. Well, . . . again** ⇒後注参照。

**136-38. little office / Will ... all to pieces** 「憎しみにみちた平民たちは、野良犬のようにわれわれをずたずたに引き裂く以外、いいことなんかしてくれない」。 **office** = service, kindness (*OED*, office, *n.* 1) **to pieces** Q1: to pieces Q2-F1: in peeces

**144-45. The task . . . drinking oceans dry** Tilley は As difficult as to number the SANDS in the sea (S91) と To drink the OCEAN dry (O9) という諺を収録している。

**147-48. Farewell . . . / Well** Qq: Farwell . . . / *Bush.* Well F1: *Bush.* Farewell . . . / Well

〔2. 3〕あらすじ・・・・・・・・・・・・・・・・・・・・・・・・・・・・・・・・・・・・・・・・・・・・・・・・・・・・・・・・・・・・・・・・・

　バークリー城にノーサンバーランドとともに向かっているボリンブルックのもとに、叔父ウスター伯に遣わされたノーサンバーランドの息子ハリー・パーシーがやってきて、物心ついて以来初対面のボリンブルックに仕えることを申し出、バークリー城に 300 の軍勢がいることを告げ、つづいてロスとウィロビーも合流する。城からヨークがやってきて、王に刃向かう甥ボリンブルックを叱責するが、リチャードによる財産没収の不当性を訴える甥の主張を聞き、自身の兵力では彼らを抑えることができないこともあり、容認せざるをえない。ボリンブルックは叔父に、王の取りまきブシー、バゴットらのいるブリストル城への同行を求め、ヨークは自身の立場上断るが、ボリンブルック一行を城に招き入れる。

・・・・・・・・・・・・・・・・・・・・・・・・・・・・・・・・・・・・・・・・・・・・・・・・・・・・・・・・・・・・・・・・・・・・・・・・・・・・・・・・・・・・・・・・・・

**1. Berkeley** ⇒ 2. 2. 119 注参照。

**4. These high wild hills** コッツウォールド丘陵 (the Cotswolds) のこと。

**5. Draws** 「～を引き伸ばす」(*OED*, draw, *v.* 54a, 87d)。

And yet your fair discourse hath been as sugar,
Making the hard way sweet and delectable.
But I bethink me what a weary way
From Ravenspurgh to Cotshall will be found
In Ross and Willoughby, wanting your company,     10
Which I protest hath very much beguiled
The tediousness and process of my travel.
But theirs is sweetened with the hope to have
The present benefit which I possess,
And hope to joy is little less in joy     15
Than hope enjoyed. By this the weary lords
Shall make their way seem short, as mine hath done
By sight of what I have, your noble company.
**BOLINGBROKE**     Of much less value is my company
Than your good words. But who comes here?     20

*Enter Harry Percy*

**NORTHUMBERLAND**     It is my son, young Harry Percy,
Sent from my brother Worcester whencesoever.
Harry, how fares your uncle?
**PERCY**     I had thought, my lord, to have learned his health of you.
**NORTHUMBERLAND**     Why, is he not with the Queen?     25
**PERCY**     No, my good Lord, he hath forsook the court,
Broken his staff of office and dispersed
The household of the King.
**NORTHUMBERLAND**            What was his reason?
He was not so resolved when last we spake together.
**PERCY**     Because your lordship was proclaimèd traitor.     30
But he, my lord, is gone to Ravenspurgh,
To offer service to the Duke of Hereford,
And sent me over by Berkeley to discover
What power the Duke of York had levied there,
Then with directions to repair to Ravenspurgh.     35

**6. your**  Qq: your  F1: our

**7. delectable**  「歓びをもたらす」（*OED*, delectable, *a*.）。

**8. bethink me**  「（間接疑問節を目的語にとって）〜かと考える」（*OED*, bethink, *v*. 8b）。通常の人称代名詞の再帰代名詞代わりの使用（Abbot, §223）。

**9. Ravenspurgh**  ⇒ 2. 1. 296 注参照。

   **Cotshall**  Cotswold の異形、[ˈkɒtsəl, -soːld] と発音（Crystal）。Qq: Cotshall  F1: Cottshold

**12. tediousness and process** = tedious process  二詞一意（hendiadys）の例。

**14. which**  Q1: which  Q2-F1: that

**22. Worcester**  ⇒ 2. 2. 58-59 注参照。

**24. thought . . . to have learned**  意図を表す hope や intend などの動詞の目的語が完了形不定詞であるとき、意図が実現しなかったことを示す（Abbott, §360）。

   **of** = from  ⇒ 1. 2. 74 注参照。

**25-30. Why . . . proclaimèd traitor**  ⇒ 2. 2. 58-59 後注参照。

**29. last we**  Qq: last we  F1: we last

**33. discover**  「（節を目的語として）〜を明かす、知らせる」（*OED*, discover, *v*. 4b）。

**35. directions**  Qq: directions  F1: direction

**NORTHUMBERLAND**   Have you forgot the Duke of Herford, boy?

**PERCY**   No, my good lord, for that is not forgot
  Which ne'er I did remember. To my knowledge
  I never in my life did look on him.

**NORTHUMBERLAND**   Then learn to know him now. This is the Duke.   40

**PERCY**   [*to Bolingbroke*]   My gracious lord, I tender you my service,
  Such as it is, being tender, raw and young,
  Which elder days shall ripen and confirm
  To more approvèd service and desert.

**BOLINGBROKE**   I thank thee, gentle Percy, and be sure   45
  I count myself in nothing else so happy
  As in a soul rememb'ring my good friends,
  And as my fortune ripens with thy love,
  It shall be still thy true love's recompense.
  My heart this covenant makes; my hand thus seals it.   50

[*Clasps Percy's hand*]

**NORTHUMBERLAND**   [*to Percy*]
  How far is it to Berkeley, and what stir
  Keeps good old York there with his men of war?

**PERCY**   There stands the castle, by yon tuft of trees,
  Manned with three hundred men, as I have heard,
  And in it are the Lords of York, Berkeley and Seymour,   55
  None else of name and noble estimate.

*Enter Ross and Willoghby*

**NORTHUMBERLAND**   Here come the Lords of Ross and Willoughby,
  Bloody with spurring, fiery-red with haste.

**BOLINGBROKE**   Welcome, my lords. I wot your love pursues
  A banished traitor. All my treasury   60
  Is yet but unfelt thanks, which, more enriched,
  Shall be your love and labour's recompense.

**ROSS**   Your presence makes us rich, most noble lord.

**36. Herford, boy?**  Q1, 2: Herfords boy?  Q3: *Hereford*, boy?  Q4, 5: *Herford*, boy?  F1: Hereford（Boy.）

**38. To my knowledge** ＝ so far as I know（*OED*, knowledge, *n.* 8b）

**41-42. tender you my service, . . . being tender** 「あなたにお仕え申しあげます…未熟な」（*OED*, tender, *v.*¹ 1; tender, *a.* 4）。Black は、シェイクスピアが動詞の tender を使ったのを忘れて軽率に形容詞の tender を使ってしまったという Clark & Wright の注記と、地口は瑕（きず）ではなく言い回しの妙（a graceful turn of speech）であるという Wilson の注記を並べて引用している。

**48-49. as my fortune ripens with thy love, / It shall be still thy true love's recompense.** 「私の運勢がお前の好意をえて上昇すれば、それが変わることなくお前の忠誠への返報となるようにしよう」。

**49. shall** ⇒ 1. 4. 50 注参照。

**still** 「つねに、変わることなく」⇒ 1. 1. 22 注参照。

**50. covenant . . . seals** 「契約…印を押す」握手を契約書への押印にたとえる比喩。

**51. stir** 「行動、活動」（*OED*, stir, *n.*¹ 2）。

**52. Keeps** 主語は York。

**53. yon** Qq: yon F1: yond

**55. Seymour** 第 4 代サンモール男爵リチャード・シーモア（Richard Seymour, fourth Baron de Saint Maur, 1345-1401）。

**56. of name** 「高名な」現代語では通常 great などの形容詞とともに用いる（*OED*, name, *n.* 7b）。

**estimate** 「名声、評判」（*OED*, estimate, *n.* 1†c の初出例）。

**58. Bloody with spurring** 「拍車によって傷ついた馬の血で汚れている」（Dawson & Yachnin）。

**61. unfelt thanks** 「手で触れられる、ものというかたちをとらない、言葉だけの感謝」（Wright）。

**unfelt** ＝ not perceived by others（Onions）

**WILLOUGHBY**   And far surmounts our labour to attain it.

**BOLINGBROKE**   Evermore thank's the exchequer of the poor,   65
    Which till my infant fortune comes to years
    Stands for my bounty. But who comes here?

*Enter Berkeley*

**NORTHUMBERLAND**   It is my lord of Berkeley as I guess.

**BERKELEY**   My lord of Hereford, my message is to you.

**BOLINGBROKE**   My lord, my answer is to 'Lancaster',   70
    And I am come to seek that name in England,
    And I must find that title in your tongue
    Before I make reply to aught you say.

**BERKELEY**   Mistake me not, my lord, 'tis not my meaning
    To raze one title of your honour out.   75
    To you, my lord, I come, what lord you will,
    From the most gracious regent of this land,
    The Duke of York, to know what pricks you on
    To take advantage of the absent time
    And fright our native peace with self-borne arms.   80

*Enter York*

**BOLINGBROKE**   I shall not need transport my words by you.
    Here comes his grace in person. My noble uncle.

*[Kneels]*

**YORK**   Show me thy humble heart and not thy knee,
    Whose duty is deceivable and false.

**BOLINGBROKE**                              My gracious uncle —

**YORK**   Tut, tut! Grace me no grace, nor uncle me no uncle.   85
    I am no traitor's uncle, and that word 'grace'
    In an ungracious mouth is but profane.
    Why have those banished and forbidden legs
    Dared once to touch a dust of England's ground?

**65. thank's** Q1-4: thanke's Q5, F1: thankes

**65. exchequer** 「財源、資力」（*OED*, exchequer, *n.* 6）。

**66. infant** 「育っていない」。文脈上「わずかなものでしかない」（*OED*, infant, *n.*[1] 5）。

**fortune** 「財産」。

**comes to years** 「成熟する」（*OED*, year[1], *n.* 5b）。

**67. Stands for** 「〜の代わりになる」（*OED*, stand, *v.* 71h）。

**70. my answer is to 'Lancaster'** 「私の答えは『ランカスター』という呼びかけにたいしてなされる（たいしてしかなされない）」ランカスターは、ボリンブルックが父ゴーントの死によって相続するはずだったが、リチャードにより剥奪された公爵位。ボリンブルックはノーサンバーランドがヘレフォードと呼んだとき（36）には反論していない。

**75. title** 「点画《i の上の・や é の´ など》」を表す tittle にかけた言葉遊びがあり、'tis not . . . your honour out (74-75) は「〔ランカスター公という称号どころか〕あなたの称号のわずかなりとも消し去ることは、私の意図ではない」の意（Chambers）。

**77. gracious regent** Q1: gratious regent Q2-F1: glorious

**82. his grace** 「閣下（王、王妃、公爵の尊称）」⇒ 1. 1. 14 注参照。

**84. gracious** 「仁慈深い（王、王妃、公爵に用いる形容詞）」（*OED*, gracious, *a.* 4b）。

**85. Grace** 「（人）を your grace と呼ぶ」（*OED*, grace, *v.* 9）。

**uncle me no uncle** 「叔父という言葉で呼ぶな」（*OED*, uncle, *v.* 1 の初出例。ただし *OED* は no uncle という補語のない F1 の読みをとっている）。

**no uncle** Qq: no vnckle F1 なし

**87. ungracious** （廃）「粗野な、無作法な」「邪悪な」（*OED*, ungracious, *a.* 3a）。王の権威に逆らうことにたいして用いられている。

**profane** 社会秩序を乱すがゆえに「瀆神的」。

**88-93. legs . . . bosom . . . pale-faced . . . arms** ボリンブルックの「脚」がイングランドの「心」の平静をかき乱し、ボリンブルックの「腕」が村むらを「顔色なからしめ」ている、という身体部位の隠喩が用いられている。

**88. those** Qq: those F1: these

But then more why: why have they dared to march          90
So many miles upon her peaceful bosom,
Frighting her pale-faced villages with war
And ostentation of despisèd arms?
Comest thou because the anointed King is hence?
Why, foolish boy, the King is left behind,          95
And in my loyal bosom lies his power.
Were I but now the lord of such hot youth
As when brave Gaunt, thy father, and myself
Rescued the Black Prince, that young Mars of men,
From forth the ranks of many thousand French,          100
O, then how quickly should this arm of mine,
Now prisoner to the palsy, chastise thee
And minister correction to thy fault!

**BOLINGBROKE**   My gracious uncle, let me know my fault.
On what condition stands it and wherein?          105

**YORK**   Even in condition of the worst degree,
In gross rebellion and detested treason.
Thou art a banished man and here art come
Before the expiration of thy time
In braving arms against thy sovereign.          110

**BOLINGBROKE**   As I was banished, I was banished Hereford;
But as I come, I come for Lancaster.
And, noble uncle, I beseech your grace
Look on my wrongs with an indifferent eye.
You are my father, for methinks in you          115
I see old Gaunt alive. O, then, my father,
Will you permit that I shall stand condemned
A wandering vagabond, my rights and royalties
Plucked from my arms perforce and given away
To upstart unthrifts? Wherefore was I born?          120
If that my cousin King be king in England,
It must be granted I am Duke of Lancaster.

**93. despisèd** 「卑しむべき」 -able という意味になる過去分詞の用法。 ⇒2. 1. 268 注参照。叛乱のために用いられているため。

**94. hence** = away (*OED*, hence, *adv*. 1b)

**95. the King is left behind** 自然的身体と政治的身体という「王のふたつの身体」観念への言及で、王の身柄が国を離れていても、その政治的身体は代理をつとめるヨークにやどる、ということ (Gurr)。

**97. lord** 「持ち主」(*OED*, lord, *n*. 2d)。

　　**the** Qq なし F1: the the があるほうが韻律どおり。

**98-100. when . . . French** ⇒後注参照。

**107. detested** = detestable ⇒2. 1. 268 注参照。

**110. braving** 「挑戦的な、これ見よがしの」(*OED*, brave, *v*. 6; braving, *ppl. a*. 1)。

**112. I come for Lancaster** 「ランカスター公爵位をえるためにやってきている」 ⇒後注参照。

**115. methinks** ⇒2. 2. 9 注参照。

**118-19. rights and royalties / Plucked from my arms perforce** ヨークの叱責に抗議して王の仕打ちの不当さを言いたてるボリンブルックは、ヨークが王を諫めて言った to seize and gripe into your hands / The royalties and rights (2. 1. 189-90) を知らずに反復しており、ヨークへの劇的皮肉となっている。

　　**royalties** ⇒2. 1. 190 注参照。

**121. If that** 従属接続詞のあとに添えられる接続詞 that の用法。⇒2. 1. 125 注参照。 **in** Q1: in Q2-F1: of

You have a son, Aumerle, my noble cousin.
Had you first died and he been thus trod down,
He should have found his uncle Gaunt a father                    125
To rouse his wrongs and chase them to the bay.
I am denied to sue my livery here,
And yet my letters patents give me leave.
My father's goods are all distrained and sold,
And these and all are all amiss employed.                        130
What would you have me do? I am a subject,
And I challenge law. Attorneys are denied me,
And therefore personally I lay my claim
To my inheritance of free descent.
**NORTHUMBERLAND**   [*to York*]   The noble Duke hath been too
    much abused.                                135
**ROSS**   [*to York*]   It stands your grace upon to do him right.
**WILLOUGHBY**   [*to York*]   Base men by his endowments are
    made great.
**YORK**   My lords of England, let me tell you this:
  I have had feeling of my cousin's wrongs
  And laboured all I could to do him right.                 140
  But in this kind to come, in braving arms
  Be his own carver and cut out his way,
  To find out right with wrong, it may not be.
  And you that do abet him in this kind
  Cherish rebellion and are rebels all.                      145
**NORTHUMBERLAND**   The noble Duke hath sworn his coming is
  But for his own, and for the right of that
  We all have strongly sworn to give him aid.
  And let him ne'er see joy that breaks that oath.
**YORK**   Well, well, I see the issue of these arms.            150
  I cannot mend it, I must needs confess,
  Because my power is weak and all ill-left.
  But if I could, by Him that gave me life,

**123. cousin**　Qq: cousin　F1: Kinsman

**126. rouse**　「（獲物）を巣から狩りだす」（*OED*, rouse, $v.^1$ 2）。

　**chase . . . bay**　「（獲物）を追いつめる」（*OED*, chase, $v.^1$ 1b; bay, $n.^4$ 3b）。

**127-28. sue . . . patents**　ここでもまたボルンブルックは、王を諫めるヨークの言葉 wrongfully seize . . . homage, (2. 1. 201-04) を知らずに反復している。

　**to sue my livery**　⇒ 2. 1. 202-04 注参照。

**129. distrained**　「（動産）を差し押さえる」（*OED*, distrain, *v.* 9）の過去分詞形。

**132. I**　Qq: I　F1 なし　　**challenge**　「～の権利を要求する」（*OED*, challenge, *v.* 5a）。　　**law**　「法が認めるもの」（*OED*, law, $n.^1$ 1†d）。

**133. personally**　= in person（*OED*, personally, *adv.* 1）

**134. of free descent**　「制約を受けない相続による」（*OED*, of, *prep.* 12a; free, *a.* 8a; descent, *n.* 10a）。

**136. It stands your grace upon to do him right**　「閣下は彼にたいして正当な扱いをしなくてはなりません」It stands sb upon to do . . . は「（人）は～しなければならない」という意味の無人称構文（*OED*, stand, *v.* 78†q）。

**137. his endowments**　「（ボリンブルック以外の手によって）与えられた（ボリンブルックの）財産」（Ure）。

**141. kind to come,**　Q1: kind to come,　Q2-F1: kind, to come　Q1 と Q2-F1 の読みでは、直後の in braving arms がかかるところが違い、Q1 のつながりを採った。

　**kind**　= manner（*OED*, kind, *n.* 8a）

　**in braving arms**　⇒ 110 注参照。

**142. Be his own carver**　「自分自身の取り分を自分で決める」現在は用いられない比喩的表現（*OED*, carver, *n.* †4）。シェイクスピアは同じ行の cut out one's way と同じ意味で carv'd out his passage（*Mac.* 1. 2. 19）という表現も使っており、ここには「食卓で包丁を使って肉を切りわける」とともに「剣をふるって戦場を突きすすむ」との意味もこめられている（Ure）。

　**cut out one's way**　「障害をぬって進む」（*OED*, cut, *v.* 24b）の比喩的用法。

**143. wrong**　Qq: wrong　F1: Wrongs

　**it may not be**　「そのようなことをしてはならない」（Ure）。it は、前の3つの不定詞を受ける形式主語。

**144. abet**　「（人）をそそのかす」（*OED*, abet, *v.* 2）。

**146-47. The noble Duke . . . for his own**　⇒ 2. 3. 112 後注参照。

**149. ne'er**　Q1, 2: neuer　Q3-5: ne're　F1: neu'r

**150. I see the issue of these arms**　「このような武装がどのような結果を招くのかわかる」。　issue「結果」（*OED*, issue, *n.* 10a）。

**151. needs**　「（must とともに用いて）ぜひとも」（*OED*, needs, *adv.* b）。

I would attach you all and make you stoop
Unto the sovereign mercy of the King.                        155
But since I cannot, be it known unto you
I do remain as neuter. So fare you well,
Unless you please to enter in the castle
And there repose you for this night.

**BOLINGBROKE**    An offer, uncle, that we will accept.       160
But we must win your grace to go with us
To Bristow Castle, which they say is held
By Bushy, Bagot and their complices,
The caterpillars of the commonwealth,
Which I have sworn to weed and pluck away.                    165

**YORK**    It may be I will go with you, but yet I'll pause,
For I am loath to break our country's laws.
Nor friends nor foes, to me welcome you are.
Things past redress are now with me past care.    *Exeunt*

[ACT II, SCENE IV]

*Enter Earl of Salisbury and a Welsh Captain*

**CAPTAIN**    My lord of Salisbury, we have stayed ten days
And hardly kept our countrymen together,
And yet we hear no tidings from the King.
Therefore we will disperse ourselves. Farewell.

**SALISBURY**    Stay yet another day, thou trusty Welshman.     5
The King reposeth all his confidence in thee.

**CAPTAIN**    'Tis thought the King is dead. We will not stay.
The bay trees in our country are all withered,
And meteors fright the fixèd stars of heaven.
The pale-faced moon looks bloody on the earth,               10
And lean-looked prophets whisper fearful change.
Rich men look sad and ruffians dance and leap,
The one in fear to lose what they enjoy,

**154. attach** 「(人)を拘束、逮捕する」(*OED*, attach, *v.* 1a)。

**156. unto** Q1: vnto Q2-F1: to

**162. Bristow** Q1-F1: Bristow ⇒2.2.134注、および2.2.134-42後注参照。

**164. caterpillars** 「芋虫、人を食い物にする強欲者」(*OED*, caterpillar, *n.* 2)。Qq、F1ともに綴りはcaterpillerとなっており、the caterpillar of the commonwealthという表現は16、17世紀によく見られ、本来の意味を失い、「強奪者、略奪者、泥棒」を意味する古い語pillerと混同されたものとされる。

**165. weed and pluck** Forkerは3.4.50-52におけるウィルツシャー、ブシー、グリーンをボリンブルックが「抜いた(plucked up)」「雑草(weeds)」と呼ぶ庭師の台詞との関連を指摘している。 ⇒後注参照。

〔2. 4〕あらすじ・・・・・・・・・・・・・・・・・・・・・・・・・・・・・・・・・・・・・・・・・・・・・・・・・・・・・・・・・・・・・

　ウェールズ人隊長が、王命を受けてウェールズに兵を集めにきたソールズベリーに、10日間待ったが、王からなんの知らせもなく、月桂樹の立ち枯れ、彗星、隕石、赤い月の出現などの現象、予言者の言葉、社会の騒擾など王の死を告げる凶兆があらわれており、リチャードは死んだと思われているため、軍を解散することを告げる。

・・・・・・・・・・・・・・・・・・・・・・・・・・・・・・・・・・・・・・・・・・・・・・・・・・・・・・・・・・・・・・・・・・・・・・・・

**6. reposeth . . . in** 「(人)に(信用など)をおく」(*OED*, repose, *v.*[1] 3)。

**8. The bay trees in our country are all withered** ⇒後注参照。
　**are all** Q1: are al Q2-F1: all are

**9. meteors** 現代では「流星」を意味するが、当時の英語では「流星」のほかに「彗星」も含む、空に一時的に見られる光を発するものを広く指す語だった(*OED*, meteor, *n.* 2)。

The other to enjoy by rage and war.

These signs forerun the death or fall of kings.                    15

Farewell. Our countrymen are gone and fled

As well assured Richard their king is dead.          *Exit*

SALISBURY    Ah, Richard, with the eyes of heavy mind

I see thy glory like a shooting star

Fall to the base earth from the firmament.                    20

Thy sun sets weeping in the lowly west,

Witnessing storms to come, woe and unrest.

Thy friends are fled to wait upon thy foes

And crossly to thy good all fortune goes.          *Exit*

**14. rage** 「暴動」Black はこの意味に相当する *OED*, rage, *n.* †3a の Vehement, violent or impetuous action（of persons）という語義を引用して、終例が 1485 年であるがエリザベス朝時代においてもこの意味があったことを指摘している。

**15. or fall** Q1: or fall Q2-F1 なし

**18. the** Q1: the Q2-F1 なし Q1 が韻律どおり。

**19-20. I see . . . firmament** 王の運命が隕石となって地上に流れ落ちる流星、沈みゆく夕日になぞらえられている。隊長の meteor についての発言（9）を受けてのもの。Newbolt は、リチャードの紋章のひとつに雲の影から現れた太陽の図柄のものがあり、それが雲のなかに沈むものとも見えることを指摘している。ソールズベリーのこの落日のイメージは、3. 3. 62-67 のボリンブルックによるリチャードを太陽にたとえるイメージ、さらに同場 178-79 の自身の運命をパエトーンの失墜にたとえるリチャードのイメージにつながるものとなっている。

[ACT III, SCENE I]

*Enter Bolingbroke, York, Northumberland, Ross, Percy, [and]*
*Willoughby, with Bushy and Green [as] prisoners*

**BOLINGBROKE**    Bring forth these men.

*[Bushy and Green stand forth]*

Bushy and Green, I will not vex your souls,
Since presently your souls must part your bodies,
With too much urging your pernicious lives,
For 'twere no charity. Yet to wash your blood                    5
From off my hands, here in the view of men
I will unfold some causes of your deaths.
You have misled a prince, a royal king,
A happy gentleman in blood and lineaments,
By you unhappied and disfigured clean.                           10
You have in manner with your sinful hours
Made a divorce betwixt his queen and him,
Broke the possession of a royal bed
And stained the beauty of a fair queen's cheeks
With tears drawn from her eyes by your foul wrongs.              15
Myself, a prince by fortune of my birth,
Near to the King in blood and near in love
Till you did make him misinterpret me,
Have stooped my neck under your injuries
And sighed my English breath in foreign clouds,                 20
Eating the bitter bread of banishment
Whilst you have fed upon my signories,
Disparked my parks and felled my forest woods,
From my own windows torn my household coat,
Razed out my imprese, leaving me no sign                        25
Save men's opinions and my living blood
To show the world I am a gentleman.

‥‥‥‥‥‥‥‥‥‥‥‥‥‥‥‥‥‥‥‥‥‥‥‥‥‥‥‥‥‥‥‥‥‥‥‥‥‥‥‥‥‥

　ボリンブルックは、王をそそのかし道をあやまらせ、自分の追放中に没収された土地を着服したとして、ブシーとグリーンの処刑をノーサンバーランドに命じ、ウェールズのグレンダワーを討伐しに出発する。

‥‥‥‥‥‥‥‥‥‥‥‥‥‥‥‥‥‥‥‥‥‥‥‥‥‥‥‥‥‥‥‥‥‥‥‥‥‥‥‥‥‥‥‥‥‥‥‥‥‥‥‥‥‥

**2. presently**　「ただちに」　⇒1. 4. 52 注参照。

**2. part**　（廃）「～から離れる」現代語にはない他動詞の用法（*OED*, part, *v.* 8†a）。

**4. urging**　「～のことを言いたてる」　⇒2. 1. 299 注参照。

**5. 'twere** ＝ it would be　⇒1. 3. 194 注参照。

**5-6. wash . . . my hands**　「お前たちの死にたいして責任がないことを示すために」この成句は、ユダヤ属州総督ピラトがキリストの処刑後に手を洗い、自分の責任を否定したとのマタイ伝の記述（Matthew, 27: 24）に由来。リチャードは、退位の意思を示す際に退位を迫るものたちについてこの表現を用いる（4. 1. 238）。劇最後のボリンブルックの台詞で、この句は「罪をつぐなう」（5. 6. 50）という聖地巡礼の目的を表すのに用いられ、ここで手を浄めようとしている彼が間接的であるにせよリチャードの血で手を再び汚したことを示す劇的皮肉となる（*OED*, wash, *v.* 3e; Shaheen, 372; Forker）。

**9. lineaments**　「姿、顔つき、性質」（*OED*, lineament, *n.* †2, 3, 2b）。

**10. unhappied**　「～を不幸にする」（*OED*, †unhappy, *v.* 1 の初出例）。

　　**clean**　「すっかり」（*OED*, clean, *adv.* 5b）。

**11-15. You have . . . foul wrongs.**　王と寵臣たちとの同性愛関係が王夫妻の仲を疎遠にさせた、というこの発言は、歴史的な裏づけがないばかりか、劇の他の部分における夫妻の関係と齟齬している（Forker）。

**11. in manner**　「いわば」（*OED*, manner, *n.*¹ 10）。Made a divorce（12）にかかる。　　**15. by**　Q1: by　Q2-F1: with

**16. prince**　「イングランドの王族男子、とくに国王、女王の息子、または孫」（*OED*, prince, *n.* 5）。ボリンブルックはエドワード三世の孫。

**20. sighed my English breath in foreign clouds**　「異境にあって、雲のなかに英語の悲嘆のため息をついた」「雲のなかにため息をつく」という表現はため息がまざって雲が増す、という考えからのもので、シェイクスピアは他のところで Adding to clouds more clouds with his deep sighs（*Rom.* 1. 1. 129）と書いている（Ure）。　　**sighed**　Q1, 2: sigh't　Q3-F1: sigh'd

**22. Whilst**　Q1: Whilst　Q2-F1: While　　**signories**　「領地」（*OED*, signory, *n.* 2）。

**23. Disparked my parks**「私の猟苑を他の用途に転用した」（*OED*, dispark, *v.*）。

**24. my own**　Q1, 2: my own　Q3-F1: mine own　　**coat**　紋章（＝ coat of arms）」（*OED*, coat, *n.* 4）。　　**25. Razed**　Qq: Rac't　F1: Raz'd

**imprese**　「盾章（＝ impresa）」（*OED*, †imprese, *n.* 1; impresa, *n.* 1）。

This and much more, much more than twice all this,
Condemns you to the death.

              [*to the lords*]    See them delivered over
To execution and the hand of Death.              30

**BUSHY**    More welcome is the stroke of Death to me
Than Bolingbroke to England. Lords, farewell.

**GREEN**    My comfort is that heaven will take our souls
And plague injustice with the pains of hell.

**BOLINGBROKE**    My Lord Northumberland, see them dispatched.    35

                [*Exit Northumberland with Busy and Green*]

[*to York*] Uncle, you say the Queen is at your house.
For God's sake fairly let her be entreated.
Tell her I send to her my kind commends.
Take special care my greetings be delivered.

**YORK**    A gentleman of mine I have dispatched          40
With letters of your love to her at large.

**BOLINGBROKE**    Thanks, gentle uncle. Come, lords, away.
To fight with Glendower and his complices.
A while to work, and after holiday.          *Exeunt*


[**ACT III, SCENE II**]

*Drums. Flourish and colours. Enter Richard, Aumerle, [Bishop of]*
*Carlisle and soldiers*


**RICHARD**    Barkloughly Castle call they this at hand?

**AUMERLE**    Yea, my lord. How brooks your grace the air
After your late tossing on the breaking seas?

**RICHARD**    Needs must I like it well. I weep for joy
To stand upon my kingdom once again.          5
Dear earth, I do salute thee with my hand
Though rebels wound thee with their horses' hoofs.
As a long-parted mother with her child
Plays fondly with her tears and smiles in meeting,

**32. Lords, farewell.**　Qq: Lords farewell.　F1 なし

**35. dispatched**　「（人）を殺す」（*OED*, dispatch, *v.* 4）。

**37. God's**　Qq: Gods　F1: Heauens

**entreated**　「（人）を遇する、扱う」（*OED*, entreat, *v.* 1）の過去分詞形。

**41. at large**　「あますところなく」（*OED*, large, *n.* 5c）。

**43. To fight with Glendower and his complices.**　Theobald ら 18 世紀の編者たちは、押韻二行連句となりそうな 42 と 44 にはさまれ、史実とも一致しないこの行をあとからの挿入と考えて削除、または括弧書きにしている（Black）。⇒ 3. 1 後注参照。

**Glendower**　オーウェン・グレンダワー（Owen Glendower c. 1354/59-c. 1416）。Prince of Wales を名のり、イングランドに抵抗して叛乱を起こし失敗したウェールズの豪族。


〔**3. 2**〕あらすじ・・・・・・・・・・・・・・・・・・・・・・・・・・・・・・・・・・・・・・・・・・・・・・・・・・・・・・・・・・・・・

　リチャードは、ウェールズのバークローリー城に到着し、アイルランドから自国に戻って、天の加護に期待し、祖国の大地が敵を苦しめることを願い、太陽のごとき自分の帰還によって夜盗さながらのボリンブルックはみずからの罪に恥じいることになる、と自信を見せている。そこへソールズベリーがやってきて、1万 2 千のウェールズ兵が王の帰還が遅いため離反したことを告げる。さらに使者スクループが、ボリンブルックの軍勢の大きさ、ブシー、グリーン、ウィルツシャー公ら寵臣の処刑の報をもたらす。彼は、追い打ちをかけるように、リチャードが一縷（いちる）の望みを託したヨークがボリンブルックに合流したことを伝え、絶望した王は軍の解散を命じフリント城に向かう。

・・・・・・・・・・・・・・・・・・・・・・・・・・・・・・・・・・・・・・・・・・・・・・・・・・・・・・・・・・・・・・・・・・・・・・・・・・・・・・・・・・・

**1. Barkloughly Castle**　バークローリー城。第 2 幕第 2 場でボリンブルックがヨークと対峙したバークリー城（Berkeley Castle、⇒ 2. 2. 119 注参照）とは別の城。ホリンシェッドでは Barclowly と綴られているが、そのような名の土地、城はなく、イーヴシャムの修道士が書いた『リチャード二世伝』では、Hertlowly または Hertlow と綴られており、それらは現在のハーレフ（Harlech）の古い形 Harddlech の異綴りとみなされている。ハーレフはウェールズ北西部の旧メリオネス（Merioneth）州（現在はグウィネズ（Gwynedd）州）にあり、エドワード二世の建てた城がある（Sugden）。

**they**　Q1: they　Q2-F1: you

**2. brooks**　「～を享受する、楽しむ」（*OED*, brook, *v.* 1）。

**3. tossing**　「揺られる」（*OED*, toss, *v.* 6b）の現在分詞形。

**4. Needs**　「ぜひとも」⇒ 2. 3. 151 注参照。

**7. wound**　「～をうねらせる」（*OED*, wind, *v.*[1] 5†a）。

So, weeping, smiling, greet I thee, my earth,                    10
And do thee favours with my royal hands.
Feed not thy sovereign's foe, my gentle earth,
Nor with thy sweets comfort his ravenous sense,
But let thy spiders that suck up thy venom
And heavy-gaited toads lie in their way,                         15
Doing annoyance to the treacherous feet
Which with usurping steps do trample thee.
Yield stinging nettles to mine enemies,
And when they from thy bosom pluck a flower,
Guard it, I pray thee, with a lurking adder                      20
Whose double tongue may with a mortal touch
Throw death upon thy sovereign's enemies.
Mock not my senseless conjuration, lords.
This earth shall have a feeling, and these stones
Prove armèd soldiers ere her native king                        25
Shall falter under foul rebellion's arms.
CARLISLE    Fear not, my lord. That Power that made you king
Hath power to keep you king in spite of all.
The means that heavens yield must be embraced
And not neglected. Else heaven would                            30
And we will not. Heaven's offer we refuse,
The proffered means of succour and redress.
AUMERLE    He means, my lord, that we are too remiss
Whilst Bolingbroke through our security
Grows strong and great in substance and in power.               35
RICHARD    Discomfortable cousin, knowest thou not
That, when the searching eye of heaven is hid
Behind the globe and lights the lower world,
Then thieves and robbers range abroad unseen
In murders and in outrage boldly here.                          40
But when from under this terrestrial ball
He fires the proud tops of the eastern pines

**11. favours**　Q1: fauours　Q2-F1: fauour

**14. spiders that suck up thy venom**　Chambers は、And not a poison-sucking envious spider / To turn the juice I take to deadly venom (Marlowe, *Edward III*, II. i. 285-86) を引用して、『リチャード二世』創作当時、蜘蛛は体内で毒を生成するのではなく、美しい花から吸いこんだ毒を使うと考えられていたことを指摘している。

**20. pray thee**　Qq: pray thee　F1: prethee

　**a lurking adder**　Tilley は SNAKE in the grass という諺的表現を収録している（S585）。

**21. double tongue**　創作当時、蛇は毒牙ではなく舌で刺すことによって毒を出すと考えられていた（Irving）。

　**double** = forked

**23. senseless conjuration**　「感覚のないもの（大地）への馬鹿げた祈願」senseless には「感覚のない」と「馬鹿げた、意味のない」のふたつの意味（*OED*, senseless, *a.* 1d, 4）がかけられ、conjuration には「超自然的な存在への祈願や呪文を用いての魔法の実践」（*OED*, conjuration, *n.* 3a）の意味がある。

**26. rebellion's**　Q1, 2: rebellions　Q3-F1: Rebellious

**27. Power**　「神」（*OED*, power, *n.*[1] 7）。

**29-32. The means . . . redress**　Qq: The meanes that heauens yeeld must be imbrac't / And not neglected. Else heauen would, / And we will not, heauens offer, we refuse, / The profered meanes of succors and redresse. Qq のみの行。we will not (31) のあとをピリオドとする Gurr のパンクチュエイションにしたがった。succors を succour とするのは Pope による校訂。

**30-31. Else heaven would / And we will not**　「そうでなければ、天が望んでいるのに、われわれのほうが望まないということになる」。

**34. security**　「油断」（*OED*, security, *n.* 3）⇒ 2. 1. 266 注参照。

**35. substance**　「財産、資産」（*OED*, substance, *n.* 16a）。

　**power**　Qq: power　F1: friends

**36-53. Discomfortable . . . sin**　リチャードは自身を太陽に、リチャードがアイルランド遠征をしているあいだに侵入したボリンブルックを夜ばたらきする盗賊にたとえる。

　**Discomfortable**　「人を落胆させる」（*OED*, discomfortable, *a.* 1）。

**38. globe and**　Qq: globe that　F1: Globe, that　Hanmer: globe and　that のままだと劇場では lightens の意味上の主語が globe だとの誤解を与えるため、Hanmer の校訂が広く受け容れられている。

**40. boldly**　Qq: bouldly　F1: bloody

And darts his light through every guilty hole,
Then murders, treasons and detested sins,
The cloak of night being plucked from off their backs,          45
Stand bare and naked, trembling at themselves?
So when this thief, this traitor, Bolingbroke,
Who all this while hath revelled in the night
Whilst we were wandering with the Antipodes,
Shall see us rising in our throne the east,                     50
His treasons will sit blushing in his face,
Not able to endure the sight of day,
But self-affrighted tremble at his sin.
Not all the water in the rough rude sea
Can wash the balm off from an anointed king.                    55
The breath of worldly men cannot depose
The deputy elected by the Lord.
For every man that Bolingbroke hath pressed
To lift shrewd steel against our golden crown
God for His Richard hath in heavenly pay                        60
A glorious angel. Then if angels fight,
Weak men must fall, for heaven still guards the right.

*Enter Salisbury*

Welcome, my lord. How far off lies your power?
SALISBURY      Nor near nor farther off, my gracious lord,
Than this weak arm. Discomfort guides my tongue                 65
And bids me speak of nothing but despair.
One day too late, I fear me, noble lord,
Hath clouded all thy happy days on earth.
O, call back yesterday, bid time return,
And thou shalt have twelve thousand fighting men.               70
Today, today, unhappy day too late,
O'erthrows thy joys, friends, fortune and thy state,
For all the Welshmen, hearing thou wert dead,

**43. light** Qq: light F1: Lightning

**every** Qq: euery F1: eu'ry Qq の読みが韻律どおり。

**46. themselves?** Q1-3: themselues? Q4, 5: themselues: F1: themselues.

**49. Whilst we were wandering with the Antipodes** Qq: VVhilst we were wandring with the Antipodes Qq のみの行。

**Antipodes** 「対蹠人（たいせきじん）」（*OED*, antephodes, *n.* †1）。「足が反対の人たち」は地球の裏側に住み、自分たちから見て逆さまに立っている人たちを意味する。地理的に言えばイングランドの対蹠点はニュージーランド南側の太平洋だが、この語には、この時代においては比喩的な用法があり（*loc. cit.*, †2）、今の文脈ではリチャードが the lower world (38)、under this terrestrial ball (41) と呼んでいる遠征先のアイルランドに住む人たちのことを指す。

**54-57. Not . . . Lord** この部分も *Englands Parnassus* に 'Kings' の見出しのもと収録されている。 ⇒2. 1. 40-66 注参照。

**55. balm** 「（戴冠式の際に国王の頭に塗る）聖油」（*OED*, balm, *n.*[1] 3）。

**off** Qq: off F1 なし F の読みが韻律どおりであるが、Forker は an anointed のふたつ目の a の音が消失すれば Qq の読みが韻律どおりとなること指摘している。

**anointed king** ⇒1. 2. 38 注参照。

**59. steel** 「剣」（*OED*, steel, *n.*[1] 3a）。

**60. God** Qq: God F1: Heauen

**65. Discomfort** 「悲しみ」（*OED*, discomfort, *n.* †2）。

**67. I fear me** 「（悪い結果について）～と思う（＝ I'm afraid）」（*OED*, fear, *v.* 3）。 me は対（直接目的）格形で再帰用法。 ⇒2. 3. 8 注参照。

**me, noble lord** Q1, 2: me noble Lo: Q3, 4: my noble Lo: Q5: my noble Lord F1:（my Noble Lord）

**70, 76, 85. twelve thousand . . . twenty thousand . . . forty thousand** リチャードは、ソールズベリーの報告では1万2千であった、去っていったウェールズ兵の数を、2万に増やして絶望の大きさを示し、王であることを思いおこさせられると、王の名はその倍の軍勢にまさるものだと虚勢を張る。 ⇒後注参照。

**72. O'erthrows** Qq: Ouerthrowes F1: Orethrowes

**state** （廃）「高い地位」（*OED*, state, *n.* †16†a）。

Are gone to Bolingbroke, dispersed and fled.

**AUMERLE**    Comfort, my liege. Why looks your grace so pale?    75

**RICHARD**    But now the blood of twenty thousand men
Did triumph in my face, and they are fled,
And till so much blood thither come again,
Have I not reason to look pale and dead?
All souls that will be safe fly from my side,    80
For time hath set a blot upon my pride.

**AUMERLE**    Comfort, my liege. Remember who you are.

**RICHARD**    I had forgot myself. Am I not king?
Awake, thou coward majesty. Thou sleepest.
Is not the King's name forty thousand names?    85
Arm, arm, my name! A puny subject strikes
At thy great glory. Look not to the ground.
Ye favourites of a king, are we not high?
High be our thoughts. I know my uncle York
Hath power enough to serve our turn. But who comes here?    90

*Enter Scrope*

**SCROPE**    More health and happiness betide my liege
Than can my care-tuned tongue deliver him.

**RICHARD**    Mine ear is open and my heart prepared.
The worst is worldly loss thou canst unfold.
Say, is my kingdom lost? Why, 'twas my care,    95
And what loss is it to be rid of care?
Strives Bolingbroke to be as great as we,
Greater he shall not be. If he serve God,
We'll serve Him too and be his fellow so.
Revolt our subjects? That we cannot mend.    100
They break their faith to God as well as us.
Cry woe, destruction, ruin and decay.
The worst is death, and Death will have his day.

**SCROPE**    Glad am I that your highness is so armed

**75. Comfort** 「元気を出してください（＝ Take comfort.）」（*OED*, comfort, *n.* †9）。シェイクスピア独自の間投詞的な用法。オーマールは discomfortable（36）という言葉が自分に向けられたのを受けて言っている。

**84. coward**　Qq: coward　F1: sluggard

**85. forty**　Qq: twenty　F1: fortie　⇒ 70, 76, 85 注参照。

**86. puny**　「身分の低い」（*OED*, puny, *a.* †1）。

**88. are . . . high?**　ここにもまた「高い／低い」という主題系が見られる（⇒ 1. 1. 109 注参照）。

　　**high** ＝ high in name and place（Black）

**92. care-tuned**　「悲しみによって調律され」、「声が悲しげな調子にあわせられた」（Gurr; *OED*, care, *n.*[1] †1a; tune, *v.* 1a, b）。

**96. care**　「心配の種」（*OED*, care, *n.*[1] 5a）。リチャードは、スクループの使った care-tuned（⇒前注参照）を受けて、care の意味を変えて答えている。

**102. and**　Qq: and　F1: Losse,

**104. armed** ＝ Morally armed, armed with fortitude（Black; cf. 'my heart prepared', 93）

To bear the tidings of calamity. 105
Like an unseasonable stormy day
Which makes the silver rivers drown their shores
As if the world were all dissolved to tears,
So high above his limits swells the rage
Of Bolingbroke, covering your fearful land 110
With hard bright steel and hearts harder than steel.
Whitebeards have armed their thin and hairless scalps
Against thy majesty. Boys with women's voices
Strive to speak big and clap their female joints
In stiff unwieldy arms against thy crown. 115
Thy very beadsmen learn to bend their bows
Of double-fatal yew against thy state.
Yea, distaff-women manage rusty bills
Against thy seat. Both young and old rebel,
And all goes worse than I have power to tell. 120
RICHARD    Too well, too well thou tell'st a tale so ill.
Where is the Earl of Wiltshire, where is Bagot,
What is become of Bushy, where is Green,
That they have let the dangerous enemy
Measure our confines with such peaceful steps? 125
If we prevail, their heads shall pay for it.
I warrant they have made peace with Bolingbroke.
SCROPE    Peace have they made with him indeed, my lord.
RICHARD    O, villains, vipers damned without redemption,
Dogs easily won to fawn on any man, 130
Snakes in my heart-blood warmed that sting my heart;
Three Judases, each one thrice worse than Judas,
Would they make peace? Terrible hell make war
Upon their spotted souls for this.
SCROPE    Sweet love, I see, changing his property, 135
Turns to the sourest and most deadly hate.
Again uncurse their souls. Their peace is made

**106-11. Like . . . steel** ボリンブルックの勢いがその名（brook ＝小川）に由来する川の水にたとえられている（Gurr）。

**106. unseasonable** 副詞的用法（*OED*, unseasonable, *a.* 1c）。

**107. makes** Q1, 2: makes Q3-F1: make

**109. rage** 「乱暴な行い」と「氾濫などの激しさ」（*OED*, rage, *n.* †3a, 4）。

**110. covering** Qq, Fc: couering F1: coueting

**111. steel** こちらには「剣」のみならず「鎧」の意味も含まれる（*OED*, steel, *n.*¹ 3a, 4）。⇒ 59 注参照。　　**112. Whitebeards** Qq: White beards F1: White Beares

**113. majesty** Q1: maiesty: Q2-5: maiestie: and F1: Maiestie, and

**114. big** 「大声で」（*OED*, big, *a.* 6）。

**117. double-fatal yew** ＝ doubly fatal 樹皮と葉、種子に毒性があるイチイ材が、殺傷能力のある長弓に用いられているため（Warburton）。　　**yew** Q1, 2: ewe Q3-5: woe F1: Eugh Hanmer: yew Q1, 2 の ewe は yew の異綴り。**state** ⇒ 72 注参照。

**118. bills** 近代初期に歩兵たちが用いた、長い柄の先端に反った刃のついた長刀のようなものや、斧と槍を組み合わせたような鉾槍（ほこ）などさまざまな形態の武器（*OED*, bill, *n.*¹ 2）。

**125. Measure** 「（土地など）に入りこむ、を進む」（*OED*, measure, *v.* 11a）。**confines** 「領土」（*OED*, confine, *n.*² †2）。

**131. Snakes . . . heart** Dawson & Yachnin は、凍てついている蛇を胸で暖めた男が生気を取りもどした蛇に噛まれる、というイソップの寓話への言及であること、To nourish a VIPER（snake）in one's bosom（Tilley V68）という諺的表現があることを指摘している。

**132. Three Judases** リチャードは 4. 1. 170 でも自身にたいする裏切り者をイスカリオテのユダにたとえている。ユダは「裏切り者」を意味する一般的な表現である（*OED*, Judas, 1）が、リチャードはあとの場面では明確に自身をイエスになぞらえている。彼は 122-25 で、ウィルツシャー、バゴット、ブシー、グリーンの 4 人の行方を尋ねるが、処刑されることなく生き残ることになるバゴットのことはこのあとも問題とされず、オーマールとスクループの彼らの運命をめぐるやりとり（141-42）でも 3 人のことしか話題にのぼらない。

**134. spotted** 「心の汚れた」（*OED*, spotted, *ppl. a* 2b）、'sinful'（Chambers）。**this** Qq: this F1: this Offence

**135-36. love . . . hate** Forker は LOVE is sweet in the beginning but sour in the ending（Tilley, L513）という諺的表現があることを指摘している。

**137. Again** un- ではじまる動作の取り消しを表す動詞などと用い「もとの状態に」（*OED*, again, *adv.* 3）。**uncurse** 「（人）への呪詛を撤回する」（*OED*, uncurse, *v.* の初出例）。

With heads and not with hands. Those whom you curse
Have felt the worst of Death's destroying wound
And lie full low, graved in the hollow ground.                    140
**AUMERLE**    Is Bushy, Green and the Earl of Wiltshire dead?
**SCROPE**    Ay, all of them at Bristow lost their heads.
**AUMERLE**    Where is the Duke my father with his power?
**RICHARD**    No matter where. Of comfort no man speak.
Let's talk of graves, of worms and epitaphs,                    145
Make dust our paper and with rainy eyes
Write sorrow on the bosom of the earth.
Let's choose executors and talk of wills.
And yet not so, for what can we bequeath
Save our deposèd bodies to the ground?                    150
Our lands, our lives and all are Bolingbroke's,
And nothing can we call our own but death
And that small model of the barren earth
Which serves as paste and cover to our bones.
For God's sake, let us sit upon the ground                    155
And tell sad stories of the death of kings,
How some have been deposed, some slain in war,
Some haunted by the ghosts they have deposed,
Some poisoned by their wives, some sleeping killed,
All murdered. For within the hollow crown                    160
That rounds the mortal temples of a king
Keeps Death his court and there the antic sits
Scoffing his state and grinning at his pomp,
Allowing him a breath, a little scene
To monarchize, be feared and kill with looks,                    165
Infusing him with self and vain conceit
As if this flesh which walls about our life
Were brass impregnable, and humoured thus
Comes at the last and with a little pin
Bores through his castle wall and farewell king!                    170

**138. With heads and not with hands** 「握手を交わしてではなく首を落とされることによって」。

**139. wound** Qq: wound F1: hand

**140. graved** 「埋葬された」（*OED*, grave, *v.*[1] 3; graved, *ppl. a.* †a)。

**142. Ay** Q: I Q2: Ye Q3-F1: Yea

**144-77. No matter ... I am a king?** リチャードがボリンブルックの勢いに、王位を追われることを意識する、この劇のターニング・ポイントとなる台詞。

**150. deposèd** 「廃位された」ゴーントのリチャードにたいする叱責の言葉（2. 1. 107-08）につづいて、今度はリチャード自身が劇の展開を先取りするかのように劇中自身の身に降りかかる最悪の事態を表す言葉を使う。

**153-54. that . . . bones** 土でできているとされる人間の身体を小宇宙＝世界の模造物とみなす表現だが、それをパイ生地にたとえている。

**model** 「模型」と「鋳型、母型」（*OED*, model, *n.* 2b, †3)。

**paste** 「パイ生地」（*OED*, paste, *n.* 1)。

**155. God's** Qq: Gods F1: Heauens

**160-70. within the hollow crown . . . farewell king!** 王冠のなかを宮廷に見立て、「死」が法学院の祝祭などで見られた茶番の王を演じ、現実の王を茶化しつつも、束の間王として君臨するあいだはその権力の大きさと身体の堅固さを過信させておきながら、最後に見すてて針で突くだけで命を奪ってしまう、という綺想。

**160. hollow crown** シェイクスピアは、スクループが処刑されたブシーらの処刑を報告する際に、彼らの埋められた大地に「中空の」という意味で添えた hollow という形容詞（140）を、リチャードに「死」が宮廷をかまえる王冠について「空洞状の」という意味で使わせ、死者の埋葬される大地と、外見だけのものにすぎない、王を死にいたらしめる王冠を結びつけている。

**162. antic** 「道化役者」（*OED*, antic, *n.* 4)。Death のこと。

**163-66. his . . . his . . . him . . . him** すべて王冠をいただいている現実の王（king, 161）を指す。

**165. monarchize** 「君主として君臨する」（*OED*, monarchize, *v.* 1)。

**166. self and vain conceit** 「自身についてのひとりよがりの思いこみ（＝ vain self-conceit）」（self は形容詞的）。

**170. through** Q1: thorough Q2-F1: through **wall** Q1: wall Q2-F1: walls

**farewell king!** ここでリチャードは、4幕1場「退位のエピソード」の前兆となる、自身の頭から王冠を取りさるという行為におよぶ（Black）。

Cover your heads and mock not flesh and blood
With solemn reverence. Throw away respect,
Tradition, form and ceremonious duty,
For you have but mistook me all this while.
I live with bread like you, feel want,                              175
Taste grief, need friends. Subjected thus,
How can you say to me, I am a king?

CARLISLE    My lord, wise men ne'er sit and wail their woes,
But presently prevent the ways to wail.
To fear the foe, since fear oppresseth strength,                    180
Gives in your weakness strength unto your foe,
And so your follies fight against yourself.
Fear and be slain. No worse can come to fight,
And fight and die is death destroying Death
Where fearing dying pays Death servile breath.                      185

AUMERLE    My father hath a power. Inquire of him
And learn to make a body of a limb.

RICHARD    Thou chid'st me well. Proud Bolingbroke, I come
To change blows with thee for our day of doom.
This ague fit of fear is overblown.                                 190
An easy task it is to win our own.
Say, Scrope, where lies our uncle with his power?
Speak sweetly, man, although thy looks be sour.

SCROPE    Men judge by the complexion of the sky
The state and inclination of the day;                               195
So may you by my dull and heavy eye.
My tongue hath but a heavier tale to say.
I play the torturer by small and small
To lengthen out the worst that must be spoken.
Your uncle York is joined with Bolingbroke                          200
And all your northern castles yielded up,
And all your southern gentlemen in arms
Upon his party.

**171. Cover your head** 王に敬意を表して脱帽している臣下たちとのあいだの垣根を取りはらう言葉。155-56でリチャードが玉座をおり地面に座ったのち、臣下たちが立ったまま王に敬意を表して脱帽して話を聞く、という所作が舞台上で行われているものと思われる。

**176. Subjected** 「〔悲しみやふつうの人間の必要など〕の影響にさらされて」という意味に、「（臣民として）服従させられて」という意味がかけられており（*OED*, subject, *v.* 5, 1）、二重の意味でリチャードを王と呼べない理由となる。

**177. How can ... king?** ⇒ 'Am I not king?'（83）参照。

**178-79. wise men ... ways to wail** Gurr は、Dent M999a の One must not bemoan a MISCHIEF but find out a remedy for it の項目に、この2行により近い、*Rom* の材源と目される Arthur Brooke, *Romeus and Juliet* の A wise man in the midst of troubles and distres, / Still stands not wailing present harm, but seeks his harm's restress が引用されていること、*3H6*, 5. 4. 1 に wise men ne'er sit and wail their loss / But cheerly seeks to redress their harms という文句が見られることを指摘して、この形が諺的表現であった可能性を指摘している。

**wise men ne'er sit and wail their woes** Qq: wisemen nere sit and waile theyr woes F1: wise men ne're waile their present woes 次行の presently にかけた F1 の読みは著者による改訂である可能性がある（Dawson & Yachnin）。

**178-182. wise ... wail ... woes / ... ways ... wail / ... fear ... foe ... fear ... / ... foe / follies ... fight** 嘆き悲しむことは敵を利することにつながる愚かなことだ、という趣旨を最初の2行では woe を中核とする w 音の頭韻、次の3行では foe を中心とする f 音の頭韻で強調している。

**182. And so your follies fight against yourself** Qq: And so your follies fight against your selfe Qq のみの行。

**183. No worse can come to fight** 「戦えば〔殺されること〕よりひどいことは起こらない」。

**185. Where** = Whereas（*OED*, where, *adv.* and *conj.* 12b）

**186. power** 「軍隊」（*OED*, power, *n.*¹ 9）。

**187. make a body of a limb** 「一本の腕（arm）と思えたものを強大な兵隊（army）にする」（Yachnin & Dawson）。

**189. change** = exchange（*OED*, change, *v.* 1）

**194. complexion** 「事物の見かけ、外見」（*OED*, complexion, *n.* 5）。

**195. inclination** 「傾向、状況」（*OED*, inclination, *n.* 7 の初出例）。

**203. party** Qq: partie F1: Faction

RICHARD        Thou hast said enough.
  [*to Aumerle*]    Beshrew thee, cousin, which didst lead me forth
  Of that sweet way I was in to despair.                          205
  What say you now? What comfort have we now?
  By heaven I'll hate him everlastingly
  That bids me be of comfort any more.
  Go to Flint Castle, there I'll pine away.
  A king, woe's slave, shall kingly woe obey.                     210
  That power I have, discharge, and let them go
  To ear the land that hath some hope to grow,
  For I have none. Let no man speak again
  To alter this, for counsel is but vain.
AUMERLE    My liege, one word.
RICHARD                            He does me double wrong         215
  That wounds me with the flatteries of his tongue.
  Discharge my followers. Let them hence away
  From Richard's night to Bolingbroke's fair day.      *Exeunt*


[ACT III, SCENE III]

*Enter, with drum and colours, Bolingbroke, York, Northumberland,*
*attendants, [and soldiers]*


BOLINGBROKE    So that by this intelligence we learn
  The Welshmen are dispersed and Salisbury
  Is gone to meet the King, who lately landed
  With some few private friends upon this coast.
NORTHUMBERLAND    The news is very fair and good, my lord.         5
  Richard not far from hence hath hid his head.
YORK    It would beseem the Lord Northumberland
  To say 'King Richard.' Alack the heavy day
  When such a sacred king should hide his head.
NORTHUMBERLAND    Your grace mistakes. Only to be brief            10
  Left I his title out.

**204. which** この時代には who 同様に人を先行詞として用いられることもあった（*OED*, which, *pron.*, 9; Abbott, §265）。

**209. Flint Castle** フリント城。ウェールズ北東部の旧州フリントシア（Flintshire）の州都フリント（Flint）北東部にあった城。ヘンリー二世に造営され、1647 年に議会政府によって解体された。次の場面ではこの城の前が舞台となる（Sugden）。

**210. kingly** 「王のような」（*OED*, kingly, *a.* 3）。

**211. them** Qq: them　F1: 'em

**212. ear** 「（土地）を耕す」（*OED*, ear, *v.*¹ 1）。

**213. again** 「答えて」（*OED*, again, *adv.* 2）。　⇒ 1. 3. 178 注。

**218. From Richard's night to Bolingbroke's fair day** 36-53 で王たる自身を太陽にたとえる比喩を用いていたリチャードが、一転して自身を夜に、ボリンブルックを太陽になぞらえている。

〔3. 3〕あらすじ‥‥‥‥‥‥‥‥‥‥‥‥‥‥‥‥‥‥‥‥‥‥‥‥‥‥‥‥‥‥‥‥‥‥

　フリント城の間近に迫り、国王側のウェールズ兵離反と国王帰国の報を受けたボリンブルックのもとにパーシーがやってきて、王が城にいることを告げる。ボリンブルックは、ノーサンバーランドを王への使者として、追放の解除とランカスター公爵領の回復を条件に武装解除と恭順を申し出る。城壁のうえに姿を現したリチャードは、はじめひざまずかないノーサンバーランドの非礼に立腹し、侵攻は叛逆であることをボリンブルックに告げるよう求めるが、ノーサンバーランドが和解の条件を告げるとそれを受け入れ、王位喪失が逃れられない運命と知り自暴自棄となって狂乱状態となる。リチャードは城の外庭におりてボリンブルックと面会し、ひざまずくボリンブルックを立たせ、要求を呑むことを告げ、さらには要求されてもいない王位の委譲さえほのめかす。

‥‥‥‥‥‥‥‥‥‥‥‥‥‥‥‥‥‥‥‥‥‥‥‥‥‥‥‥‥‥‥‥‥‥‥‥‥‥‥‥‥‥‥‥

**1. intelligence** （可算名詞）「一片の情報」この用法は現代語にない（*OED*, intelligence, *n.* 7†b）。

**6-8. Richard . . . 'King Richard.'** このノーサンバーランドが王を「リチャード」と呼び捨てにしたことでヨークにたしなめられるエピソードは、場面終盤でリチャードがボリンブルックを「ボリンブルック王（King Bolingbroke）」（173）と呼ぶのと対になり、劇の転換点となるこの場面にあって重要な意味をもつものとなっている。

**7. beseem** 「〜するのが（人）にふさわしい」（*OED*, beseem, *v.* 2b）。

YORK                    The time hath been,
   Would you have been so brief with him, he would
   Have been so brief with you to shorten you,
   For taking so the head, your whole head's length.
**BOLINGBROKE**   Mistake not, uncle, further than you should.     15
YORK   Take not, good cousin, further than you should,
   Lest you mistake. The heavens are o'er our heads.
**BOLINGBROKE**   I know it, uncle, and oppose not myself
   Against their will. But who comes here?

                    *Enter Percy*

   Welcome, Harry. What, will not this castle yield?     20
PERCY   The castle royally is manned, my lord,
   Against thy entrance.
**BOLINGBROKE**
   Royally?
   Why, it contains no king?
PERCY                    Yes, my good lord,
   It doth contain a king. King Richard lies     25
   Within the limits of yon lime and stone
   And with him are the Lord Aumerle, Lord Salisbury,
   Sir Stephen Scrope, besides a clergyman
   Of holy reverence, who, I cannot learn.
NORTHUMBERLAND   O, belike it is the Bishop of Carlisle.     30
**BOLINGBROKE**   [*to Northumberland*]   Noble lord,
   Go to the rude ribs of that ancient castle.
   Through brazen trumpet send the breath of parley
   Into his ruined ears, and thus deliver:
   Henry Bolingbroke     35
   On both his knees doth kiss King Richard's hand
   And sends allegiance and true faith of heart
   To his most royal person, hither come
   Even at his feet to lay my arms and power,

**11-13. The time . . . shorten you**　Qq: The time . . . him, / He would . . . so briefe to shorten you　F1: The time hath beene, / Would you . . . would / Haue beene so briefe with you, to shorten you,

**12-13. brief . . . brief**　「（王という称号を省略することで）言葉少なである…（命令を下すのに）簡潔である」　**with you**　Qq なし　F1: with you

**13-14. shorten you . . . your whole head's length**　つまり、斬首すること。

**14. taking so the head**　「称号を省略すること」と「（馬が騎手の統御を受けずに走るように）自由に振る舞うこと」（*OED*, head, *n.*¹ 13a, 64）。

**15. Mistake**　「〜の言葉を誤解する」と「〜に不当なことをする」（*OED*, mistake, *v.* 4, †2a）。

**16. Take**　「〜を理解する」と「〜をつかむ、とる」（*OED*, take, *v.* 47a, 2）。

**17. o'er our heads**　Q1, 2: ouer our heads　Q3-5: ouer your heads　F1: ore your head

**18. oppose**　語の意味は「（人、もの）を〜と（*against*）敵対関係におく」（*OED*, oppose, *v.* 6）。だが、文脈上「敵対関係にあるとみなす」の意。

**20. this castle**　フリント城のこと。

**21. royally is manned**　パーシーは man を「（砦や船など）に人員を配置する」の意味で使い「国王側によって防備が固められている」という意味で言ったのにたいして、ボリンブルックは man を「（場所）に人を住まわせる」の意に解して「国王がいる」と理解している（*OED*, man, *v.* 1, 2）。

**23-24. Royally? / . . . king?**　Qq: Royally, . . . King.　F1: Royally? . . . King?　Steevens: Royally! / . . . king?　パンクチュエイションは F1 に、行割は Steevens にしたがった。　**26. yon**　Qq: yon　F1: yond

**27. are**　Q1: are　Q2-F1 なし　**31. lord**　Qq: Lords　F1: Lord

**32. rude ribs**　「無骨な脇腹」城壁を指す比喩で、前場でもリチャードが身体を砦にたとえている。rib には壁面の「横木」の意味もある（*OED*, rib, *n.*¹ 10）。

**33. send the breath of parley**　breath には「管楽器に吹きこまれる呼気」（*OED*, breath, *n.* 3c）の意味があるが、ここでは「吹鳴」の意味で使われている。「喇叭を鳴らして交渉申しこみの合図を送る」を意味する sound a parley（*OED*, parley, *n.*¹ 2）に基づく表現。

**34. his ruined ears**　「砲撃で崩れたフリント城の胸壁の狭間や窓」を耳にたとえたもの（his = its、城を人間の身体にたとえる比喩が 32 からつづいている）。しかし、「打ちひしがれたリチャードの耳」と解し、自身が優位に立っているとの認識を示す言葉ととる解釈もある（Dawson & Yachnin）。

**35-38. Henry . . . come**　Malone による行割り。Qq は . . . hands, / . . . heart / . . . come で終わる 3 行。F1 は . . . kisse / . . . allegeance / . . . come で終わる 3 行。

**36. On both**　Qq: on both　F1: vpon　**38. most**　Q1, 2: most　Q3-F1 なし

143

Provided that my banishment repealed                    40
And lands restored again be freely granted.
If not I'll use the advantage of my power
And lay the summer's dust with showers of blood
Rained from the wounds of slaughter'd Englishmen,
The which how far off from the mind of Bolingbroke    45
It is such crimson tempest should bedrench
The fresh green lap of fair King Richard's land,
My stooping duty tenderly shall show.
Go signify as much while here we march
Upon the grassy carpet of this plain.                   50

[*Northumberland with Trumpet goes to the walls*]

Let's march without the noise of threatening drum,
That from this castle's tottered battlements
Our fair appointments may be well perused.
Methinks King Richard and myself should meet
With no less terror than the elements                   55
Of fire and water, when their thund'ring shock
At meeting tears the cloudy cheeks of heaven.
Be he the fire, I'll be the yielding water.
The rage be his whilst on the earth I rain
My waters — on the earth and not on him.                60
March on, and mark King Richard how he looks.

*The trumpets sound [a] parley without, and answer within. Then a flourish.*
*Enter on the walls, Richard, Carlisle, Aumerle, Scrope [and] Salisbury*

See, see, King Richard doth himself appear
As doth the blushing discontented sun
From out the fiery portal of the east
When he perceives the envious clouds are bent           65
To dim his glory and to stain the track
Of his bright passage to the occident.

**40-41. Provided . . . granted** 「追放の撤回と土地の回復が無条件に認められれば」名詞＋過去分詞が抽象名詞となる（my banishedment repealed ＝ the repeal of my banishment; lands restored ＝ the restoration of lands）ラテン語風語法。

**43. lay the . . . dust** 「埃をしずめる」(*OED*, lay, *v*.¹ 3a)。

**45-48. The which . . . shall show** この部分の構文は以下のとおり。主語＋動詞が My stooping duty tenderly shall show (48)、show の目的語となる節が how far off from the mind of Bolingbroke / It is (45-46)、It (46) は直後の (that) such . . . land (46-47) を受けるが、内容的には I'll use . . . Englishmen (42-44) を受ける The which (45) の言い直しとなっている。the which については 1. 1. 90 注を参照せよ。

**53. appointments** 「軍備、軍装」(*OED*, appointment, *n*. 9)。

**55-57. elements . . . heaven** 雷は大気中における火と水の要素の衝突によって発生すると考えられていた。

**52. tottered** 「ぼろぼろになった」(*OED*, † tottered, *ppl. a.* 1)。もともとは tattered の異綴りだが、のちに「よろめかせる」という意味の totter という動詞と同化された語。Q1, 2: tottered　Q3-F1: tatter'd

**56. shock** Q1: shocke　Q2-F1: smoake

**59. whilst** Qq: whilst　F1: while

　**rain** Qq: raigne　F1: raine

**62-67. See, see . . . to the occident** 休戦交渉のためにフリント城から姿を現したリチャードをボリンブルックは雲に隠れそうになり不機嫌な太陽にたとえる。

**65. envious** 「悪意ある」(*OED*, envious, *a*. †2)。

**66. track** Qq: tracke　F1: tract

**YORK**    Yet looks he like a king. Behold, his eye,
        As bright as is the eagle's, lightens forth
        Controlling majesty. Alack, alack, for woe        70
        That any harm should stain so fair a show.
**RICHARD**    [*to Northumberland*]    We are amazed, and thus long
            have we stood
        To watch the fearful bending of thy knee
        Because we thought ourself thy lawful king.
        And if we be, how dare thy joints forget        75
        To pay their awful duty to our presence?
        If we be not, show us the hand of God
        That hath dismissed us from our stewardship,
        For well we know no hand of blood and bone
        Can gripe the sacred handle of our sceptre        80
        Unless he do profane, steal or usurp.
        And though you think that all as you have done
        Have torn their souls by turning them from us
        And we are barren and bereft of friends,
        Yet know my master, God omnipotent,        85
        Is mustering in his clouds on our behalf
        Armies of pestilence, and they shall strike
        Your children yet unborn and unbegot
        That lift your vassal hands against my head
        And threat the glory of my precious crown.        90
        Tell Bolingbroke, for yon methinks he stands,
        That every stride he makes upon my land
        Is dangerous treason. He is come to open
        The purple testament of bleeding War,
        But ere the crown he looks for live in peace        95
        Ten thousand bloody crowns of mothers' sons
        Shall ill become the flower of England's face,
        Change the complexion of her maid-pale peace
        To scarlet indignation and bedew

**69. lightens forth** 「〜を稲妻のように放つ」(*OED*, lighten, *v.*[2] 7)。リチャードを、気象現象を司りしばしば雷として姿を現すユーピテルにたとえている。

**73. watch** 「〜を待ち望む」(*OED*, watch, *v.* 12b)。

**76. awful duty** 膝を屈して礼をすること (i.e. 'thy duty of showing awe', Chambers)。

　　**awful** 「畏敬の念にみちた」(*OED*, awful, *a.* 6) の初出例。

**77. hand** 「署名」(*OED*, hand, *n.* 17)。

**78. stewardship** 「執事の職」の比喩的な意味で「地上における神の代理人たる王であること」(*OED*, stewardship, *n.* 1)。

**79. blood and bone** flesh and bone 同様に「生身の人間」を意味する (*OED*, bone, *n.* 3a)。

**81. profane** (絶対用法、または自動詞)「瀆神的な言動をする」(*OED*, profane, *v.* 2 初出例は 1690 年となっている)。

**83. torn their souls** 「(忠誠を誓った私から) 心を引き離す」と「(罪深いことをして罰として) 自身の魂に危害をおよぼす」(*OED*, tear, *v.*[1] 5a, 3d)。

　　**turning them** 「関心や心などを向ける」(*OED*, turn, *v.* 27)。

　　**them** = themselves ⇒ 2. 3. 8 注参照。

**89. That** 先行詞は Your (88)。所有格の代名詞が関係代名詞の先行詞となるケースについては Abbott, §218 を参照せよ。

　　**vassal** 「臣民、臣下の」(*OED*, vassal, *n.* and *a.* 4)。

**91. yon** Qq: yon F1: yond

　　**stands** Qq: stands F1: is

**93. open** Qq: open F1: ope

**94. purple testament of bleeding War** 「血まみれの『戦争』の遺贈を伝える血染めの遺書」purple は詩的表現で血の色を表す形容詞 (*OED*, purple, *a.* 2d; testament, *n.* 1)。

**95-96. crown . . . crowns** 「王冠 … 頭」(*OED*, crown, *n.* 2, 17b)。

**98. her** Qq: her F1 なし

Her pastor's grass with faithful English blood. 100

NORTHUMBERLAND   The King of Heaven forbid our lord the King

Should so with civil and uncivil arms

Be rushed upon. Thy thrice noble cousin,

Harry Bolingbroke, doth humbly kiss thy hand,

And by the honourable tomb he swears 105

That stands upon your royal grandsire's bones,

And by the royalties of both your bloods,

Currents that spring from one most gracious head,

And by the buried hand of warlike Gaunt,

And by the worth and honour of himself, 110

Comprising all that may be sworn or said,

His coming hither hath no further scope

Than for his lineal royalties and to beg

Enfranchisement immediate on his knees,

Which on thy royal party granted once 115

His glittering arms he will commend to rust,

His barbèd steeds to stables and his heart

To faithful service of your majesty.

This swears he as he is a prince and just,

And as I am a gentleman I credit him. 120

RICHARD   Northumberland, say thus the King returns:

His noble cousin is right welcome hither,

And all the number of his fair demands

Shall be accomplished without contradiction.

With all the gracious utterance thou hast 125

Speak to his gentle hearing kind commends.

*[Northumberland with Trumpets returns to Bolingbroke]*

[*to Aumerle*]   We do debase ourselves, cousin, do we not,

To look so poorly and to speak so fair?

Shall we call back Northumberland and send

Defiance to the traitor and so die? 130

**102. civil and uncivil arms** 「自国民でありながら礼節を欠いて叛乱する軍」（*OED*, civil, *a*. 2; uncivil, *a*. 3)。

**103-20. Thy . . . him.** ノーサンバーランドは、追放の解除と領地の回復という要望（35-41）とそれがかなえられない場合の武力行使の脅し（42-48）というメッセージをリチャードに伝えるようボリンブルックに命じられ、前者のみを伝えて、後者を言わずにおき、命じられていない誓言（103-20）を付け加えている。

**103. rushed** Qq: rusht  F1: rush'd

**105. tomb** ウェストミンスター大聖堂にあるエドワード三世の墓を指す。

**108. head** 「(河川の) 源泉」= fountain-head（*OED*, head, *n*.¹ 16)。

**112. scope** 「目的」（*OED*, scope, *n*.² 2a)。

**113. lineal royalties** 「直系相続によって継承された、国王から委譲された（領地の）管轄権」、royalties はさらに「王(族)の特権」も含意している（*OED*, lineal, *a*. 2a; royalty, *n*. 5a, 6a.）。2. 1. 190 注参照。

**114. Enfranchisement** 「投獄、隷属、服従などからの解放」ここでは「追放の解除」を指す（*OED*, enfranchisement, *n*. 1)。

**115. Which on thy royal party granted once** 「そのことを王様がひとたび認められれば」関係代名詞句。Which の先行詞は royalties（113）と Enfranchisement（114）。

**on thy royal party** 「王様のほうで」（*OED*, party, *n*. 5†b)

**116. commend** 「～に（*to*...）ゆだねる」（*OED*, commend, *v*. 1)。

**117. barbèd** 「装飾馬具につけた」（*OED*, barbed, *ppl. a*.²)。

**119. a prince and** Q1, 2: princesse  Q3-5: a Prince  F1: a Prince, is  採用した読みは Charles J. Sisson, *New Readings in Shakespeare*, 2 vols. (Cambridge: Dawsons, 1956) II. 24 による提案。Sisson は、Q1 の植字工は原稿にあった &（*et* の書記体をつづけて書いたもの）を書記体の *es* と読み違えて princesse と植字し、Q3, F の植字工は Q1 の読みにたいする修正を試みたが不十分な結果に終わったと推定している。

**121. returns** 「答えとして～と言う」（*OED*, return, *v*.¹ 19b の初出例)。

**126. commends** 「『よろしく』という挨拶」（*OED*, †commend, *n*. 3)。

**127. ourselves** Qq: our selues  F1: our selfe

**AUMERLE**   No, good my lord. Let's fight with gentle words
Till time lend friends, and friends their helpful swords.
**RICHARD**   O God, O God, that e'er this tongue of mine,
That laid the sentence of dread banishment
On yon proud man, should take it off again                    135
With words of sooth! O that I were as great
As is my grief or lesser than my name,
Or that I could forget what I have been,
Or not remember what I must be now!
Swell'st thou, proud heart? I'll give thee scope to beat        140
Since foes have scope to beat both thee and me.

[*Northumberland returns to the walls*]

**AUMERLE**   Northumberland comes back from Bolingbroke.
**RICHARD**   What must the King do now? Must he submit?
The King shall do it. Must he be deposed?
The King shall be contented. Must he lose                      145
The name of King? A God's name let it go.
I'll give my jewels for a set of beads,
My gorgeous palace for a hermitage,
My gay apparel for an almsman's gown,
My figured goblets for a dish of wood,                         150
My sceptre for a palmer's walking staff,
My subjects for a pair of carvèd saints
And my large kingdom for a little grave,
A little, little grave, an obscure grave.
Or I'll be buried in the king's highway,                      155
Some way of common trade, where subjects' feet
May hourly trample on their sovereign's head,
For on my heart they tread now whilst I live,
And buried once, why not upon my head?
Aumerle, thou weep'st, my tender-hearted cousin.              160
We'll make foul weather with despisèd tears.

**133-35. O . . . that . . . should . . .** 「ああ、〜するとは」悲しみ、怒りなどの感情を表す感嘆文（*OED*, that, *conj.* 1e）。

**133. mine** 前の台詞まで royal 'we' を使っていたリチャードは、この台詞からIという代名詞を用いはじめる。

**135. yon** Qq: yon F1: yond

**take it off again** 「それ（the sentence of dread banishment, 134）を撤回する」（*OED*, take, *v.* 85g の初出例）。

**136. sooth** 「へつらい」しばしばシェイクスピアが用いている「真実」ではなく、動詞 soothe からの連想で生じた意味（*OED*, sooth, *n.* †8）の初出例。

**O that . . . were** 「ああ、〜であればよいのに」願望を表す感嘆文（*OED*, that, *conj.* 3c）。

**140. Swell'st** 「傲りたかぶる」と「膨らむ」（*OED*, swell, *v.* 7b, 1）。

**scope to beat** 「鼓動を打つ場所」（*OED*, scope, *n.*² 8a; beat, *v.*¹ 13）。

**141. scope to beat both thee and me** 「お前（リチャードの心臓）と俺をつづけさまに打擲する意図と機会」（*OED*, scope, *n.*² 2a, 7a; beat, *v.*¹ 1a）。

**144-45. Must he be deposed? / The King shall be contented** 廃位が避けがたいことをリチャードが認める最初の言葉が、Must he ...? / The King shall ... を3度くり返す首句反復（anaphora）のなかで発されている。

**146. A God's** Qq: a Gods F1: o' Gods

**149. almsman's** 「施しを受ける貧民の」（*OED*, almsman, *n.* 1）。

**150. figured**「文様や飾りをほどこした」（*OED*, figured, *ppl. a.* 4）。

**155. the king's highway** 「天下の大道、国王が管轄する大街道」（*OED*, highway, *n.* 1）。

**156. way of common trade** 「だれでも通行できる道」（*OED*, trade, *n.* †1）。

Our sighs and they shall lodge the summer corn
And make a dearth in this revolting land.
Or shall we play the wantons with our woes
And make some pretty match with shedding tears,                    165
As thus to drop them still upon one place
Till they have fretted us a pair of graves
Within the earth and, therein laid, 'There lies
Two kinsmen digged their graves with weeping eyes'?
Would not this ill do well? Well, well, I see                     170
I talk but idly and you laugh at me.
[*to Northumberland*]   Most mighty prince, my Lord
    Northumberland,
What says King Bolingbroke? Will his majesty
Give Richard leave to live till Richard die?
You make a leg and Bolingbroke says 'Ay.'                         175
**NORTHUMBERLAND**   My lord, in the base court he doth attend
To speak with you. May it please you to come down?
**RICHARD**   Down, down I come like glistering Phaëton,
Wanting the manage of unruly jades.
In the base court? Base court where kings grow base             180
To come at traitors' calls and do them grace.
In the base court? Come down? Down court, down king!
For night-owls shriek where mounting larks should sing.
                    [*Exeunt Richard and his followers from above*]

[*Northumberland returns to Bolingbroke*]

**BOLINGBROKE**   What says his majesty?
**NORTHUMBERLAND**                     Sorrow and grief of heart
Makes him speak fondly like a frantic man                         185

                [*Enter Richard and his followers below*]

Yet he is come.
**BOLINGBROKE**   Stand all apart

**162. lodge** 「(風雨が作物)をなぎたおす」(*OED*, lodge, *v.* 5 の初出例)。主語
となる「ため息と涙(sighs and they)」を風雨にたとえている。

**163. revolting** 「叛乱を起こす」(*OED*, revolting, *ppl. a.* 1 の初出例)。

**164. play the wantons with** 「〜をもてあそぶ」(*OED*, wanton, *n.* 4)。

**165. make some pretty match** 「すばらしい競い合いをする」(*OED*, match,
*n.*¹ 7)。

**168-69. 'There lies . . . weeping eyes'?** リチャードは自分たちの墓石にきざま
れた墓碑銘を想像している。

**170. ill** 「不幸、悲運」(*OED*, ill, *n.* 5)。

**171. laugh** Qq: laugh F1: mock

**173-74. King Bolingbroke . . . his majesty . . . Richard . . . Richard** リ
チャードがノーサンバーランドに向かってボリンブルックを「ボリンブルック
王」と呼ぶこのエピソードは、ノーサンバーランドが王を「リチャード」と呼
び捨てにしたことでヨークにたしなめられる場面冒頭のエピソード(6-8)と
対をなしている。

**176-82. in the base court . . . come down . . . Down, down I come . . . In the
base court? Base court . . . grow base . . . In the base court? Come down?
Down court, down king!** この劇の高低の主題のクライマックス的台詞。上
舞台から主舞台におりていく物理的な移動とあわせて、王位喪失を観念したリ
チャードの墜落感を端的に示している。

**178-79. Down . . . jades** 城の胸壁に姿を現したときに東の空に昇る太陽にた
とえられた(62)リチャードが、ここでは自身を、馬車の制御を誤って地上
に落ち大火災をもたらした太陽神ヘリオスの子パエトーンにたとえている。

**180. court?** Qq: court, F1: Court?

**182. court? Come down?** Qq: court come downe: F1: Court come down:
Capell: court? Come down?

**183. 1, 185. 1 [*Exeunt . . . above*], [*Enter . . . below*]** 台詞のなかに見られ
た、リチャードとボリンブルックの力関係を表す高低の主題が、城の胸壁に見
立てられた上舞台から城の外庭に見立てられる平舞台におりるリチャードの劇
場内での動きによって可視化される。

**185. fondly** 「愚かしい話しぶりで」(*OED*, fondly, *adv.* †1)。

And show fair duty to his majesty.

*He kneels down*

My gracious lord.

**RICHARD**    Fair cousin, you debase your princely knee    190
To make the base earth proud with kissing it.
Me rather had my heart might feel your love
Than my unpleased eye see your courtesy.
Up, cousin, up. Your heart is up, I know,

*[Raises Bolingbroke]*

Thus high at least, *[Indicates the crown]* although your knee be low.    195

**BOLINGBROKE**    My gracious lord, I come but for mine own.

**RICHARD**    Your own is yours and I am yours and all.

**BOLINGBROKE**    So far be mine, my most redoubted lord,
As my true service shall deserve your love.

**RICHARD**    Well you deserve. They well deserve to have    200
That know the strong'st and surest way to get.
*[to York]*    Uncle, give me your hands. Nay, dry your eyes.
Tears show their love, but want their remedies.
*[to Bolingbroke]*    Cousin, I am too young to be your father,
Though you are old enough to be my heir.    205
What you will have I'll give, and willing too,
For do we must what force will have us do.
Set on towards London, cousin, is it so?

**BOLINGBROKE**    Yea, my good lord.

**RICHARD**                                     Then I must not say no.

*Flourish. Exeunt*

[ACT III, SCENE IV]

*Enter the Queen with her two Ladies*

**QUEEN**    What sport shall we devise here in this garden

**190. debase** 「〜をおとしめる」（*OED*, debase, *v*. †2）。

**192. Me rather had** ＝ I had rather that　初期近代英語にしばしば見られる、現代語でも使う I had, *or* would, rather . . . と古い無人称構文（To）me（it）were lever . . . というふたつの構文の混同から生じた語法（*OED*, have, *v*. 22c; Abbott, §230）。

**194-95. Your heart is up, I know, / Thus high at least,〔*Indicates the crown*〕although your knee be low**　リチャードは、へりくだってひざまずいていても、ボリンブルックの野心がめざす高みが王位であることを示すために、自身の王冠を指さす。

**198. redoubted**　「畏怖すべき」-able の意になる過去分詞形の用法。　⇒2. 1. 268 注参照。

**200. deserve**　Qq: deserue　F1: deseru'd

**202. hands**　Qq: handes　F1: Hand

**203. want**　「〜を欠いている、もっていない（＝ lack）」（*OED*, want, *v*. 2）。

**204-05. I am too young to be your father, / Though you are old enough to be my heir**　史実ではリチャードとボリンブルックは同い年（Black）。

**206-07. What you will . . . will have us do.**　Dawson & Yachnin は、この場面、とりわけ外庭におけるボリンブルックとの会見で、求められないうちに白旗をあげるようなリチャードの振る舞いについて、「みずから運命の転落を演出している（orchestrating his own fall）」と評している。

〔3. 4〕あらすじ・・・・・・・・・・・・・・・・・・・・・・・・・・・・・・・・・・・・・・・・・・・・・・・・・・・・・・・・・・・・・・・・・・

　悲嘆にくれる王妃の気持ちをなんとか引きたてようと、侍女たちが娯楽を提案している。そこへ庭師たちがやってきて、王妃らは彼らの会話を盗み聞きすることにする。庭師は王国を庭にたとえ、その手入れを怠ったことをリチャード失脚の原因とし、国王が廃位されることを告げる手紙がヨーク公の周囲に届いているとまことしやかに語る。聞き捨てならないと思った王妃は庭師の前に姿を現し、その情報の出所を問いつめ、だれもが知っていることと知らされ、自身の不運を嘆き、悪い報せをもたらした庭師を呪詛しながらロンドンに向かう。

・・・・・・・・・・・・・・・・・・・・・・・・・・・・・・・・・・・・・・・・・・・・・・・・・・・・・・・・・・・・・・・・・・・・・・・・・・・・・・・・・・・・・・・・・・・・・・・・

To drive away the heavy thought of care?

LADY    Madam, we'll play at bowls.

QUEEN    'Twill make me think the world is full of rubs

And that my fortune runs against the bias.    5

LADY    Madam, we'll dance.

QUEEN    My legs can keep no measure in delight

When my poor heart no measure keeps in grief.

Therefore no dancing, girl. Some other sport.

LADY    Madam, we'll tell tales.    10

QUEEN    Of sorrow or of joy?

LADY                      Of either, madam.

QUEEN    Of neither, girl.

For if of joy, being altogether wanting

It doth remember me the more of sorrow.

Or if of grief, being altogether had    15

It adds more sorrow to my want of joy.

For what I have I need not to repeat

And what I want it boots not to complain.

LADY    Madam, I'll sing.

QUEEN               'Tis well that thou hast cause,

But thou shouldst please me better wouldst thou weep.    20

LADY    I could weep, madam, would it do you good.

QUEEN    And I could sing, would weeping do me good,

And never borrow any tear of thee.

*Enter a Gardener and two Men*

But stay, here come the gardeners.

Let's step into the shadow of these trees.    25

My wretchedness unto a row of pins,

They'll talk of state, for every one doth so

Against a change. Woe is forerun with woe.

*[Queen and Ladies stand apart]*

**2. care** 「悲しみ」。 ⇒2.2.79注参照。

**3. bowls** 「ローンボウリングの試合」（bowl, *n.*² 3a）。

**4. rubs** 「（ローンボウリングで）地面の凸凹などの球の進行を妨げる障害物」から生じた一般的な「障害物」（*OED*, rub, *n.*¹ 2a, †b）。

**5. bias** 「（ローンボウリングの）球の進む方向をそらす力」（*OED*, bias, *n.* 2）。

**7-8. measure . . . measure** 「（とくにゆるやかで荘重な）踊り」と「限度、ちょうどよい加減」（*OED*, measure, *n.* 20, 12c）。

**11. joy** Qq: griefe F1: Griefe 採用した読みは Rowe (ed. 3) による校訂。

**13-16. For if of joy . . . want of joy** 「もし楽しい話なら、そんなものはまったくないため、悲しいことをますます思いおこさせる。もし悲しい話なら、そんなものしかないため、楽しいことのない状況に悲しみを付け加える」という意味の、joy と grief、wanting と sorrow という対義語を用いて対句的に表現を重ねる王妃のこの台詞は、この劇の特徴である、悲惨な状況におかれた登場人物が発する言葉遊びの顕著な例となっている。 ⇒2.1.74, 85注参照。

**14. remember** 「（人）に〜を思いおこさせる」。 ⇒1.3.268注参照。

**18. want** 「〜を欠いている、もっていない」 ⇒3.3.203注参照。

**21-23. I could weep . . . tear of thee.** 「お妃様、泣いて差しあげましょう、それがあなたのためになるのなら」と言う侍女にたいして王妃が「歌ってあげましょう、泣いてもらうことが私のためになるのなら。そうしたらもうお前から涙を借りたりはしないわ」と答えるここでも、言葉遊びが哀れを誘う。

**24. come** Q1: come Q2-5: commeth F1: comes

**26. My wretchedness unto a row of pins** 「私の（大きな）惨めさを（あなたがたのつまらない）何本もの針にかけてもいいわ」針は価値のないもののたとえで、王妃は庭師たちがきっと政治の話をはじめる（27-8）ということを断言するために、自分の大きな惨めさを賭ければ、侍女たちが何本も針を賭けてもおよばないとしている（*OED*, pin, *n.*¹ 3b）。

**pins** Qq: pines F1: Pinnes

**27. They'll** Qq: The will F1: They'll

**28. Against** 「〜を前にして、〜にそなえて」（*OED*, against, *prep.* 19）。

**GARDENER**  [*to one Man*]  Go bind thou up young dangling
    apricocks,

Which, like unruly children, make their sire           30

Stoop with oppression of their prodigal weight.

Give some supportance to the bending twigs.

[*to the other Man*]  Go thou and like an executioner

Cut off the heads of too-fast-growing sprays

That look too lofty in our commonwealth.          35

All must be even in our government.

You thus employed, I will go root away

The noisome weeds which without profit suck

The soil's fertility from wholesome flowers.

**MAN**  Why should we in the compass of a pale        40

Keep law and form and due proportion,

Showing as in a model our firm estate,

When our sea-wallèd garden, the whole land,

Is full of weeds, her fairest flowers choked up,

Her fruit-trees all unpruned, her hedges ruined,     45

Her knots disordered and her wholesome herbs

Swarming with caterpillars?

**GARDENER**                  Hold thy peace.

He that hath suffered this disordered spring

Hath now himself met with the fall of leaf.

The weeds which his broad-spreading leaves did shelter,    50

That seemed in eating him to hold him up,

Are plucked up root and all by Bolingbroke,

I mean the Earl of Wiltshire, Bushy, Green.

**MAN**  What, are they dead?

**GARDENER**              They are, and Bulingbroke

Hath seized the wasteful King. O, what pity is it      55

That he had not so trimmed and dressed his land

As we this garden! We at time of year

Do wound the bark, the skin of our fruit trees,

**29. young**  Q1: yong  Q2-5: yon  F1: yond

**apricocks**  apricot の 16-18 世紀の語形。Chambers は、この劇が描く出来事が起こった 1399 年にはこの果実がイングランドにはもたらされていないとしてこの言及が時代錯誤的であることを指摘している。*OED* に収録された apricot の 初 出 例 は 1551 年 (*OED*, apricot, *n.*)。Q1: Aphricokes  Q2: Aphricocks  Q3, F1: Apricocks  Q4, 5: Apricockes  ⇒4. 1. 40 注、および 5. 2. 23-28 注参照。

**30. sire**  (詩)「父親」(*OED*, sire, *n.* 6)。

**31. prodigal**  「過度の」Forker は聖書 Luke, 15: 11-32 の放蕩息子の寓話への言及の可能性を指摘している (*OED*, prodigal, *a.* 2, *n.* 2)。

**32. supportance**  「支え、支持」(*OED*, †supportance, *n.* 3 の初出例)。

**34. too-**  Qq: two-  F: too-

**sprays**  「小枝」(*OED*, spray, *n.*[1] 2a)。

**38. noisome**  「有害な」(*OED*, noisome, *a.* 1)。

**weeds**  ⇒2. 3. 165 注、および 50-52 注参照。

**which**  Q1: which  Q2-F1: that

**40. in the compass of a pale**  「柵のなかで」(*OED*, compass, *n.*[1] 7a; pale, *n.*[1] 3)。

**42. firm estate**  「安定した状態」(*OED*, firm, *a.* 2; estate, *n.* 1)。

**43. sea-wallèd garden**  リチャードの手によって国土が賃貸に出されていることを嘆くゴーントの台詞のなかの England, bound in with the triumphant sea (2.1.61) を想起させる表現。

**45. unpruned**  「剪定されていない」(*OED*, unpruned, *ppl. a.*[2] の初出例)。

**46. knots**  「整形庭園の幾何学紋様など複雑な図形を描く花壇」(*OED*, knot, *n.*[1] 7)。

**50-52. The weeds . . . by Bolingbroke**  ⇒2. 3. 165 注、および後注参照。

**52. plucked**  Q1, 2: pluckt  Q3-5: puld  F1: pull'd

**54-57. They . . . year**  Capell による行割り。Qq、F1 は They are. / . . . king, / . . . trimde, / . . . year, / で終わる 4 行。

**56. trimmed and dressed his land**  国を適切に統治することを「土地を耕し庭園に剪定や施肥を行う」ことにたとえる隠喩 (*OED*, trim, *v.* †2; dress, *v.* 13c)。

**57. garden!**  Q1, 2: garden  Q3: garden,  Q4-F1: Garden,  Capell: garden!

**58. Do**  Qq: Do  F1: And

Lest being over-proud in sap and blood
With too much riches it confound itself.                    60
Had he done so to great and growing men,
They might have lived to bear and he to taste
Their fruits of duty. Superfluous branches
We lop away that bearing boughs may live.
Had he done so, himself had borne the crown,               65
Which waste of idle hours hath quite thrown down.
MAN    What, think you the King shall be deposed?
GARDENER    Depressed he is already, and deposed
'Tis doubt he will be. Letters came last night
To a dear friend of the good Duke of York's,              70
That tell black tidings.
QUEEN    O, I am pressed to death through want of speaking!

*[Queen and Ladies come forward]*

Thou, old Adam's likeness set to dress this garden,
How dares thy harsh rude tongue sound this unpleasing news?
What Eve, what serpent, hath suggested thee                75
To make a second fall of cursèd man?
Why dost thou say King Richard is deposed?
Dar'st thou, thou little better thing than earth,
Divine his downfall? Say where, when and how
Cam'st thou by this ill tidings? Speak, thou wretch.      80
GARDENER    Pardon me, madam. Little joy have I
To breathe this news; yet what I say is true.
King Richard he is in the mighty hold
Of Bolingbroke. Their fortunes both are weighed.
In your lord's scale is nothing but himself               85
And some few vanities that make him light;
But in the balance of great Bolingbroke
Besides himself are all the English peers,
And with that odds he weighs King Richard down.

**59. in** Q1: in Q2-F1: with

**59. over-proud** 「(植物について) 樹液、液汁が豊富な」(*OED*, proud, *a.* 7d の初出例)。

**62. bear** 「実をつける」(*OED*, bear, $v.^1$ 42c、ただし絶対用法の用例は 14 世紀末のものしか収録されていない)。

**66. of** Qq: of F1: and

**69. doubt** = feared (*OED*, doubt, *v.* 5b) 語形に関しては 1. 4. 20 注を参照せよ。 **doubt** Qq: doubt F1: doubted

**70. good** Q1, 2: good Q3-F1 なし

**72. pressed to death through want of speaking** 「どうしても話さずにはいられない」。重罪で訴追されながら罪状を黙秘する被疑者に課した、答えるか死ぬまで胴体のうえに重しを載せつづける「苛酷拷問 (*peine forte et dure*)」を比喩として用いており、直訳すれば「話せないために死に至る拷問にかけられている」(Malone; *OED*, press, $v.^1$ 1b; want, $n.^2$ 2c)。

**73. dress** 「〜を耕す」 ⇒ 56 注参照。

**80. Cam'st** Q1: Canst Q2-F1: Cam'st

**82. breathe** 「〜を告げる、言う」 ⇒ 2. 1. 1-2 注参照。 **this** Q1: this Q2-F1: these

**83. hold** 「拘禁」(*OED*, hold, $n.^1$ 4)。

**84-89. Their fortunes . . . King Richard down.** 天秤ばかりの一方の皿にリチャードを、他方の皿にイングランドのすべての貴族を味方につけたボリンブルックを載せるというこの比喩では、重さでまさるボリンブルックの載った皿がさがりリチャードが持ちあげられることになるが、庭師は政治的な力の差を逆説的に表現する。次場にも、リチャードとボリンブルックの状況を綱の両端についたふたつの水桶の上下動にたとえる比喩が見られる (⇒ 4. 1. 183-88 注参照)。

**85. lord's** 「夫の」(*OED*, lord, *n.* 2a)。

**87. balance** 「天秤ばかり (balance) の皿 (= scale)」(*OED*, balance, *n.* †2)。

**89. weighs . . . down** 「〜に重くのしかかる、〜を押しさげる」(*OED*, weigh, $v.^1$ 18a)。

Post you to London and you will find it so.                    90
I speak no more than every one doth know.
QUEEN    Nimble mischance, that art so light of foot,
Doth not thy embassage belong to me,
And am I last that knows it? O, thou think'st
To serve me last that I may longest keep              95
Thy sorrow in my breast. Come, ladies, go
To meet at London London's king in woe.
What, was I born to this, that my sad look
Should grace the triumph of great Bolingbroke?
Gard'ner, for telling me these news of woe                100
Pray God the plants thou graft'st may never grow.

_Exit_ [_with Ladies_]

GARDENER    Poor Queen, so that thy state might be no worse
I would my skill were subject to thy curse.
Here did she fall a tear. Here in this place
I'll set a bank of rue, sour herb of grace.              105
Rue even for ruth here shortly shall be seen
In the remembrance of a weeping queen.              _Exeunt_

**90. you will**　Qq: you will　F1: you'll

**99. triumph**　「凱旋式」本来的な意味は勝利を飾った将軍とその軍が行う古代ローマの凱旋行進で、その際には敗軍の捕虜も栄光に彩りを添えるために行進に加わった。王妃は自身を捕虜にたとえている（*OED*, triumph, *n.* 1）。

**100. these**　Qq: these　F1: this

**101. Pray God**　Qq: Pray God　F1: I would

**104. fall**　Q1: fall　Q2-F1: drop

**105. bank of rue**　「ヘンルーダの花壇」「後悔、悲しみ」を表す同音異義語 rue との連想から「悲嘆」、「悔い改め」の象徴とされる花（*OED*, bank, *n.*[1] 1, †3; rue, *n.*[1] 1; rue, *n.*[2] 1）。

**106. ruth**　「哀れみ、憐憫」（*OED*, ruth[1], *n.* 1）。

[ACT IV, SCENE I]

*Enter as to the Parliament, Bolingbroke, Aumerle, Northumberland, Percy,*
*Fitzwater, Surrey, [Bishop of] Carlisle, Abbot of Westminster. [Another*
*Lord] herald [and] officers*

**BOLINGBROKE**    Call forth Bagot.

*Enter Bagot*

Now, Bagot, freely speak thy mind,
What thou dost know of noble Gloucester's death,
Who wrought it with the King and who performed
The bloody office of his timeless end.                               5
**BAGOT**    Then set before my face the Lord Aumerle.
**BOLINGBROKE**    [*to Aumerle*]    Cousin, stand forth and look
    upon that man.

[*Aumerle comes forward*]

**BAGOT**    My Lord Aumerle, I know your daring tongue
    Scorns to unsay what once it hath delivered.
    In that dead time when Gloucester's death was plotted        10
    I heard you say, 'Is not my arm of length
    That reacheth from the restful English court
    As far as Calais to mine uncle's head?'
    Amongst much other talk that very time
    I heard you say that you had rather refuse              15
    The offer of an hundred thousand crowns
    Than Bolingbroke's return to England,
    Adding withal how blest this land would be
    In this your cousin's death.
**AUMERLE**                           Princes and noble lords,
    What answer shall I make to this base man?              20
    Shall I so much dishonour my fair stars
    On equal terms to give him chastisement?

〔**4. 1**〕あらすじ・・・・・・・・・・・・・・・・・・・・・・・・・・・・・・・・・・・・・・・・・・・・・・・・・・・・・・・・・・・・・・・・・・・・・・・・・・・・・・・・・・・・・・・・・・・

　議会における場面。ボリンブルックに呼び出されて登場したバゴットが、グロスター暗殺の謀議に加わっていたとの咎でオーマールを告発すると、オーマールが決闘のしるしの手袋を投げ、フィッツウォーター、パーシーらが挑戦に応じる。フィッツウォーターが、オーマールはさらに追放中のモーブリーに刺客を送ったと主張し、ボリンブルックが、真相を確かめるためにモーブリーの追放解除を主張すると、彼がヴェネツィアで客死したことをカーライル主教が告げ、ボリンブルックは、決闘について後日沙汰を下すことにする。ヨークが登場し、リチャードの王位委譲の意思を告げ、ボリンブルックは即位の意思を表明する。するとカーライルが、神に選ばれた国王が本人不在の場で臣下によって裁かれることの不当性を訴え、王の交替が国に混乱をもたらすと主張し、叛逆罪で逮捕される。退位に疑義が生じないように、リチャードによる自身の罪科告白を求める平民院の要求を認めるかという、ノーサンバーランドの問いかけを受けて、ボリンブルックはリチャードの召喚を命じる。ヨークに伴われてリチャードが登場し、ボリンブルックに王冠を渡すことをしぶり愁嘆場を演じる。リチャードはさらに、ノーサンバーランドが迫る、訴追された罪状の読みあげを拒み、罪の書かれた書物である自身の姿を読むためにと、鏡をもってくるよう求める。鏡を受けとったリチャードは、恥辱をこうむった自分の相貌を以前と変わらぬように見せる鏡を割り、ボリンブルックのいないところに行かせてほしいと懇願し、ロンドン塔送りを申しわたされる。ボリンブルックが戴冠式日程を決めて退場すると、あとに残ったカーライルとオーマールは戴冠を阻止する陰謀について相談をはじめる。

・・・・・・・・・・・・・・・・・・・・・・・・・・・・・・・・・・・・・・・・・・・・・・・・・・・・・・・・・・・・・・・・・・・・・・・・・・・・・・・・・・・・・・・・・・・・・・・・・・・・・・・・・・

**4. wrought it with the King**　「〔グロスター暗殺を〕王にそそのかした」と「王とともにその実行に加わった」（Ure; *OED*, work, *v.* 30b, 10）。　⇒後注参照。

**9. once it hath**　Qq: once it hath　F1: it hath once

**10. dead**　「致命的な」、「静まりかえった」（*OED*, dead, *a.* †9, 18a）。

**11-13. Is . . . head**　「王はどこまでも届く腕をもつ」（Kings have long arms）という諺（Tilley, K87）があり、この台詞は 1. 2. 4-5 のゴーントの言葉と同様にグロスター殺害へのリチャードの関与を示唆するものとなっている。

**13. mine**　Qq: mine　F1: my　　**17-19. Than . . . death**　Capell による行割り。Qq, F1 ともに . . . withall, / . . . death で終わる 2 行。

**14-19. Amongst . . . death**　ボリンブルックの追放はグロスターの死よりあとのことなので、グロスター暗殺の謀議の際に、追放されたボリンブルックの帰国にたいする強い嫌悪をオーマールが口にしたということはありえない。

**21-22. Shall I . . . chastisement?**　オーマールは公爵、バゴットはジェントリー。

**21. stars**　「（人の運命にたいする星の影響によって与えられた）社会的地位」（*OED*, star, *n.*[1] 3c）。　　**22. him**　Q1: them　Q2: my　Q3-F1: him

Either I must, or have mine honour soiled
With the attainder of his slanderous lips.

[*Throws down his gage*]

There is my gage, the manual seal of death                    25
That marks thee out for hell. I say thou liest
And will maintain what thou hast said is false
In thy heart-blood, though being all too base
To stain the temper of my knightly sword.
**BOLINGBROKE**    Bagot, forbear. Thou shalt not take it up.    30
**AUMERLE**    Excepting one, I would he were the best
    In all this presence that hath moved me so.
**FITZWATER**    [*to Aumerle*]    If that thy valour stand on sympathy,
    There is my gage, Aumerle, in gage to thine.

[*Throws down his gage*]

By that fair sun which shows me where thou stand'st,          35
I heard thee say, and vauntingly thou spak'st it,
That thou wert cause of noble Gloucester's death.
If thou deniest it twenty times, thou liest,
And I will turn thy falsehood to thy heart,
Where it was forgèd, with my rapier's point.                 40
**AUMERLE**    Thou dar'st not, coward, live to see that day.

[*Takes up gage*]

**FITZWATER**    Now by my soul I would it were this hour.
**AUMERLE**    Fitzwater, thou art damned to hell for this.
**PERCY**    Aumerle, thou liest. His honour is as true
    In this appeal as thou art all unjust,                    45
    And that thou art so, there I throw my gage
    To prove it on thee to the extremest point
    Of mortal breathing. [*Throws down his gage*] Seize it if thou darest.
**AUMERLE**    And if I do not, may my hands rot off

**24. attainder**　「非難」（*OED*, attainder, *n.* †2）。

**24. 1.** 〔*Throws down his gage*〕　これを皮切りに、機械的で茶番のような、決
闘のしるしとなる手袋の投げつけあいが行われる。ここでオーマールが投げた
手袋をバゴットはボリンブルックに止められ（30）拾わない。オーマールは
さらに、34. 1でフィッツウォーターが、48. 1でパーシーが、55. 1でもうひと
りの貴族が投げた手袋を拾い（41. 1; 51. 1; 57. 1）、自分のもう一方の手袋を投
げ（⇒ 57注参照）、サリーに手袋を投げられた（70. 1）フィッツウォーター
がもう片方の手袋を投げ返す（77. 1）と、両方を投げてしまったため借りた
手袋を投げる（85. 1）。こうして8つの手袋が投げられ、受けとられなかった
3つが床のうえに残り、ボリンブルックが These differences shall all rest
under gage . . .. (86) でおさめることになる混乱した状況をはっきりと示す。

**25. manual seal of death**　「死を約束する署名」（*OED*, manual, *a.* 1b）。「手
の」を意味する manual という語を用いて決闘のしるしである手袋を契約書
の署名にたとえた比喩だが、シェイクスピアは、ホリンシェッド『年代記』（6:
512）で頭巾（hood）となっている決闘のしるしを手袋に変えてこの言葉遊び
を可能にしている。

**26. I say**　Q1: I say　Q2-F1 なし

**29. temper**　「鍛造によってもたらされた強度と粘性（をもつ刃）」（*OED*,
temper, *n.* 5）。

**31. one**　ボリンブルックのこと。

**32. that hath moved me so**　先行詞は前行の he。

**33. If that thy valour stand on sympathy**　「（決闘に応じるという）お前の勇
気が（身分の）一致を条件とするなら」（*OED*, stand, *v.* 74c; sympathy, *n.*
2）。フィッツウォーターは男爵であるためバゴットに代わって決闘の相手を申
し出ている。　　**sympathy**　Qq: simpathie　F1: sympathize

**35. which**　Q1: which　Q2-F1: that

**39. turn**　「〜をつっ返す」（*OED*, turn, *v.* †21†c の初出例）。

**40. rapier's point**　Johnson は、細身で先のとがった諸刃の長剣ラピアーは16
世紀になって移入されたものであるため、この台詞を時代錯誤的としている。
*OED* に収録されている rapier の初出例は1553年（*OED*, rapier, *n.* a）。
⇒ 3. 4. 29注、および 5. 2. 23-28注参照。

**41. that**　Qq: that　F1: the　　　**43. Fitzwater**　Qq: Fitzwaters　F1: Fitzwater

**44. His honour**　「閣下」王に用いられる his majesty、王や王族、貴族に用い
られる highness、grace と同種の尊称で、高位の人全般に用いられる（*OED*,
honour, *n.* 4b）。　⇒ 1. 1. 14注参照。

**47-48. the extremest point / Of mortal breathing**　「死（この世で生きている
最後の瞬間）」（*OED*, extreme, *a.* 3; point, *n.*¹ 24a）。⇒ 2. 2. 72注。

167

And never brandish more revengeful steel                        50
Over the glittering helmet of my foe.

*[Takes up gage]*

**ANOTHER LORD**    I task the earth to the like, forsworn Aumerle,
And spur thee on with full as many lies
As may be hollowed in thy treacherous ear
From sun to sun. There is my honour's pawn.                     55

*[Throws down his gage]*

Engage it to the trial if thou dar'st.
**AUMERLE**    Who sets me else? By heaven, I'll throw at all.

*[Takes up gage]*

I have a thousand spirits in one breast
To answer twenty thousand such as you.
**SURREY**    My Lord Fitzwater, I do remember well               60
The very time Aumerle and you did talk.
**FITZWATER**    'Tis very true. You were in presence then,
And you can witness with me this is true.
**SURREY**    As false, by heaven, as heaven itself is true.
**FITZWATER**    Surrey, thou liest.
**SURREY**                            Dishonourable boy,           65
That lie shall lie so heavy on my sword
That it shall render vengeance and revenge
Till thou the lie-giver and that lie do lie
In earth as quiet as thy father's skull,
In proof whereof there is my honour's pawn.                     70

*[Throws down his gage]*

Engage it to the trial if thou dar'st.
**FITZWATER**    How fondly dost thou spur a forward horse!

*[Takes up gage]*

**52-59. ANOTHER . . . you.**　F1 にない Qq のみの行。

**52. task the earth to the like**　「地面に同様の〔＝私の決闘のしるしを受けとめるという〕務めを課す」（*OED*, task, *v.* 2b)。

**53. lies**　「お前は嘘つきだという非難」（*OED*, lie, *n.*[1] 2b)。

**54. hollowed**　「叫ぶ」を意味する hollo の異形 hollow の過去分詞形。

**55. From sun to sun**　「日の出から日の入りまで」（*OED*, sun, *n.*[1] 5)。Qq: From sinne to sinne　Capell: From sun to sun

**56. Engage it to the trial**　「それを（受けとって）決闘の約束のしるしにしろ」。trial = trial by combat（*OED*, engage, *v.* 2; trial, *n.*[1] 1b)。

**57.　sets . . . throw**　「（金額）を賭ける」から派生した「（人）に決闘を申し入れる」（*OED*, set, *v.*[1] 14b)。set は次の文の「（骰子）を振る」の意の throw と縁語となっているが、そちらは手袋を投げて決闘を挑むことも含意しており、Forker はここでオーマールが 24. 1 につづいてもう一方の手袋を投げると考え、85.1 で手袋を借りる根拠としている。

**62. ’Tis**　Qq: Tis　F1: My Lord, / ’Tis

**66. That lie shall lie so heavy on my sword**　「その嘘つきという非難（lie）をわが剣に重くのしかから（lie）せよう」。　⇒ 53 注参照。

**68-69. thou the lie-giver and that lie do lie / In earth**　「おれを嘘つきだと言うお前（thou lie-giver）とその嘘だとの非難（that lie）が地中に横たわる（lie)」。　⇒ 53 注参照。

**70. my**　Q1, 4, 5: my　Q2, 3, F1: mine

**71. Engage it to the trial if thou dar’st**　56 の正確なくり返し。

If I dare eat or drink or breathe or live,
I dare meet Surrey in a wilderness
And spit upon him whilst I say he lies                    75
And lies and lies. There is my bond of faith
To tie thee to my strong correction.

*[Throws down his second gage]*

As I intend to thrive in this new world
Aumerle is guilty of my true appeal.
Besides, I heard the banished Norfolk say                 80
That thou, Aumerle, didst send two of thy men
To execute the noble Duke at Calais.
**AUMERLE**    Some honest Christian trust me with a gage.
That Norfolk lies here do I throw down this,
If he may be repealed to try his honour.                  85

*[Borrowing a gage, throws it down]*

**BOLINGBROKE**    These differences shall all rest under gage
Till Norfolk be repealed. Repealed he shall be
And, though mine enemy, restored again
To all his lands and signories. When he is returned,
Against Aumerle we will enforce his trial.               90
**CARLISLE**    That honourable day shall never be seen.
Many a time hath banished Norfolk fought
For Jesu Christ in glorious Christian field,
Streaming the ensign of the Christian cross
Against black pagans, Turks and Saracens,                95
And, toiled with works of war, retired himself
To Italy, and there at Venice gave
His body to that pleasant country's earth
And his pure soul unto his captain Christ,
Under whose colours he had fought so long.               100
**BOLINGBROKE**    Why, Bishop, is Norfolk dead?

**74. in** = even in

**76. my bond of faith** = gage   **my**   Q1 なし   Q2: the   Q3-5, F1: my

**78. this new world**   ボリンブルックが支配する新しい時代。

**85. repealed**   「～を追放先から呼びもどす」の過去分詞形。   ⇒ 2. 2. 49 注参照。

**85.1**〔*Borrowing a gage . . .*〕   ⇒ 57 注参照。

**86. These differences shall all rest under gage**   「この争いは決闘の挑戦がなされたままで預かりということにしておこう」（*OED*, difference, *n.* 3a; gage, *n.*[1] 1b)。

**89. he is**   Qq: he is   F1: he's

**91-100. That honourable day . . . so long.**   ⇒後注参照。

**90. we**   1. 1 でボリンブルックとモーブリーの決闘の申し入れをリチャードが裁いたのと同様に、劇後半がはじまるこの場面でフィッツウォーターとオーマールらの決闘の申し入れをボリンブルックが裁くが、彼はまだ国王となっていないこの時点で国王の用いる代名詞を使用しており、106 でもくり返す。

**91. never**   Qq: neuer   F1: ne'er

**100. colours**   「（通例複数形で）軍旗」（*OED*, colour, *n.* 7a)。

**CARLISLE**   As surely as I live, my lord.
**BOLINGBROKE**   Sweet peace conduct his sweet soul to the bosom
  Of good old Abraham. Lords appellants,
  Your differences shall all rest under gage                                    105
  Till we assign you to your days of trial.

*Enter York*

**YORK**   Great Duke of Lancaster, I come to thee
  From plume-plucked Richard, who with willing soul
  Adopts thee heir and his high sceptre yields
  To the possession of thy royal hand.                                    110
  Ascend his throne, descending now from him,
  And long live Henry, of that name the fourth!
**BOLINGBROKE**   In God's name I'll ascend the regal throne.
**CARLISLE**   Marry, God forbid!
  Worst in this royal presence may I speak,                                    115
  Yet best beseeming me to speak the truth.
  Would God that any in this noble presence
  Were enough noble to be upright judge
  Of noble Richard. Then true noblesse would
  Learn him forbearance from so foul a wrong.                                    120
  What subject can give sentence on his king,
  And who sits here that is not Richard's subject?
  Thieves are not judged but they are by to hear
  Although apparent guilt be seen in them,
  And shall the figure of God's majesty,                                    125
  His captain, steward, deputy, elect,
  Anointed, crownèd, planted many years,
  Be judged by subject and inferior breath,
  And he himself not present? O, forfend it, God,
  That in a Christian climate souls refined                                    130
  Should show so heinous, black, obscene a deed.
  I speak to subjects, and a subject speaks,

**102. surely**　Q1: surely　Q2-F1: sure

**103-04. to the bosom / Of good old Abraham**　「安らかな眠りに」。Luke, 16: 22 に由来する慣用表現（*OED*, bosom, *n.* 1b）。

**104. Lords appellants**　「（重罪や反逆罪の）上訴人の方々」（*OED*, appellant, *a.* 1a, *n.* 1）。　⇒1. 1. 34 注参照。

**106. we**　⇒90 注参照。

**106.1 *Enter York*** 　⇒後注参照。

**107. Great Duke of Lancaster**　ボリンブルックはここで劇中はじめて、父から引き継ぐはずで王に奪われたランカスター公爵という称号で呼ばれる。彼がそう呼ばれるもう一度の機会は、獄中のリチャードによる呪詛の言葉のなかの Henry of Lancaster（5. 5. 102）との呼びかけ。ちなみにこの劇はリチャードのゴーントにたいする Old John of Gaunt, time-honoured Lancaster（1. 1. 1）という呼びかけではじまる。

**108. plume-plucked**　「羽をむしられた、貶められた」（*OED*, plume, *n.* 6）。

**109. thee**　Q1: the　Q2-F1: thee

**111. Ascend his throne, descending now from him**　前場のリチャードの舞台上における動きによって示された、ボリンブルックとリチャードの運命の上昇と下降を端的に言い表す言葉。

**112. Henry, of that name the fourth**　Q1-3: Henry fourth of that name　Q4, 5: *Henrie*, fourth of that name　F1: *Henry*, of that Name the Fourth　F1 が韻律どおり。

**114-49. Marry . . . woe.**　⇒後注参照。

**114. God**　Qq: God　F1: Heauen

**117. Would God that**　「神が〜と思し召しますように」　⇒2. 2. 100 注参照。

**119. noblesse**　Q1: noblesse　Q2-F1: Noblenesse

**120. Learn**　「（人）に（こと）を教える」（*OED*, learn, *v.* 4c）。

**forbearance**　「差し控えること」（*OED*, forbearance, *n.* 1 の初出例）。

**123. but**　「〜することなしには」（*OED*, but, *conj.* 14）。

**126. deputy,**　Qq: deputy,　F1: Deputie

**129. forfend**　Qq: forfend　F1: forbid

**130. climate**　「地域」（*OED*, climate, *n.* †1†b）。

Stirred up by God thus boldly for his king.
My Lord of Herford here, whom you call king,
Is a foul traitor to proud Herford's king                          135
And if you crown him, let me prophesy
The blood of English shall manure the ground
And future ages groan for this foul act.
Peace shall go sleep with Turks and infidels
And in this seat of peace tumultuous wars                          140
Shall kin with kin and kind with kind confound.
Disorder, horror, fear and mutiny
Shall here inhabit, and this land be called
The field of Golgotha and dead men's skulls.
O, if you raise this house against this house,                     145
It will the woefullest division prove
That ever fell upon this cursèd earth.
Prevent it, resist it, let it not be so,
Lest child, child's children, cry against you woe.
NORTHUMBERLAND    Well have you argued, sir, and for your pains    150
Of capital treason we arrest you here.
My Lord of Westminster, be it your charge
To keep him safely till his day of trial.

[*Carlisle is taken into custody*]

May it please you, lords, to grant the commons' suit?
BOLINGBROKE    Fetch hither Richard, that in common view           155
He may surrender. So we shall proceed
Without suspicion.
YORK                        I will be his conduct.    *Exit* [*with officers*]
BOLINGBROKE    Lords, you that here are under our arrest,
Procure your sureties for your days of answer.
Little are we beholding to your love                                160
And little looked for at your helping hands.

**133. God** Qq: God F1: Heauen

**137. manure** 「（土地）を肥やす」（*OED*, manure, *v.* 3）。

**144. Golgotha and dead men's skulls** この言い換えは a place of dead mens skull（Mark, 15: 22）としている主教聖書にしたがうもの。欽定訳聖書では a place of skull となっている（Noble, 61-62）。キリストが十字架にかけられた土地の名 Golgotha は「頭蓋骨」を意味するヘブライ語のラテン語音訳。

**145. raise** Qq: raise F1: reare

**148. let** Q1: let Q2-F1: and let

**150. SP** Northumberland ⇒後注参照。

**151. Of capital treason** 「極刑に値する叛逆罪の咎で」同じ行の arrest にかかる副詞句（*OED*, capital, *a.* 2b）。

**154-317. May . . . fall** エリザベス朝に出版された Q1-3 になく、ジェイムズ朝になって出版された Q4 以降の四つ折本と F1 の本文にのみおさめられた部分。一般的には、エリザベス朝時代に出版検閲によって削除された部分に代わる部分がジェイムズ朝時代の再演時に増補されたとされる。　⇒解説 11 ページ参照。

**154. commons' request** この内容は 221-26 で明らかにされる。　⇒後注参照。

**commons'** Q4, 5: common F: Commons

**155. SP** Bolingbroke Q4 なし F1: *Bull.* Forker は、頭書きのない Q4 の読みは F1 とは違う上演台本に由来するか植字工による誤りのどちらかであると指摘している。

**155-57. Fetch . . . conduct.** F1 による行割り。Q4: . . . view / . . . suspition / . . . conduct. の 3 行に印刷。

**155. Fetch hither Richard** ボリンブルックのこの言葉は平民院の要求にしたがうことをうながすノーサンバーランドへの答えとなっているが、同時に王を裁きの場に立ちあわせることを求めるカーライルの主張に沿うものともなっている（Forker および 154 後注参照）。

**157. conduct** 「案内者」（*OED*, conduct, *n.*[1] †3）。

**158. Lords, you that here are under our arrest** オーマール、パーシーら決闘裁判の当事者たち。決闘裁判は国王が裁判官となって行われるもので、当事者たちはその管理下に置かれる。

**here are** Q4, 5: are here, are F1: here are

**159. sureties** 「保証人」（*OED*, surety, *n.* 7）。

**160. beholding** 「恩義をこうむっている（＝ beholden）」シェイクスピアには現在分詞と過去分詞の混同がしばしば見られる（*OED*, beholding, *ppl. a.*, †1; Abbott, §372）。

**161. looked** Q4, 5: looke F1: look'd Q4, 5 の現在形の読みでも意味は通じるが、F1 の過去形の読みのほうがボリンブルックの抜け目なさを感じさせる。

175

*Enter Richard and York [with officers bearing the crown and sceptre]*

**RICHARD**    Alack, why am I sent for to a king
  Before I have shook off the regal thoughts
  Wherewith I reigned? I hardly yet have learned
  To insinuate, flatter, bow and bend my knee.            165
  Give sorrow leave awhile to tutor me
  To this submission. Yet I well remember
  The favours of these men. Were they not mine?
  Did they not sometime cry 'All hail' to me?
  So Judas did to Christ, but He in twelve            170
  Found truth in all but one, I in twelve thousand none.
  God save the King! Will no man say 'Amen'?
  Am I both priest and clerk? Well then, Amen.
  God save the King although I be not he,
  And yet Amen if heaven do think him me.           175
  To do what service am I sent for hither?
**YORK**    To do that office of thine own good will
  Which tired majesty did make thee offer —
  The resignation of thy state and crown
  To Henry Bolingbroke.
**RICHARD**      [*to York*]   Give me the crown. [*Takes crown*]    180
  [*to Bolingbroke*]   Here, cousin, seize the crown. Here, cousin,
  On this side my hand and on that side yours.
  Now is this golden crown like a deep well
  That owes two buckets filling one another,
  The emptier ever dancing in the air,           185
  The other down, unseen and full of water.
  That bucket down and full of tears am I,
  Drinking my griefs, whilst you mount up on high.
**BOLINGBROKE**    I thought you had been willing to resign.
**RICHARD**    My crown I am, but still my griefs are mine.    190
  You may my glories and my state depose,

**165. knee.**　Q4, 5: limbes?　F1: Knee.

**166-70. Give . . . twelve**　F1による行割り。Q4は . . . submission: / . . . men, / . . . hayle / . . . twelue、で終わる4行。

**166. Give . . . leave . . . to**　「～が～することを許してくれ」(*OED*, leave, *n.*[1] 1a, c)。　**tutor**　Q4, 5: tutor F1: tuture

**168. favours**　「顔つき」(*OED*, favour, *n.* 9)。

**169. sometime**　Q4, 5: sometimes　F1: sometime

**170. So Judas did to Christ**　⇒後注参照。

**171. Found . . . none**　1行12音節のアレクサンダー格の詩行。Forker は、そのことが12と12,000という対比を強調していること、one と none という同一行内の韻が見られること、次の行から数カ所に渡ってリチャードの台詞に押韻二行連句が見られることをあげて、この場面におけるリチャードの台詞の詩的強度が他の登場人物の台詞と比べて際立っていることを指摘している。押韻二行連句となっているのは、172-75、187-88、191-92、195-98（ボリンブルックの台詞も含めて187-98）、200-01、213-20。リチャードの台詞の詩的技巧としては206-14の首句反復もあげられる（⇒l. 206-14注参照）。

**173. priest and clerk**　英国国教会の典礼における司式者（priest = officiant）と助手（clerk = server）(*OED*, priest, *n.* 4b; clerk, *n.* 2b)。司式者が祈祷し、助手は「アーメン」と受ける。To play (be) both PRIEST and clerk は諺的表現 (Dent, P587.1)。

**178. tired majesty**　「王位にあって疲れはてていること」。

**180. Henry**　Q4, 5: Harry　F1: Henry

**180-82. Give . . . yours.**　Wells による行割り。Q4, 5は Sease the Crowne Heer Coosin, on this side my hand, and on that side yours: の2行。F1は Giue me the Crown. Here Cousin, seize y[e] Crown / Here Cousin, on this side my Hand, on that side thine. の2行で、下に示す異同がある。

**180-81. Give me the crown / Here, cousin**　Q4, 5なし　F: Giue me the Crown. Here Cousin,

**182. and**　Q4, 5: and F なし　**yours**　Q4, 5: yours F1: thine

**183-88. Now . . . high.**　リチャードは、王冠の受け渡しを行う自身とボリンブルックの状況を、井戸の、1本の綱の両端にあるふたつの桶で水の入れ換えを行って、空になったほうが宙に舞い、水の入ったほうが下降するさまにたとえることによって、ここでも高低の主題を導入する。前場の庭師による天秤ばかりの比喩では多くの味方をもつボリンブルックが重みでさがる側であったが、こちらでは悲しみに沈むリチャードが涙の重みでさがる側となっている。⇒3. 4. 84-89注参照。

**184. owes** = has　**188. griefs**　Q4, 5: griefe　F1: Griefes

**190. My crown I am** = My crown I am willing to resign

But not my griefs. Still am I king of those.

**BOLINGBROKE**     Part of your cares you give me with your crown.

**RICHARD**     Your cares set up do not pluck my cares down.

My care is loss of care, by old care done.         195

Your care is gain of care, by new care won.

The cares I give I have, though given away.

They tend the crown, yet still with me they stay.

**BOLINGBROKE**     Are you contented to resign the crown?

**RICHARD**     Ay, no — no, ay, for I must nothing be.       200

Therefore, no 'no', for I resign to thee.

Now mark me how I will undo myself.

I give this heavy weight from off my head,

[*Gives crown to Bolingbroke*]

And this unwieldy sceptre from my hand,

[*Takes up sceptre and give it to Bolingbroke*]

The pride of kingly sway from out my heart.       205

With mine own tears I wash away my balm;

With mine own hands I give away my crown;

With mine own tongue deny my sacred state;

With mine own breath release all duteous oaths.

All pomp and majesty I do forswear;           210

My manors, rents, revenues I forgo;

My acts, decrees and statutes I deny.

God pardon all oaths that are broke to me;

God keep all vows unbroke are made to thee.

Make me, that nothing have, with nothing grieved,    215

And thou with all pleased, that hast all achieved.

Long mayst thou live in Richard's seat to sit,

And soon lie Richard in an earthly pit.

'God save King Henry', unkinged Richard says,

'And send him many years of sunshine days.'      220

**194-97. Your . . . away** 「あなたに責任（care）が生じたからと言って私の責任（care）が減るわけではない。私の悲しみ（care）は気遣うもの（care）を失ったことである、たとえそのための気遣い（care）で消耗しているとしても。あなたの心配（care）は気遣うもの（care）をえたことである、たとえそれが慎重（care）に手に入れたばかりのものであっても。こうして私は気遣うもの（cares）を譲りわたしても、その代わりに悲しみ（cares）をえることとなった」（*OED*, care, *n.*[1] 4, 1, 5, 3, 2）。

**194. set up** 「〜を生じさせる、確立する」の過去分詞形（*OED*, set, *v.*[1] 154z）。この過去分詞の用法については 3. 3. 40-41 注を参照。

**pluck . . . down** 「〜を弱める、減じる」（*OED*, pluck, *v.* 3†b）シェイクスピアはこのふたつの熟語動詞を使って次のような一節も書いている。this great work ― / Which is almost to pluck a kingdom down / And set another up（*2H4*, 1. 3. 48-50） **200-20. Ay . . . days.** ⇒後注参照。

**200. Ay, no ― no, ay** 肯定と否定をくり返すこの答えは、ay を I と綴っている Q4, 5, F1 の本文から ay に I をかけた言葉遊びであることがわかる。「〔王位を委譲する気が〕ある」が「ない」に変わる（Ay, no）のは「私はいないも同然（I, no）」だからで、その理由が直後の「というのも〔王位を委譲した〕私はなんでもないものに違いないから」によって説明される。次に「ない」が「ある」に変わる（no, ay）のも同様に「ないというのは私と同じ（no, I）」だからで、そのため「だから『ない』などということはないのだ。私は王位を譲る」（201）ということになる。Q4, 5: I, no no I　F1: I, no; no, I:

**201. no 'no'** Q4: no no　F1: no, no　引用符の付加は Wilson による校訂。

**204. unwieldy** 「（大きく重いために）扱いづらい」（*OED*, unwieldy, *a.* 3b）。

**205. pride** 「物々しい装飾」（*OED*, pride, *n.*[1] 7）。

**206-14. With mine own . . . thee** 206-09 で With mine own、211-12 で My、213-14 で God と、行のはじまりで同一語句をくり返す首句反復（anaphora）という修辞技法が用いられている。さらにこの部分の最後の 2 行（213-14）から台詞の終わり（220）まで押韻二行連句がつづく。

**206. With . . . balm** リチャードは 3. 2. 54-55 で「荒海のすべての水をもってしても聖別された王の聖油を洗い流すことはできない」と言っている。

**209. release all duteous oaths** = release my subjects from all the oaths of allegience which they dutifully swore to me (Forker)

**duteous oaths** Q4, 5: duties rites　F1: dutious Oathes

**214. are** = that are（関係代名詞主格の省略）

**are made** Q4, 5: that sweare　F1: are made

**218. earthly** Q4, F1: earthy　Q5: earthly　**pit** 「墓穴」（*OED*, pit, *n.*[1] 3）。

**219. Henry** Q4, 5: Harry　F1: Henry

**unkinged** 「王位を奪われた」（*OED*, unkinged, *ppl. a.*[1]）の初出例。

What more remains?

*[Northumberland gives a paper to King Richard]*

**NORTHUMBERLAND**     No more, but that you read
These accusations and these grievous crimes
Committed by your person and your followers
Against the state and profit of this land,
That by confessing them the souls of men                      225
May deem that you are worthily deposed.
**RICHARD**     Must I do so? And must I ravel out
My weaved-up follies? Gentle Northumberland,
If thy offences were upon record,
Would it not shame thee in so fair a troop                    230
To read a lecture of them? If thou wouldst,
There shouldst thou find one heinous article
Containing the deposing of a king
And cracking the strong warrant of an oath,
Marked with a blot, damned in the book of heaven.            235
Nay, all of you that stand and look upon me
Whilst that my wretchedness doth bait myself,
Though some of you with Pilate wash your hands,
Showing an outward pity, yet you Pilates
Have here delivered me to my sour cross                       240
And water cannot wash away your sin.
**NORTHUMBERLAND**     My lord, dispatch. Read o'er these articles.

*[Presents the paper again]*

**RICHARD**     Mine eyes are full of tears; I cannot see.
And yet salt water blinds them not so much
But they can see a sort of traitors here.                     245
Nay, if I turn mine eyes upon myself,
I find myself a traitor with the rest,
For I have given here my soul's consent

**221-26. No more . . . deposed**　ノーサンバーランドが平民院の要求に応じるか
と尋ねたのにたいしてボリンブルックがリチャードを召喚し（154-57）、召喚
されたリチャードにたいしてノーサンバーランドが要求するのがこのことであ
るため、この劇では平民院の要求の内容は、リチャードが書面にされた自身の
罪状を読みあげて認めることとなっている。⇒ 4. 1. 154 後注参照。

**227. ravel out**　「～を明らかにする」（*OED*, ravel, *v.*¹ 7c の初出例）。文字どお
りの意味は「（撚りあわされたもの、織られたもの）を解きほぐす」（ravel, *v.*¹
6a）。

**228. weaved-up**　比喩的には「～たくらむ、作りあげる」、文字どおりの意味は
「～を織りあげる」（*OED*, weave, *v.*¹ 1e, 1）の過去分詞形。前行 ravel out の
対義語。

**follies**　Q4, 5: Folly　F1: follyes

**230. troop**　「大勢の人たち」（*OED*, troop, *n.* 1d）。

**231. lecture**　「読むこと」（*OED*, lecture, *n.* 1）。　read の同族目的語となって
いる。

**234. cracking**　「（約束、誓いなど）をやぶる」（*OED*, crack, *v.* 12）の動名詞
形。

**235. book of heaven**　Dawson & Yachnin は、1. 3. 201 でモーブリーが言及
する book of life のことである可能性を指摘している。Shaheen はここを主
教聖書の I will not blot out his name out of the book of life（Rev., 3: 5）の
反響とみなしている。

**236. all**　Q4, 5 なし　F1: all

**me**　Q4, 5 なし　F1: me

**237. Whilst that**　⇒ 2. 1. 125 注参照。

**bait**　「～に襲いかかる、責めさいなむ」（*OED*, bait, *v.*¹ 4）。「（犬が獲物）に
襲いかかる」という意味の動詞の比喩的用法。

**238-41. Though . . . sin**　リチャードは Mat., 27: 24-26 に基づいて自身をキリ
ストに、周囲のものたちをピラトにたとえている。wash your hands（238）
と wash away your sin（241）については 3. 1. 5-6 注を参照せよ。

**245. sort**　「一団」（*OED*, sort, *n.*² †17a）。

T'undeck the pompous body of a king,
Made glory base and sovereignty a slave,                    250
Proud majesty a subject, state a peasant.

NORTHUMBERLAND    My lord —

RICHARD    No lord of thine, thou haught insulting man,
Nor no man's lord. I have no name, no title —
No, not that name was given me at the font,                 255
But 'tis usurp'd. Alack the heavy day
That I have worn so many winters out
And know not now what name to call myself.
O that I were a mockery king of snow
Standing before the sun of Bolingbroke                      260
To melt myself away in water-drops.
Good King, great King, and yet not greatly good,
And if my word be sterling yet in England,
Let it command a mirror hither straight
That it may show me what a face I have                      265
Since it is bankrupt of his majesty.

BOLINGBROKE    Go some of you and fetch a looking-glass.

                                        [*Exit an attendant*]

NORTHUMBERLAND    Read o'er this paper while the glass doth come.

                    [*Presents the paper again*]

RICHARD    Fiend, thou torments me ere I come to hell.

BOLINGBROKE    Urge it no more, my Lord Northumberland.    270

NORTHUMBERLAND    The commons will not then be satisfied.

RICHARD    They shall be satisfied. I'll read enough
When I do see the very book indeed
Where all my sins are writ, and that's myself.

                    *Enter one with a glass*

Give me that glass and therein will I read.                 275

**249. T'undeck**　Q4, 5: To vndecke　F: T'vndeck

**250. and**　Q4, 5: and　F1: a

**251. state**　「高い地位」。⇒ 3. 2. 72 注参照。

**253. haught**　（古）「傲慢な（= haughty）」（*OED*, haught, *a.* 1）。

**254. Nor**　Q4, 5: Nor　F1: No, nor

**255. not that name was given me at the font**　「洗礼式で与えられ名前をもっ
ていない」つまり王の称号だけでなく、リチャードという名も失ったというこ
と。

　**was** = that was　関係代名詞主格の省略。　⇒ 1. 1. 50 注参照。

　**font**　「洗礼盤」（*OED*, font, *n.*[1] 1）。

**256. 'tis usurp'd**　フロワッサールの年代記や *Traison* に記されている、ボリン
ブルック支持者のあいだで流された、リチャードが王家の正嫡子ではなくボル
ドーの聖職者の庶子でジョンと名づけられたとする噂への言及である可能性が
指摘されている（Black）。その場合にはリチャードが権利のないリチャード
という名（と王という地位）を占有しているということになる。この噂への言
及可能性を考えなければ、王位を奪われたことによって自分の名前も奪われ
た、という誇張表現ということになる（Forker）。

**259. mockery**　「まがいものの」名詞の限定的（形容詞的）用法（*OED*,
mockery, *n.* 4）。

　**mockery king**　Q4: mockerie King　F1: Mockerie, King

**263. word**　Q4, 5: name　F1: word

　**sterling**　（廃）「（通貨以外のものについて）通用する」（*OED*, sterling, *a.*
2†c）。

**264. straight**　「ただちに」⇒ 2. 1. 215 注参照。

**275-79. Give . . . prosperity**　F1 にしたがった読み、行割り。Q4 は . . . yet? /
. . . this / . . . woundes? / . . . prosperitie! で終わる 4 行で下に示す異同があ
る。

**275. that**　Q4, 5: the　F1: that

　**and therein will I read**　Q4, 5 なし　F1: and therein will I reade

[*Takes the glass and looks in it*]

No deeper wrinkles yet? Hath sorrow struck
So many blows upon this face of mine
And made no deeper wounds? O flatt'ring glass,
Like to my followers in prosperity
Thou dost beguile me. Was this face the face                    280
That every day under his household roof
Did keep ten thousand men? Was this the face
That like the sun did make beholders wink?
Is this the face that faced so many follies,
That was at last outfaced by Bolingbroke?                       285
A brittle glory shineth in this face,
As brittle as the glory is the face,

[*Throws down the glass*]

For there it is cracked in a hundred shivers.
Mark, silent King, the moral of this sport:
How soon my sorrow hath destroyed my face.                      290
**BOLINGBROKE**    The shadow of your sorrow hath destroyed
The shadow of your face.
**RICHARD**                     Say that again.
The shadow of my sorrow? Ha, let's see.
'Tis very true, my grief lies all within
And these external manners of laments                           295
Are merely shadows to the unseen grief
That swells with silence in the tortured soul.
There lies the substance, and I thank thee, King,
For thy great bounty, that not only givest
Me cause to wail but teachest me the way                        300
How to lament the cause. I'll beg one boon
And then be gone and trouble you no more.
Shall I obtain it?

**278. flatt'ring**　Q4, 5: flattering　F1: flatt'ring

**280-82. Thou . . . men?**　は F1 にしたがった読み、行割り。Q4 は . . . vnder his / . . . men? で終わる 2 行で下に示す欠落と相違がある。

**280-87. Was this . . . is the face**　この部分の修辞技巧と押韻については解説 15-16 ページを参照せよ。

**280. Thou dost beguile me.**　Q4, 5 なし　F1: Thou do'st beguile me.

**face the face**　Q4, 5: face　F1: Face, the Face

**282. ten thousand men**　⇒後注参照。

**282-83. Was this the face / That like the sun did make beholders wink?**　Q4, 5 なし　F1: Was this the Face, / That like the Sunne, did make beholders winke?

**283. wink**　「目をつむる」（*OED*, wink, *v.*¹ †1a）。

**284. Is**　Q4, 5: Was　F1: Is

**that**　Q4, 5: that　F1: which

**284-85. that . . . That**　ともに先行詞は the face (284)。

**That**　Q4, 5: And　F1: That

**outfaced**　「～を顔色なからしめる」（*OED*, outface, *v.* 1）の過去分詞形。

**286. brittle**　「壊れやすい、束の間の」（*OED*, brittle, *a.* 3）。

**288. shivers**　「破片」（*OED*, shiver, *n.*¹ 1）。

**289. sport**　「芝居」（*OED*, sport, *n.*¹ 5†d の最後の用例）。リチャードは自身の演じている愁嘆場を芝居にたとえている。

**291-92. shadow . . . shadow**　「実体とかけ離れた姿…鏡に映った像」（*OED*, shadow, *n.* 6a, 5a）。ボリンブルックは、リチャードが悲しみをよそおっていると考えている。

**292-99. Say . . . givest**　は F にしたがった読み。Q4, 5 は各行の行末が . . . face. / . . . sorrow; / . . . my griefe / . . . manners / . . . vnseene, / sorrow: . . . giuest で終わる 7 行で下に示す相違と欠落がある。

**295. manners**　Q4, 5: manners　F1: manner

**298. There lies the substance,**　Q4, 5 なし　F1: There lyes the substance:

**There** ＝ in the soul

**299. For thy great bounty,**　Q4, 5 なし　F1: For thy great bountie,

**303. Shall I obtain it?**　Q4, 5 なし　F1: Shall I obtaine it?

**BOLINGBROKE**     Name it, fair cousin.

**RICHARD**    Fair cousin? I am greater than a king,

  For when I was a king, my flatterers                                        305

  Were then but subjects; being now a subject

  I have a king here to my flatterer.

  Being so great I have no need to beg.

**BOLINGBROKE**    Yet ask.

**RICHARD**    And shall I have?                                              310

**BOLINGBROKE**    You shall.

**RICHARD**    Then give me leave to go.

**BOLINGBROKE**    Whither?

**RICHARD**    Whither you will, so I were from your sights.

**BOLINGBROKE**    Go some of you convey him to the Tower.            315

**RICHARD**    O, good — 'convey'. Conveyers are you all,

  That rise thus nimbly by a true king's fall.

>                          [*Exit Richard under guard*]

**BOLINGBROKE**    On Wednesday next we solemnly set down

  Our coronation: lords, prepare yourselves.

>                *Exeunt. Manent Carlisle, Westminster and Aumerle*

**WESTMINSTER**    A woeful pageant have we here beheld.               320

**CARLISLE**    The woe's to come. The children yet unborn

  Shall feel this day as sharp to them as thorn.

**AUMERLE**    You holy clergymen, is there no plot

  To rid the realm of this pernicious blot?

**WESTMINSTER**    My lord,                                                    325

  Before I freely speak my mind herein,

  You shall not only take the sacrament

  To bury mine intents, but also to effect

  Whatever I shall happen to devise.

  I see your brows are full of discontent,                                     330

  Your hearts of sorrow and your eyes of tears.

  Come home with me to supper. I'll lay

  A plot shall show us all a merry day.                          *Exeunt*

**303-04. cousin . . . cousin** 第1幕では王がボリンブルックに cousin と呼びか
け、決闘のとき最贔にならないようにそう呼ぶのを差し控えるが、ここではい
まや王となったボリンブルックが同じ呼びかけをするとリチャードが色をな
す。 ⇒ 1. 1. 186 注参照。　**cousin?** Q4, 5: Coose, why?　F1: Cousin?

**304-08. I . . . beg** 王であるときは追従するのは臣下たちだけだったが、臣下
となったいまや王に追従され、王であったときよりも偉くなったとリチャード
が自嘲するこの件は、死に瀕したゴーントが、やせ衰えた自身についてその名
にかけて自虐的なことを言うのは、追従者たちにたぶらかされて死んだも同然
の王に追従するためだと言った劇序盤の件（2. 1. 84-91）を思いおこさせる。
追従者たちによって王位を失うにいたったリチャードが、そうした自身の愚行
に気づかないでいたことにたいする皮肉が感じとれる。

　**RICHARD . . . beg.** は F1 にしたがった行割り。Q4, 5 は . . . but subiects, /
. . . heere / . . . beg で終わる3行となっている。

**307. to** = as, for（*OED*, to, *prep.* 11b）。

**316. 'convey'** リチャードは、前行でボリンブルックが通常の「護送する」と
いう意味で使った語を、「盗む」の婉曲表現（*OED*, convey, *v.* 6b）のような
悪い意味を意識させるようにくり返している。

**317. That . . . fall** ここにも上昇と下降の主題が見られる。リチャードは自分
を護送しようと立ちあがったものを王位につくボリンブルックと重ねあわせ
て、王位を失って墜落した自身と対比している。

**318-19. On Wednesday . . . yourselves.** Q1-3: Let it be so, and loe on
wednesday next, / We solemnly proclaime our Coronation, / Lords be
ready all.　Q4-F1: On Wednesday next, we solemnly set downe / Our
Coronation: Lords, prepare your selues.　Q1 では直前のカーライル逮捕
（150-53）にたいする反応（Let it be so）からはじまっていた台詞が、Q4, F
では、154-317 におけるリチャードの愁嘆場とロンドン塔への護送につづく台
詞となり、カーライルの逮捕にたいする反応の部分がなくなっている一方、直
前にくるリチャードの退場にたいする反応も含まない台詞となっている。　⇒
後注参照。

**318. On . . . set down** 「～の予定を（特定の日時に）に定める」（*OED*, set,
143e (d) の初出例）。

**320. pageant** 語の本来的な意味は中世の聖史劇を演じた移動式舞台であるが、
広く「芝居の一場面」を指すような意味で使われた（*OED*, pageant, *n.* 1）。
Q1-3 ではリチャード廃位とボリンブルック擁立、カーライルの逮捕などの一
連の出来事を指し、Q4 と F1 ではリチャードの愁嘆場を指す。

**327. take the sacrament** 「（誓いをたてるために）聖餐を授かる」。

[ACT V, SCENE I]

*Enter Queen with Ladies*

QUEEN   This way the King will come. This is the way
   To Julius Caesar's ill-erected tower,
   To whose flint bosom my condemnèd lord
   Is doomed a prisoner by proud Bolingbroke.
   Here let us rest, if this rebellious earth     5
   Have any resting for her true king's queen.

*Enter Richard and [a] guard*

   But soft, but see, or rather do not see
   My fair rose wither. Yet look up, behold,
   That you in pity may dissolve to dew
   And wash him fresh again with true-love tears.    10
   Ah thou, the model where old Troy did stand,
   Thou map of honour, thou King Richard's tomb,
   And not King Richard! Thou most beauteous inn,
   Why should hard-favoured Grief be lodged in thee
   When Triumph is become an alehouse guest?    15
RICHARD   Join not with Grief, fair woman, do not so
   To make my end too sudden. Learn, good soul,
   To think our former state a happy dream,
   From which awaked, the truth of what we are
   Shows us but this. I am sworn brother, sweet,    20
   To grim Necessity, and he and I
   Will keep a league till death. Hie thee to France
   And cloister thee in some religious house.
   Our holy lives must win a new world's crown,
   Which our profane hours here have thrown down.    25
QUEEN   What, is my Richard both in shape and mind
   Transformed and weakened? Hath Bolingbroke
   Deposed thine intellect? Hath he been in thy heart?

〔**5. 1**〕あらすじ……………………………………………………………………

　リチャードと王妃の別れの場面。運命を受け容れ、フランスへの帰国を勧める
リチャードの変容を王妃は悲しむ。ノーサンバーランドが登場し、ボリンブルッ
クが心を変えてリチャードを北方のポンフレット城に送り、王妃はフランスに帰
されることになったと告げる。リチャードはノーサンバーランドに、王となった
ボリンブルックが、即位の手助けをした彼を警戒することになると警告するも、
彼は意に介さず、リチャードは悲しむ妃をなだめて別れを告げる。

……………………………………………………………………………………………

**2. Julius . . . tower**　ロンドン塔はウィリアム征服王によって建てられたもので
あるが、ストウによればユリウス・カエサルが建てたとするのが「一般的な考
え方」であったという（John Stow, *A Survey of London* [1598], D3ᵛ）。
　**ill-erected**　「建てられた目的と結果がよくない」の意でその悪い結果のなか
にはリチャードが拘禁されることも含まれる（Forker）。

**3. flint bosom**　「石造りの建物の内部」（*OED*, flint, *n.* 8a; bosom, *n.* 4）。
⇒5. 5. 20参照。　　　**7. soft**　「静かに、待て」（*OED*, soft, *adv.* 8）。

**8. My fair rose**　薔薇は存在の大いなる連鎖のなかで植物の最上位を占め、王
を表すのに用いられた。

**11. the . . . stand**　「（城壁だけが残る）トロイのあった場所さながらのもの」。
　**model**　「設計図」（*OED*, model, *n.* †1）。実体を失った廃墟を表す比喩。

**12. map of honour**　map は17世紀の用法では通例「（美徳や性質などの）体
現者」（*OED*, map, *n.*¹ 2†b）という意味で、外見が内面を映しだしているこ
とを強調する語だが、前後の文脈から判断して、ここでは外見と内面が一致し
ない「見かけだけ名誉高く見えるもの」を意味していると思われる。

**13-15. Thou . . . guest?**　悲しみに沈むリチャードと勝利の祝い（*OED*,
triumph, *n.* †4）の歓びにひたるボリンブルックをそれぞれ「美しい邸」
（*OED*, inn, *n.* †1）と「居酒屋」にたとえ、それぞれの感情がそれらの建物
に不似合いな客として訪れている、とする隠喩が用いられている。

**14. hard-favoured**　「人相の悪い」（*OED*, hard-favoured, *a.*）。

**19. truth**　「実体」（*OED*, truth, *n.* 7）。

**20. sworn brother**　本来の意味は「（互いに運命をともにすると誓いを立てた騎
士道上の）義兄弟」、転じて「（互いに裏切らない）親友」（*OED*, sworn, *ppl.
a.* 1）。　　　**21. Necessity**　「困窮」　⇒1. 3. 276-77注参照。

**22. Hie thee** ＝ Hie thyself　⇒2. 3. 8注参照。

**23. cloister thee** ＝ cloister thyself「修道院に入れ」（*OED*, cloister, *v.* 1）。
⇒前注参照。　　　**25. thrown**　Qq: throwne　F1: stricken　Forker は、F1
の stricken がここに2音節が必要であることを示すものとみなし、しばしば
throwen と綴られた thrown を2音節と考えている。

**28. Deposed**　「（性質、感情など）を取りさる」（*OED*, depose, *v.* †2）。

The lion dying thrusteth forth his paw
And wounds the earth if nothing else with rage          30
To be o'erpowered, and wilt thou pupil-like
Take the correction mildly, kiss the rod
And fawn on rage with base humility,
Which art a lion and the king of beasts?
RICHARD    A king of beasts, indeed. If aught but beasts     35
    I had been still a happy king of men.
    Good sometimes Queen, prepare thee hence for France.
    Think I am dead and that even here thou takest
    As from my deathbed thy last living leave.
    In winter's tedious nights sit by the fire          40
    With good old folks and let them tell thee tales
    Of woeful ages long ago betid.
    And ere thou bid good night, to quite their griefs,
    Tell thou the lamentable tale of me
    And send the hearers weeping to their beds.         45
    For why the senseless brands will sympathize
    The heavy accent of thy moving tongue
    And in compassion weep the fire out,
    And some will mourn in ashes, some coal-black,
    For the deposing of a rightful king.               50

*Enter Northumberland*

NORTHUMBERLAND    My lord, the mind of Bolingbroke is changed.
    You must to Pomfret, not unto the Tower.
    And, madam, there is order ta'en for you.
    With all swift speed you must away to France.
RICHARD    Northumberland, thou ladder wherewithal          55
    The mounting Bolingbroke ascends my throne,
    The time shall not be many hours of age
    More than it is ere foul sin gathering head
    Shall break into corruption. Thou shalt think

**32. Take** 「(仕打ちなど)を甘受する」(*OED*, take, *v.* 34b)。

　**the correction** Q1: the correction　Q2-F1: thy Correction

　**correction mildly,**　Qq: correction, mildly　F1: Correction mildly

**34. the**　Q1: the　Q2-F1: a

**36. I had been** ＝ I would have been　⇒ 1. 3. 194 注参照。

**37. sometimes**　⇒ 1. 2. 54 注参照。Q1-2: sometimes　Q3-F1: sometime

　**hence** ＝ to go hence　⇒ 1. 2. 56 注参照。

**39. thy**　Q1: thy　Q2-F1: my

**41. thee**　Q1: the　Q2-F1: thee

**42. woeful ages long ago betid**　「ずっと前にあった悲しいとき」ages のあと
に主格の関係代名詞が省略されており、betid は「(出来事など)が起こる」
(*OED*, betide, *v.* 1)の過去形。　**betid**　Q1: betidde　Q2-F1: betide　Q1
の綴りは betide の過去形 betid の異形。

**43. quite**　「(してもらったこと)に返礼する」(*OED*, quit, †quite, *v.* 11b)
　Qq: quite　F1: quit

　**griefs**　「悲しみのもと」(*OED*, grief, *n.* 7a)。tales / Of woeful ages (41-
42) のこと。　Q1: griefes　Q2-F1: griefe

**44. tale**　Qq: tale　F1: fall

**46. For why** ＝ for which reason 「その〔王妃が語る悲しい話の〕ために」関
係副詞としての用法 (*OED*, why, *adv.* 8b)。現代語的に言えば、from
whence の from と同様に for は重複的。Abbott, §75 参照。　**why:**　Qq:
why,　F1: why?

　**sympathize**　「〜に呼応する」(*OED*, sympathize, *v.* †3 の初出例)。

**47. heavy accent**　「悲しい話しぶり」(*OED*, heavy, *a.*[1] 25a; accent, *n.* 4)。
⇒ 2. 2. 3 注参照。

　**moving**　「心を動かす、憐れみを感じさせる」(*OED*, moving, *ppl. a.* 2c)。

**48. weep . . . out**　「泣いてその涙で(火)を消す」(*OED*, weep, *v.* 8c の初出例)。

**52. You must to Pomfret**　⇒ 1. 2. 56 注参照。

　**Pomfret**　ポンフレット。正式にはポンテフラクト (Pomtefract)、ヨークシ
ア州ウェスト・ライディングにある古い町。ノルマン人の征服のあとイルバー
ト・ド・レイシー (Ilbert de Lacy) によって建てられた城があり、リチャー
ド二世の幽閉と死の舞台となる (Sugden)。

**53. there is order ta'en**　「取りはからいがなされている」(*OED*, order, *n.* 14)。

**54. you must away to France**　⇒ 1. 2. 56 注参照。

**55. Northumberland, thou ladder**　この劇で多用される上下運動の比喩のひと
つ。

**58-59. gathering head / Shall break into corruption**　「(できもの)が腫れあ
がり破れて膿をながす」(*OED*, head, *n.* 14; corruption, *n.* 3)。

Though he divide the realm and give thee half          60
It is too little, helping him to all.
He shall think that thou, which knowest the way
To plant unrightful kings, wilt know again,
Being ne'er so little urged another way,
To pluck him headlong from the usurped throne.          65
The love of wicked men converts to fear,
That fear to hate and hate turns one or both
To worthy danger and deservèd death.
**NORTHUMBERLAND**  My guilt be on my head, and there an end.
Take leave and part, for you must part forthwith.          70
**RICHARD**  Doubly divorced! Bad men, you violate
A twofold marriage, 'twixt my crown and me
And then betwixt me and my married wife.
[*to Queen*]  Let me unkiss the oath 'twixt thee and me —
And yet not so, for with a kiss 'twas made.          75
[*to Northumberland*]  Part us, Northumberland: I towards
    the north,
Where shivering cold and sickness pines the clime;
My wife to France, from whence set forth in pomp
She came adornèd hither like sweet May,
Sent back like Hallowmas or short'st of day.          80
**QUEEN**  And must we be divided? Must we part?
**RICHARD**  Ay, hand from hand, my love, and heart from heart.
**QUEEN**  [*to Northumberland*]  Banish us both and send the
    King with me.
**NORTHUMBERLAND**  That were some love but little policy.
**QUEEN**  Then whither he goes, thither let me go.          85
**RICHARD**  [*to Queen*]  So two together weeping make one woe.
Weep thou for me in France, I for thee here.
Better far off than, near, be ne'er the near.
Go count thy way with sighs, I mine with groans.
**QUEEN**  So longest way shall have the longest moans.          90

**61. helping . . . to** 「(人) が～を (to) える手助けをする」(*OED*, help, *v.* 7)。現在分詞が使われているが文脈上完了の意味。

**63. plant** 「(人) をよくない目的で地位につける」(*OED*, plant, *v.* 2c)。

**unrightful** *OED* は「不正な」のような倫理的な意味のみをあげているが、Onions が指摘するように「正当な権利をもたない」という意味。

**know** = know how (*OED*, know, *v.* 12a)。

**again** 「もとの状態に、反対に」the way / To plant unrightful kings (62-63) にたいして To pluck him headlong from the usurped throne (65) が元にもどす行いであるということ。 ⇒3. 2. 137 注参照。

**64. Being ne'er so little urged** 「そそのかされることがどんなにわずかであっても」ne'er so は直後の副詞、形容詞と結びついて「いかに～であっても」(*OED*, never, *adv.* 4)。

**another way** 「今度は反対に」urged にかかる副詞句。

**66. men** Qq: men F: friends

**67. one or both** 「邪悪なふたり (wicked men)」(66) の「一方または双方」

**69. My guilt be on my head** Forker は、ここにキリストの処刑後責任を逃れようとするピラトにたいして民衆が答えた「その血の責任は、われわれとわれわれの子孫の上にかかってもよい (His blood be on us, and on our children)」(Matthew, 27: 25) の反響を聞きとり、この劇のキリスト＝リチャード、ピラト＝ボリンブルックという構図においてノーサンバーランドが皮肉にも知らずに損な立場に身を置いてしまっていることを指摘している。

**70. part . . . part** 「別れる…立ち去る」(*OED*, part, *v.* 6a, 7a)。

**71. divorced** 「(夫婦) を離婚させる」という意味とそれから派生した「(ふたつのもの) を分離する、引き離す」という比喩的な意味がある (*OED*, divroce, *v.* 1, 4)。　**you** Qq: you F1: ye

**74. unkisss** 「キスをして～をとり消す (= undo by a kiss)」(Onions)。

**76-78. I towards the north . . . My wife to France** ⇒1. 2. 56 注参照。

**77. pines the clime** 「その地域を痛めつける」(*OED*, pine, *v.* †1; clime, *n.* 2)。

**78. wife** Qq: wife F1: Queene

**set forth** 「飾りたてる」(*OED*, set, *v.*¹ 144g) の過去分詞形。

**79-102.** ⇒解説 p.16 参照。

**80. Hallowmas** 「諸聖人の祝日 (11 月 1 日 = All Saints' Day)」。

**short'st of day** シェイクスピアの時代では冬至は12 月 10 日だった。

**84. S.P. Northumberland** Qq: King.　F1: North.

**were** ⇒1. 3. 194 注参照。

**88. near . . . near** 「もっと近くにいても、それよりさらに〔会えるほど〕近くにはいない」near は nigh の比較級。

RICHARD    Twice for one step I'll groan, the way being short,
    And piece the way out with a heavy heart.
    Come, come, in wooing sorrow let's be brief,
    Since, wedding it, there is such length in grief.
    One kiss shall stop our mouths, and dumbly part.                95
    Thus give I mine and thus take I thy heart.

*[They kiss]*

QUEEN    Give me mine own again. 'Twere no good part
    To take on me to keep and kill thy heart.

*[They kiss again]*

    So now I have mine own again, be gone
    That I may strive to kill it with a groan.                    100
RICHARD    We make woe wanton with this fond delay.
    Once more, adieu. The rest let Sorrow say.          *Exeunt*

[ACT V, SCENE II]
*Enter Duke and Duchess of York*

DUCHESS    My lord, you told me you would tell the rest,
    When weeping made you break the story off,
    Of our two cousins' coming into London.
YORK    Where did I leave?
DUCHESS                        At that sad stop, my lord,
    Where rude misgoverned hands from windows' tops            5
    Threw dust and rubbish on King Richard's head.
YORK    Then, as I said, the Duke, great Bolingbroke,
    Mounted upon a hot and fiery steed,
    Which his aspiring rider seemed to know,
    With slow but stately pace kept on his course              10
    Whilst all tongues cried 'God save thee, Bolingbroke!'
    You would have thought the very windows spake,

**92. piece the way out**　「道筋（の長さ）を補う」（*OED*, piece, *v.* 7）。つまり、短い道筋を（悲しみ沈む心で歩くことで）より長く感じる、ということ。

**97. ’Twere**　⇒ 1. 3. 194 注参照。

　**part**　「振る舞い、行い」（*OED*, part, *n.* †11）。

〔**5. 2**〕あらすじ……………………………………………………………………

　市民たちがリチャードに冷たい眼差しを向けごみを投げつける一方、ボリンブルックにたいしては歓呼で迎えた、新王のロンドン入市の様子をヨークが妻に語っているところに、オーマールが帰宅。胸元からのぞいた手紙によって、オックスフォードでの槍試合のおりに王を暗殺するカーライルの陰謀に彼が加わっていたことが発覚する。ヨークはとめる妻を振りきって王に告げに出かけ、妻は息子に父親を追い越して先に王のもとに行って赦しを乞うよう命じ、自身もあとを追うことにする。

………………………………………………………………………………………

**2. off**　Q1: of　Q2-5 なし　F1: off

**5. misgoverned**　「抑制できない、手に負えない」（*OED*, misgoverned, *ppl. a.* †2 の初出例）。

**9. aspiring**　「野心に燃える」（*OED*, aspirng, *ppl. a.* 1）。

**11. Whilst**　Q1: Whilst　Q2-F1: While　　**thee**　Qq: the　F1: thee

So many greedy looks of young and old
Through casements darted their desiring eyes
Upon his visage, and that all the walls         15
With painted imagery had said at once
'Jesu preserve thee! Welcome, Bolingbroke!'
Whilst he, from the one side to the other turning,
Bare-headed, lower than his proud steed's neck,
Bespake them thus: 'I thank you, countrymen',    20
And thus still doing, thus he passed along.

DUCHESS    Alack, poor Richard! Where rode he the whilst?

YORK    As in a theatre the eyes of men,
After a well-graced actor leaves the stage,
Are idly bent on him that enters next,         25
Thinking his prattle to be tedious,
Even so, or with much more contempt, men's eyes
Did scowl on gentle Richard. No man cried 'God save him',
No joyful tongue gave him his welcome home,
But dust was thrown upon his sacred head,    30
Which with such gentle sorrow he shook off,
His face still combating with tears and smiles,
The badges of his grief and patience,
That had not God for some strong purpose steeled
The hearts of men, they must perforce have melted    35
And barbarism itself have pitied him.
But heaven hath a hand in these events,
To whose high will we bound our calm contents.
To Bolingbroke are we sworn subjects now,
Whose state and honour I for aye allow.    40

*Enter Aumerle*

DUCHESS    Here comes my son Aumerle.

YORK                                  Aumerle that was,
But that is lost for being Richard's friend,

**15. and that** thought（12）のふたつ目の目的節を導く。

**16. painted imagery** 「描かれた絵」建物の窓からのぞく人びとの顔を、建物の外壁にたらされた布に描かれた、吹き出しに発言の書かれた絵にたとえている。

**18. the one** Qq: the one F1: one

**21. still** ＝ always ⇒ 1. 1. 22 注参照。

**22. Alack** Qq: Alac F1: Alas　　**rode** Q1: rode Q2-F1: rides

**23-28. As ... Richard** Chambers は、16 世紀に誕生した大衆演劇へのこの言及が時代錯誤的であることを指摘している。⇒ 3. 4. 29 注、および 4. 1. 40 注参照。

**24. well-graced** 「魅力にあふれ」ているため「（観客たちから）贔屓にされる」（*OED*, graced, *ppl. a.* の初出例）。

**25. idly** 「熱意なく」（*OED*, idly, *adv.* 2）。

**28. scowl on** 「〜にしかめっ面をする」（*OED*, scowl, *v.* 1）。

　**gentle** Qq: gentle F1 なし

**33. badges** 「しるし」（*OED*, badge, *n.* 2a）。

**36. barbarism** ＝ the very savages (Verity) 提喩（synecdoche）の一種。

**38. To . . . contents** 「天の賢き思し召しに静かに満足することにしよう」。

　**bound** 「〜を枠内にとどめる」（*OED*, bound, *v.*¹ 1b）。

**40. allow** 「〜を称賛する」（*OED*, allow, *v.* 1）。

**41-43. Aumerle that was . . . now.** リチャードを支持したオーマールは、ボリンブルック即位とともに、オーマール公爵位を剥奪され、それ以前からのラトランド伯爵という称号で呼ばれるようになる（Holinshed, 3: 513）。

And, madam, you must call him Rutland now.
I am in Parliament pledge for his truth
And lasting fealty to the new-made King.                              45

**DUCHESS**  Welcome, my son. Who are the violets now
That strew the green lap of the new-come spring?

**AUMERLE**  Madam, I know not, nor I greatly care not.
God knows I had as lief be none as one.

**YORK**  Well, bear you well in this new spring of time              50
Lest you be cropped before you come to prime.
What news from Oxford? Do these jousts and triumphs hold?

**AUMERLE**  For aught I know, my lord, they do.

**YORK**  You will be there, I know.

**AUMERLE**  If God prevent it not, I purpose so.                     55

**YORK**  What seal is that that hangs without thy bosom?
Yea, lookst thou pale? Let me see the writing.

**AUMERLE**  My lord, 'tis nothing.

**YORK**                                  No matter then who see it.
I will be satisfied. Let me see the writing.

**AUMERLE**  I do beseech your grace to pardon me.                    60
It is a matter of small consequence,
Which for some reasons I would not have seen.

**YORK**  Which for some reasons, sir, I mean to see.
I fear, I fear —

**DUCHESS**           What should you fear?
'Tis nothing but some bond that he is entered into              65
For gay apparel 'gainst the triumph day.

**YORK**  Bound to himself? What doth he with a bond
That he is bound to? Wife, thou art a fool.
Boy, let me see the writing.

**AUMERLE**  I do beseech you, pardon me. I may not show it.        70

**YORK**  I will be satisfied. Let me see it, I say.

*He plucks it out of his bosom and reads it*

**44. pledge** 「保証人」（*OED*, pledge, *n.* 1）。

**truth** 「忠誠」（*OED*, truth, *n.* 1a）。 ⇒ 2. 2. 101 注参照。

**46. violets** 新王の寵臣をスミレの花にたとえている。

**47. strew** 「～の表面にまき散らされている」（*OED*, strew, *v.* 3）。

**49. I had as lief be none as one** 「そんなもの〔寵臣〕でないほうがましだ」（*OED*, lief, *adv.* 1d）。

**50. bear you** = bear yourself「振る舞う」（*OED*, bear, *v.*[1] 4）。 ⇒ 2. 3. 8 注参照。

**52. Do these jousts and triumphs hold?** Qq: do these iusts & triumphs hold? F1: Hold those Iusts & Triumphs?

**triumphs** 「（馬上槍試合＝ joust のような）盛大な祝祭」（*OED*, triumph, *n.* †4）。

**hold** 「開催される、行われる」（*OED*, hold, *v.* 26）。

**55. it** Qq, F1 なし Capell: it

**56. seal** 「印影（印章を蠟に押して帯状の羊皮紙で書状につけたもの）」（*OED*, seal, *n.*[2] 1）。

**58. see** Qq: see F1: sees

**59. I will be satisfied** 「納得のいく説明を聞きたい」（*OED*, satisfy, *v.* 7）。

**62. Which . . . I would not have seen** 「それを見られたくない」have は一般動詞。

**65. bond** Qq: band F1: bond

**66. 'gainst** Q1: gainst Q2-F1: against

**day** Q1: day Q2-F1 なし

**67. Bound to himself?** 借用書は債権者がもっているものなので、証文をオーマールがもっているとすれば、自分から借金したということなのか、との疑問。

Treason, foul treason! Villain, traitor, slave!

**DUCHESS**   What is the matter, my lord?

**YORK**   [*Calls offstage*]

Ho! Who is within there?

[*Enter Servingman*]

Saddle my horse.

God for His mercy, what treachery is here!                     75

**DUCHESS**   Why, what is it, my lord?

**YORK**   Give me my boots, I say. Saddle my horse.

[*Exit Servingman*]

Now by mine honour, by my life, by my troth

I will appeach the villain.

**DUCHESS**                     What is the matter?

**YORK**   Peace, foolish woman.                                80

**DUCHESS**   I will not peace. What is the matter, Aumerle?

**AUMERLE**   Good mother, be content. It is no more

Than my poor life must answer.

**DUCHESS**                     Thy life answer?

**YORK**   [*to Servingman offstage*]

Bring me my boots. I will unto the King.

*Servingman enters with his boots*

**DUCHESS**   Strike him, Aumerle. Poor boy, thou art amazed.     85

[*to Servingman*]

Hence, villain! Never more come in my sight!

**YORK**   Give me my boots, I say.

[*Servingman helps York put on his boots, then exit*]

**DUCHESS**                     Why, York, what wilt thou do?

Wilt thou not hide the trespass of thine own?

Have we more sons or are we like to have?

Is not my teeming date drunk up with time,                     90

**73. What is**　Qq: What is　F1: What's

**74. Who is**　Qq: who is　F1: who's

**75. God**　Qq: God　F1: Heauen

**76. is it**　Qq: is it　F1: is't

**78. by my life, by my troth**　Qq: by my life, by my troth　F1: my life, my troth,　Forker は、最初の by が二度くり返されているためにこの行が1音節多い行となる Qq の読みについて、韻律の乱れを、登場人物の感情の高ぶりを伝える技法と考えている。　　**troth**「忠誠」(*OED*, troth, *n*. 1)。

**79. appeach**「〜を訴える」(*OED*, †appeach, *v*. 2)。

**80. Peace**「黙れ、静かにしろ」(*OED*, peace, *v*. 1)。

**81. Aumerle**　Qq: Aumerle　F1: Sonne

**83. answer**「(罪)を償う」(*OED*, answer, *v*. 6)。

**85. amazed**「呆然としている、われを忘れている」(*OED*, amazed, *ppl. a.* †1)。

**88. thine own**「わが子、身内」(*OED*, own, *a*. 3)。

**90. teeming date**「妊娠可能な期間」(*OED*, teeming, *ppl. a.*[1] 1; date, *n.*[2] 2b)。

　　**drunk up**「尽きている」(「飲み尽くされた」の比喩的用法 *OED*, drink, *v*. 2a)。

And wilt thou pluck my fair son from mine age
And rob me of a happy mother's name?
Is he not like thee? Is he not thine own?

**YORK**   Thou fond mad woman,
Wilt thou conceal this dark conspiracy?                    95
A dozen of them here have ta'en the sacrament
And interchangeably set down their hands
To kill the King at Oxford.

**DUCHESS**                     He shall be none.
We'll keep him here. Then what is that to him?

**YORK**   Away, fond woman. Were he twenty times my son,    100
I would appeach him.

**DUCHESS**                  Hadst thou groaned for him
As I have done, thou wouldst be more pitiful.
But now I know thy mind. Thou dost suspect
That I have been disloyal to thy bed
And that he is a bastard, not thy son.                      105
Sweet York, sweet husband, be not of that mind.
He is as like thee as a man may be,
Not like to me or any of my kin,
And yet I love him.

**YORK**                  Make way, unruly woman.        *Exit*

**DUCHESS**   After, Aumerle. Mount thee upon his horse.     110
Spur post, and get before him to the King
And beg thy pardon ere he do accuse thee.
I'll not be long behind. Though I be old,
I doubt not but to ride as fast as York.
And never will I rise up from the ground                    115
Till Bolingbroke have pardoned thee. Away, be gone.  *Exeunt*


[ACT V, SCENE III]

*Enter Bolingbroke [as] King, Percy and other Lords*

**95. dark** 「邪悪な」（*OED*, dark, *a*. 4）。

**98-99. He . . . to him?** F1 にしたがった行割り。Qq は . . . heere / . . . him? で
終わる2行になっている。

**100-01. Away . . . appeach him.** Qq にしたがった行割り。F1 は . . . my / . . .
him. で終わる2行となっている。

**101-02. Hadst . . . done** Rowe にしたがった行割り。Qq、F1 は Hadst . . .
done で1行となっている。

**108. or** Qq: or F1: nor

**109. Make way** 「道を空けろ」（*OED*, way, *n*.¹ 6a, 25c）。

**110. After** 「あとを追いなさい」運動の動詞の省略。⇒ 1. 2. 56 注参照。

**111. post** 「（早馬のように）速く」（*OED*, post, *adv*. b）。

〔**5. 3**〕**あらすじ**‥‥‥‥‥‥‥‥‥‥‥‥‥‥‥‥‥‥‥‥‥‥‥‥‥‥‥‥‥‥‥

　ヘンリー四世王となったボリンブルックは酒場に入りびたり悪い仲間とつきあ
う息子の素行の悪さに頭を痛めている。そこへオーマールが訪れ、罪を告白する
という条件で赦しを乞い、部屋に鍵をかけて罪の告白をはじめようとしていると
ころへ父親ヨークが現れる。ヨークは、息子が加担している叛逆について話すと
言って扉を開けさせ、オーマールのもっていた手紙を新王に見せ、処罰を強く求
める。遅れて助命嘆願にやってきた夫人の登場で場面は一気に茶番へと変わる。
彼女の心からの、強引な言葉に気おされてボリンブルックはオーマールを赦すが、
その一方で、陰謀勢力の弾圧に乗り出す。

‥‥‥‥‥‥‥‥‥‥‥‥‥‥‥‥‥‥‥‥‥‥‥‥‥‥‥‥‥‥‥‥‥‥‥‥‥‥‥‥

**BOLINGBROKE**   Can no man tell me of my unthrifty son?
  'Tis full three months since I did see him last.
  If any plague hang over us, 'tis he.
  I would to God, my lords, he might be found.
  Inquire at London 'mongst the taverns there,                    5
  For there they say he daily doth frequent
  With unrestrainèd loose companions,
  Even such they say as stand in narrow lanes
  And beat our watch and rob our passengers,
  Which he, young wanton and effeminate boy,                    10
  Takes on the point of honour to support
  So dissolute a crew.
**PERCY**   My lord, some two days since I saw the Prince
  And told him of those triumphs held at Oxford.
**BOLINGBROKE**   And what said the gallant?                    15
**PERCY**   His answer was he would unto the stews
  And from the common'st creature pluck a glove
  And wear it as a favour, and with that
  He would unhorse the lustiest challenger.
**BOLINGBROKE**   As dissolute as desperate. Yet through both    20
  I see some sparks of better hope which elder years
  May happily bring forth.

*Enter Aumerle amazed*

But who comes here?
**AUMERLE**   Where is the King?
**BOLINGBROKE**   What means our cousin that he stares and
    looks so wildly?
**AUMERLE**   God save your grace. I do beseech your majesty    25
  To have some conference with your grace alone.
**BOLINGBROKE**   [*to Lords*]   Withdraw yourselves and leave us
    here alone.

                              [*Exeunt Percy and the other Lords*]

**1. me**　Qq: of　F1 なし

**unthrifty son**「浪費家の息子」*1H4, 2H4, H5* に登場するハル王子（のちのヘンリー五世）のこと。

**2. full**　「（数詞とともに用いて）丸々」（*OED*, full, *adv.* 2a）。

**4. God**　Qq: God　F1: heauen

**7. unrestrainèd**「無軌道な」（*OED*, unrestrained, *ppl. a.* 2）。

**loose**「勝手気ままな」（*OED*, loose, *a.* 1c）。

**9. beat . . . rob**　Qq: beate . . . rob　F1: rob . . . beate

**passengers**「通行人」（*OED*, passenger, *n.* 1b）。

**10. Which** = as to which　節のなかの文法的要素となっておらず、副詞的に用いられる which の用法（Abbot, §272 参照）。

**11. Takes on the point**　= undertakes as a point of（Black; *OED*, take, *v.* 17）

**14. those**　Qq: those　F1: these

**16. stews** = brothels（*OED*, stew, *n.*[2] 4a）

**19. unhorse**「〜を馬から引きずり下ろす」（*OED*, unhorse, *v.* 1）。

**21. years**　Qq: yeares　F1: dayes

**22. happily**「たぶん」と「好運なことに」（*OED*, happily, *adv.* 1, 2）。

**bring forth**「（結果）をもたらす」（*OED*, bring, *v.* 16a）。

**24. What means our cousin that he stares and / looks so wildly?**　Qq: What meanes our cosen, that he stares and lookes so wildly.　F1: What meanes our Cosin, that hee stares / And lookes so wildely?

**26. conference**「会話、話し合い」（*OED*, conference, *n.* 4a）。

What is the matter with our cousin now?

**AUMERLE**    For ever may my knees grow to the earth, [*Kneels*]

My tongue cleave to the roof within my mouth,           30

Unless a pardon ere I rise or speak.

**BOLINGBROKE**    Intended or committed was this fault?

If on the first, how heinous e'er it be,

To win thy after-love I pardon thee.

**AUMERLE**    Then give me leave that I may turn the key        35

That no man enter till my tale be done.

**BOLINGBROKE**    Have thy desire.

*[Aumerle locks the door]*

*The Duke of York knocks at the door and crieth*

**YORK**    [*Within*]    My liege, beware, look to thyself.

Thou hast a traitor in thy presence there.

**BOLINGBROKE**    [*to Aumerle*]

Villain, I'll make thee safe. [*Draws his sword*]        40

**AUMERLE**    Stay thy revengeful hand. Thou hast no cause to fear.

**YORK**    [*Within*]    Open the door, secure, foolhardy King.

Shall I for love speak treason to thy face?

Open the door or I will break it open.

*[Bolingbroke unlocks the door.] Enter York*

**BOLINGBROKE**    What is the matter, uncle? Speak,        45

Recover breath. Tell us how near is danger

That we may arm us to encounter it.

**YORK**    Peruse this writing here, and thou shalt know

The treason that my haste forbids me show.

*[Presents the paper]*

**AUMERLE**    Remember, as thou read'st, thy promise past.        50

I do repent me. Read not my name there.

My heart is not confederate with my hand.

**29. grow to the earth** 「地面に根づく」（*OED*, grow, *v.* 3b）。

**30. the roof within my mouth** 「口蓋」（*OED*, roof, *n.* 3a）。 **the roof** Q1-F1: my roofe　Dyce: the roof　Q1-F1 の読みは植字工が同じ行の my mouth に影響されたと考えられている。

**31. Unless a pardon** = unless a pardon be granted

**33. If on the first** = if the former

**34. after-love** 「のちの忠誠」。

**35. I** Q1 なし　Q2-F1: I may

**36. be** Qq: be　F1: me

**40. safe** 「人に危害を加えられない状態の」（*OED*, safe, *a.* 10）。

**42. secure** 「油断した」（*OED*, secure, *a.* 1）。　⇒ 2. 1. 266 注参照。

**43. Shall I for love speak treason to thy face?** 「私が忠誠心からあなたに面と向かって刃向かうような言葉遣いをする（前行で foolhardy と呼んでいることを指して）ようなことがあるだろうか」（Ure）。ただし、Black、Dawson & Yachnin は、Q1 の句読法にしたがって Shall I を Let me のような意味にとり「忠誠心からあなたにたいして（オーマールの）叛逆のことをお伝えさせてください」と解している。

　**face?** Q1: face,　Q2-F: face?

**47. us** = ourself　再帰代名詞代わりの人称代名詞。⇒ 1. 1. 5 注、および 2. 3. 8 注参照。

**49. treason** Qq: treason　F1: reason

　**that my haste forbids me show** 急いできたせいで息が荒れて口で説明することができない、ということ。

**50. past** 「さきほど交わされた」動詞 pass（*OED*, pass, *v.* 20）の過去分詞形。

**51. repent me** = repent myself　「後悔している」repent は無人称構文をとる動詞なので、現代では稀だが、再帰用法がこの動詞の本来的な使い方（*OED*, repent, *v.* 1）。　⇒ 2. 3. 8 注参照。

**52. confederate** 「結託している（= confederated）」（*OED*, confederate, *a.* 1 の比喩的用法の初出例）。　⇒ 1. 4. 20 注参照。

YORK    It was, villain, ere thy hand did set it down.
　　I tore it from the traitor's bosom, King.
　　Fear and not love begets his penitence.　　　　　　　　55
　　Forget to pity him lest thy pity prove
　　A serpent that will sting thee to the heart.

BOLINGBROKE    O, heinous, strong and bold conspiracy!
　　O, loyal father of a treacherous son!
　　Thou sheer, immaculate and silver fountain　　　　　60
　　From whence this stream through muddy passages
　　Hath held his current and defiled himself,
　　Thy overflow of good converts to bad
　　And thy abundant goodness shall excuse
　　This deadly blot in thy digressing son.　　　　　　　65

YORK    So shall my virtue be his vice's bawd
　　And he shall spend mine honour with his shame,
　　As thriftless sons their scraping fathers' gold.
　　Mine honour lives when his dishonour dies
　　Or my shamed life in his dishonour lies.　　　　　　70
　　Thou kill'st me in his life. Giving him breath,
　　The traitor lives, the true man's put to death.

DUCHESS    [*Within*]    What ho, my liege! For God's sake, let me in.

BOLINGBROKE    What shrill-voiced suppliant makes this eager cry?

DUCHESS    [*Within*]    A woman and thy aunt, great King, 'tis I.　75
　　Speak with me, pity me, open the door.
　　A beggar begs that never begged before.

BOLINGBROKE    Our scene is altered from a serious thing
　　And now changed to 'The Beggar and the King'.
　　My dangerous cousin, let your mother in.　　　　　80
　　I know she's come to pray for your foul sin.

　　　　　[*Aumerle opens the door.*] Enter Duchess [*of York*]

YORK    [*to Bolingbroke*]    If thou do pardon whosoever pray,
　　More sins for this forgiveness prosper may.

**53. it** ＝〔thy ＝ Aumerle's〕name (51)

**54. it** ＝ this writing (48)

**58. strong** （廃）「(罪などが) ひどい、はなはだしい」（*OED*, strong, *a.* 11†e）。

**60. immaculate** 「汚点のない、汚れのない (比喩的)」（*OED*, immaculate, *a.* 1）。

**62. held** Q1, 2: held Q3-5: hald F1: had

**63. converts** （廃）「(ものが) 形や性質を変える」（*OED*, convert, *v.* 11†e）。

**65. digressing** （廃）「正道をはずれた」（*OED*, digress, *v.* 3）。60 行目からの澄んだ泉から流れる小川の比喩がつづいている。

**68. scraping** 「金を貪欲にかき集める」（*OED*, scraping, *ppl. a.*, 2）。

**69-72, 74-135. Mine . . . art** ヨーク、ヨーク公夫人、ボリンブルック、オーマールの会話が押韻二行連句になっている。 ⇒解説 p. 14 参照。

**73. God's** Qq: Gods F1: heauens

**74. shrill-voiced** Q1, 2: shril voice Q3-5: shril voic'd F1: shrill-voic'd

**75. thy** Qq: thy F1: thine

**77. beggar** （廃）「嘆願者」（*OED*, beggar, *n.* 3）。 Q1-4: beggar Q5, F1: Begger *OED* は「嘆願者」という意味では、F1 の読みである begger という綴りのほうが適切であることを指摘している（*OED*, beggar, *n.* †3）。

**78-79. Our scene . . . King** 演劇性への言及がこの場面のコミカルなトーンを端的に示している。

**79. 'The Beggar and the King'** 女嫌いであった伝説上のアフリカ王コフェチュア（Cophetua）と乞食の娘との恋を歌った大衆歌謡の題への言及。シェイクスピアは *2H4*, 5. 3. 102、*Rom.*, 2. 1. 14、*LLL*, 1. 2. 109 でもこの歌に言及している。

　**Beggar** Qq: Beggar F1: Begger

**80. dangerous** （廃）「危害を及ぼす」（*OED*, dangerous, *a.* 5）。

**81. she's** Qq: she is F1: she's

　**pray** 「懇願する」（*OED*, pray, *v.* 5b）。

This festered joint cut off, the rest rest sound.

This let alone will all the rest confound.                                85

**Duchess**   O King, believe not this hard-hearted man.

Love loving not itself none other can.

**York**   Thou frantic woman, what dost thou make here?

Shall thy old dugs once more a traitor rear?

**Duchess**   Sweet York, be patient. [*to Bolingbroke*] Hear me,

gentle liege.                                                           90

[*Kneels*]

**Bolingbroke**   Rise up, good aunt.

**Duchess**                                    Not yet, I thee beseech.

For ever will I walk upon my knees

And never see day that the happy sees

Till thou give joy, until thou bid me joy

By pardoning Rutland, my transgressing boy.                              95

**Aumerle**   Unto my mother's prayers I bend my knee. [*Kneels*]

**York**   Against them both my true joints bended be. [*Kneels*]

Ill mayst thou thrive if thou grant any grace.

**Duchess**   Pleads he in earnest? Look upon his face.

His eyes do drop no tears; his prayers are in jest;                      100

His words come from his mouth, ours from our breast.

He prays but faintly and would be denied;

We pray with heart and soul and all beside.

His weary joints would gladly rise I know;

Our knees still kneel till to the ground they grow.                      105

His prayers are full of false hypocrisy,

Ours of true zeal and deep integrity.

Our prayers do outpray his; then let them have

That mercy which true prayer ought to have.

**Bolingbroke**   Good aunt, stand up.

**Duchess**                                    Nay, do not say 'Stand up.'   110

Say 'Pardon' first and afterwards 'Stand up.'

**84. This . . . sound.** Noble は「もしあなたの片手または片足が、罪を犯させ
るなら、それを切って捨てなさい。両手、両足がそろったままで、永遠の火に
投げ込まれるよりは、片手、片足になって命に入る方がよい。」(Wherefore
if thy hand or thy foot offend thee, cut them off, and cast them from
thee: it is better for thee to enter into life halt or maimed, rather than
having two hands or two feet to be cast into everlasting fire. Matthew,
18: 8) の反響を指摘している。

**joint** 「手足」(Schmidt)。*OED* はこの意味を収録していない。

**rest rest**　Qq: rest rest　F1: rest rests

**85. confound** (廃)または (古)「〜を破滅させる、だめにする」(*OED*, confound,
*v.* 1)。

**87. Love loving not itself none other can** 「自身を愛することのできない愛はだ
れも愛することができない」Ure は「自身を (itself)」は「自身の子」を意味
すると注記している。

**105. still**　Qq: still　F1: shall

**108. outpray**　「(相手の懇願) をしのぐ」(*OED*, outpray, *v.* 1 の初出例)。

**109. prayer**　Qq: prayer　F1: prayers

**110. SP** **Bolingbroke**　Q1: *yorke*　Q2-5: *King H.*　F1: *Bul.*

**111. Say**　Qq: Say　F1: But

And if I were thy nurse thy tongue to teach,
'Pardon' should be the first word of thy speech.
I never longed to hear a word till now.
Say 'Pardon', King. Let pity teach thee how.                    115
The word is short but not so short as sweet,
No word like 'pardon' for kings' mouths so meet.
**YORK**   Speak it in French, King. Say '*Pardonne moi.*'
**DUCHESS**   [*to York*]   Dost thou teach pardon pardon to destroy?
  Ah, my sour husband, my hard-hearted lord,                   120
  That sets the word itself against the word!
  [*to Bolingbroke*]   Speak 'Pardon' as 'tis current in our land.
  The chopping French we do not understand.
  Thine eye begins to speak; set thy tongue there
  Or in thy piteous heart plant thou thine ear                 125
  That, hearing how our plaints and prayers do pierce,
  Pity may move thee 'Pardon' to rehearse.
**BOLINGBROKE**   Good aunt, stand up.
**DUCHESS**                              I do not sue to stand.
  Pardon is all the suit I have in hand.
**BOLINGBROKE**   I pardon him as God shall pardon me.          130

*[York and Aumerle rise]*

**DUCHESS**   O, happy vantage of a kneeling knee!
  Yet am I sick for fear. Speak it again.
  Twice saying 'Pardon' doth not pardon twain,
  But makes one pardon strong.
**BOLINGBROKE**                        I pardon him
  With all my heart.

*[Duchess rises]*

**DUCHESS**                   A god on earth thou art.           135
**BOLINGBROKE**   But for our trusty brother-in-law and the Abbot,
  With all the rest of that consorted crew,

**118. 'Pardonne moi.'** 「（願いを聞きいれられないことを）お赦しください」。

**121. That sets the word itself against the word!** 「それは同じ言葉同士に喧嘩をさせることになる」 直前に、王に「赦す」と言ってほしいと迫る公爵夫人の言葉にたいして、ヨークが反対の意味になるようにフランス語に言い換えて、「（願いを聞きいれられないことを）お赦しください」と言うよう王に求めたことばかりでなく、オーマールの「母親の懇願にあわせて跪きます」にたいして、ヨークが「そのふたりの懇願を聞かぬよう跪きます」と言う（96-97）など、この件におけるヨークの、妻と子の言葉を同じ言葉でひっくり返して喜劇的興趣を盛りあげる、言葉遣いの特徴を端的に言い表わしている。5. 5. 13-14で同じ表現がくり返される。

**122. current** 「通用している」（*OED*, current, *a.* 6）。

**123. chopping** 「（言葉の意味を変えて）屁理屈をこねる」（*OED*, chop, *v.*² †5, 8）。

**127. rehearse** （廃）「〜と言う」（*OED*, rehearse, *v.* 1†c）。

**130. God** Qq: God F1: heauen

**133. twain** （廃）「〜をふたつに分ける」（*OED*, twain, *v.*）。

**135. A god on earth thou art** 「地上における神の代理人」という王権神授説に関する考えを端的に表わす言葉が、その意味と無関係な文脈で発されている。

**136. brother-in-law** エクセター公爵ジョン・ホランドのこと。⇒2. 1. 281注参照。

**and the** Qq: and the F1: the

**137. consorted** 「盟約を交わした」（*OED*, consorted, *ppl. a.*）。

**crew** 「連中（軽蔑的）」（*OED*, crew, *n.*² 4）。

Destruction straight shall dog them at the heels.
Good uncle, help to order several powers
To Oxford or where'er these traitors are.                    140
They shall not live within this world, I swear,
But I will have them if I once know where.
Uncle, farewell, and cousin, adieu.
Your mother well hath prayed and prove you true.
**DUCHESS**    Come, my old son. I pray God make thee new.    145

*Exeunt*


**[ACT V, SCENE IV]**

*Enter Sir Piers [of] Exton and Servants*


**EXTON**    Didst thou not mark the King, what words he spake?
'Have I no friend will rid me of this living fear?'
Was it not so?
**SERVANT**        These were his very words.
**EXTON**    'Have I no friend?' quoth he. He spake it twice
And urged it twice together, did he not?                    5
**SERVANT**    He did.
**EXTON**    And speaking it, he wishtly looked on me
As who should say 'I would thou wert the man
That would divorce this terror from my heart',
Meaning the King at Pomfret. Come, let's go.                10
I am the King's friend and will rid his foe.        *Exeunt*


**[ACT V, SCENE V]**

*Enter Richard alone*


**RICHARD**    I have been studying how I may compare
This prison where I live unto the world,
And for because the world is populous
And here is not a creature but myself,

**139-40. to order several powers / To** 「〜にそれぞれ部隊を派遣するように」（「「（軍隊）に〜への（*to . . .*）派遣命令を下す」という用法を定義している *OED*, order, *v.* 7b の初出例は 17 世紀後半だが、これは 7a の、人を目的語としそのあとに to 不定詞をとる用法から運動の動詞が省略されたもの。　⇒ 1. 2. 56 注参照。

**145. God**　Qq: God　F1: heauen

〔**5. 4**〕あらすじ……………………………………………………………………………………

　サー・ピアーズ・オヴ・エクストンは、ボリンブルックの「この生きている恐怖を私から取りのぞいてくれる友はいないのか」という言葉を、リチャード暗殺を自分に遠回しに依頼するものと理解したことを従者に告げる。

…………………………………………………………………………………………………

**2. will** = who will　主格関係代名詞の省略。　⇒ 1. 1. 50 注参照。

**3. These**　Qq: These　F1: Those

**4-5. He spake it twice / And urged it twice together, did he not?**　⇒後注参照。

**7. wishtly**　「強く望んで（= wishly）」（*OED*, † wishly, *adv.*）。Q1, 2: wishtly　Q3-F1: wistly

**8. would**　「（仮定法の目的節をとって）〜であればいいのにと願う（= wish）」（*OED*, wish, *v.* 36）。

**10. the King at Pomfret**　⇒ 5. 1. 52 参照。

〔**5. 5**〕あらすじ……………………………………………………………………………………

　獄中で夢想にふけり、王位を追われたわが身の境遇を嘆いているリチャードのもとへ、かつての厩番が訪れ、ボリンブルックが入市行進の際リチャードの馬に乗っていたことを悲しげに語る。牢番がエクストンの差し向けた毒入りの食事をもって登場し、厩番を帰す。いつもしている食事の毒味をエクストンの指示でこのときばかりはしない牢番をリチャードが打ちすえているところへ、エクストンが現われ刺殺する。

…………………………………………………………………………………………………

**1. studying how I may**　「どうしたら〜できるものかとよく考える」（*OED*, study, *v.* 2†d）。

　**I may**　Q1: I may　Q2-F1: to

**3. for because** = because　for cause that . . . という表現の名残で because の前にしばしば for がつけられていた（*OED*, because, *conj.* 1; cause, *n.* 6）。

I cannot do it. Yet I'll hammer't out.     5
My brain I'll prove the female to my soul,
My soul the father, and these two beget
A generation of still-breeding thoughts,
And these same thoughts people this little world
In humours like the people of this world,     10
For no thought is contented. The better sort,
As thoughts of things divine, are intermixed
With scruples and do set the word itself
Against the word, as thus: 'Come, little ones',
And then again,     15
'It is as hard to come as for a camel
To thread the postern of a small needle's eye.'
Thoughts tending to ambition, they do plot
Unlikely wonders: how these vain weak nails
May tear a passage through the flinty ribs     20
Of this hard world, my ragged prison walls,
And, for they cannot, die in their own pride.
Thoughts tending to content flatter themselves
That they are not the first of Fortune's slaves,
Nor shall not be the last, like silly beggars     25
Who sitting in the stocks refuge their shame,
That many have and others must sit there,
And in this thought they find a kind of ease,
Bearing their own misfortunes on the back
Of such as have before endured the like.     30
Thus play I in one person many people
And none contented. Sometimes am I king,
Then treasons make me wish myself a beggar,
And so I am. Then crushing penury
Persuades me I was better when a king,     35
Then am I kinged again, and by and by
Think that I am unkinged by Bolingbroke

**5. hammer't out**　「それを考えだす」鉄の鍛造の比喩（*OED*, hammer, *v.* 2）。
Qq: hammer it　F1: hammer't

**7. beget**　「（子）をつくる」通常は父親が「（子）をもうける」ことを意味するが、両親を主語にして使うこともある（*OED*, beget, *v.* 2）。

**8. generation**　「子供たち」（*OED*, generation, *n.* †3）。
**still-breeding**　「つねに子を産みつづける」。⇒ 1. 1. 22 注参照。

**9. people**　「（場所）に住む、の住民となる」（*OED*, people, *v.* 2）。
**this little world**　「小宇宙（= microcosm）」（*OED*, †little world）、つまりリチャード自身の身体のこと。リチャードは自身が閉じこめられている牢獄を指してこの言葉を使っているが、それを世界と考えるのに必要な住人がいないため、脳を母親、魂を父親に、そしてそれらが産みだす思考をその世界の住人と見立てることによって、ようやく牢獄という空間がリチャードの身体と重なりあい「小宇宙」となっている。

**10. humours**　「気質」（*OED*, humour, *n.* 4）。

**13-14. set . . . word**　5. 3. 121 のヨーク公夫人のヨーク公に関する言葉をくり返すもの。　**word . . . word**　Qq: word . . . word　F1: Faith . . . Faith
Jowett & Taylor は、F1 の読みを、シェイクスピアが 5. 3. 121 の反復となるのを避けるために改変したものと考えている。

**14-15. Against . . . again**　Wells による行割り。Qq, F1 は 1 行に印刷。

**14. 'Come, litttle ones'**　'Suffer little children to come vnto me'（Luke 18: 16）を踏まえたもの（Noble）。

**15. again**　「〜に答えて」（*OED*, again, *adv.* 2）。

**16-17. It . . . eye.**　'For it is easier for a Camel to go thorow a needles eye, then for a rich man to enter into the kingdome of God'（Luke 18, 25）を踏まえたもの（Noble）。

**17. thread**　「（狭いところ）を通り抜ける」（*OED*, thread, *v.* 4a の初出例）。
**small**　Qq: small　F1 なし

**20. tear**　「（引き裂いて穴）をあける」（*OED*, tear, *v.*¹ 1b の初出例）。
**through**　Qq: thorow　F1: through　**flinty ribs**　「燧石のように硬い（迫持を支える）力骨」（*OED*, rib, *n.*¹ 10b）。⇒ 5. 1. 3 注参照。

**26-27. refuge . . . That**　「〜と考えることによって恥辱から逃れる」that は理由を表す説を導く（*OED*, that, *conj.* 2a）。

**27. sit**　Q1, 2: set　Q3-F1: sit　**29. misfortunes**　Qq: misfortunes　F1: misfortune

**31-32. Thus . . . contented.**　演劇の比喩が 5. 3. 78-79 と対照的に深刻さを表す。

**31. person**　Q1: prison　Q2-F1: person

**33. treasons make**　Qq: treasons make　F1: Treason makes

**37. unkinged**　⇒ 4. 1. 219 注参照。

And straight am nothing. But whate'er I be,
Nor I nor any man that but man is
With nothing shall be pleased till he be eased      40
With being nothing.

*The music plays*

Music do I hear?
Ha, ha, keep time. How sour sweet music is
When time is broke and no proportion kept!
So is it in the music of men's lives.
And here have I the daintiness of ear      45
To check time broke in a disordered string,
But for the concord of my state and time
Had not an ear to hear my true time broke.
I wasted time and now doth Time waste me,
For now hath Time made me his numb'ring clock.      50
My thoughts are minutes and with sighs they jar
Their watches on unto mine eyes, the outward watch,
Whereto my finger like a dial's point
Is pointing still in cleansing them from tears.
Now sir, the sound that tells what hour it is      55
Are clamorous groans, which strike upon my heart,
Which is the bell. So sighs and tears and groans
Show minutes, hours and times. But my time
Runs posting on in Bolingbroke's proud joy,
While I stand fooling here, his Jack of the clock.      60
This music mads me. Let it sound no more,      [*Musick ceases*]
For though it have holp madmen to their wits,
In me it seems it will make wise men mad.
Yet blessing on his heart that gives it me,
For 'tis a sign of love and love to Richard      65
Is a strange brooch in this all-hating world.

**38. be**　Qq: be　F1: am

**39-41. Nor . . . nothing.**　「私にせよ、ただの人間ならだれにせよ、（死んで）無となるまではなにごとにも満足することはない」。

**42. time**　「リズム」または「テンポ」（*OED*, time, *n.* 12†a, b）。

**43. proportion**　「リズム」（*OED*, proportion, *n.* 10†a, b）。

**45. daintiness**　「えり好みのうるささ」（*OED*, daintiness, *n.* 3）。

**46. check**　Qq: check　F1: heare

**49. I wasted time and now doth Time waste me**　「私が時間を無駄にしたため、『時』の神はいま私を破滅させている」（*OED*, waste, *v.* †5a）。

**51-54. My thoughts . . . tears**　「私の考えが一分一分であり、カチカチという音のようにため息の音をたてて夜の時間が進むのを見張り役の目に見せ、涙をぬぐう私の指が時計の針のようにそこを指す」。悲しい思いにひたって眠れずにこぼれる涙を指でぬぐう状況を、ため息を時計の音、目を時計の目盛り、指を時計の針に見立てて、時計の動きになぞらえている。次の文（55-57）では、うめき声が1時間ごとに鳴るベルの音に見立てられる。

**51. jar**　（廃）「カチカチと音を立て（時）を進める」（*OED*, jar, *v.*¹ †2）の初出例。

**52. watches**　「（夜の）時間」夜の時間をヘブライ人は3つに、ギリシャ人は4つまたは5つに、ローマ人は4つに分けたが、その時間区分（Heb. *ashmōreth*, Gr. φυλακή, L. *vigilia*）を指す。古代中国の「更」に相当（*OED*, watch, *n.* 4）。

**55. Now sir**　架空の対話相手への呼びかけ。

**56. which**　Qq: which　F1: that

**58. hours and times**　Qq: times, and houres　F1: Houres, and Times　「分、時」と並ぶF1の読みが正しいものと見える。

**60. Jack of the clock**　「時打ちジャック《古い教会堂などの大型時計のベルを打つハンマーを持った機械仕掛けの人形》」（*OED*, jack, *n.*¹ 6, 37）。

　**of the**　Qq: of the　F1: o'th'

**62. holp**　help の古い過去分詞形。

**63. wise**　「正気の」（*OED*, wise, *a.* 4）。

**66. strange brooch**　「類い稀な宝飾品」（*OED*, strange, *a.* †8; brooch, *n.* †2）。

*Enter a Groom of the Stable*

**GROOM**    Hail, royal Prince!
**RICHARD**                            Thanks, noble peer.
  The cheapest of us is ten groats too dear.
  What art thou? And how comest thou hither,
  Where no man never comes but that sad dog                    70
  That brings me food to make misfortune live?
**GROOM**    I was a poor groom of thy stable, King,
  When thou wert king, who travelling towards York
  With much ado at length have gotten leave
  To look upon my sometimes royal master's face.              75
  O, how it earned my heart when I beheld
  In London streets that coronation day
  When Bolingbroke rode on roan Barbary,
  That horse that thou so often hast bestrid,
  That horse that I so carefully have dressed.                80
**RICHARD**    Rode he on Barbary? Tell me, gentle friend,
  How went he under him?
**GROOM**    So proudly as if he disdained the ground.
**RICHARD**    So proud that Bolingbroke was on his back?
  That jade hath eat bread from my royal hand;                85
  This hand hath made him proud with clapping him.
  Would he not stumble? Would he not fall down,
  Since pride must have a fall, and break the neck
  Of that proud man that did usurp his back?
  Forgiveness, horse. Why do I rail on thee,                  90
  Since thou, created to be awed by man,
  Wast born to bear? I was not made a horse,
  And yet I bear a burthen like an ass,
  Spurred, galled and tired by jauncing Bolingbroke.

  *Enter Keeper to Richard with meat*

**67-68. Thanks, noble peer. / The cheapest of us is ten groats too dear** 厩番<sup>うまや</sup>

がリチャードに royal Prince (67) と呼びかけたことにたいして、リチャード
は、自分はいまや王でなく貴族となり彼と同等だということで彼に noble
peer と呼びかけ、投獄されている囚人の身である自分がいまここにいるふた
りのうちの価値の低いほうだとして、noble、royal とも金貨の名前であるた
めその価値にかけて言葉遊びをしている。当時のイングランドの貨幣単位は、
£1 (1 ポンド) = 20 s. (シリング) = 240 d. (ペンス) で、noble は 6 s. 8 d.
= 80 d. であるから 10 s. = 120 d. に相当する royal と呼ばれると 10 groats
(= 40 d.) 高すぎだと答えている (*OED*, royal, *n.*<sup>1</sup> 2; noble, *n.* 2a; groat, *n.*
2; dear, *a.* 6a)。

**70. never** Q1-4: neuer Q5, F1: euer

**76. it earned** 「(人を主語とする自動詞、または人を与格の目的語とする無人称
構文で) (人) がひどく嘆く」(*OED*, †earn, *v.*<sup>3</sup> 2)。

**earned** Qq: ernd F1: yern'd

**78. roan** 「糟毛<sup>かすげ</sup> (灰色に白いさし毛のまざった馬の毛色) の」(*OED*, roan, *a.*
a)。

**Barbary** 「バーバリー (エジプト以外の北アフリカの旧称) 産の馬」(*OED*,
Barbary, *n.* 4†c) に由来する馬の名前。

**79. bestrid** Qq: bestride F1: bestrid

**83. he** Qq: he F1: he had

**85. hath eat** eat は過去分詞形。

**88. pride . . . fall** PRIDE will have a fall (Tilley, P581) は Pride goes
before a destruction, a haughty spirit before a fall (Proverbs, 16: 18) に
基づく諺。

**94. Spurred, galled** Qq: Spurrde, galld, F1: Spur-gall'd,

**jauncing** 「(馬を) 跳ねまわらせる」と「(馬が) 跳ねまわる」(*OED*,
jaunce, *v.* a, b)。

**KEEPER**  [*to Groom*]   Fellow, give place. Here is no longer stay.   95
**RICHARD**  [*to Groom*]   If thou love me, 'tis time thou wert away.
**GROOM**   What my tongue dares not, that my heart shall say.

*Exit*

**KEEPER**   My lord, will't please you to fall to?
**RICHARD**   Taste of it first, as thou art wont to do.
**KEEPER**   My lord, I dare not. Sir Pierce of Exton,   100
  Who lately came from the King, commands the contrary.
**RICHARD**   The devil take Henry of Lancaster and thee!
  Patience is stale and I am weary of it.

*[Beats Keeper]*

**KEEPER**   Help, help, help!

*The murderers, Exton and his Servants, rush in*

**RICHARD**   How now! What means Death in this rude assault?   105
  Villain, thy own hand yields thy death's instrument.

*[Seizes a Servant's weapon and kills him with it]*

Go thou and fill another room in hell.

*[Kills another Servant.] Here Exton strikes him down*

That hand shall burn in never-quenching fire
That staggers thus my person. Exton, thy fierce hand
Hath with the King's blood stained the King's own land.   110
Mount, mount, my soul. Thy seat is up on high
Whilst my gross flesh sinks downward here to die. *[Dies]*
**EXTON**   As full of valour as of royal blood.
  Both have I spilled. O, would the deed were good,
  For now the devil that told me I did well   115
  Says that this deed is chronicled in hell.
  This dead King to the living King I'll bear.
  *[to Keeper and remaining Servants]*

**98. fall to** 「(食事に) とりかかる」(*OED*, fall. *v.* 67†e)。

**99. Taste of** 「～の毒味をする」(*OED*, taste, *v.* 6c, 12a) の命令形。

  **art** Q1-4: art　Q5, F1: wert

**102. The devil take Henry of Lancaster and thee!** ⇒後注参照。

**106. thy own** Q1-4: thy owne　Q5, F: thine owne

**109. staggers** 「～を殴ってよろめかせる」(*OED*, stagger, *v.* 6a の初出例)。

  **my person** 「ほかならぬ本人の身柄」、「王の身体」を含意する言葉 (*OED*, person, *n.* 5a, †b)。Chambers は「リチャードは、王位の放棄を余儀なくされながらも、最後に王威を取りもどしている」と注記している。

**111-12. Mount, mount, my soul. Thy seat is up on high / Whilst my gross flesh sinks downward here to die.** エクストンに刺されたリチャードの最後の言葉。リチャードの霊魂は天に昇り、肉体は下方へと降下する、というこの部分にも高低の主題が見られ、high と die の押韻が鮮烈な印象を残す。

**114. spilled** 「(勇気あるもの) を殺す」と「(王の血) をこぼす」(*OED*, spill, *v.* 2, 10a)。

Take hence the rest, and give them burial here.          *Exeunt*

[ACT V, SCENE VI]

*Flourish. Enter Bolingbroke, York with with other lords and attendants*

**BOLINGBROKE**    Kind uncle York, the latest news we hear
Is that the rebels have consumed with fire
Our town of Ciceter in Gloucestershire,
But whether they be ta'en or slain we hear not.

*Enter Northumberland*

Welcome, my lord. What is the news?                         5
**NORTHUMBERLAND**    First, to thy sacred state wish I all
    happiness.
The next news is I have to London sent
The heads of Salisbury, Spencer, Blunt, and Kent.
The manner of their taking may appear
At large discoursèd in this paper here.                        10

*[Presents a paper]*

**BOLINGBROKE**    We thank thee, gentle Percy, for thy pains
And to thy worth will add right worthy gains.

*Enter Fitzwater*

**FITZWATER**    My lord, I have from Oxford sent to London
The heads of Brocas and Sir Bennet Seely,
Two of the dangerous consorted traitors                       15
That sought at Oxford thy dire overthrow.
**BOLINGBROKE**    Thy pains, Fitzwater, shall not be forgot.
Right noble is thy merit, well I wot.

*Enter Percy and Carlisle [as prisoner]*

**PERCY**    The grand conspirator, Abbot of Westminster,

・・・・・・・・・・・・・・・・・・・・・・・・・・・・・・・・・・・・・・・・・・・・・・・・・・・・・・・・・・・・・・・・

　ボリンブルックがヨークにシシターの叛乱のことを話しているところへ、ノーサンバーランド、フィッツウォーターが謀反人の討伐を報告。パーシーがカーライルをつれて登場すると、ボリンブルックは仇敵ではあってもカーライルを処罰せずに隠遁を命じる。次いでリチャードの棺とともに登場したエクストンが暗殺を報告するが、ボリンブルックは彼を呪詛し追放を言いわたし、リチャードの死を悼み、聖地への巡礼を決意する。

・・・・・・・・・・・・・・・・・・・・・・・・・・・・・・・・・・・・・・・・・・・・・・・・・・・・・・・・・・・・・・・・・・・・・・・・・・・・・・・・・・・・・・・・・・・・・・・・・・・・・

**3. Ciceter**　シシター（'sisitər)、現在のサイレンセスター（Cirencester）。イングランド南部グロスターシア州の町（Kökeritz, 'Cicester'; Sugden, 'Cirencester'）。

**8. Salisbury, Spencer, Blunt**　Q1: Oxford, Salisbury, Blunt　Q2-5: Oxford, Slisbury　F1: *Salsbury, Spencer, Blunt*　Qq が叛乱と無関係のオックスフォード伯の名をあげているのは、シェイクスピアがホリンシェッド『年代記』に頻出する地名と混同したとも、植字工が直後（13）に出てくる地名と混同したともとれる。オックスフォード伯をスペンサーに代える F1 の読みはホリンシェッドが伝える歴史的事実に沿う内容となっており、Qq の誤りを正すものとなっている。

**Spencer**　トマス・ル・デスペンサー（Thomas le Despenser, 1373-1400) リチャードに授けられたグロスター伯位をヘンリー四世に剥奪されていた。

**Blunt**　サー・トマス・ブラント（Sir Thomas Blunt, -1400）。リチャード支持者のひとり。

**Kent**　ケント伯は、サリー公トマス・ホランド（Thomas Holland, Duke of Surrey, 1374-1400）の公位剥奪後の称号。4. 1 に登場。

**9. taking**　「逮捕、拘束」（*OED*, taking, *vbl.n.* 2a）。

**11. Percy**　ノーサンバーランドの名はヘンリー・パーシー（Henry Percy）。

**14. Brocas**　サー・バーナード・ブロカス（Sir Bernard Brocas, c.1354-1400）。リチャードの最初の妃アン・オヴ・ボヘミアに侍従として仕えた同名の父をもち、鹿狩り犬監督官（Master of Buckhounds）としてリチャードに仕えた。ホリンシェッド『年代記』では sir Leonard Brokas となっている（3: 516）。

**Sir Bennet Seely**　ホリンシェッド『年代記』では sir Benet Cilie knight となっている。正確な素性はわからず、姓は Scheveley、Sely、Shelley などとも綴られる（Davis 参照）。

**15. consorted**　⇒ 5. 3. 137 注参照。

**17. Fitzwater**　Q1-3: Fitz.　Q4, 5: Fitz　F1: Fitzwaters

　**not**　Q1: nor　Q2-F1: not

With clog of conscience and sour melancholy                    20
Hath yielded up his body to the grave.
But here is Carlisle living, to abide
Thy kingly doom and sentence of his pride.
**BOLINGBROKE**    Carlisle, this is your doom:
Choose out some secret place, some reverend room              25
More than thou hast, and with it joy thy life.
So as thou livest in peace, die free from strife,
For though mine enemy thou hast ever been,
High sparks of honour in thee have I seen.

*Enter Exton [and Servants bearing] the coffin*

**EXTON**    Great King, within this coffin I present          30
Thy buried fear. Herein all breathless lies
The mightiest of thy greatest enemies,
Richard of Bordeaux, by me hither brought.
**BOLINGBROKE**    Exton, I thank thee not, for thou hast wrought
A deed of slander with thy fatal hand                         35
Upon my head and all this famous land.
**EXTON**    From your own mouth, my lord, did I this deed.
**BOLINGBROKE**    They love not poison that do poison need,
Nor do I thee. Though I did wish him dead,
I hate the murderer, love him murdered.                       40
The guilt of conscience take thou for thy labour
But neither my good word nor princely favour.
With Cain go wander through shades of night
And never show thy head by day nor light.        *[Exit Exton]*
Lords, I protest my soul is full of woe                       45
That blood should sprinkle me to make me grow.
Come mourn with me for what I do lament
And put on sullen black incontinent.
I'll make a voyage to the Holy Land
To wash this blood off from my guilty hand.                   50

**20. clog** 「(罪人の足につける) おもり木」(*OED*, clog, *n.* 2)。

**22. abide** 「従容として (処分など) を待つ」(*OED*, abide, *v.* 15)。

**25. reverend** 「敬意を表するに値する、神聖な」(*OED*, reverend, *a.* 3a, †b)。
Q1-3: reuerent  Q4-F1: reuerend  Q1-3 の読みは reverent だが、その綴り
は「(人について) 敬意をいだく」の意味で、敬意の対象となるものを指す意
味の場合は現代語では revenrend の綴りを用いる。

**26. More than thou hast** 「これまで選んできたのよりも神聖な」または「いま
幽閉されている場所よりも広い」(Newbalt)。

**33. Richard of Bordeaux** エクストンはリチャードについて、王と呼ぶことを
避けるように出生地を加えて呼んでいる。

**34. wrought** 「(行為) を行った」動詞 work の「(行為) を行う」、「(もの) を
作りだす」などの意味のときに使われる、古い過去分詞形 (*OED*, work, *v.* 1.)。

**35. A deed of slander** 「非難を招く行い」(*OED*, slander, *n.* †3)。
**slander**  Q1: slaunder  Q2-F1: Slaughter

**43. Cain** カイン。弟アベルを殺し人類最初の殺人者として国を追われ流浪の
身 (a fugitive and a vagabond,) となった (Genesis 4: 12)。 ⇒ 1. 1. 104-
05 注参照。
**shades**  Q1: shades  Q2-F1: the shade

**45-46. Lords . . . grow** 味方の離反の報に接して、「嘆きの奴隷 (woe's
slave)」となって「王のように君臨する嘆き (kingly woe)」にしたがうしか
ないとあきらめ、軍を解散して「育つ見込み (some hope to grow)」のある
土地に行かせるよう命じるリチャードの言葉 (3. 2. 210-14)、および国王廃位
の噂という「嘆かわしい知らせ (these news of woe)」を告げた庭師に接ぎ
木した植物が「育たないように (may never grow)」と呪詛する王妃の言葉
(3. 4. 100-01) を反響する言葉。

**46. me** 「私のために」利害を表わす与格 (*OED*, me. *pers.pron.* 2b)。

**47. what** Qq: what  F1: that

**48. incontinent** 「すぐに」(*OED*, incontinent, *adv.*)。

**49-50. I'll . . . hand.** ここの言葉遣いからは、王が考えているのは、十字軍遠
征ではなく巡礼のように思われる (Gurr)。この劇につづくシェイクスピアの
『ヘンリー四世』二部作では、十字軍遠征を行えないことがしばしば話題にな
る (*1H4*, 1. 1. 19-29, 48, 102, *2H4*, 3. 1. 108, 4. 4. 3-4, 4. 5. 209-10, 238)。ホリ
ンシェッド『年代記』ではヘンリー四世による十字軍派遣は統治最終年 (1413
年) の記述 (3: 540) のみに見られる。「罪深い私の手からこの血を洗い落と
すために」という表現は退位のエピソードのリチャードの呪詛の言葉を思いお
こさせる (⇒ 4. 1. 238-41 注参照)。

March sadly after. Grace my mournings here
In weeping after this untimely bier.          *Exeunt*

**51. mournings**　Qq: mournings　F1: mourning

**52. untimely bier**　「時期尚早な死を迎えたリチャードの棺」転位修飾語
（transferred epithet）。

# 後 注

**1. 1.** ホリンシェッド『年代記』に記録されている、1398年4月29日にウィンザーで開かれた、ボリンブルックによるモーブリー告発の聴聞会にあたる場面。そこにいたる経緯は以下のとおり。シュルーズベリーで同年1月27日に開始された議会期間中の1月30日にボリンブルックがモーブリーを訴える提案をするが、リチャードは早々に議会を終了させる。その結果、この訴えは3月19日に議会の委員会で取りあげられ、ふたりが出頭して訴えとそれにたいする反論を行う。王は和解を要請したが聞き入れられなかった。次いで4月29日に、再度ふたりは王の前に出頭し、ボリンブルックが、兵士の給料の使い込み、グロスター暗殺、18年間に起こったすべての陰謀の罪で、モーブリーを訴える。双方国王のとりなしを受け容れず、コヴェントリーで決闘が行われることになる。決闘の日取りに関しては、8月の月曜日という記録と、シェイクスピアが採用した聖ランベルトゥスの日（9月17日）という記録があるという（Holinshed, 3: 493-94）。

**1. 1. 3. Henry Herford** この劇の主人公となるボリンブルックの劇中もっとも多用される呼び名であるこの名については、Q1, F1ともに現行綴りのHereford (hérəfərd 3音節) と古い形 Herford (həːrfərd 2音節) を併用している。本書では1行10音節あるいは12音節という韻律から判断して両者を使い分ける。この名前の出現箇所とQ1, F1における綴りに関しては以下のとおり。name の欄には、当該箇所で添えられている名前、他の称号などをあわせた呼び名全体を記した。

| act | sc. | line | name | Q1 | F1 |
|---|---|---|---|---|---|
| 1 | 1 | 3 | Henry Herford | Herford | Herford |
| 1 | 1 | 27 | Cousin of Herford | Herford | Hereford |
| 1 | 2 | 46 | Herford | Hereford | Herford |
| 1 | 2 | 47 | Herford's | Herefords | Herfords |
| 1 | 3 | 1 | Harry Herford | Herford | Herford |
| 1 | 3 | 21 | the Duke of Hereford | Herford | Herford |
| 1 | 3 | 35 | Harry of Hereford, Lancaster and Derby | Herford | Herford |
| 1 | 3 | 55 | Cousin of Herford | Herford | Herford |
| 1 | 3 | 100 | Harry of Hereford, Lancaster and Derby | Herford | Herford |
| 1 | 3 | 104 | Harry of Hereford, Lancaster and Derby | Herford | Herford |
| 1 | 3 | 113 | Henry of Hereford, Lancaster and Derby | Herford | Herford |
| 1 | 3 | 140 | cousin Herford | Hereford | Herford |

| 1 | 4 | 2 | high Herford | Hereford | Herford |
|---|---|---|---|---|---|
| 1 | 4 | 3 | high Herford | Hereford | Herford |
| 2 | 1 | 144 | Harry Duke of Herford | Hereford | Herford |
| 2 | 1 | 145 | Herford's | Herefords | Herfords |
| 2 | 1 | 165 | Herford's | Herefords | Herfords |
| 2 | 1 | 190 | banished Hereford | Hereford | Herford |
| 2 | 1 | 191 | Herford | Hereford | Herford |
| 2 | 1 | 195 | Herford's | Herefordes | Herfords |
| 2 | 1 | 201 | Herford's | Herefords | Herfords |
| 2 | 1 | 232 | the Duke of Hereford | Hereford | Hereford |
| 2 | 1 | 279 | Harry Duke of Herford | Herford | Herford |
| 2 | 2 | 89 | Herford's | Hereford's | Herfords |
| 2 | 3 | 32 | the Duke of Hereford | Hereford | Hereford |
| 2 | 3 | 36 | the Duke of Herford | Herefords | Hereford |
| 2 | 3 | 69 | My lord of Hereford | Hereford | Hereford |
| 2 | 3 | 111 | banished Hereford | Hereford | Hereford |
| 4 | 1 | 135 | proud Herford's king | Herefords | Herfefords |

ただし、劇の後半では主として Bolingbroke という呼び名が使用される。King、Bolingbroke、Lancaster、Herford、Hereford という呼び名の幕ごとの使用頻度は以下のとおり。

| Act | King | Bol | Lan | Her | Here |
|---|---|---|---|---|---|
| 1 | 0 | 2 | 0 | 9 | 6 |
| 2 | 0 | 5 | 1 | 9 | 5 |
| 3 | 1 | 24 | 0 | 0 | 0 |
| 4 | 1 | 5 | 1 | 2 | 0 |
| 5 | 10 | 14 | 1 | 0 | 0 |
| total | 12 | 50 | 3 | 20 | 11 |

なお、Henry、Harry という名前が呼ばれるのは、称号に添えられる場合も合めて、Henry 7 回（1. 1. 3; 1. 3. 113; 3. 3. 35; 4. 1. 112, 179, 219; 5. 5. 102）、Harry 6 回（1. 3. 1, 35, 100, 104; 2. 1. 279; 3. 3. 104）。

**1. 1. 87-108. Look . . . spent** ホリンシェッド『年代記』によれば、ボリンブルックを擁護する騎士が、このボリンブルックの台詞同様に、兵士への前渡し金の横領、近年のあらゆる謀叛への関与、グロスターの殺害画策の3点でモーブリーを告発している（3: 494）。

**1. 1. 100. Duke of Gloucester's death** 初代グロスター公トマス・オヴ・ウッドストック（Thomas of Woodstock, 1st Duke of Gloucester, 1355-1397）は、リチャード二世とボリンブルックから見て叔父（リチャードの父エドワード黒

太子とボリンブルックの父ジョン・オヴ・ゴーントの弟）。その殺害はモーブリーによる拘禁中の出来事だった。ホリンシェッド『年代記』は王がモーブリーにグロスターの拘禁を命じたと伝えており、その死にも関与したとする（3: 489）が、ここでボリンブルックは、殺害をモーブリーの企てとして、王の関与に触れないでいる。

**1. 1. 126-41. Three . . . it** 1395 年にモーブリーとオーマールは王女イザベルのリチャードとの婚礼のためにフランス王と交渉を行い、多額の費用を負担している。ホリンシェッド『年代記』によれば、モーブリーは、告発への反論のなかで、前渡し金の着服とジョン・オヴ・ゴーントにたいする待ち伏せについてこの台詞とほぼ同じ内容の発言をしているが、グロスターの死に関してなにも言っていない（3: 494）。

**1. 1. 132-34. For Gloucester's death . . . that case** ホリンシェッドが伝えるモーブリーの返答（3: 494）にないシェイクスピアの創作。ただし「〔グロスターを〕殺さず、不名誉なことにもそのことに関して〔王に〕誓ったつとめを怠った」という内容は、グロスター拘禁後、モーブリーがグロスター暗殺の密命をはたさず王の不興を買ったという記述（3: 488）に沿うものとなっている。

**1. 1. 162-63. When, Harry, when? / Obedience bids I should not bid again** Harold F. Brooks によれば、原稿では 1 行であったものを、Q の植字工がそのまま組んだのち、Obedience bids 以降で 1 行となることに気づいて、163 行をあらたに組んだが、前行の obedience bids を削除し忘れたため、この句のくり返しが起こったという（Ure）。

**1. 1. 195. 1 *Exit Gaunt*** Dawson & Yachnin は、このト書きについて、場面同士のあいだに間隔をあけず、前場の最後までいた登場人物は次場には登場しないというエリザベス朝演劇の慣習に触れて、ゴーントが次の場面冒頭に登場するための退場であると推測している。

**1. 1. 204. Lord Marshal** 史実ではモーブリーが軍務伯（Earl Marshal）であるために、決闘に当たってサリー公爵が臨時の軍務伯に就任している。

**1. 2** 種本のホリンシェッド『年代記』にない、シェイクスピアが創作した場面。作者不詳の先行作品『ウッドストック』（*Woodstock*）に、夫の死に悲嘆してゴーントに復讐をうながすグロスター公爵夫人が登場する。

**1. 3** この場面の出来事については、種本のホリンシェッド『年代記』は、前夜のボリンブルックによる王のもとへの来訪、当日朝のモーブリーによる王のもとへの来訪からはじめて、決闘の中止、追放の言い渡しに加えて、モーブリーの出発とその後の運命、エルタム宮殿でのボリンブルックの王への辞去、出立の際の人びととの歓呼を伝えている（3: 494-95）。

**1. 3. 122. 1-2. *Richard . . . combatants*** ホリンシェッド『年代記』によれば判決が伝えられるまで 2 時間かかったという（3: 495）。

**1. 3. 208-10. Thy sad aspect . . . Plucked four away** ここでは、ボリンブ

ルックの追放期間短縮は、リチャードが追放を言い渡した直後ゴーントの悲しみを見て言いだしたものとなっているが、ホリンシェッドは後日ボリンブルックがエルタム宮殿に別れの挨拶をしにきた際に言いわたしたと伝えている（3：495）。

**1.3.232-33. Thy son is . . . a party-verdict gave** ボリンブルックを追放に処す顧問院の決定にたいしてゴーントが関与していることは、ホリンシェッド『年代記』では、この劇の 4.1.114-49 の素材となっている、廃位にたいするカーライルの反対演説のなかで述べられている（3：512）。

**1.4** この場面の、オーマールが報告する追放されたボリンブルックの見送りと、リチャードと忠臣たちのアイルランドの叛乱に関するやりとりはシェイクスピアの創作。

**1.4.23. Bushy, Bagot here and Green** Q1 ではブシーが場面最初に王とともに登場し（1.4.0.1 注参照）、ここでこれまで王と話をしていたことになっていながら、52 行目に「ブシーが知らせをもって登場」とのト書きがあり、登場人物の登場について劇作家が執筆中に考えを変えたものと思われる。Gurr は、劇作家が最初のト書きを書いてから 52 行目までのあいだに変更を思いつき、ブシーのあとにバゴットとグリーンの名前も書いてあった台詞に、ブシーだけはここにいないことがわかるように here の位置をずらすなどの変更の印をつけたが、Q1 の植字工が消去の印と勘違いした可能性を指摘している。F1 では、場面最初に登場し王と話をしているのがバゴットとグリーンになっており、変更を反映したものとなっている。しかしながら、*Bushy : heere Bagot* だと here と Bagot の最初の音でアクセントがつづくことになり、Q6 は同じ登場人物の登場パターンでありながら、弱強格の韻律に沿う韻律パターンとなっており、変更をうまく処理した本文となっている。

　なお、この佞臣 3 人について、ホリンシェッド『年代記』は、リチャードが手に入れたグロスターらの領地を貴族たちの維持に利用したとする記述のなかで、王がなにをしようと臣下たちのなかに苦言を呈するものがなくなり、人びとが顧問官たちを「最悪の手先（the worst creatures）」とみなしとくに彼ら 3 人に「こっそりと大きな憎しみ」をいだいていたと記している（3：493）。

**1.4.45-52. We are . . . make for Ireland presently.** ホリンシェッド『年代記』には王国領土の賃貸、白紙徴税勅許状の発行、ゴーントの領地の没収について、それぞれ「王がウィルツシャー伯ウィリアム・スクループ、大蔵卿ジョン・ブシーとふたりの騎士サー・ジョン・バゴットとサー・ヘンリー・グリーンに王国の領土を賃貸に出したという噂があった」（3：496）、「多くの白紙の勅許状が案出されロンドン市にもたらされ、多くの富裕な市民たちが喜んで押印し、あとになって大きな負担となるとわかった。同様の勅許状は王国内の全州に送られ、人びとのあいだに大きな不満が高まった。というのも、人びとが喜んで押印すると、役人たちがその勅許状に思いのままの請求金額その他を書

き入れたからである」(3: 496)、「〔ゴーントの〕死が国民の王にたいするさらなる憎しみをつのらせるきっかけとなった。というのも、王は彼のすべての財産を奪いとり、合法的な相続によってヘレフォード公爵に相続されるはずだった彼の土地からの地代のすべてを受けとりもしたからである」(3: 496) との記述があるが、それらすべてをアイルランドの叛乱平定のための戦費捻出のためのものとした (51-52) のはシェイクスピアの創作である。

**2.1** リチャードのゴーント訪問はシェイクスピアの創作。リチャードによるゴーントの領地没収とヨークの離反はホリンシェッド『年代記』の記述 (3: 496) に基づくが、そちらでは、ヨークはリチャードの仕打ちに怒り心頭に発し見切りをつけるものの、面と向かって抗議は行っていない。この場面に王が翌日アイルランドに向かう旨の発言がある (217-18) が、ゴーントの死は1399年の2月3日、王の出発は4月 (3: 496) で、シェイクスピアは2ヶ月ぐらいの期間で起こったことを2日での出来事としている。

**2.1. 167-68. prevention of poor Bolingbroke / About his marriage** ホリンシェッド『年代記』によれば、追放中のボリンブルックはパリに滞在し、フランス王シャルル七世の従姉妹で、ベリー公の娘マリーと婚約を交わしたが、リチャードは不忠を理由にその結婚を妨害している (3: 495)。

**2.1. 219-20. we create ... England** リチャードが、自身のいだくゴーントの財産没収の計画に抗議して憤然として席を立ったヨークを、アイルランド遠征中の摂政に指名することはあきらかに無謀な行いである。リチャードのこうした振る舞いについて、ホリンシェッド『年代記』は、グロスターの叛乱鎮圧のあと、リチャードは「あらゆる叛乱を根絶やしにしたと信じこんで、自分は生きているどの君主よりも高い位に就いていると考えて、それまで以前に比べてだれが敵でだれが味方かに頓着しなくなった」と書いている (3: 493)。

**2.2** シェイクスピアの創作になる場面。ダニエル同様シェイクスピアは史実に反して王妃を成人女性として描いている。

**2.2. 49-51. The banished Bolingbroke ... is safe arrived / At Ravenspurgh** ホリンシェッド『年代記』は、沿岸で状況を探ったのち1399年7月初頭にボリンブルックが60名たらずをしたがえてラヴェンスパーから上陸したと記している (3: 498)。

**2.2. 58-59. the Earl of Worcester / Hath broken his staff, resigned his stewardship** ノーサンバーランドの弟、初代ウスター伯は1399年9月29日に王室家政長官職を退いている (Fryde, 77)。ホリンシェッド『年代記』は、「職責を表わす標である職杖を折って」職を辞したのは、「王の命令か、王が兄のノーサンバーランド伯を叛逆者と宣言したためか」(3: 499-500) としているが、シェイクスピアは、ここでも次場 (2.3.30) でもノーサンバーランドが叛逆者とされたことへの不満からとしている。

**2.2. 86. your son was gone before I came** ホリンシェッド『年代記』では、

オーマールは王の命令を受け、王のアイルランド遠征に合流している（3: 497）。

**2. 2. 97.　An hour before I came the Duchess died**　ホリンシェッド『年代記』によれば、グロスター公未亡人の死は、ヘンリーの戴冠後に、アイルランドからの帰還中に疫病で他界した息子の死の悲しみからのこととされている（3: 514）。シェイクスピアはその時期を早めて、直前のオーマール離反の報につづけることによって、悲報が連続するようにしている（Dawson & Yachnin）。Ure は、これによって、グロスター公未亡人役の俳優が 5 幕でヨーク公夫人役を演じることが可能になることを指摘している。

**2. 2. 134-42.　Well, . . . again**　グリーンとブシーがウィルツシャー伯のいるブリストル城に行き、バゴットが王のいるアイルランドに行くという 3 人の落ち延び先は、ホリンシェッド『年代記』3: 498 の記述に基づいている。

**2. 3**　ホリンシェッド『年代記』の、帰国したボリンブルックがノーサンバーランドをはじめ多くのものの歓迎を受けバークリー城に向かった（1399 年 7 月 27 日到着）という記述と、上陸したボリンブルックとの対峙にそなえて兵を集めたがうまくいかなかったヨークがアイルランドから戻るリチャードを迎えるため同じバークリー城に滞在したという記述（3: 498）に基づくが、ボリンブルックの、のちに『ヘンリー四世・第 1 部』でハルと対決することになるパーシーとの対面、ロスとウィロビーの合流、ヨークとの対峙はシェイクスピアの創作。父親の財産を没収され、法的措置もとることができなかったというボリンブルックの主張は、ホリンシェッド『年代記』のゴーントの死に際する財産没収に関する記述（3: 496）の言語的影響が見られる。

**2. 3. 98-100.　when . . . French**　ヨークがフランスで黒太子とともに戦ったという記録はなく、これはシェイクスピアの創作。Paul Reyher, 'Notes sur les sources de "Richard II"', *Revuede l'enseignement des langues vavantes*, xli（1924）158-68 は、作者不詳の劇『ウッドストック』で黒太子の亡霊が眠っているグロスターのところにあらわれて言う、Had I the vigour of my former strength, / When thou beheldst me fight at Crècy field / Where hand to hand took King John of France / And his bold sons my captive prisoners, / I'd shake these stiff supportrs of thy bed and drag thee from this dull security（*Woodstock*, 5. 1. 67-72）を引用して、この箇所の材源としているが、Forker は使われている語に類似が見られないことを理由にその可能性を否定している（490-91）。

**2. 3. 112.　I come for Lancaster**　ホリンシェッド『年代記』によれば、ボリンブルックは上陸してダンカスターに到着すると、支援する貴族たちに、「父親からの相続と妻の所有権によって自分のものとなった土地以外要求しない」と誓ったという（3: 496）。

**2. 3. 165.　weed and pluck**　Forker はこの部分と 3. 4. 50-52 に関して *Traison*, 92-3/247 における即位後のヘンリー四世のウェストミンスター修道

院長の共謀者処刑後の演説との類似を指摘している。　⇒3.4.50-52後注参照。

2.4　ホリンシェッド『年代記』3: 496における、ソールズベリーによるウェールズでの援軍急募の失敗についての記述に基づく場面。

**2.4.8.　The bay trees in our country are all withered**　Dawson & Yachnin は、このウェールズにおける月桂樹の立ち枯れへの言及を、ホリンシェッド『年代記』が伝える、リチャードのアイルランド遠征前の、アイルランドではなくイングランドで、国中の月桂樹が立ち枯れしたのちふたたび緑を取りもどし、未曾有の出来事の前兆と考えられたとの記述（3: 496）から想をえたものと指摘している。

3.1　ブシー、グリーンの処刑はホリンシェッド『年代記』3: 498の記述に基づくが、そちらでは処刑されたもののなかにウィルツシャー伯爵も入っている。ホリンシェッドは、史実では2年後に当たる、リチャードがボリンブルックにとらえられたときにオーウェン・グレンダワーが王に仕えていたことを伝えている（3: 513）が、彼はウェールズに逃れ、そのあとなにも起こらず、また、この劇も今後彼に触れることはない。

3.2　アイルランドから帰還したリチャードのウェールズ到着、ボリンブルックの勢力にたいする彼の狼狽、ソールズベリーによるウェールズ軍の解散の報、寵臣処刑の報、絶望したリチャードによる自軍の解散命令は、ホリンシェッド『年代記』（3: 499）に依拠。同書によれば、リチャードは、バークローリー城からコンウェイ城に移動してソールズベリーと会見したのち、国家にたいする犯罪者を裁く議会の開催と、身柄の安全を保証したうえでのボリンブルックとの会見を提案するノーサンバーランドにだまされて、コンウェイ城を出て身柄を拘束される（3: 500）が、シェイクスピアはその経過を劇化していない。

**3.2.70, 76, 85.　twelve thousand … twenty thousand … forty thousand**　ホリンシェッド『年代記』では、リチャードの帰還が遅れたせいで離反した兵士の数は forty thousand となっている（3: 499）。

3.3　バークローリー城におけるリチャードの、ボリンブルックの使者ノーサンバーランドとの、次いでボリンブルックとの会見は、ホリンシェッド『年代記』（3: 501）に基づくが、前場の注に記したようにそちらには王が拘禁されたことが記されており、会見はそのあとの出来事となっている。また、ホリンシェッドによれば、王とボリンブルックとの会見では、カンタベリー主教もおり、彼は王にたいして身柄の安全を保証したが、廃位は身体に傷をつけるものでないためその保証は「ピラト」の言葉のようであったという。

3.4　基本的にシェイクスピアによる創作。

**3.4.50-52.　The weeds … by Bolingbroke**　Forker はこの部分と2.3.165に関して *Traison*, 92-3/247における即位後のヘンリー四世のウェストミンスター修道院長の共謀者処刑後の演説との類似を指摘している。　⇒2.3.165後注参照。

4.1 シェイクスピアはホリンシェッド『年代記』にある以下の7つの記述にも
とづいてひとつの場面を作りあげている。(1) 9月29日ロンドン塔における
リチャードによる退位証書への署名の報告（3: 504）、(2) ボリンブルックの戴
冠の日取り決定（3: 507）、(3) バゴットによるオーマール告発、(3: 511)、(4)
フィッツウォーターによるオーマール告発（3: 512）、(5) カーライルによる平
民院の国王訴追要求への反対演説（3: 512、劇ではリチャード廃位、ボリンブ
ルック擁立への反対演説）、(6) モーブリーの客死についての報告（3: 495、
⇒ 4.1.91-100 後注参照）、(7) ウェストミンスターの陰謀（3: 514）。ホリンシ
ェッドの記述によればQ1-3 のようにリチャードは議会に姿を現わさない。

4.1.4 **wrought it with the King** Ure は、シェイクスピアが、ホリンシ
ェッド『年代記』の、10月15日に議会に提出されたバゴットの申立書中に見ら
れる、二様に解すことができる、以下の言葉をもとに、「王をそそのかす」と「王
とともに実行に加わる」という多義性をはらんだ台詞を書いた可能性を指摘し
ている。「彼〔オーマール〕は、王の意向に沿うため、前述の公爵〔グロスタ
ー公〕とそのほかの貴族たちにたいしてなされたすべてのことに関して、彼〔オ
ーマール自身／リチャード〕が手を下すようにした（set him in hand with all
that was done)」(3: 512)。

4.1.91-100. **That honourable day ... so long** ホリンシェッド『年代記』
では、モーブリーの客死については、1.3 の出来事となっている決闘中止、追
放の言い渡しのあと、出国の記述につづけて記されている（3: 495）。

4.1.106.1 *Enter York* ホリンシェッド『年代記』ではリチャード退位の意
志を伝えるにあたってヨーク公は関与しておらず（3: 504）、Forker はシェイ
クスピアがヨーク大主教の関与をヒントにヨーク公を登場させた可能性を指摘
している（497）。Wilson は、この場面にヨーク公が登場するのはフロワサール、
ホールの年代記の影響であることを示唆している（198-99）。

4.1.114-49. **Marry ... woe.** シェイクスピアはカーライルによるこの反対演
説を、ホリンシェッド『年代記』が伝える、9月29日の議会における決闘騒
ぎと国王退位の意志伝達から3週間以上がすぎた10月22日に提出された平民
院による国王の訴追と廃位の理由公表の要求にたいするカーライル主教の反対
演説（3:512）をもとに作っている。それをリチャード廃位、ボリンブルック
擁立への反対演説に流用したために、演説前半（114-33）は材源に基づき、そ
れ以降はシェイクスピアの創作となっている。そのため、不在の国王を裁くこ
とを批判する最初の論点（121-29）は劇の文脈からはずれたものとなっている。

4.1.150. SP Northumberland ホリンシェッド『年代記』ではカーライル
を逮捕したのは当時軍務伯だったウェストムアランド伯（3: 512）。ノーサンバ
ーランド伯はその前任者。

4.1.154. **commons' request** ホリンシェッド『年代記』が1599年10月22
日に提出されたとする、リチャードに判決を下し、退位の根拠となる罪状を明

らかにすることを求める平民院の要求（3: 512）を指すものと思われる。カーライルの国王廃位と新王擁立への反対演説（114-49）はその要求への反対演説を材源としている。ノーサンバーランドがリチャードに、自身の犯した罪科の読みあげを迫る（221-26）ことから、この劇では国王による自身のおかした罪状を読みあげ認めることが要求の内容となっているものと思われる。 ⇒221-26 注参照。

**4. 1. 170. So Judas did to Christ** Wilson は、*Traison* に見られる、ノーサンバーランドをユダにたとえる記述と自身を「ゆえなくして敵の手に売り渡されたわれらの救世主」を思いおこすように求めるリチャードの言葉（49/197-98; 52/201）を引いている。

**4. 1. 200-20. Ay ... days** リチャードが議会で退位を認めるこの台詞はシェイクスピアの創作ということになるが、ホリンシェッド『年代記』の 9 月 29 日におけるロンドン塔でのリチャードの退位宣言についての記述（3: 503-04）におおむね一致している。そちらには、その際の王の態度について、「敵の手に落ちあらゆる救いをあきらめていた王は、… 求められるあらゆることに承諾し … 王冠（roiall crwone）と王の威厳を捨て、自発的にそれらから退かされた（voluntarilie was deposed）」（強調引用者）という、退位がけっして自発的とは言えるものではなかったことを示す記述が見られる。また、王の象徴物、財産、法、臣下の忠誠の誓いなどあらゆるものを捨てるとの宣言（203-14）も、ホリンシェッドがつづけて収録しているリチャードの退位証書に沿うものとなっている。

**4. 1. 282. ten thousand men** ホリンシェッド『年代記』はボリンブルックの戴冠式日程の決定とリチャードにたいする忠誠の誓い破棄の記述のあとにつづくリチャードの宮廷についての記述のなかでこの数字を示している（3: 508）。

**4. 1. 318-19. On Wednesday ... yourselves** ホリンシェッド『年代記』によればヘンリー四世の戴冠式は 10 月 13 日月曜日に行われている（3: 507, 511）。Ure は、シェイクスピアが『年代記』で戴冠式の日付を急いで探し、カーライルの逮捕に関する段落が「次の水曜日」（3: 512）ではじまっているので誤った可能性を指摘している。

**5. 1** リチャードと王妃の別れはホリンシェッド『年代記』になく、おおむねシェイクスピアの創作と考えられるが、唯一フランスに帰る前の夫妻を描いているのはダニエルの『ランカスター家とヨーク家の内戦、最初の四巻』の2.71-98 で、その影響を受けていることが見受けられる。

**5. 2** ホリンシェッド『年代記』ではリチャードのロンドン塔移送はボリンブルックのロンドン入りの翌日の出来事ということになっているが、ボリンブルックは歓呼をもって迎えられ、リチャードは悪意あるものたちに連れさられそうになったと記されている（3: 501）。ダニエル『四巻』にはリチャードの前をボリンブルックが馬に乗って行進する記述（2. 66-77）があり、その影響も考え

られる。オーマールの裏切り発覚についてはホリンシェッド『年代記』に記述がある（3: 515）ほかにホール（17-18）に依拠している可能性も指摘されている。ヨーク公夫人の役割はシェイクスピアの創作で、1399 年の段階でヨーク公夫人は後妻でありオーマールの実の母親ではなかった。

**5.3**　1-22 で語られるのちにヘンリー五世となるハルの青年時代の無軌道はヘンリー五世の治世中から喧伝されておりほぼ伝説となっていたが、材源となった可能性があるのはトマス・エリオット『為政者論』（fols. 122-23ᵛ）など。場面の主な出来事に関しては、前場におけるのと同様にホリンシェッドとともにホールに依拠している可能性がある。ヨーク公夫人については前場同様シェイクスピアの創作。

**5.4**　ホリンシェッド『年代記』における、ヘンリー四世によるため息まじりのつぶやきをサー・ピアーズ・オヴ・エクストンが聞きとめていたという一節（3: 517）に依拠。

**5.4.4-5.　He . . . not?**　ホリンシェッド『年代記』における新王の言葉は以下のとおりで、「くり返した」というのはシェイクスピアの創作。Haue I no faithfull fréend which will deliuer me of him, whose life will be my death, and whose death will be the preseruation of my life? (3: 517)

**5.5**　リチャード殺害に関しては、ホリンシェッド『年代記』の前場の材源につづく部分（5: 517）に記されている。

**5.5.102.　The devil . . . thee!**　材源のホリンシェッド『年代記』（3: 517）からそのままとった言葉。

**5.6**　ホリンシェッド『年代記』3: 515-17 の素材を凝縮。

［編注者紹介］

篠崎　実（しのざき　みのる）
1959年神奈川県に生まれる。
東京大学文学部卒業、同大学院修了。
現在、千葉大学人文科学研究院教授。
［著書］高橋康也編『シェイクスピア・ハンドブック』（共著、新書館出版）
［論文］「『舞台まるごとを鏡にして』──『気質なおし』に見るジョンソンのキャリア創出」、『Shakespeare Journal』第6巻所収、「『嘆かわしい一幕』──『リチャード二世』検閲説をめぐって」、日本シェイクスピア協会編『シェイクスピアとの往還　日本シェイクスピア協会創立60周年記念論集』（研究社）所収など
［訳書］C・ノリス『デリダ──もうひとつの西洋哲学史』（共訳、岩波書店）、ピーター・ゲイ『官能教育』全2巻（共訳、みすず書房）など

〈大修館シェイクスピア双書 第2集〉

リチャード二世
©Minoru Shinozaki, 2022　　　　　　　NDC 932／xiv, 239p／20cm

初版第1刷──2022年12月20日

編注者─────篠崎　実
発行者─────鈴木一行
発行所─────株式会社 大修館書店
　　　　　　　〒113-8541 東京都文京区湯島2-1-1
　　　　　　　電話 03-3868-2651（販売部）　03-3868-2293（編集部）
　　　　　　　振替 00190-7-40504
　　　　　　　［出版情報］https://www.taishukan.co.jp

装丁・本文デザイン─────井之上聖子
印刷所────広研印刷
製本所────ブロケード

ISBN 978-4-469-14268-6　Printed in Japan

## 大修館 シェイクスピア双書 (全12巻)
### THE TAISHUKAN SHAKESPEARE

| | | |
|---|---|---|
| お気に召すまま | *As You Like It* | 柴田稔彦 編注 |
| ハムレット | *Hamlet, Prince of Denmark* | 高橋康也・<br>河合祥一郎 編注 |
| ジュリアス・シーザー | *Julius Caesar* | 大場建治 編注 |
| リア王 | *King Lear* | Peter Milward 編注 |
| マクベス | *Macbeth* | 今西雅章 編注 |
| ヴェニスの商人 | *The Marchant of Venice* | 喜志哲雄 編注 |
| 夏の夜の夢 | *A Midsummer-night's Dream* | 石井正之助 編注 |
| オセロー | *Othello* | 笹山　隆 編注 |
| リチャード三世 | *King Richard the Third* | 山田昭広 編注 |
| ロミオとジュリエット | *Romeo and Juliet* | 岩崎宗治 編注 |
| テンペスト | *The Tempest* | 藤田　実 編注 |
| 十二夜 | *Twelfth Night; or, What You Will* | 安西徹雄 編注 |

## 大修館 シェイクスピア双書 第2集 (全8巻)
### THE TAISHUKAN SHAKESPEARE 2nd Series